The Frozen Dead

BERNARD MINIER

The Frozen Dead

Translated by Alison Anderson

MULHOLLAND
BOOKS
HODDER

First published as *Glacé* in France in 2011 by XO Éditions

First published in Great Britain in 2013 by Mulholland Books
An imprint of Hodder & Stoughton
An Hachette UK company

1

A CIP catalogue record for this title is
available from the British Library

Trade Paperback ISBN 978 1 444 73225 2
eBook ISBN 978 1 444 73227 6

Printed and bound in Great Britain by Clays Ltd, St Ives plc

Hodder & Stoughton policy is to use papers that are natural,
renewable and recyclable products and made from wood grown in
sustainable forests. The logging and manufacturing processes are
expected to conform to the environmental regulations of
the country of origin.

Hodder & Stoughton Ltd
338 Euston Road
London NW1 3BH

www.hodder.co.uk

To the memory of my father
To my wife, my daughter and my son

To Jean-Pierre Schamber
and Dominique Matos Ventura,
who changed everything

TRANSLATOR'S NOTE

The French justice system is somewhat different from that elsewhere. Under French law, when it is believed that a crime has been committed, an officer of the crime unit will inform the district public prosecutor, who in turn appoints an examining magistrate to the case.

Investigations are conducted under the supervision of these magistrates, who answer to the Ministry of Justice. Crimes may be investigated by police commissioners from the crime unit, along with commissioned officers of the gendarmerie.

The Frozen Dead

FROM:
DIANE BERG
GENEVA

TO:
DR WARGNIER
WARGNIER PSYCHIATRIC INSTITUTE
SAINT-MARTIN-DE-COMMINGES

Diane Berg – Curriculum vitae
Psychologist, Swiss Federation of Psychologists (FSP)
Specialist in Forensic Psychology (SSPL)

Date of Birth: 16 July 1976
Nationality: Swiss

Diplomas:
2002: Master of advanced studies in clinical psychology (DES),
University of Geneva. Dissertation: 'Instinctual Economy, Necrophilia
and Dismembering among Compulsive Killers'.

1999: Degree in psychology, University of Geneva. Dissertation:
'Aspects of Childhood Fear among Children Eight to Twelve Years
of Age'.

1995: Secondary School Diploma in classical and Latin studies
1994: Cambridge First Certificate in English as a foreign language

Professional Experience:
2003 – present: Private Practice, psychotherapy and forensic
psychology, Geneva

2001 – present: Assistant to Professor Pierre Spitzner at the Faculty
of Psychology and Educational Sciences (FPSE), University of Geneva

1999–2001: Intern in psychology, Institute of Forensic Psychology, University of Geneva
Intern in psychology, Medical Services of Champ-Dollon Prison

PROFESSIONAL ASSOCIATIONS:
International Academy of Law and Mental Health (IALMH)
Geneva Association of Psychologists-Psychotherapists (AGPP)
Swiss Federation of Psychologists (FSP)
Swiss Society of Forensic Psychology (SSPL)

INTERESTS:
Classical music (ten years of violin), jazz, reading
Sports: swimming, running, diving, potholing, parachute jumping

Prologue

Dgdgdgdgdgd – taktaktak – ddgdgdgdgdg – taktaktak

Sounds: the regular clicking of the cable and, intermittently, of wheels over towers as the cable car passed over, causing the cabin to judder. Then the ever-present wailing of the wind, a fluty sound, like the cries of children in distress. Finally the voices of the passengers in the cabin as they shouted to make themselves heard above the din. There were five of them, including Huysmans.

Dgdgdgdgdgd – taktaktak – ddgdgdgdgdg – taktaktak

'Shit! I don't like going up there in this weather,' one of them said.

Huysmans watched in silence for the lower lake to appear, a thousand metres below, through the gusts of snow swirling round the cabin. The cables seemed peculiarly slack, tracing a double curve that drooped lazily into the grey background.

The clouds parted. The lake appeared. Briefly. For a moment it looked like a puddle beneath the sky, a simple splash of water between the peaks and the strips of tattered cloud against the summits.

'What the fuck does the weather have to do with it?' said someone else. 'We're going to spend a week stuck underneath that fucking mountain no matter what.'

The hydroelectric power station at Arruns: perched two thousand metres high with a series of halls and tunnels burrowed seventy metres underground. The longest tunnel stretched for eleven kilometres, feeding the water from the upper lake to the pressure pipelines: pipes a metre and a half in diameter that ran down the mountain to force the water from the upper lake to the thirsty turbines of the production facilities down in the valley. There was only one way into the station's interior, deep in the mountain: through an access shaft from the top of the station, then down a hoist and along a tunnel on board two-seated tractors while the gates were closed. Eight kilometres of tunnels for a voyage lasting a good hour, into the heart of darkness.

3

The other way to get to the station's entrance was by helicopter – but only in emergencies. A pad had been built near the upper lake, accessible in good weather.

'Joachim is right,' said the oldest among them. 'With weather like this, the chopper wouldn't even be able to land.'

They all knew what this meant. Once the gates were opened, thousands of cubic metres of water from the upper lake would come roaring down into the tunnel they had just used. In the event of an accident, it would take two hours to drain the tunnel again, another hour through the tunnel by tractor to get back to the access shaft, fifteen minutes to get back up to the open air, ten to go down by cable car to the production facility and another half-hour by road to reach Saint-Martin-de-Comminges – provided the road wasn't blocked.

If there were an accident, they wouldn't be able to reach the hospital for four hours or more. And the power station was getting old . . . It had been in operation since the 1920s. Every winter, before the snows melted, they spent four weeks up there, cut off from the world, for the maintenance and repair of machines from another era. A difficult, dangerous job.

Huysmans watched as an eagle glided on the belly of the wind, roughly a hundred metres from the cabin.

Silence.

He turned to gaze at the dizzying frozen expanses below.

Three enormous pressure pipelines dropped vertiginously towards the abyss, moulded to the flank of the slope. The valley had vanished from their field of vision some time ago now. The last support tower was visible three hundred metres further down, standing there alone in the midst of the fog, where the flank of the mountain created an escarpment. Now the cable car was climbing straight to the access shaft. If the cable were to break, the cabin would fall several dozen metres before smashing like a nutshell against the rock face. In the blizzard it was swinging like a basket on a housewife's arm.

'Hey, chef! What's for dinner this time?'

'Nothing organic, that's for sure.'

Only Huysmans did not laugh; he was watching a yellow minibus on the road to the power station's offices down in the valley. The manager's. Then the bus too disappeared from view, swallowed by banks of clouds like a stagecoach surrounded by Indians.

4

Every time he went up there he felt he was on the verge of discovering some fundamental truth about his existence. But he could not determine what it was.

Huysmans turned to look towards the peak.

They were nearing the terminus of the cable car – a metal scaffold clinging to the start of the access shaft. Once the cabin had come to a halt, the men would set off down a series of footbridges and staircases until they came to the concrete blockhouse.

The wind was howling violently. It must be at least minus ten degrees.

Huysmans narrowed his gaze.

There was something unusual about the shape of the scaffold.

Something that shouldn't be there . . .

Like a shadow between the steel girders and cross-braces, swept by the gusts of wind.

It's an eagle, he thought; *an eagle's got caught in the cables and pulleys.*

No, that would be absurd. And yet that's what it was: a huge bird, its wings spread wide. Maybe a vulture, imprisoned in the superstructure, tangled in the bars and railings.

'Hey, look at that!'

Joachim's voice. He'd seen it, too. The others turned to look at the platform.

'Christ almighty! What is it?'

It's no bird, that's for sure, thought Huysmans.

He felt a vague anxiety welling inside. The thing was hanging above the platform, just below the cables and pulleys, as if suspended in the air. It looked like a giant butterfly, a dark, evil butterfly staining the whiteness of snow and sky.

'Fuck! What is that thing?'

The cabin was preparing to stop. They were nearly there. The shape grew larger.

'Holy mother of God!'

It was no butterfly; nor was it a bird.

The cabin stopped; the doors opened automatically.

An icy gust thick with snowflakes whipped their faces. But no one got out. They stood there staring at this work of madness and death. They already knew that they would never forget what they had just seen.

The wind was screaming around the platform. It was no longer children's cries that Huysmans could hear, but something tormented, awful screams hidden by the howling of the wind. They all took a step further back into the cabin.

Fear struck them head on like a locomotive at full steam. Huysmans rushed over to the headphones and rammed them over his ears.

'Is that the main station? Huysmans here! Call the gendarmerie, quick! Tell them to get up here right away. There's a dead body. The sickest thing you've ever seen!'

PART I
The Man Who Loved Horses

I

The Pyrenees. Diane Berg watched them loom into sight as she drove over the hill. A white barrier, still quite far away, stretching the entire breadth of the horizon, hills breaking like waves against it. A raptor tracing circles in the sky.

Nine o'clock in the morning, the tenth of December.

Judging by the road map on the dashboard, she should take the next exit and head south, towards Spain. She had neither GPS nor sat nav on board her elderly Lancia. She saw a signpost above the motorway: 'Exit 17, Montréjeau/Spain, 1,000 m.'

Diane had spent the night in Toulouse. A budget hotel, a tiny room with a tiny television and a bath made of moulded plastic. During the night she had started awake to the sound of repeated screaming. Her heart pounding, she sat up at the head of the bed, on full alert, but the hotel remained perfectly silent, and she was beginning to think she had merely dreamt it when suddenly the screaming started again, louder than ever. Her stomach tied itself in knots until she realised it was only cats fighting below her window. She had trouble getting back to sleep after that. Only the day before she had still been in Geneva, celebrating her departure with colleagues and friends. She had gazed at her surroundings, there in her room at the university, and wondered what the view from her next room would be.

In the hotel car park, as she was unlocking her Lancia, melted snow sliding from car roofs all around her, she grasped that she was leaving her youth behind. And she knew that before a week or two had gone by she would have forgotten her life from before. A few months from now she would have changed, utterly and profoundly. In light of where she would be staying for the next twelve months, how could it be otherwise? 'Just be yourself,' her father had advised. As she pulled out of the little rest area back onto the motorway, already busy with traffic, she wondered if the changes would be positive ones. Someone once said that there are adaptations that are more like amputations, and she could only hope that this would not be the case for her.

She could not stop thinking about the Institute.

All those people shut away in there.

All day long the previous day, Diane had been haunted by this thought: *I'll never manage. I won't be up to it. Even though I've prepared myself, and I'm the best person for the job, I have absolutely no idea what to expect. And the people there will see right through me.*

She was thinking of them as people, human beings, and not . . . *monsters.*

And yet that is what they were: individuals who were genuine monsters, people as far removed from her own self and her parents and everyone she knew as a tiger is from a cat.

Tigers . . .

That was how she had to think of them: unpredictable, dangerous, capable of inconceivable cruelty. *Tigers shut away in the mountain* . . .

When she came to the tollbooth, she discovered she'd been so absorbed by her thoughts that she had no clue where she'd put her ticket. The operator gave her an exasperated look as she searched frantically through the glove box and her handbag. Yet there was no hurry: there was no one in sight.

At the next roundabout she headed for Spain and the mountains. After a few kilometres the flat plain came to an abrupt end. The first foothills of the Pyrenees rose from the earth and the road was surrounded by round, wooded knolls that were nothing like the high, ridged summits she could see in the distance. The weather changed, too; the snowflakes were falling more thickly.

She came out of a bend and the road suddenly gave onto a land-scape of rivers, forests and white plains. There was a Gothic cathedral perched on the summit of a hill, with a little town surrounding it. Through the swishing of the windscreen wipers the landscape began to resemble an old etching.

Spitzner had warned her: 'The Pyrenees are nothing like Switzerland.'

Along the side of the road the snowdrifts rose ever higher.

Diane saw the flashing lights through the snowflakes before she came upon the roadblock. The snow was falling heavily now. Policemen stood in the thick of it, waving their luminous batons. Diane noticed that they were armed. One van and two motorcycles were parked in the dirty slush on the verge, beneath two tall pine trees. She rolled down her window and in no time her seat was wet from the thick, fluffy snowflakes.

'Your papers, please, mademoiselle.'

She leaned over to the glove compartment. She could hear a string of messages crackling on their radios, blending with the rhythm of the windscreen wipers and the sharp accusations of her exhaust pipe. She felt the chill damp upon her face.

'Are you a reporter?'

'Psychologist. I'm on my way to the Wargnier Institute.'

The gendarme studied her, leaning on her open window. A tall, blond fellow, who must have been well over six foot. Beneath the fabric of sounds woven by the radios she could make out the river rushing through the forest.

'What are you doing in this part of the world? Switzerland isn't exactly next door.'

'The Institute is a psychiatric hospital; I'm a psychologist. Do you see the connection?'

He handed back her papers.

'Here you are, you can go.'

As she turned the ignition, she wondered whether the French police always checked on motorists in this way, or if something had happened. The road wound its way round several bends, following the meandering river (known as a '*gave*', according to her guidebook) as it flowed through the trees. Then the forest vanished, giving way to a plain that must have been at least five kilometres wide. A long, straight avenue took her past petrol stations and deserted campsites, banners flapping sadly in the wind, fine houses with the air of Alpine chalets, and a string of advertising hoardings vaunting the merits of the nearby ski resorts.

'IN THE HEART OF THE VALLEY, SAINT-MARTIN-DE-COMMINGES, POPULATION 20,863' – according to the brightly coloured sign. Above the town, grey clouds obscured the peaks, torn here and there by a glow that sculpted the ridge of a summit or the profile of a pass like the sweep of a beam of light. At the first round-about, Diane drove past the sign for the town centre and took a little street on the right, behind a building where a large display window proclaimed in neon letters, 'Sport & Nature.' 'It's not a very enter-taining place for a young woman.' She recalled Spitzner's words as she drove down the streets to the familiar, reassuring monologue of her windscreen wipers.

The road headed uphill. She caught a brief glimpse of huddled roofs at the bottom of the slope. On the ground the snow was turning into a black slush that splattered the underneath of the car. 'Are you sure you want to go there, Diane? It won't have much in common with Champ-Dollon.' Champ-Dollon was the name of the Swiss prison where, after she had graduated, she had conducted a number of forensic assessments and taken on casework dealing with sex offenders. She'd had to assess serial rapists, paedophiles, cases of interfamilial sexual abuse – an administrative euphemism for incestuous rape. She had also been called on as a joint evaluator to conduct credibility tests on minors who claimed to be the victims of sexual abuse, and she had discovered, to her horror, how easily such an undertaking could be skewed by the evaluator's own ideological and moral prejudices, often to the detriment of all objectivity.

'I've heard strange things about the Wargnier Institute,' Spitzner had said.

'I spoke to Dr Wargnier on the telephone. He made an excellent impression on me.'

'Wargnier is very good,' Spitzner conceded.

She knew, however, that Wargnier would not be there to welcome her, that it would be his successor as head of the Institute, Dr Xavier, a Quebecois from the Pinel Institute in Montreal. Wargnier had retired six months earlier. He was the one who had gone over her application and given it his approval, before leaving his post; he had also warned her in the course of their numerous telephone conversations how difficult her task would be.

'It's not an easy place for a young woman, Dr Berg. And I'm not just referring to the Institute; I mean the area around it. That valley . . . Saint-Martin . . . You're in the Pyrenees, the Comminges region. The winters are long, and there's not much to do. Unless you like winter sports, of course.'

'I am Swiss, don't forget,' she replied, a touch of humour in her voice.

'In that case, I have one piece of advice: don't let yourself get too absorbed in your work, keep some time for yourself – and spend your free hours outside. It's a place that can become . . . *disturbing* . . . after a while.'

'I'll bear that in mind.'

'And another thing: I won't be here to help you get settled. My successor, Dr Xavier from Montreal, will have that honour. He's a practitioner with a very good reputation, very enthusiastic. He's due to arrive here next week. As you know, they're ahead of us over there with regard to the treatment of aggressive patients. I think it will be very interesting for you to compare your points of view.'

'I agree.'

'In any case, we've needed an assistant to the director of the establishment for quite a while now. I didn't delegate enough.'

Diane was once again driving under a canopy of trees. The road continued to climb until it reached a narrow wooded valley that seemed to be enveloped in a stifling, noxious intimacy. She cracked her window open and a penetrating fragrance of leaves, moss, needles and wet snow tickled her nostrils. The sound of a nearby torrent almost drowned the purr of the engine.

'A lonely place,' she said out loud, to give herself courage.

She drove cautiously through the gloom of the winter morning. Her headlights grazed the trunks of fir and beech trees. An electricity cable followed the road; branches leaned against it as if they no longer had the strength to support themselves. From time to time the forest opened out to reveal a barn with a moss-covered slate roof – closed, abandoned.

She glimpsed some buildings further along, past a bend in the road. They reappeared as she came out of the bend – several houses of concrete and wood with large picture windows, backed up against a forest. To reach them, a drive led down from the road, over a metal bridge above the water then across a snowy meadow. Obviously deserted, run down. She did not know why, but those empty buildings, lost deep in this valley, caused her to shiver.

Then a rusting sign at the entrance to the drive: 'LES ISARDS HOLIDAY CAMP.'

Still no hint of the Institute. Not even a signpost. It looked as if the Wargnier was not exactly looking for publicity. Diane began to wonder if she had taken the wrong road. The National Geographical Institute map, scale 1/25,000, lay open on the passenger seat next to her. One kilometre and a dozen bends further along she spotted a lay-by bordered by a stone parapet. She slowed down and turned the wheel. The Lancia bounced over the potholes, churning up splatters of mud. She grabbed the map and got out of the car. The damp air enveloped her like a clammy sheet.

Heedless of the falling snow, she unfolded the map. The buildings of the holiday camp were designated by three little rectangles. She gauged the approximate distance she had come, following the winding thread of the *départementale* road. Two more rectangles appeared slightly further along; they met in the shape of a T, and although there were no indications as to the nature of the buildings, it could hardly be anything else, for the road came to an end at that point, and there were no other symbols on the map.

She was almost there . . .

She turned round, walked as far as the parapet – and saw them.

Further upstream, on the opposite shore, higher up on the slope: two long stone buildings. In spite of the distance she could tell how huge they were. A giant's architecture. The same Cyclopean style that was everywhere in the mountains, be it power plants or dams or hotels from an earlier century. That's what it was: the lair of a Cyclops. *Except that there is not just one Polyphemus deep inside that cave – there are several.*

Diane wasn't the type to be easily daunted; she had often travelled to places where tourists were warned not to go; since adolescence she had taken up sports that entailed a certain amount of risk. As a child and then an adult she had always had a taste for adventure. But something about the view there before her made her stomach lurch. It wasn't a question of physical risk. No, it was something else. A leap into the unknown . . .

She took out her mobile and dialled. She didn't know whether there would be a mast in the area to relay her call, but after three rings a familiar voice replied.

'Spitzner here.'

Her sense of relief was instantaneous. His warm, firm, calm voice had always been able to soothe her and banish her doubts. It was Pierre Spitzner – her mentor in the department – who had first got her interested in forensic psychology. An intensive SOCRATES course on children's rights had brought her closer to this discreet, charming man, devoted husband and father of seven children. The famous psychologist had taken her under his wing in the Faculty of Psychology and Educational Sciences; he had enabled the chrysalis to become a butterfly – even if such an image would undoubtedly have seemed far too conventional to Spitzner's demanding mind.

'It's Diane. Am I disturbing you?'

'Of course not. How is it going?'

'I'm not there yet . . . I'm on the road . . . I can see the Institute from here.'

'Is something wrong?'

Good old Pierre. Even over the telephone he could tell from the slightest shift in her voice.

'No, everything's fine. It's just that . . . their aim was to isolate these guys from the outside world. They've stuck them in the most sinister, remote place they could find. This valley gives me goose-bumps . . .'

She was immediately sorry she'd said that. She was behaving like an adolescent left to her own resources for the first time – or a frustrated student in love with her supervisor and doing everything she could to attract his attention. She told herself he must be wondering how she'd manage to cope if the mere sight of the buildings was causing her to panic.

'Come on,' he said. 'You've already seen your fair share of paranoids and schizophrenics and sex offenders, right? Tell yourself that it won't be any different there.'

'They weren't all murderers. In fact, only one of them was.'

His image sprang to mind: a thin face, irises the colour of honey staring at her with a predator's greed. Kurtz was a genuine sociopath. The only one she had ever met. Cold, manipulative, unstable. Not a trace of remorse. He had raped and killed three mothers; the youngest was forty-six and the eldest seventy-five. That was his thing, mature women. Not to mention the ropes, ties, gags, slipknots . . . Every time she struggled *not* to think about him, he would settle into her consciousness, with his ambiguous smile and wildcat gaze. This reminded her of the sign Spitzner had nailed to the door of his office: 'Don't think of an elephant.'

'It's a bit late in the game to be doubting yourself, don't you think, Diane?'

His words made her blush.

'You'll be up to it, I'm sure. You have the dream profile for the job. I'm not saying it'll be easy, but you'll manage, I know you will.'

'You're right,' she said. 'I'm being ridiculous.'

'Not at all. Anyone in your shoes would react the same way. I know the reputation that place has. Don't let that get to you. Focus on your work. And when you come back to us, you will be the greatest specialist on psychopathic disorders in all the cantons. I have to let you go now, Diane. The dean's expecting me, to talk about finances. You know what he's like: I'm going to need all my wits about me. Good luck. Keep me posted.'

Dial tone. He'd hung up.

The silence, interrupted only by the sound of the stream, draped itself over her like a wet canvas. The *plop* of a big clump of snow falling from a branch made her jump. She put her mobile into the pocket of her down jacket, folded the map and climbed back into the car.

Then she backed round to leave the lay-by.

A tunnel. The beam of her headlights glanced over the black, streaming walls. No overhead lighting, a bend immediately beyond it. And the first sign, at last, on a white fence: 'CHARLES WARGNIER INSTITUTE FOR FORENSIC PSYCHIATRY.' She turned slowly and drove over a bridge. The road climbed suddenly and sharply, following a few hairpin bends through the fir trees and the snowdrifts – she was afraid her old banger might skid on the icy slope. She had neither snow tyres nor chains. But quickly enough the road flattened out.

One last bend and they were there, very close now.

She pressed deeper into her seat when the buildings came to meet her through the snow, mist and woods.

Eleven fifteen in the morning, Wednesday, the tenth of December.

2

Snow-covered fir trees. Imagine them from above, from a sheer, vertical perspective. A ribbon of road leading straight and deep between these same fir trees, trunks wrapped in mist. Treetops hurtling by. At the end of the road, among the trees, a Cherokee Jeep like a plump beetle was driving beneath the tall conifers. Its headlights pierced the swirling mists. The snow plough had left huge drifts on either side. In the distance white mountains blocked the horizon. The forest came to an abrupt end. The road wound in a tight bend round a rocky slope before continuing alongside a quick-running stream. The stream met a small weir covered in a rush of roiling water. Beyond the other bank, the black mouth of a hydroelectric power station was visible in the gaping side of the mountain. On the verge, a road sign: 'SAINT-MARTIN-DE-COMMINGES: BEAR COUNTRY – 7 KM.'

Servaz looked at the sign as he drove past.

A Pyrenean bear painted against a background of mountains and fir trees.

Pyrenean bears, yeah, right! Newly introduced Slovenian bears, more like, which the local shepherds would be only too happy to have at the other end of their rifle.

According to the shepherds, the bears strayed too close to inhabited areas; they attacked the herds; they were even becoming a danger to humans. *The only species that is dangerous to humans is other humans,* thought Servaz. With each passing year he saw more and more corpses in the morgue in Toulouse. And they hadn't been killed by bears. *Sapiens nihil affirmat quod non probat.* 'A wise man asserts nothing he cannot prove,' he mused. He slowed down as the road curved before leading back into the woods – no longer tall conifers, this time, more like a nondescript undergrowth full of thickets. He could hear the burbling mountain stream through the car window, slightly open despite the chill. Its clear song almost drowned the music from the

CD player: Mahler's Fifth Symphony, the allegro. A music full of anxiety and feverishness, which seemed appropriate for what lay ahead.

Suddenly there before him were the revolving lights of the squad cars, and figures silhouetted against the road, waving their luminous batons.

Those useless gendarmes . . . When the gendarmerie had no clue how to start an investigation, they set up roadblocks.

He remembered what Antoine Canter had said to him that very morning, at the regional crime unit in Toulouse: 'It happened last night, in the Pyrenees. A few kilometres from Saint-Martin-de-Comminges. Cathy d'Humières called it in. I think you've worked with her before, right?'

Canter was a colossus of a man, with the rugged accent of the Southwest, a former rugby player with a vicious streak who liked to dominate his opponents in the scrum, a cop who'd worked his way up from the bottom to become deputy chief of the local crime unit. The skin on his cheeks was pockmarked with little craters, like sand pitted by rain; his huge iguana's eyes watched Servaz closely.

'*It* happened? What happened?' Servaz asked.

The corners of Canter's mouth were sealed with a white deposit, and now he parted his lips: 'No idea.'

Servaz stared at him, taken aback.

'What do you mean?'

'She wouldn't say on the phone, just that she was waiting for you, and she wants the utmost discretion in the matter.'

'And that's it?'

'Yes.'

Servaz looked at his boss, bewildered.

'Saint-Martin, isn't that where that asylum is?'

'The Wargnier Institute,' confirmed Canter, 'a psychiatric establishment unique in France, even in Europe. That's where they lock up murderers who've been judged insane.'

Someone had escaped, committed a crime while on the run? That would explain the roadblocks. Servaz slowed down. He recognised the MAT 49 sub-machine guns and the Browning BPS-SP shotguns among the weapons the officers were carrying. He rolled down his window. Scores of snowflakes drifted on the cold air. He waved his card in the gendarme's face.

18

'Which way?'

'You have to go to the hydroelectric station.' The man raised his voice to talk over the messages spurting from the radios, his breath a cloud of white condensation. 'A dozen kilometres or so from here, in the mountains. At the first roundabout on the way into Saint-Martin, you take a right. Then right again at the next roundabout. Follow the signs for Lac d'Astau. Then just keep going.'

'Whose idea were these roadblocks?'

'Public prosecutor. Routine procedure. We open the boot, check their papers. You never know.'

'Uh-huh,' said Servaz doubtfully.

He started the car again, turned up the volume on the CD player. The horns of the scherzo filled the small space. He took his eyes from the road for a moment to grab the cold coffee he had stashed in the drinks holder. The same ritual, every time: he always prepared himself in the same way. He knew from experience that the first day, the first hour of an investigation are decisive. That it's when he must be awake, focused and open-minded. Coffee to wake up, music to focus – and to empty his mind. *Caffeine and music . . . And today, fir trees and snow,* he thought, looking at the side of the road with the first flutterings of a cramp in his stomach. Servaz was a city-dweller at heart. Mountains felt like hostile territory to him. He remembered that it had not always been like that, however; when he was a child, his father used to take him walking in these valleys every year. Like a good teacher, he explained all about the trees and rocks and clouds, and young Martin Servaz listened while his mother spread a blanket on the springtime grass and opened the picnic basket, calling her husband a pedant and a crushing bore. Halcyon days when innocence reigned over the world. As he stared at the road, Servaz wondered whether the real reason he had never come back here was because his memory of these valleys was inextricably connected to that of his parents.

When will you get round to some spring-cleaning up there, for Christ's sake?

For a while he'd been seeing a shrink. After three years had gone by, however, the shrink himself had thrown in the towel: 'I'm sorry, I wanted to help you but I can't. I have never met such resistance.' Servaz had smiled and answered that it didn't matter. At the time he was thinking mostly of the positive impact the end of his treatment would have on his budget.

He looked around him again. So much for the frame; only the painting was missing. Canter said he knew nothing. And Cathy d'Humières, the public prosecutor for Saint-Martin, had insisted he come alone. *Why is that?* He hadn't told her, however, that it suited him; he led an investigation team of seven, and his men (in fact six men and one woman) had enough to deal with already. The day before, they had wound up an investigation into the murder of a homeless man. His battered and half-drowned body had been found in a pond, not far from the motorway Servaz had just taken near the village of Noé. They hadn't needed more than forty-eight hours to find the culprits: the tramp, who was sixty or more, had been spotted a few hours before his death in the company of three adolescents from the village. The eldest was seventeen, the youngest twelve. To begin with they had denied it, then, fairly quickly, confessed. No motive. And no remorse, either. The eldest just said, 'He was a social reject, a bum . . .' Not one of them had a file with the police or the social services. Kids from good families. Normal educations, none of them running with a bad crowd. Everyone taking part in the investigation said the boys' indifference made their blood run cold. Servaz could still see their chubby faces, their large, pale, attentive eyes staring at him fearlessly, even defiantly. He had tried to work out which one was the ringleader – in this sort of thing there is always a leader – and he thought he had figured it out. It wasn't the eldest boy, but the middle one. A boy whose name, ironically, was Clément . . .

'Who told on us?' the kid had asked in the presence of his lawyer, who was baffled because the boy had refused to talk to him, as was his right, under the pretext that the man was 'a moron'.

'I'm the one who asks the questions round here,' said the policeman.

'I'll bet it's that old cow Schmitz. She's such a slag.'

'Calm down and watch your language,' said the lawyer; he'd been hired by the boy's father.

'You're not in the playground,' Servaz pointed out. 'You know what you risk, you and your mates?'

'This is premature,' protested the lawyer feebly.

'She'll get her head bashed in, that bitch. Watch if she doesn't get killed. I'm fucking mad.'

'Stop swearing,' shouted the lawyer, beside himself.

'Are you listening to me?' said Servaz, getting annoyed. 'You risk

20

twenty years in prison. Do the maths: when you get out, you'll be old.'

'Please,' said the lawyer. 'No—'

'Old like you, you mean? How old are you? Thirty? Forty? It's not bad, your velvet jacket! Must be worth a fortune. Why are you picking on me, huh? We didn't do it! We didn't fucking do anything! Honestly we didn't. Are you idiots or what?'

To defuse his rising anger, Servaz reminded himself that this was an adolescent who'd never been in trouble. Who'd never run foul of the police. No trouble at school, either. The lawyer had turned very pale and was sweating profusely.

'You're not in some TV series here,' said Servaz calmly. 'You're not going to get out of it. It's already wrapped up. You're the idiot here.'

Any other teenager would have reacted. But not this one. Not this boy named Clément; the boy named Clément did not even seem to realise what he'd been accused of. Servaz had already read articles about minors like this who raped, killed and tortured, and who seemed perfectly unaware of the horror of their deeds. As if they'd been involved in some video game or role play that had simply gone wrong. Until that day Servaz had refused to believe they existed. The media, exaggerating as usual. And now here he was, faced full on with the phenomenon. And what was even more terrifying than the apathy of the three young murderers was the fact that there was nothing at all exceptional anymore about the case. The world had become a huge laboratory for increasingly demented experimentation, where God, the devil or random luck stirred the contents of the test-tubes.

Once he got home, Servaz took a long time scrubbing his hands, got undressed and stayed in the shower until all the hot water was gone, as if to decontaminate himself. After that, he took his Juvenal down from the bookshelf and opened it to Satire XIII: 'What day is there, however festive, which fails to disclose theft, treachery and fraud: gain made out of every kind of crime, and money won by the dagger or the bowl? For honest men are scarce; hardly so numerous as the gates of Thebes.'

These kids, we're the ones who've made them the way they are, he'd thought, closing the book. *What sort of future do they have? None. Everything's going to the dogs. You have bastards who fill their pockets and waltz round on TV while these kids' parents get the sack and look like losers to their children. Why don't they rebel? Why don't they set fire to banks, luxury boutiques and the corridors of power, instead of schools and buses?*

I'm reasoning like an old fart, he told himself afterwards. Was it because he was about to turn forty in a few weeks? He'd left his team in charge of the three kids. This would be a welcome diversion – even if he didn't know what lay ahead.

He followed the gendarme's instruction and bypassed Saint-Martin. Immediately after the second roundabout the road began to climb, and he caught a glimpse of the white roofs of the town below him. He pulled over onto the verge and climbed out. The town spread further across the valley than he'd thought. Through the gloom he could just make out the huge snowy fields he'd driven past on his way in, as well as an industrial zone and some campsites to the east, on the other side of the river. There were also some council estates, long low buildings. The town centre, with its skein of little streets, was spread at the foot of the highest of the surrounding mountains. Along the fir-covered slopes a double row of cable cars inscribed a vertical fault.

The mist and the snowflakes created a distance between the town and him, blurring the details, and Servaz sensed that Saint-Martin was not a town that gave itself easily to strangers, that you had to approach from an angle, not face on.

He climbed back into the Jeep. The road still headed up. In summer, there would be luxuriant vegetation, an overabundance of greenery, thorns, moss, which even the snow could not hide in winter. And everywhere the sound of water: springs, torrents, streams . . . With the window down, he went through a few villages where half the houses were boarded up. A new road sign: 'HYDROELECTRIC POWER PLANT, 4 KM.'

The fir trees vanished. As did the mist. No more nature, only walls of ice the height of a man by the side of the road, and a violent, boreal light. He put the Cherokee on the black-ice setting.

At last the power plant appeared, with its typical industrial-age architecture: a titanic stone building with tall, narrow windows, crowned with a wide slate roof holding back huge drifts of snow. Behind it, three gigantic pipes headed up the mountain as if to conquer it. The car park was busy. Vehicles, men in uniform – and journalists. A van from the regional TV channel with a big satellite dish on its roof and a few unmarked cars. Servaz noticed the press badges on the windscreens. A Land Rover, three Peugeot estate cars, two Transit vans, all of them in the colours of the gendarmerie, and one van with an elevated roof, which he recognised as a mobile laboratory. There was also a helicopter waiting on a landing pad.

Before leaving the car, he gave himself a quick glance in the rear-view mirror. He had circles under his eyes, and his cheeks were hollow, as usual – he looked like a guy who'd spent the night on the town, and yet that was hardly the case – but he figured, too, that no one would think he was forty years old. With his fingers he combed his thick brown hair as best he could, rubbed his two-day beard to wake himself up and gave a tug to his trousers. Good Lord, he'd lost some more weight.

A few snowflakes caressed his cheeks, but it was nothing like down in the valley. It was very cold. He should have put on warmer clothes. The reporters and the cameras and microphones turned to look at him – but no one recognised him and their curiosity faded at once. He headed for the building, climbed three steps and showed his card.

'Servaz!'

A voice rolling through the foyer like a snow cannon. Servaz turned towards the figure heading in his direction. A tall, slender woman in her fifties, elegantly dressed. Hair dyed blonde, a scarf tossed over an alpaca coat. Catherine d'Humières had come in person, instead of sending one of her deputies: Servaz felt a sudden rush of adrenaline.

Her profile, her sparkling eyes, like a raptor's. People who did not know her were intimidated. As were those who did know her. Someone told Servaz one day that she made incredible spaghetti alla puttanesca. Servaz wondered what she put in it. Human blood? She took his hand briefly, a firm handshake as powerful as a man's.

'Remind me – what sign are you, Martin?'

Servaz smiled. At their very first meeting, when he had just started at the Toulouse crime unit and she was still only one deputy public prosecutor among others, she had asked him that same question.

'Capricorn.'

She acted as if she hadn't noticed his smile.

'Well, that explains your cautious, controlled and phlegmatic side, doesn't it?' She gave him an intense, searching look. 'So much the better. We'll find out whether you'll still be controlled and calm after this.'

'After what?'

'Follow me, I'll introduce you.'

She led him across the foyer, their steps ringing out in the vast space. For whom had all these buildings in the mountain been constructed? Some imminent race of supermen? Everything about them seemed to proclaim confidence in a radiant, colossal industrial future; an era of faith that had disappeared long ago, he mused. They headed towards a glassed-in cubicle. Inside there were filing cabinets and a dozen or so desks. They wove their way past them to join a little group in the middle. D'Humières made the introductions: Captain Rémi Maillard, head of the gendarmerie in Saint-Martin; Captain Irène Ziegler, from the research unit in Pau; the mayor of Saint-Martin – a short, broad-shouldered fellow with a lion's mane and a burnished face – and the manager of the power plant, an engineer who looked like an engineer: short hair, glasses and a sporty air in his rollneck jumper and lined parka.

'I've asked Commandant Servaz to give us a hand. When I was a deputy public prosecutor in Toulouse, I often had reason to call on his services. His team assisted us in getting to the bottom of several sticky cases.'

'Assisted us in getting to the bottom of . . .' That was d'Humières all over. It was just like her to want to get right in the middle of the photograph. But he immediately told himself that it wasn't really fair to think like that: he knew she was a woman who loved her job – and who did not keep track of either her time or her sweat. That was something he appreciated. Servaz liked conscientious people. He thought that he too belonged to this category: conscientious, tough, probably boring.

'Commandant Servaz and Captain Ziegler will be handling the investigation jointly.'

Servaz saw Captain Ziegler's fine face crumple. Once again he told himself that this must be a major incident. An investigation that was handled jointly by the police and the gendarmerie was an inexhaustible source of quarrels, rivalry and withholding of evidence – but that too was a sign of the times. And Cathy d'Humières was sufficiently ambitious never to lose sight of the political angle. She had climbed up all the rungs: assistant public prosecutor, deputy public prosecutor . . . She had become head of the public prosecutor's office in Saint-Martin five years earlier and Servaz was sure she did not intend to stop there when she was doing so well: the office in Saint-Martin was too small, too far from the spotlight, for someone whose ambition was as consuming as hers. He was convinced that in the next year or two she would make presiding judge at a more important tribunal.

Now he asked, 'Was the body found here, at the power plant?'

'No,' answered Maillard, pointing to the ceiling, 'up there, at the cable car terminus, two thousand metres up.'

'Who uses the cable car?'

'The workers who go up to maintain the machines,' answered the plant manager. 'It's a sort of underground factory that functions by itself; it channels the water from the upper lake into the three pressure pipelines you can see outside. The cable car is the only way to get up there under normal circumstances. There is of course the helicopter pad – but that's only used in the event of a medical emergency.'

'There's no path, no road?'

'There's a path that goes up there in the summer. In the winter it's buried under metres of snow.'

'You mean that whoever did this used the cable car? How does it work?'

'Nothing could be simpler: there's a key; then you press a button to start it. And another big red button to bring everything to a halt if there's a problem.'

'The keys are kept in a locker, here,' Maillard interrupted, pointing to a metal box on the wall. 'It seems to have been forced open. The body had been strung up on the last support tower, at the very top. There can be no doubt: the perpetrator must have used the cable car to transport it.'

'No fingerprints?'

'No visible traces, in any case. We've got hundreds of latent prints in the cabin. The samples have been sent to the lab. We're in the process of getting all the employees' prints to compare them.'

He nodded.

'And what was the body like?'

'Decapitated. And dismembered: the skin peeled back on either side like great wings. You'll see it on the video: a truly macabre sight. The workers still haven't recovered.'

25

Servaz stared at the gendarme, all his senses suddenly on alert. Even though this was an era of extreme violence, this incident was far from ordinary. He noticed that Captain Ziegler wasn't saying anything, just listening attentively.

'Any make-up?' He shook his hand. 'Fingertips cut?'

In French police jargon, 'make-up' meant hindering identification of the victim by destroying or removing anything that could be used for ID: face, fingers, teeth . . .

The officer opened his eyes wide, astonished.

'What . . . you mean they didn't tell you?'

Servaz frowned.

'Tell me what?'

He saw Maillard cast a panicked look at Ziegler, then the prosecutor.

'The body,' stammered the gendarme.

Servaz felt he was about to lose his patience – but he waited for what came next.

'It was a horse.'

'*A horse?*'

Servaz looked at the rest of the group, incredulous.

'Yes. A horse. A thoroughbred, probably a year old, according to what we know.'

Now it was Servaz's turn to look at Cathy d'Humières.

'You made me come all the way up here for a *horse?*'

'I thought you knew,' she said defensively. 'Didn't Canter tell you anything?'

Servaz thought back to Canter in his office and the way he'd feigned ignorance. *He knew.* And he also knew that Servaz would have refused to come all this way for a horse, since he had the murder of the homeless man on his hands.

'I've got three kids who've murdered a homeless bloke and you drag me up here for a nag?'

D'Humières's reply was instantaneous, conciliatory but firm.

'It's not just any horse. A thoroughbred. A very expensive animal. Which in all likelihood belonged to Éric Lombard.'

So that's it, he thought. Éric Lombard, the son of Henri Lombard and grandson of Édouard Lombard . . . A financial dynasty, captains of industry, entrepreneurs who had reigned over this patch of the

Pyrenees, over the *département* and even over the region, for six decades or more. With obviously unlimited access to all the ante-chambers of power. In this part of the world, Éric Lombard's thoroughbreds were indisputably more important than some murdered homeless man.

'And bear in mind that not far from here there's an asylum full of dangerous lunatics. If one of them did this, it means he's roaming around somewhere out there.'

'The Wargnier Institute . . . Have you called them?'

'Yes. They say that none of their inmates are missing. And in any case none of them are allowed out, even temporarily. They swear that it's impossible to get over the wall, that the security is draconian – several restraining walls, biometric security measures, staff who've been hand-picked and so on . . . We'll double-check it all, naturally. But the Institute has a good reputation – given both its notoriety and the unusual nature of its inmates.'

'A horse!' said Servaz again.

Out of the corner of his eye he saw Captain Ziegler emerge at last from her reserve with a faint smile. That smile, which he alone had noticed, went some way towards defusing his growing anger. Captain Ziegler had lake-deep green eyes, and beneath the cap of her uniform her blonde hair was pulled back into a chignon: he suspected it must be quite beautiful. On her lips, only a trace of colour.

'So what is the purpose of all the roadblocks?'

'We'll keep them there until we are sure that none of the inmates from the Wargnier Institute have escaped,' answered d'Humières. 'I don't want to be accused of negligence.'

Servaz said nothing. But his thoughts were racing. D'Humières and Canter had got their orders from high up. It was always the same. No matter how good they were as bosses, far superior to the majority of careerists who filled the prosecutors' offices and ministries, they, like everyone else, had developed an acute sense of danger. Someone at the top, perhaps the minister himself, had decided this whole ridiculous production would be a good idea, in order to be of service to Éric Lombard, a personal friend to the highest authorities of the State.

'And where is Lombard now?'

'In the US, a business trip. We want to be sure it's one of his horses before we contact him.'

'One of his stewards did report the disappearance of a horse this morning,' explained Maillard. 'The stall was empty. The description matches. He should be here shortly.'

'Who found the horse? The workers?'

'Yes, on their way up there.'

'Do they go up there often?'

'At least twice a year: at the beginning of winter and just before the snows melt,' answered the plant manager. 'It's an old factory, with old machines. They have to have regular maintenance, even if they do operate automatically. The last time the workers went up there was three months ago.'

Servaz noticed that Captain Ziegler hadn't taken her eyes off him.

'Do we know the time of death?'

'According to the initial examination, sometime during the night,' said Maillard. 'The autopsy will give us more exact details. In any event, it looks as though whoever put the horse up there knew that the workers were about to go up there too.'

'And at night? Isn't there any security at the plant?'

'There is. Two watchmen, with an office at the end of this building. They say they didn't see or hear anything.'

Servaz hesitated, frowning.

'Yet you can't just move a horse like that, can you? Even dead. You need something to tow it with at the very least. A van. There were no visitors, no cars? Nothing at all? Maybe they were asleep and they don't dare say as much? Or maybe they were watching a match on the telly. Or a film. And how are you supposed to load the carcass onto the cable car, get it up there, string it up, get back down – that all takes time. How many people would it take to carry a horse, anyway? Does the cable car make a noise when it's operating?'

'Yes,' said Captain Ziegler, intervening for the first time. 'You can't help but hear it.'

Servaz turned his head. Captain Ziegler was wondering the same thing as he was. *Something wasn't right.*

'Do you have an explanation?'

'Not yet.'

'We'll have to interrogate the watchmen separately,' he said. 'That means today, before we let them go.'

'We've already separated them,' answered Ziegler calmly, with authority. 'They're in two different rooms; we've got an eye on them. They . . . were waiting for you.'

Servaz noticed the icy glance Ziegler gave d'Humières. Suddenly the ground began to vibrate. It was as if the vibration were spreading through the entire building. For a moment, his mind completely elsewhere, he thought it might be an avalanche or an earthquake, and then he understood: it was the cable car. Ziegler was right: you could not help but hear it. The door to the cubicle opened.

'They're on their way down,' announced a subordinate.

'Who is?'

'The body,' explained Ziegler. 'With the cable car. And the investigators. They've finished their work up there.'

The crime scene investigators: the mobile laboratory belonged to them. In it would be photographic equipment, cases for storing biological swabs and sealed items to be sent for analysis to the IRCGN – the central Institute for Criminal Research of the Gendarmerie Nationale, in Rosny-sous-Bois, in the Paris region. There was bound to be a refrigerator, too, for the most perishable samples. All this fuss over a horse.

'Let's go,' he said. 'I want to see the star of the day, the winner of the Grand Prix de Saint-Martin.'

As they went back out, Servaz was astonished to see how many reporters there were. He could have understood if they'd been there for a murder – but for a horse! It looked as if the private little worries of a billionaire like Éric Lombard were a newsworthy topic for the celebrity press.

He tried as best he could to avoid getting his shoes wet as he walked along, and he sensed that Captain Ziegler was still watching him attentively.

Then all of a sudden he saw it.

A vision from hell . . . If hell could be made of ice.

He forced himself to look, despite his disgust. The horse's remains were held in place by wide straps looped round the carcass and attached to a big forklift truck equipped with a little motor and pneumatic jacks. Servaz knew that this same type of forklift might have been used by whoever hung the horse up there . . . They were taking it out of the cable car. Servaz saw that the cabin was very big. He recalled the vibrations a few moments ago. How could the watchmen have failed to notice anything?

Reluctantly, he turned to focus his attention on the animal. He didn't know anything about horses, but it seemed to him that this one must have been a fine specimen. His long tail was a brush of black, shining strands darker than the hair on his coat, which was the colour of roasted coffee, with cherry-red glints. The splendid beast seemed to have been sculpted from a smooth, polished exotic wood. His legs were the same coal-black colour as the tail and what was left of the mane. A multitude of little icicles whitened the corpse. Servaz assumed that if the temperature down here was below zero, it must be several degrees colder up there. Perhaps the gendarmes had used a blowtorch or soldering iron to melt the ice around the attachments. Other than that, the animal was no more than a wound – with two huge flaps of skin pulled back from the body and hanging along its flanks like folded wings.

A dizzying fear had overcome everyone gathered there.

Where the skin had been peeled back, the flesh was bared, every muscle distinctly visible, as in an anatomy diagram. Servaz glanced around him: Ziegler and Cathy d'Humières were pale; the plant manager looked as if he'd seen a ghost. Servaz himself had rarely seen anything so unbearable. To his great dismay he realised that he was so used to the sight of human suffering that he was far more shocked and disturbed by the sight of an animal's pain.

Then there was the head. Or rather its absence; instead, a huge gaping wound just above the throat. This absence made the whole picture so strange that it was hard to stomach. Like artwork proclaiming the utter madness of the artist. And indeed, this vision was indisputable proof of insanity – and Servaz could not help but think again of the Wargnier Institute: it was hard not to see a connection, in spite of the director's assertion that none of his inmates could have escaped.

Instinctively he had to admit that Cathy d'Humières's fears were well founded: this was not just some business about a horse. It gave you shivers down your spine, the way the animal had been killed.

The sudden roar of an engine caused them to turn round.

A big Japanese four-wheel drive tore up the road and came to a sudden halt a few metres away. The cameras instantly turned to focus on the vehicle. In all likelihood they were hoping for a glimpse of Éric Lombard, but they could have spared themselves the trouble: the man who stepped out of the car was in his sixties, with an iron-grey crew-cut. His height and build were those of a military man or a retired lumberjack. He was also wearing a lumberjack's checked flannel shirt. The sleeves were rolled up to reveal powerful forearms, and he did not seem to feel the cold. Servaz saw that he did not take his eyes off the carcass. He did not even notice their presence; circling their little group, he strode quickly over to the horse. Then Servaz saw his broad shoulders sag.

When the man turned to look at them, his bloodshot eyes were shining. With pain – but also anger.

'What bastard did this?'

'Are you André Marchand, Monsieur Lombard's steward?'

'I am.'

'Do you recognise this animal?'

'Yes, it's Freedom.'

'Are you sure of that?' asked Servaz.

'Of course.'

'Could you be more explicit? His head is missing.'

The man glared at him. Then he shrugged and turned back to the animal's remains.

'Do you think there are many bay yearlings like him in the region? He's as recognisable to me as your brother or sister is to you. With or without his head.' He pointed to the left foreleg. 'He has this white stocking halfway up his pastern, for example.'

'His what?' asked Servaz.

'The white stripe above the hoof,' translated Ziegler. 'Thank you, Monsieur Marchand. We're going to have the carcass taken to the stud farm in Tarbes for an autopsy. Was Freedom receiving any kind of medical treatment?'

Servaz could not believe his ears: they were going to perform a toxicology examination on a horse.

'He was in perfect health.'

'Did you bring his papers?'

'They're in the 4x4.'

The steward went to rummage in the glove compartment and came back with a pile of papers.

'Here is his registration card and the booklet that goes with it.'

Ziegler looked through the documents. Over her shoulder Servaz could see a multitude of columns, boxes and slots filled in with a tight, precise handwriting. And sketches of horses, face on and in profile.

'Monsieur Lombard adored this horse,' said Marchand. 'He was his favourite. He was born at the academy. A magnificent yearling.'

His voice was filled with rage and sorrow.

'*Yearling?*' whispered Servaz to Ziegler.

'A thoroughbred no older than a year.'

While she was going through the documents, he could not help but admire her profile. She was attractive, with an aura of authority and competence. He thought she must be in her thirties. She wasn't wearing a wedding ring. Servaz wondered whether she had a boyfriend or was single. Unless she was divorced, like him.

'Apparently you found the stall empty this morning,' he said to the breeder.

Marchand gave him another sharp look that reflected all the disdain an expert feels towards a philistine.

'Most certainly not. None of our horses sleep in a stall,' he sniffed. 'They all have loose boxes. Or free stabling, or daytime paddocks with shelters, so they can be together. I did find his box empty, that is true. And signs that the stable had been broken into.'

Servaz didn't know the difference between a stall and a box, but it seemed fairly important to Marchand.

'I hope you're going to find the bastards who did this,' said Marchand.

'Why did you use the plural?'

'For heaven's sake, do you think a man on his own could carry a horse up there? I thought there was supposed to be security round the power plant.'

No one seemed prepared to answer that question. Cathy d'Humières, who had been standing to one side until now, walked up to the steward.

'Please tell Monsieur Lombard that we will do everything in our power to find the perpetrator. He can call me at any time. Tell him that.'

Marchand studied the high-ranking official standing there before him as if he were an ethnologist and she the representative of some utterly bizarre Amazon tribe.

'I will tell him,' he said. 'I would also like to recover the body after the autopsy. Monsieur Lombard will probably want to bury it on his land.'

'*Tarde venientibus ossa,*' declared Servaz.

He thought he could detect a hint of astonishment in Captain Ziegler's eyes.

'That's Latin,' she said. 'And it means?'

'"Those who come late to dine will find only bones." I'd like to go up there.'

She looked deep into his eyes. She was almost as tall as he was. Servaz could tell that the body beneath her uniform was firm, supple, muscular. A beautiful, healthy, uncomplicated girl. He was reminded of his wife, Alexandra, when she was young.

'Before or after you question the watchmen?'

'Before.'

'I'll take you there.'

'I can go on my own,' he said, pointing to the cable car station. She gave a vague wave of her hand.

'This is the first time I've ever met a cop who speaks Latin,' she said with a smile. 'The cable car has been cordoned off. We'll take the chopper.'

Servaz went pale.

'Are you the pilot?'

'Surprised?'

3

The helicopter aimed for the side of the mountain like a mosquito buzzing over an elephant. The huge slate roof of the power plant, the car park full of vehicles were both abruptly left behind – too suddenly for Servaz's taste, as his stomach lurched.

Below them, their white boiler suits barely visible against the whiteness of snow, the investigators went to and fro from the cable car station to the mobile lab, carrying the small cases with the samples they'd taken. Viewed from on high, their scurrying seemed ridiculous: the bustle of a colony of ants. Servaz hoped they knew their jobs. It wasn't always the case: the training of crime scene investigators frequently left a lot to be desired. Lack of time, lack of means, insufficient budgets – always the same refrain, in spite of all the politicians' speeches promising a rosier future. Then the horse's body was wrapped in its bag, zipped up, placed on a huge gurney and rolled over to an ambulance, which sped off with its sirens wailing – as if there were some urgency for the poor beast.

Servaz looked straight ahead through the Plexiglas bubble.

The sky had cleared. The three giant pipelines that emerged from the back of the building climbed up the mountainside; the cable car followed the same path. He ventured another look downward – and instantly regretted it. The plant was already far below on the valley floor, and the cars and vans were shrinking before his eyes, insignificant spots of colour sucked up by the altitude. The pipes now plunged towards the valley like ski-jumpers from the top of their ski-jump: a dizziness of stone and ice to take your breath away. Servaz went pale, swallowed and concentrated on the summit ahead of him. The coffee he had drunk from the vending machine in the foyer was floating somewhere in his oesophagus.

'You don't look very well.'

'No problem. Everything's fine.'

'Do you suffer from vertigo?'

'No . . .'

Captain Ziegler smiled beneath her headphones. Servaz could no longer see her eyes behind her dark glasses – but he could admire her suntan and the faint blonde down on her cheeks shining in the harsh light reflecting from the ridge.

'All this carry-on for a horse,' she said suddenly.

He understood that, like him, she did not think much of such an investment of resources, and she was taking the opportunity to let him know that while no one could hear. He wondered whether her superiors had twisted her arm. And whether she had complained.

'Don't you like horses?' he said teasingly.

'I like horses a great deal,' she replied, not smiling, 'but that's not the problem. We have the same concerns as you: a lack of resources, material, staff – and the criminals are always two paces ahead. So, to spend this much energy on an animal . . .'

'At the same time, if there's someone out there capable of doing that to a horse . . .'

'Yes,' she conceded, so forcefully that he thought she must share his fear.

'Fill me in on what happened up there.'

'Do you see the metal platform?'

'Yes.'

'That's where the cable car arrives. That's where the horse was hanging, from the support tower, just below the cables. They had really staged it. You'll see, on the video. From a distance, the workers thought it was a bird.'

'How many workers?'

'Four, plus the cook. The upper platform of the cable car leads to the access shaft to the underground plant: that's the concrete thing you can see behind the platform. With the help of a crane they can send equipment down the shaft and then load it onto tractors with trailers. Seventy metres below, the shaft opens out into a tunnel in the heart of the mountain. That's quite a way down, seventy metres. They use the same tunnel that channels the water from the upper lake to the pressure pipelines in order to gain access to the plant: the floodgates are kept closed the time it takes for the men to go through.'

Now the helicopter was flying directly above the platform wedged into the mountainside like a derrick. It was practically hanging in space – once again Servaz felt the vertigo tying knots in his stomach.

35

And beneath the platform the slope took a sudden dizzying downward plunge. The lower lake was visible a thousand metres below, among the peaks, with its huge dam in the form of an arc.

Servaz could see footprints in the snow around the platform where the investigators had taken their samples. Yellow plastic rectangles with black numbers wherever they had found clues. And halogen projectors still magnetised to the metal pillars. For once it hadn't been difficult to cordon off the scene of the crime, he thought, but the cold must have given them some trouble.

Captain Ziegler pointed to the support tower.

'The workers didn't even get out of the cable car. They called the main office and went straight back down. They were scared to death. It could be they were afraid the lunatic who did it was still somewhere nearby.'

Servaz observed the young woman. The more he listened to her, the more he felt his interest growing, and the number of his questions with it.

'In your opinion, could one man, unaided, hoist the body of a dead horse up to that height and attach it in the middle of the cables? It seems it would be difficult, no?'

'Freedom was a yearling, so he would have weighed about two hundred kilos,' she replied. 'Even if you take off his head and neck, it would still mean nearly a hundred and fifty kilos of meat to carry around. Having said that, you saw the forklift just now: a device like that can move enormous loads. The thing is, even if you do suppose that a man could drag a horse around by means of a cart or a truck, he couldn't have hung it to the tower like that by himself. And besides, you were right: he would have needed a vehicle to get it up there.'

'And the night watchmen didn't see anything.'

'And there are two of them.'

'And they didn't hear anything.'

'And there are two of them.'

Neither Servaz nor Ziegler needed to be reminded that seventy per cent of those who commit a homicide are identified within twenty-four hours of the crime. But what if the victim is a horse? That was the type of question which probably didn't figure in police statistics.

'It's too easy,' said Ziegler. 'It's what you think. Too easy. Two watchmen and a horse. Why on earth would they want to do that?

If they'd wanted to take it out on one of Éric Lombard's horses, why would they go and stick the animal at the top of the cable car, in their own workplace, where they'd be the prime suspects?'

Servaz thought about what she had just said. Why indeed? On the other hand, could they really not have heard a thing?

'And besides, why would they do it?'

'No one is simply a watchman, or a cop,' he said. 'Everyone has their secrets.'

'Do you?'

'Don't you?'

'Yes, but there is the Wargnier Institute,' she hastened to add, while manoeuvring the helicopter. (Servaz again held his breath.) 'There is bound to be at least one guy in there who could do something like this.'

'You mean someone who managed to slip out and back in again without the staff at the Institute noticing?' He thought for a moment. 'Go all the way to the riding academy, kill the horse, get it out of its box and load it onto a vehicle all by himself? And all the while no one notices a thing in either place? And then cut it up into pieces, get it up the mountain and—'

'Right, OK, it's absurd,' she interrupted. 'And it still brings us back to where we started: how on earth could someone, even a lunatic, manage to hang the horse up there without anyone's help?'

'Two lunatics, say, who escape without being seen, then go mildly back to their cells without trying to run away? It makes no sense!'

'Nothing makes sense in this case.'

The chopper suddenly banked to the right to go round the mountain – or was it the mountain that was leaning the opposite way? Servaz couldn't really tell, and he gulped again. The platform and the blockhouse entrance vanished behind them. Masses of rock flashed by the Plexiglas bubble; then a lake appeared, much smaller than the one further down. Its surface, tucked in the hollow of the mountain, was covered with a thick crust of snow and ice; it resembled the crater of a frozen volcano.

Servaz saw a house on the shore of the lake, built right up against the rock face, near a dam.

'The upper lake,' said Ziegler. 'And the workers' residential "chalet". They get up here on a funicular which climbs straight from the depths of the mountain into the house; it's connected to the

37

underground plant. That's where they sleep, eat and live once their work day is over. They spend five days here, then go back down to the valley for the weekend, for a period of three weeks. They have all the mod cons, even satellite television – but it's still a pretty tough job.'

'Why don't they come up this way to get to the plant, rather than closing down the underground river?'

'The power plant doesn't have a helicopter. This pad, like the landing area down below, is only used by mountain rescue in extreme emergencies. And even then only when the weather allows it.'

The helicopter began a gentle descent towards a flat surface carved out amid a chaos of scattered patches of fresh snow and moraines. They were surrounded by a cloud of powdery snow. Servaz could just make out a huge H beneath the drifts.

'We're lucky,' she said into the headset. 'Five hours ago, when the workers discovered the body, we couldn't have got this far, because of the awful weather!'

The helicopter's landing skids touched down. Servaz felt alive again. Solid ground – even at more than two thousand metres. But they'd have to go back down again the same way, and the very thought of it made his stomach churn.

'If I've understood correctly, when the weather's bad, once the tunnel is filled with water, the workers are prisoners of the mountain. What do they do if there's an accident?'

Captain Ziegler made an eloquent grimace.

'They have to empty out the tunnel again and go back to the cable car through the access shaft. It takes at least two hours, maybe three, to get to the main station.'

Servaz would have liked to know what sort of bonuses these guys got for taking such risks.

'Who does the plant belong to?'

'The Lombard Group.'

The Lombard Group. The investigation was only just getting started and this was the second time the name had come up. Servaz imagined a loose conglomeration of enterprises, subsidiaries, holding companies, not just in France but in all likelihood abroad as well, an octopus whose tentacles reached everywhere, with money in its limbs instead of blood, flowing by the billions from the extremities to the heart. Servaz was no expert on business, but like most people nowadays he knew more or less what the word 'multinational' meant. Could an old factory like this one still be profitable to a group like Lombard's?

The rotation of the blades slowed and the whistling of the turbine faded and died.

Silence.

Ziegler put down her headset, opened the door and stepped out. Servaz followed. They walked slowly towards the frozen lake.

'We're at two thousand metres up here,' said the young woman. 'You can tell, can't you?'

Servaz took a deep breath of pure ether, intoxicating, icy. His head was spinning slightly – perhaps because of the helicopter ride, or the altitude. But it was a sensation more exalting than it was disturbing, not unlike, he supposed, the thrill that deep-sea diving could bring. He wondered if there was a similar thrill at high altitude. He was awed by the beauty and wildness of the place. The mineral solitude, a white, luminous desert. The shutters to the house were closed. Servaz imagined what the workers must feel every morning as they opened the windows onto the lake before they went down into the darkness. But perhaps that was all they could think about, in fact: the day ahead down there in the depths of the mountain, the deafening noise and artificial light, the long, trying hours in store.

'Are you coming? The tunnels were dug in 1929, and the plant was built the following year,' she explained, as they walked towards the house.

The eaves of the roof were supported by thick, rough stone pillars, forming a porch which all the windows looked out onto except one, on the side. Servaz noticed a retaining sleeve for a satellite dish on one of the pillars.

'Have you had a look in the tunnels?'

'Of course. Our men are still in there. But I don't think we're going to find anything up here. The man – or men – didn't come this far. It was enough to get the horse into the cable car, hang it up there and then go back down.'

She opened the wooden door. Inside, all the lamps were on. All the rooms were furnished: the bedrooms had two beds; the living room had a television, two sofas and a dresser; there was a large kitchen with a refectory table. Ziegler led Servaz to the back of the house, where it became part of the rock face; there was a small room that seemed to serve both as a security door and a hall, with metal

39

lockers and coat pegs on the wall. Servaz could see the yellow wire-mesh gate to the funicular at the back of the room and behind it the black hole of a tunnel dug into the dark bowels of the mountain.

She motioned to him to climb on board, closed the gate behind them, then pressed a button. The motor immediately got underway and the cabin shuddered. It began to move slowly along the shining rails down a forty-five-degree slope, vibrating slightly. Along the wall of black rock, visible through the fence, neon lights punctuated their descent at regular intervals. Eventually they came out into a large room built in the rock, brilliantly lit by more rows of neon lights. A workshop full of machine tools, pipes and cables. Technicians wearing white boiler suits, like the men down at the main facility, were bustling about here and there.

'I'd like to question these workers right away. Don't let them go home.'

'What do you have in mind?'

'Nothing special at the moment. At this stage an investigation is like a crossroads in the forest: all the paths look alike, but there's only one right one. To stay up here like this in the mountain, cut off, far from everything, it must create bonds but tension as well. They have to have strong nerves.'

'Could it be former workers with a grudge against Lombard? But then why go to so much trouble? When someone wants to take revenge on their employer, they show up at the workplace all of a sudden with a weapon; then they take it out on their boss or colleagues before they do themselves in. They don't go to the bother of stringing a horse up on top of a cable car.'

Servaz knew she was right.

'Let's find out if anyone now working or who has worked at the power plant over the last few years has a history of mental disorders,' he said. 'Especially anyone who's in the crews that come up here.'

'Good idea!' she shouted, to make herself heard above the noise. 'And the watchmen?'

'Workers first, then the watchmen. We'll spend the night on it if need be.'

'For a horse!'

'For a horse,' he echoed.

'We're lucky. As a rule the racket here is infernal! But they've closed the floodgates and the lake water isn't flowing.'

40

Servaz thought that, as far as noise went, it was already pretty bad.

'How does it work?' he asked, raising his voice.

'I don't really know! The dam at the upper lake fills when the snows melt. The water goes through the underground tunnels into the pressure pipelines, which then channel the water to the hydraulic generating sets in the plant, down in the valley. The power from the falling water drives the turbines. They say the water is put through the turbines "in a cascade", something like that. The turbines convert the driving force of the water into mechanical energy; then the alternators transform that energy into electricity, which is sent out onto high-tension lines. The power plant produces fifty-four million kilowatt hours per year – in other words, enough for a town of thirty thousand inhabitants.'

Servaz could not help but smile at her learned presentation.

'For someone who says they don't know, you seem to be very informed.'

He swept his gaze over the cavern of black rock lined with wire-mesh and metal structures fitted with bundles of cables, rows of neon lights, ventilation pipes, then the enormous machines from another age, control panels, the concrete floor . . .

'Fine,' he said. 'Let's go back up: we won't find anything here.'

The sky had darkened by the time they went back out. Sombre, shifting clouds passed above the frozen crater, which suddenly took on a sinister air. A violent wind drove the snowflakes before it. The surroundings, quite abruptly, had come to reflect the crime: something dark, chill, chaotic – where the desperate neighing of a horse could easily go unheard in the howling wind.

'We'd better hurry,' Ziegler urged. 'The weather's turning.'

Her blonde hair danced in the gusts, unruly strands coming loose from her chignon.

4

'Mademoiselle Berg, I will not hide the fact that I am puzzled as to why Dr Wargnier insisted on hiring you. What I mean is, clinical psychology, genetic psychology, Freudian theory – all this . . . *hotch-potch*. On balance, I would have preferred even the Anglo-Saxon clinical method.'

Dr Francis Xavier was sitting behind a big desk. He was a small man, still young, very well groomed; his hair was dyed, and he wore extravagant red glasses; beneath his lab coat was a tie with an exuberant floral pattern. He spoke with a slight Quebecois accent.

Diane let her gaze wander over to the DSM-IV, the *Diagnostic and Statistical Manual of Mental Disorders*, published by the American Psychiatric Association, the only book on his desk. She frowned slightly. She did not like the way the discussion was going, but she waited for the little man to finish showing his hand.

'Please understand, I am a psychiatrist. And – how to put it? – I cannot see what purpose you might serve for our establishment . . . No offence intended . . .'

'I . . . I am here in order to perfect my knowledge and training, Dr Xavier. Dr Wargnier must have explained this to you. Moreover, before he left, your predecessor hired me as his assistant and gave his approval to my absence – sorry, my presence here. He made a commitment to the University of Geneva on behalf of this establishment. If you were against my coming, you might have let us know before—'

'In order to *perfect your knowledge and training*?' Xavier pinched his lips slightly. 'Where do you think you are? Some university department? The murderers who are waiting for you at the end of these corridors,' he said, pointing to the door of his office, 'are even more horrific than the worst creatures ever to haunt your nightmares, Mademoiselle Berg. They are our nemesis. Our punishment for having killed God, for having created societies where evil has become the norm.'

This last sentence seemed a touch grandiloquent to her. As did everything else about Dr Xavier. But the way in which he had said it – with a curious mixture of fear and delight – made her shudder. She could feel the hair on the back of her neck standing on end. *He's afraid of them. They come to haunt him at night when he's asleep, or perhaps he can hear them screaming from his room.*

She stared at the unnatural colour of his hair and was reminded of the character Gustav von Aschenbach in *Death in Venice*, who dyes his hair, eyebrows and moustache for the sake of a beautiful young man he has seen on a beach and to delude himself about the approach of death. And never realises how desperate and pathetic his efforts really are.

'I am an experienced forensic psychologist. I have seen over a hundred sex offenders in three years.'

'And how many murderers?'

'One.'

He flashed her a mean little smile, then looked again at her file.

'*Degree* in psychology, master of advanced studies in clinical psychology from the University of Geneva,' he recited, his red glasses sliding down his nose.

'I worked for four years for a private psychotherapy and forensic psychology practice. I was entrusted with civil and criminal evaluations for the judicial authorities. It's there on my CV.'

'Any internships in penal institutions?'

'An internship with the medical services at Champ-Dollon Prison, as a joint expert for forensic examinations, and the supervision of sex offenders.'

'International Academy of Law and Mental Health, Geneva Association of Psychologists-Psychotherapists, Swiss Society of Forensic Psychology . . . Good, good, good . . .'

He let his gaze settle upon her again. She had the unpleasant impression she was facing a jury.

'There is just one thing . . . You absolutely do not have the experience required for this type of patient: you are young; you still have a great deal to learn; you could – completely unintentionally, of course, through your inexperience – *ruin* everything we have been trying to accomplish. Which could turn out to be an additional source of distress for our clientele.'

'What do you mean?'

'I am sorry, but I must ask you to refrain from any contact with our seven most dangerous residents, the ones in Unit A. And I do not need an assistant; I already have the head nurse to assist me.'

She was silent for so long that he eventually raised an eyebrow. When she spoke, her voice was calm but firm.

'Dr Xavier, the reason I am here is those men in Unit A. Dr Wargnier must have told you that. You must have our correspondence in your files. The terms of our agreement are perfectly clear: not only did Dr Wargnier authorise me to see the seven inmates in Unit A, he also asked me to compile a report once my interviews were completed, particularly in the case of Julian Hirtmann.'

She could see him bristle. His smile vanished.

'Mademoiselle Berg, Dr Wargnier is no longer in charge of this establishment. I am.'

'In that case, I have no business here. I will have to refer the matter to your regulatory authority, and to the University of Geneva. And Dr Spitzner. I have come a long way, Doctor. You might have spared me this useless journey.'

She stood up.

'Mademoiselle Berg, now, please!' said Xavier, sitting up and spreading his hands. 'Don't get carried away! Sit down, sit down, please! You are welcome here. Do not misunderstand me: I have nothing against you. I am sure you will do your best. And who knows? Perhaps . . . perhaps another point of view, a – shall we say – "inter-disciplinary" approach could contribute to our understanding of these *monsters.* Yes, yes – why not? All that I ask of you is not to have any more contact than is absolutely necessary, and to adhere strictly to the internal regulations. The tranquillity of our institute depends upon a fragile equilibrium. The security measures here may be ten times more stringent than in any other psychiatric institution, but any breach of protocol could have incalculable consequences.'

Francis Xavier got up and walked round the desk.

He was even shorter than she had thought. Diane was five foot five and Xavier was clearly the same height – allowing for his heel-pieces. The immaculate white lab coat floated on him.

'Come with me. I will show you around.'

He opened a cupboard. Lab coats hanging all in a row. He took one and handed it to Diane. She caught a whiff of washing powder, and something musty.

He brushed against her. He laid his hand on Diane's arm; his nails were, she saw, very well groomed, perhaps too well groomed.

'They are truly terrifying individuals,' he said smoothly, looking her in the eyes. 'Forget what they are, forget what they have done. Concentrate on your work.'

She remembered Wargnier's words on the telephone: he had said virtually the same thing.

'I've already dealt with sociopaths,' she objected, but her voice lacked confidence, for once.

A strange look flashed briefly through his red glasses.

'None like these ones, mademoiselle. *None like these ones.*'

White walls, white floor, white neon lights . . . Like most people in the West, Diane associated the colour with innocence, candour and virginity. And yet there were vile murderers living in the midst of all this whiteness.

'Originally, white was the colour of death and mourning,' said Xavier, as if reading her thoughts. 'This is still the case in the East. White is also a limit value – like black. Finally, it is the colour which is associated with rites of passage. This is a rite of passage for you at this moment, wouldn't you say? But I am not the one who chose the décor – I've only been here for a few months.'

Steel gates slid open and closed as they passed through; electronic locks clunked in the thickness of the walls. Xavier's short figure strode ahead.

'Where are we?' she asked, counting the closed-circuit cameras, the doors, the emergency exits.

'We are leaving the administration offices to enter the actual psychiatric unit. This is the first security barrier.'

Diane watched as he inserted a magnetic card into a box fitted on the wall, which read the card and spat it back out. The metal gate opened. On the far side was a glass cubicle, where two guards in orange boiler suits sat under the electronic surveillance screens.

'At present we have eighty-eight patients who are considered dangerous, capable of committing acts of violence. Our clientele have been sent here from penal institutions and other psychiatric establishments in France, but also from Germany, Switzerland, Spain . . . These individuals have mental health issues, compounded with delinquency, violence and criminality. Patients who turned out to be too violent to stay in the hospitals that had initially taken them in, detainees whose psychosis is too severe to be treated in prison, or murderers who have been ruled irresponsible by the courts. Our clientele requires a highly qualified staff, and an infrastructure that will guarantee both their security and that of the staff and visitors. We are in Ward C at the moment. There are three levels of security: low, medium and high. This is a low-level area.'

Diane raised an eyebrow every time Xavier talked about the clientele.

'The Wargnier Institute has shown itself to be uniquely competent in the treatment of aggressive, dangerous, violent patients. Our practice is founded on the highest, most modern standards. In the initial stages we carry out a psychiatric and criminological evaluation, which includes, in particular, fantasy analysis and plethysmography.'

She started. Plethysmography consisted of measuring a patient's reactions to audio and video stimuli showing a variety of scenarios and partners, such as the sight of a naked woman or child.

'You are using aversion therapy with subjects who are shown to have deviant profiles when they are subjected to the plethysmographic test?'

'Precisely.'

'It's not as if aversive plethysmography has received unanimous approval,' she said.

'Here it works,' answered Xavier firmly.

She felt him stiffen. Whenever anyone spoke of aversion therapy, Diane thought of *A Clockwork Orange*. Aversion therapy meant associating a recording of a deviant fantasy – visions of rape, naked children and so on – with very unpleasant or even painful sensations: electric shock or inhaling ammonia, for example, instead of the pleasant sensations the patient usually associated with the fantasy. Systematic repetition of the experience was supposed to produce a lasting change in the subject's behaviour. A sort of Pavlovian conditioning, in other words, as tested on sex abusers and paedophiles in certain countries, like Canada.

Xavier was playing with the button of the pen sticking out of his chest pocket.

'I know that many practitioners in this country are sceptical about the behaviour therapy approach. It is a practice that has its roots in the Anglo-Saxon countries and the Pinel Insitute in Montreal, which is where I came from. We have obtained remarkable results. But obviously your French colleagues find it difficult to acknowledge such an empirical method, particularly one from the other side of the Atlantic. They fault it for overlooking such fundamental notions as the unconscious, the superego and the implementation of impulses in repression strategies . . .'

Behind his glasses his eyes were gazing at Diane with an exasperating indulgence.

'Many people in this country still favour an approach that takes the findings of psychoanalysis into greater consideration, which involves reshaping the deepest layers of a personality. In so doing they overlook the fact that the total absence of guilt or emotion displayed by major psychopathic perverts will always cause their efforts to fail. With this type of patient, only one thing works: reconditioning.' His voice flowed over the word like a stream of icy water. 'One must make the subject responsible for his treatment, thanks to an entire range of rewards and punishments, and thus create conditioned behaviour. We also conduct risk assessments at the request of the judicial or medical authorities,' he continued, stopping outside yet another door made of Securit glass.

'Haven't the majority of studies shown that most of these assessments do not serve much purpose?' asked Diane. 'Some of them maintain that, half the time, psychiatric risk assessments are wrong.'

'So they say,' conceded Xavier. 'But more often than not it turns out the risk has been overevaluated. If there is any doubt, in our evaluation report we systematically advise continuing detention or prolonging hospitalisation. And then,' he added, with a smile of absolute fatuousness, 'these evaluations correspond to a deeply rooted need in our societies, Mademoiselle Berg. The courts ask us to resolve a moral dilemma in their place, a dilemma which in all truth *no one is capable of resolving*: how can one be sure that the measures taken with regard to a particular dangerous individual will meet the needs required for the protection of society, and yet not infringe upon the basic rights of that individual? No one has an answer to this question. Therefore the courts pretend to believe that psychiatric evaluations are reliable. No one is fooled, of course. But it allows the judicial machine, which is constantly threatened with obstruction, to go on turning, while maintaining the illusion that judges are wise people and that they make informed decisions – something which, I might add in passing, is the greatest lie of all the lies on which our democratic societies are founded.'

A new black box was fitted into the wall, much more sophisticated than the previous one. It contained a little screen and sixteen buttons for typing a code, as well as a large red sensor where Xavier now placed his right index finger.

'Obviously, we don't have this type of problem with our residents. They have given ample proof of their dangerousness. This is the second security barrier.'

There was a little glassed-in office on the right. Once again Diane saw two figures behind the glass; she was sorry to see Xavier walk right by them without stopping. She would have liked him to introduce her to the rest of the staff. But she was already convinced he would do nothing of the sort. The two men watched through the glass as she went by. Diane suddenly wondered what sort of welcome she would have. Had Xavier spoken about her to anyone? Was he insidiously planning to make life difficult for her?

For a fraction of a second she indulged in a nostalgic memory of her student room, her friends at the university, her office in the department . . . Then she thought of someone. She felt a flush come to her cheeks, and hastened to consign the image of Pierre Spitzner to the deepest recesses of her mind.

Servaz looked at himself in the mirror in the flickering glow of the neon light. He was wan. He leaned with both hands on the chipped edge of the sink and tried to breathe calmly. Then he bent down and splattered cold water onto his face.

His legs could hardly hold him; he had the strange sensation he was walking on soles filled with air. The return journey by helicopter had been a rough one. The weather had taken a definite turn for the worse and Captain Ziegler had to keep a tight grip on the controls. Battered by the gusting wind, the chopper had made its descent swaying from side to side like a life raft on a raging sea. The moment the skids touched the ground, Servaz rushed to the toilets to throw up.

He turned round, his thighs pressed against the row of sinks. Graffiti profaned some of the stall doors: 'Bib the King of the Mountain' (the usual boasting). 'Sofia is a bitch' (followed by a mobile telephone number). 'The manager is a filthy bastard' (a lead?). Then a drawing of several small Keith Haring-like characters, buggering each other in single file.

Servaz took out the small digital camera that Margot had given him for his most recent birthday, went over to the doors and photographed them one by one.

Then he went back out and along the corridor to the foyer.

Outside it had started snowing again.

'Feeling better?'

He detected sincere indulgence in Irène Ziegler's smile.

'Yes.'

'Why don't we go and question the workers?'

'If you don't mind, I'd rather interrogate them on my own.'

He saw Captain Ziegler's lovely face go blank. He could hear Cathy d'Humières speaking to the journalists outside: stereotypical fragments, the usual bureaucratic style.

'Have a look at the graffiti in the toilets and you'll understand why,' he said. 'There are things they might be more likely to reveal in the presence of a man . . . things they'd keep silent about if a woman were present.'

'Fine. But don't forget that there are two of us on this investigation, Commandant.'

The five men watched as he came in, their gazes filled with a mixture of anxiety, weariness and anger. Servaz remembered they'd been held in this room since morning. Clearly someone had brought them food and drink. Scattered over the large conference table were empty cups, full ashtrays and the remains of pizza and sandwiches. Their stubble had grown and they were as hairy as castaways on a desert island, except for the cook – a fellow with a shiny bald head and earlobes pierced with multiple rings.

'Hello,' said Servaz.

No answer. But they sat up imperceptibly. In their eyes he could see they were surprised by his appearance. They'd been told a commandant from the crime unit was coming, yet there before them was a man who could be a teacher or a journalist, a fit forty-something, his cheeks covered in stubble, wearing a velvet jacket and worn jeans. Servaz shoved to one side a pizza box smudged with grease and a plastic cup with cigarette butts floating in a puddle of coffee. Then he sat on the edge of the table, ran a hand through his brown hair and turned to them.

He inspected them closely. One by one. Lingering each time for a few tenths of a second. They all lowered their eyes – except for one.

'Who saw it first?'

A man sitting in a corner of the room raised his hand. He was wearing a short-sleeved sweatshirt with the logo 'University of New York' over a checked shirt.

'What's your name?'

'Huysmans.'

Servaz took his notebook from his jacket.

'Tell me what you saw.'

Huysmans sighed. His patience had been sorely tested over recent hours, and he was not a particularly patient person by nature. He had already told his story at least half a dozen times, so this time his delivery was somewhat mechanical.

'You came back down without setting foot on the platform. Why was that?'

Silence.

Finally the man who had just spoken confessed, 'Fear. We were afraid the guy might still be somewhere nearby – or hiding in the tunnels.'

'What makes you think it's a man?'

'Can you picture a woman doing something like that?'

'Have there been any quarrels or disagreements among the workers?'

'It's like everywhere,' said another man. 'Drunken brawls, stuff about women, some guys just don't get along. That's all.'

'What's your name?' asked Servaz.

'Gratien Etcheverry.'

'Life up there must be pretty tough, no?' said Servaz. 'The danger, the isolation, living one on top of the other – it must create tension.'

'The men who get sent up there have their heads screwed on, Commissaire. The manager must have told you. If they don't, they stay down here.'

'It's commandant, not commissaire. Still, when it's stormy, with the bad weather and everything, you could easily blow a fuse, right?' he insisted. 'I've been told it's really hard to get to sleep at that altitude.'

'That's true.'

'Can you explain it to me?'

'The first night you're so knackered from the altitude and the work that you sleep like a log. But then you start sleeping less and less. The last nights maybe only two or three hours at the most. It's the mountain that does it. We catch up at the weekend.'

Servaz looked at them again. Some of them were nodding in agreement.

He stared at these tough men, guys who'd never had any higher education and made no claims on genius; nor had they gone after easy money; no, they went about wordlessly carrying out a thankless task in the public interest. The men were roughly his age – between forty and fifty; the youngest might have been thirty. He was suddenly ashamed about what he was doing. Then he caught the cook's fleeting gaze again.

'Did this horse mean anything to any of you? Did you know it? Had you ever seen it?'

They stared back at him, astonished, then slowly shook their heads.

'Have there already been accidents up there?'

'Several,' said Etcheverry. 'The last one was two years ago: a guy lost his hand.'

'What is he doing now?'

'He works down here, in the office.'

'His name?'

Etcheverry hesitated. He turned red. He looked at the others, embarrassed.

'Schaab.'

Servaz figured he would have to find out more about this Schaab: *a horse loses his head/a worker loses his hand* . . .

'Any fatal accidents?'

Etcheverry shook his head again.

Servaz turned to the eldest. A sturdy bloke in a short-sleeved T-shirt that enhanced his muscular arms. He was the only one, along with the cook, who hadn't spoken yet – and the only one who hadn't lowered his gaze when Servaz looked at them. Moreover, a gleam of defiance showed in his pale eyes. A flat, wide face. A cold gaze. *Narrow-minded, incapable of nuance, won't tolerate uncertainty,* thought Servaz.

'Are you the one who's been here the longest?'

'Yup,' said the man.

'How long have you been working here?'

'Up there or down here?'

'Both.'

'Twenty-three years up there. Forty-two in all.'

A flat voice, with no inflection. Smooth as a mountain lake.

'What is your name?'

'What's it to you?'

'I'm the one asking the questions, right? So, what's your name?' said Servaz, equalling the man's offhand manner.

'Tarrieu,' barked the man, annoyed.

'You're how old?'

'Sixty-three.'

'How well do you all get along with management? You can speak openly: it will go no further than these walls. In the toilet just now I saw some graffiti saying, "The manager is a bastard."'

Tarrieu made a face that was half scornful, half amused.

'That's true. But if this were some sort of revenge, he's the one we would have found up there. Not that horse. Don't you think, *Officer*?'

'Who said anything about revenge?' retorted Servaz in the same tone. 'You want to conduct this investigation for me? You want to join the force?'

There was some sniggering. Servaz watched as Tarrieu's face flushed bright red, like a cloud of ink spreading through water. Clearly the man was capable of violence. But to what degree? That was the eternal question. Tarrieu opened his mouth to reply, then at the last minute thought better of it.

'No,' he said at last.

'Are any of you familiar with the riding academy?'

The cook with the earrings raised his hand awkwardly.

'Your name?'

'Marousset.'

'You go horse-riding, Marousset?'

Tarrieu spluttered with laughter; the others copied him. Servaz felt his anger welling up.

'No . . . I'm the cook . . . From time to time I go to lend a hand to Monsieur Lombard's cook, at the chateau . . . when they have parties – birthdays, Bastille Day . . . The stables are just next door.'

Marousset had big, pale eyes with pupils no bigger than the head of a pin. And he was sweating profusely.

'So had you already seen that horse?'

'I'm not interested in horses. Maybe . . . There are loads of horses over there . . .'

'And do you see Monsieur Lombard very often?'

Marousset shook his head.

'I go there just once a year . . . maybe twice . . . and I hardly leave the kitchen . . .'

'But you've spotted him now and again, all the same, haven't you?'

'Yes.'

'Does he come to the plant at all?'

'Lombard, here?' said Tarrieu sarcastically. 'For Lombard this plant is a grain of sand. Do you look at every blade of grass when you mow the lawn?'

Servaz turned to the others. They confirmed this with a slight nod.

'Lombard doesn't live round here,' continued Tarrieu in the same provocative tone. 'Paris, New York, the Caribbean, Corsica . . . He doesn't give a damn about this plant. He only keeps it because it said in his old man's will that he had to hang on to it. But he really doesn't give a toss.'

Servaz nodded. He wanted to say something biting. But what would be the point? Perhaps Tarrieu had his reasons. Perhaps one day he'd had a run-in with some incompetent or bent copper. *People are icebergs*, he thought. *Beneath the surface there's this enormous mass of the things they don't tell you, a mass of pain and secrets. No one is really what they seem.*

'Can I give you some advice?' said Tarrieu suddenly.

Servaz froze, on the defensive. But his tone had changed: the hostility was gone, and along with it the wariness and sarcasm.

'I'm listening.'

'The watchmen,' said the senior man. 'Rather than wasting your time with us, you'd do better to question the watchmen. Shake them up a bit.'

Servaz gave him an intense look.

'Why?'

Tarrieu shrugged.

'You're the cop here,' he said.

Servaz went down the corridor and out through the swing doors, moving abruptly from an overheated atmosphere to the icy chill of the foyer. Flashbulbs were popping outside, flooding the foyer with their brief glow, casting large, menacing shadows. Servaz saw Cathy d'Humières climbing into her car. Night was falling.

'Well?' asked Ziegler.

'They probably have nothing to do with it, but I want an additional background check on two of them. The first is Marousset, the cook. The other one is called Tarrieu. And then someone called Schaab: the guy who lost his hand in an accident last year.'

'And why the other two?'

'Just checking.'

He pictured Marousset's gaze again.

'I want to get in touch with the drug unit as well, see if they don't have a file on the cook.'

Captain Ziegler gave him a close look, but she didn't add anything.

'How are we doing checking out the immediate vicinity?'

'We've been questioning everyone who lives along the road to the power plant, in the event that someone might have seen a vehicle go by during the night. So far, nothing.'

'Anything else?'

'Graffiti on the outside walls of the plant. If there are any taggers lurking about the neighbourhood, they might have seen or heard something. With everything that went into this crime, there had to be a preparatory stage, researching the location. Which takes us back to the watchmen. Maybe they know who left the graffiti. And why didn't they hear anything?'

Servaz thought back to what Tarrieu had said. Maillard came up to them. He was taking notes on a little pad.

'And the Wargnier Institute?' said Servaz. 'On the one hand we have a crime that, clearly, has been committed by a lunatic; on the other a bunch of criminal madmen locked away only a few kilometres from here. Even if the director of the Institute swears that none of his residents got over the wall, we'll have to look into it thoroughly.' He glanced first at Ziegler then at Maillard. 'Have you got a staff psychiatrist?'

Ziegler and Maillard looked at each other.

'A profiler is supposed to get here in a day or two,' replied Irène Ziegler.

Servaz frowned imperceptibly. *A profiler for a horse* . . . He knew that the gendarmerie were a few lengths ahead of the police in this respect, as in others, but he wondered if this wasn't overdoing it a bit: even the gendarmerie ought not to be mobilising its specialists as easily as all that.

Éric Lombard really did have a long reach . . .

'You're lucky we're here,' said Ziegler ironically, rousing him from his thoughts. 'Otherwise you would have had to call in an independent expert.'

He didn't pick up on it. He knew what she was driving at: since they weren't prepared to train their own profilers, the way the gendarmerie did, the cops often had to make do with outside experts – shrinks who were not always properly qualified for this type of work.

'But it is only a horse, after all,' he said, without conviction.

He looked at Irène Ziegler. She wasn't smiling now. On the contrary, he could detect the tension and worry on her features. She gave him a searching look. *She's not taking this business at all lightly anymore*, he thought. Like him, she must be beginning to think that something far more serious lay behind this macabre deed.

5

'Have you read *The Time Machine?*'

They were walking down long, deserted corridors. The sound of their footsteps rang out and filled Diane's ears, together with the psychiatrist's chatter.

'No,' she replied.

'H. G. Wells, a socialist. He was interested in technological progress, social justice and the class struggle. He was the first to explore themes like genetic engineering in *The Island of Doctor Moreau* or mad scientists in *The Invisible Man*. In *The Time Machine* he imagined his narrator travelling into the future, where he discovers that England has become a sort of earthly paradise inhabited by a peaceful, carefree population, the Eloi.' Never taking his eyes from her, he slotted his card into yet another box. 'The Eloi are the descendants of the privileged members of the bourgeoisie. Over thousands of years, they have attained such a degree of comfort and stability that their intelligence has withered, to the point where they have the intellectual wherewithal of a five-year-old. As they haven't had to make the slightest effort for centuries, they tire very easily. Sweet, cheerful creatures, but also terrifyingly indifferent: when one of their kind is drowning in plain sight of the others, not one of them raises a finger to try and help.'

Diane was only half listening; she was trying to pick up a sign of life, of human presence – and to remember her way through this labyrinth.

'When night falls, the narrator discovers another, even more terrifying reality: the Eloi are not alone. Beneath the earth there lives a second race, hideous, dreadful people, the Morlocks. They are the descendants of the proletariat. Little by little, because of their masters' greed, they have evolved away from the upper classes to become a distinct race, as ugly as the others are gracious. They are forced to live deep in tunnels and shafts. They have grown so unaccustomed to the light that they only leave their lair after nightfall. That is why the minute the sun sets, the Eloi flee their idyllic countryside in fear to huddle together in their ruined palaces. Because the Morlocks, in order to survive, have become cannibals . . .'

Diane was beginning to feel exasperated by the psychiatrist's incessant chatter. What was he driving at? Clearly, he loved to hear himself talk.

'Is that not a fairly accurate description of our own society, Mademoiselle Berg? On the one hand, the Eloi, whose intelligence and will have been diminished by well-being and the absence of danger, while their selfishness and indifference have increased. On the other hand, there are predators to remind them of the old lesson: fear. You and I are Eloi, Mademoiselle Berg . . . and our residents are Morlocks.'

'Isn't that a rather simplistic view?'

He ignored her remark.

'Would you like to know the moral of this story? For of course there is one. Wells thought that diminishing intelligence was a natural consequence of the . . . disappearance of danger. An animal living in perfect harmony with its environment is a pure mechanism. Nature only calls upon intelligence if habit and instinct do not suffice. It can only develop where there is change – *and where there is danger.*'

He gave her a long look, with a grin on his face.

'Tell me about the staff,' she said. 'We haven't come across very many people up to now. Is everything automatic?'

'We employ thirty or so nursing auxiliaries. Along with six nurses, a doctor, a sexologist, a head cook, seven kitchen and dining-room staff and nine maintenance men – all of them part-time, of course, due to budget restrictions, with the exception of three night-time nursing auxiliaries, the head nurse, the cook . . . and myself. So there are six of us who sleep on site. In addition to the guards, who, I hope, do not sleep.' He gave a curt little laugh. 'With you, it will make seven.'

'Six, for . . . eighty-eight patients?'

How many guards? she immediately wondered. She thought of this immense building at night, emptied of its staff, with eighty-eight dangerous psychotics locked up along its deserted corridors, and shuddered.

Xavier seemed to notice her uneasiness. His smile spread at the same time as his gaze wrapped itself round her, as black and slimy as a puddle of oil.

'As I explained, our security systems are not only numerous, they are superfluous. The Wargnier Institute has not had a single escape or even an incident of note since its foundation.'

'What sort of medicines do you use?'

'The use of anti-obsessional agents has proven more efficient than classical substances, as you know. Our basic treatment consists in associating a hormone-based medication of the LHRH variety with an SSRI antidepressant. This treatment directly impacts the production of sexual hormones and reduces obsessive disorders. Of course, it's a treatment that is totally ineffective with our seven residents in Unit A . . .'

They had just come out into a big hall, at the foot of a staircase through whose slatted stairs a rough stone wall could be seen. Diane assumed these were the impressive walls she had seen on arriving, with their rows of tiny windows like those of a prison. The stone walls, the concrete stairway, the cement floor: Diane wondered what the building had originally been designed for. Yet there was a picture window looking out onto the mountains slowly being swallowed by the night. She was surprised by how quickly it was growing dark beyond the window. She had not noticed the time go by. Suddenly a silent shadow fell upon her and she swallowed a gasp of surprise.

'Mademoiselle Berg, may I introduce our head nurse, Élisabeth Ferney. How are our "champions" this evening, Lisa?'

'They're rather nervous. I don't know how, but they've already heard about the power plant.'

A cold, authoritarian voice. The head nurse was a tall woman in her forties with features that were rather severe but not altogether unpleasant. Chestnut hair, a superior air, a direct but defensive gaze. On hearing her words Diane remembered the roadblock as she drove up there.

'I was stopped by the gendarmerie on my way,' she said. 'What happened?'

Xavier did not even bother to reply. Diane hardly seemed to matter to him. Lisa Ferney focused her brown eyes on her, then turned to stare at the psychiatrist.

'You don't actually intend to take her to Unit A this evening, do you?'

'Mademoiselle Berg is our new . . . *psychologist,* Lisa. She will be here for a while. And she will have access to everything.'

Once again the nurse's gaze lingered on Diane.

'In that case, I suppose we will be seeing a fair amount of each other,' said Lisa Ferney as she climbed up the stairs.

The concrete stairway led to a new door at the very top of the building. This one was not made of glass but of very thick steel with a rectangular porthole. Through the porthole Diane saw a second, identical door. A double-entrance security door – like the ones in submarines or in bank vaults. Above the steel doorway a camera was filming them.

'Good evening, Lucas,' said Xavier, looking up at the lens. 'Open up.'

A dual LED lamp went from red to green and Xavier opened the heavy armoured door. Once they were inside, they waited in silence for the first door to lock again. In this confined space, above the mineral, metallic odour, Diane could smell the head nurse's perfume. Suddenly, coming from beyond the second door, a long scream startled her. A sound which took a long time to fade.

'With the seven residents of Unit A,' said Xavier, who did not seem to have noticed the scream, 'as I told you, we practise a particular kind of aversion therapy. A sort of "behavioural reconditioning".' It was the second time he had mentioned this, and once again Diane stiffened. 'I'll say it again, these individuals are pure sociopaths: no remorse, no empathy, no hope of a cure. Other than this reconditioning, we go no further than a minimal therapy, such as regularly checking their serotonin levels: too little serotonin in the blood is an indicator of violence and impulsiveness. Otherwise, our goal is never to give them the opportunity to cause harm. These monsters are afraid of nothing. They know they will never get out. No amount of threats, no authority can reach them.'

There was a bleep and Xavier placed his manicured fingers on the second armoured door.

'*Welcome to hell, Mademoiselle Berg.* But not this evening. No, Lisa is right, not this evening. Tonight I'll go in alone: Lisa will walk you back.'

Servaz stared at the second watchman.

'So, you didn't hear a thing?'

'No.'

'Because of the telly?'

59

'Or the radio,' replied the man. 'If we're not watching the telly, we've got the radio on.'

'Full volume?'

'Fairly loud, yeah.'

'And what were you watching or listening to last night?'

The watchman sighed. Between the gendarmes and this copper, this was the third time he'd had to tell his version of the facts.

'A football match, Marseille versus Atlético Madrid.'

'And after the match you put on a DVD, is that right?'

'Yes.'

The neon light caused his skull to shine. His hair was close-shaven and Servaz could see a big scar through it. The moment he'd come into the room he'd decided to adopt a casual, friendly manner with the man. With this sort of person you had to get into his space right away, make it clear to him who was in charge.

'What film did you watch?'

'Some horror B-movie: *The Night Has Eyes*.'

'And how was the volume?'

'Loud, I said.'

Servaz's silences were unnerving the watchman. He felt he had to explain: 'My colleague is kind of deaf. Besides, we're all alone here. So who's to care?'

Servaz nodded understandingly. Almost word for word what his co-worker had said.

'A football match lasts how long, as a rule?'

The watchman looked at him as if he'd just landed from another planet.

'Forty-five minutes, times two . . . Plus half-time and stoppages . . . Two hours. Give or take.'

'And the film?'

'Dunno . . . Hour and a half, two hours . . .'

'What time did the match start?'

'It was the Europa League – eight forty-five.'

'Hmm . . . Which would take us to around half past midnight . . . And did you do the rounds after that?'

The watchman looked down, sheepish.

'No.'

'Why not?'

'We watched another film.'

Servaz leaned closer. He caught a glimpse of his reflection in the window. Outside it was pitch black. The temperature must have fallen well below zero.

'Another horror film?'

'No . . .'

'What, then?'

'A porn flick . . .'

Servaz raised an eyebrow and put on his best cruel, depraved smile. For a split second he looked like a cartoon character.

'Hmm, I see . . . Until what time?'

'Dunno. Two in the morning, I suppose.'

'Blimey! And then?'

'Then what?'

'Then did you do your rounds?'

This time the watchman's shoulders drooped noticeably.

'No.'

'Another film?'

'No, we went to sleep.'

'Aren't you supposed to do night rounds?'

'Yes.'

'How often?'

'Every two or three hours.'

'And last night you didn't do a single one, is that correct?'

The watchman was staring at the toes of his shoes. He seemed completely absorbed in the contemplation of a tiny mark.

'No . . .'

'I didn't hear you.'

'*No.*'

'Why not?'

This time the watchman raised his head.

'Listen, who . . . who would think of coming up here in the middle of winter? There's never a soul . . . It's deserted . . . So what's the point of doing any rounds?'

'But that's what you're paid for, after all? What about the graffiti on the walls?'

'Kids who come up here now and again . . . But only when the weather's fine.'

Servaz leaned a little closer, his face a few inches from the watchman's.

'So, if a car had come up during the film, you wouldn't have heard it?'

'No.'

'And the cable car?'

The watchman hesitated for a split second. Servaz caught it.

'Same.'

'Are you sure?'

'Uh . . . yeah.'

'And the vibrations?'

'What vibrations?'

'The cable car vibrates. I felt it. You didn't feel it last night?'

Another hesitation.

'We were caught up in the film.'

He was lying. Servaz was absolutely sure of it. A fabric of lies they'd woven, together, before the gendarmes arrived. The same answers, the same hesitations.

'One match plus two films, that takes about five hours,' calculated Servaz, as if he were a restaurant owner working out the bill. 'But when you watch a film, it's not noisy all the time, right? You've got silent stretches in a film. Even a horror film . . . *especially* a horror film . . . When the tension rises, when the suspense is at a peak . . .' Servaz leaned even closer. His face was practically touching the watchman's. He could smell his bad breath – and his fear. 'The actors don't spend the whole time screaming and getting their throats cut, do they? And the cable car, how long does it take to get up there? Fifteen minutes, twenty? Same on the way down. You see what I'm getting at? It would be one hell of a coincidence if the racket the cable car makes were completely drowned out by the film, no? What d'you think?'

The watchman looked at him, a hunted beast.

'I dunno,' he said. 'Maybe it was before . . . or during the match . . . Either way we didn't hear anything.'

'Do you still have the DVD?'

'Uh . . . yeah.'

'Right, we'll do a little reconstruction – to see if it is actually possible that your very private little show could have drowned out all that noise. And we'll try it with a football match, too. And even a porn movie. Why not? – may as well do things properly.'

Servaz could see the sweat running down the watchman's face.

'We'd had a few drinks,' he muttered, so quietly that Servaz had to ask him to repeat what he'd said.

'Pardon?'

'We'd been drinking . . .'

'A lot?'

'Fair amount.'

The watchman raised his hands, palms upward.

'Look . . . you can't imagine what it's like up here, in the middle of winter, Commissaire. Have you had a look around you? When it gets dark, you feel like you're alone on earth. It's as if . . . as if you were in the middle of nowhere . . . on a desert island, yeah . . . An island lost in the middle of an ocean of snow and ice,' he added, with surprising lyricism. 'No one down at the plant gives a damn what we do here at night. To them we're invisible, we don't exist. All they want is to make sure no one comes to sabotage the equipment.'

'For a start, it's commandant, not commissaire. Be that as it may, someone did manage to get up here, break the door, start up the cable car and load a dead horse on board,' said Servaz patiently. 'That all takes time. And doesn't go unnoticed.'

'We'd closed the shutters. There was a blizzard last night. And the heating doesn't work properly. So we get cosy, we have a little drink to get warm, and we put on the telly or the music with the volume on loud so we can't hear the wind. Pissed as we were, we might have thought it was the noise from the storm. So we didn't do our job, fair enough – but we didn't have anything to do with the horse.'

One point for him, thought Servaz. It was not hard to imagine what a storm up here would be like. The wind gusting, the snow, the old deserted buildings full of draughts, shutters and doors creaking . . . An instinctive fear, of the kind which gripped man's most distant forebears on their first encounter with the unbridled fury of the elements. Even tough nuts like these two.

He hesitated. The two watchmen's versions matched. And yet he still didn't believe them. No matter which way he turned the problem, Servaz was sure of at least one thing: *they were lying*.

'Well?'

'Their stories tally.'

'Yes.'

'A little too neatly.'

'That's what I think.'

Maillard, Ziegler and Servaz had gathered in a windowless little room lit by a pale neon light. On the wall a poster proclaimed, 'Occupational medicine, prevention and evaluation of workplace hazards,' with instructions and a telephone number. Fatigue was apparent on the faces of the two gendarmes. Servaz knew it must be the same with him. At this time and in this place, they all felt as if they had come to the end of everything: the end of tiredness, the end of the world, the end of the night.

Someone had brought coffee. Servaz looked at his watch: five thirty-two. The manager of the plant had gone home two hours earlier, with a grey face and red eyes, after he had said goodbye to everyone. Servaz frowned when he saw Ziegler typing on a little laptop. In spite of her fatigue she was concentrating on her report.

'They agreed on what they were going to say before we had time to separate them,' he concluded, gulping down his coffee. 'Either because they're the ones who did it or because they have something else to hide.'

'What do we do?' asked Ziegler.

He thought for a moment, crumpled his polystyrene cup and tossed it towards the basket, but missed.

'We've got nothing on them,' he said, leaning over to pick it up. 'We let them go.'

Servaz pictured the watchmen. He didn't trust either one of them. He'd met truckloads of blokes like them in seventeen years in the profession. Before the interview Ziegler had told him that their names had shown up in the criminal offences database – which didn't really mean much: there were twenty-six million offences recorded there, some of which were categorised as fifth class, applicable to minor offences – to the great displeasure of civil liberties activists, who had given the French police a Big Brother Award for having set up an 'information-age watchtower'.

But he and Ziegler had also discovered that the two watchmen had criminal records. Both of them had served what were several fairly short prison sentences, given the crimes they'd committed: assault and battery, death threats, unlawful detention, extortion and an entire range of violent crimes, some of them against their partners. Yet in spite of criminal records as voluminous as a Who's Who, both of them together had not spent more than five years in jail. They'd come across as mild as lambs during their interviews, swearing that they'd learned their lesson and were back on the straight and narrow. Their professions of faith were identical, their sincerity null and void: the usual blah-blah, which only a lawyer could even pretend to swallow. Instinctively, Servaz had sensed that if he weren't a cop, and had asked them the same questions in a deserted car park somewhere, they'd have given him a rough time and taken a certain pleasure in hurting him.

He wiped his hand over his face. There were circles under Irène Ziegler's lovely eyes and he found her even more attractive. She had removed her uniform jacket, and the neon lights played in her blonde hair. He looked at her neck. There was a small tattoo emerging from under her collar. A Chinese ideogram.

'Let's take a break and get a few hours' sleep. What's the programme for tomorrow?'

'The riding academy,' she said. 'I sent the men to cordon off the box. The crime scene investigators will take care of it tomorrow.'

Servaz remembered there'd been mention of breaking and entering.

'We'll start with the staff at the stables. Someone must have heard or seen something. Captain,' he said, turning to Maillard, 'I don't think we'll need you. We'll keep you posted.'

Maillard nodded.

'There are two questions that are an absolute priority. Where has the horse's head got to? And why go to all the trouble of hanging the horse up at the top of a cable car line? It must mean something.'

'The plant belongs to the Lombard Group,' said Ziegler, 'and Freedom was Éric Lombard's favourite horse. So obviously he's their target.'

'An accusation?' suggested Maillard.

'Or revenge.'

'Revenge can also be an accusation,' said Servaz. 'A man like Lombard is bound to have enemies, but I can't imagine a simple business rival going to such lengths. I think we need to look, rather, at his employees, the ones who've been fired, or who have a past history of psychiatric problems.'

'There's another hypothesis,' said Ziegler, snapping her laptop shut. 'Lombard is a multinational with subsidiaries in a lot of countries: Russia, South America, South-East Asia . . . It could be they've crossed paths with the mafia or some organised crime ring, at one point or other.'

'Good thought. Let's keep all these possibilities in mind and rule nothing out for the time being. Is there a decent hotel anywhere round here?'

'There are fifteen or more hotels in Saint-Martin,' Maillard replied. 'Depends what sort of place you're looking for. If I were you, I'd try the Russell.'

Servaz made a note of the name, still thinking about the watchmen, their silence, their awkwardness.

'Those guys are afraid,' he said suddenly.

'What?'

'The watchmen: something or someone has frightened them.'

6

Servaz was startled awake by his mobile. He looked at the time on the clock radio: eight thirty-seven. *Shit!* He hadn't heard the alarm; he should have asked the owner of the hotel to wake him up. Irène Ziegler would be coming for him in twenty minutes. He grabbed the telephone.

'Servaz here.'

'How'd it go up there?'

Espérandieu's voice . . . As usual, his assistant was at the office before everyone else. Servaz could see him now, reading a Japanese manga or trying out the latest police software applications, dressed in a designer jumper his wife had chosen, a lock of hair falling over his brow.

'Hard to say,' he replied, heading towards the bathroom. 'Let's just say it's not like anything we've ever known.'

'Drat, I wish I'd seen it.'

'You'll see it on the video.'

'What does it look like?'

'It looks like a horse hanging from the support tower of a cable car, at an altitude of two thousand metres,' answered Servaz, adjusting the temperature of the shower with his free hand.

There was a brief silence.

'A horse? On top of a cable car?'

'Yes.'

The silence lingered.

'Fuck,' said Espérandieu bluntly, sipping something a little too close to the speaker.

Servaz would have wagered it was something sparkling rather than a plain coffee. Espérandieu was a specialist in chemicals: chemicals to wake him up, chemicals to go to sleep, for memory, for energy, against coughs, colds, headaches and stomach upsets . . . The most incredible thing was that Espérandieu was not some ageing copper nearing retirement, but a young crime unit sleuth who'd only just turned thirty. In great shape. Who went running along the Garonne three times a week. Absolutely no issues with his cholesterol or his triglycerides, but he dreamt up a whole host of imaginary evils, some of which, by virtue of his zeal, eventually became reality.

'When will you be back? We need you here. The kids are claiming that the police *beat them.* Their lawyer says the old woman's a drunk,' continued Espérandieu. 'That her testimony is worthless. He's asked the examining magistrate to release the oldest one immediately. The other two have gone home.'

Servaz pondered this for a moment.

'And fingerprints?'

'Not until tomorrow.'

'Call the deputy public prosecutor. Tell him to drag it out for the older boy. We know it's them: the prints will talk. Have him speak to the magistrate. And tell the lab to get a move on.'

He hung up. He was wide awake now. Once he was out of the shower he dried off quickly and put on clean clothes. He brushed his teeth and inspected himself in the mirror above the sink, thinking about Irène Ziegler. He was surprised to see he was taking longer than usual to check his face. He wondered what sort of image he projected to the gendarme. A guy who was still young, not bad-looking, but utterly drained by fatigue? A cop who was sort of stubborn, but efficient? A divorced man whose solitude was plain to see, both on his face and in the state of his clothes? If he'd had to describe himself, what would he have seen? Without a doubt the shadows under his eyes, the wrinkles around his mouth and the vertical line between his brows – he looked as if he'd just come out of the spin cycle of a washing machine. Still, he remained convinced that despite the extent of the damage something youthful and passionate rose to the surface. Good God! What had got into him all of a sudden? He suddenly felt like some teenager in heat; he shrugged and went out onto the balcony.

The Russell Hotel was located in the upper part of Saint-Martin, and his room looked out over the town's rooftops. With his hands on the railing he watched the shadows ebbing from the narrow streets, giving way to a luminous dawn. At nine o'clock in the morning, the sky above the mountains was as bright and transparent as a crystal dome. Up there, at two thousand five hundred metres, the glaciers would be emerging from shadow, sparkling in sunlight, even though the sun was still hidden. Straight ahead of him lay the old town, the historic centre. On the left, beyond the river, council housing. On the other side of the broad basin, two kilometres away, a high wooded slope rose like a wave, scarred with a wide trench of cable cars. From his perch Servaz could see figures darting through the shadow of the little streets in the centre of town, on their way to work; there were the headlights of delivery vans; adolescents perched on back-firing mopeds on their way to their colleges and lycées; tradesmen rolling up their iron shutters. Servaz shivered. Not because it was cold, but because he had just thought again of that horse hanging up there, and the person or persons responsible.

He leaned over the railing. Ziegler was waiting for him downstairs, lounging against her squad car. She'd swapped her uniform for a rollneck jumper and leather jacket. She was smoking, a bag slung over her shoulder.

Servaz went down to join her and invited her for a coffee. He was hungry and he wanted something to eat before they set off. She checked her watch, made a face, then finally stepped away from the car to follow him back inside. The Russell was a hotel from the 1930s; the rooms were poorly heated; the corridors, with high moulded ceilings, were endless and gloomy. But the dining room, a vast veranda with vases of flowers on the tables, offered a breathtaking view. Servaz sat down at a table near the picture window and ordered a black coffee and a buttered slice of bread, and Ziegler asked for a fresh orange juice. At the next table were some Spanish tourists – the first of the season – speaking loudly, punctuating their sentences with lusty-sounding words.

When he turned his head, a detail caught his attention and left him puzzled: not only was Irène Ziegler not in uniform, that morning she had also clipped a fine silver ring to her left nostril, and it shone in the light from the window. It was the sort of jewellery he expected to see on his daughter, not on an officer of the gendarmerie. *Times have changed*, he thought.

'Sleep all right?' he asked.

'No. I ended up having to take half a sleeping tablet. And you?'

'I didn't hear the alarm. At least the hotel is quiet; most of the tourists haven't arrived yet.'

'They won't be here for another two weeks. It's always quiet this time of year.'

'Up above those cable cars,' said Servaz, pointing to the double line of support towers on the mountain opposite, 'is there a ski resort?'

'Yes, Saint-Martin 2000. Forty kilometres and twenty-eight downhill runs, including six black, four chair lifts, ten tow lifts. But there's also a resort at Peyragudes, fifteen kilometres from here. Do you ski?'

A joking rabbit-like smile appeared on Servaz's face.

'The last time I put on a pair of skis, I was fourteen years old. It didn't make for a very good memory. I'm not exactly . . . *sporty*.'

'Yet you look fit,' said Ziegler with a smile.

'As do you.'

Oddly enough, it made her blush. The conversation was hesitant. Last night they were two police officers deep in the same investigation, exchanging professional observations. This morning they were awkwardly trying to get acquainted.

'May I ask you a question?'

He nodded.

'Yesterday you asked for a further inquiry into three of the workers. Why?'

The waiter brought their order. He looked as old and sad as the hotel itself. Servaz waited until he had left to tell her about his interview with the five men.

'That guy Tarrieu,' she said, 'what sort of impression did he make on you?'

Servaz pictured the man's flat, massive face, his cold stare.

'An intelligent man, but full of anger.'

'Intelligent. That's interesting.'

'Why?'

'All the dramatic staging . . . this *madness* . . . I think whoever did it is not only mad but also intelligent. Highly intelligent.'

'In that case, we can rule out the watchmen,' he said.

'Perhaps. Unless one of them is faking.'

She took her laptop from her bag and opened it on the table, between her orange juice and Servaz's coffee. He had the same thought he'd had earlier: times were changing; a new generation of investigators was taking over. She might lack experience but she was also more in sync with her era – and the experience would come in any case.

She typed something and he took a moment to look at her. She was very different from the day before, when he'd seen her in her uniform. He stared at the little tattoo on her neck, the Chinese ideogram that was just visible above her rollneck collar. He was reminded of Margot. What was it with this fashion for tattoos? That, and piercing. Should he allot some sort of significance to them? Ziegler had a tattoo and a ring in her nose. Maybe she had other secret jewels elsewhere: in her belly button, or even her nipples or down below; he'd read about that somewhere. The idea of it unsettled him. He suddenly wondered what the private life of a woman like her consisted of, yet he was only too aware that his own private life over the last few years had been a desert. He brushed the thought aside.

'Why the gendarmerie?' he asked.

She looked up, hesitated for a moment.

'Oh,' she said, 'you mean why did I go into the gendarmerie?'

He nodded, not taking his eyes off her. She smiled.

'Job security, I suppose. And to not be doing the same thing as everyone else.'

'Which is?'

'I was at university, studying sociology. I hung out with a very free-thinking crowd. I even lived in a squat. Cops, gendarmes, they were the enemy: fascists, guard dogs for the people in power, the outpost of reactionary thinking – the police were the ones who protected bourgeois comfort and oppressed the immigrants, the homeless or just people who were down on their luck . . . My father was a gendarme. I knew he wasn't like that, but I still thought my university friends were right and my father was the exception, that was all. And then after university, when I saw my revolutionary friends becoming doctors, solicitors, bank workers or HR managers, talking more and more about money, investments, rates of return and all that, I started to ask myself questions. Since I was unemployed at the time, I ended up taking the entrance exam.'

As simple as that, he thought.

'Servaz, that's not a name from round here,' she said.

'Nor is Ziegler.'

'I was born in Lingolsheim, not far from Strasbourg.'

He was going to reply in turn when Ziegler's mobile began to vibrate. She made a gesture of apology and answered. He saw her frown as she listened. She switched off the phone and looked at him blankly.

'That was Marchand. He's found the horse's head.'

'Where?'

'At the riding academy.'

They left Saint-Martin by a different road from the one he had come in on. At the edge of town they drove past the headquarters of the mountain gendarmerie, whose representatives were called on with increasing frequency to help with the media coverage of high-risk sports.

Three kilometres further along they left the main road for a secondary route. Now they were driving across a wide plain surrounded by mountains, still a certain distance away, and Servaz felt that he could breathe a bit. Before long the land on either side of the road began to be fenced off. The sun was shining, dazzling on the snow.

'This is the estate of the Lombard family,' announced Irène Ziegler.

She drove fast, despite the bumps. They came to a crossing that led to a forest track. Two horsemen wearing riding caps watched them go by, a man and a woman. Their mounts had the same black and brown coat as the dead horse. *Bay*, recalled Servaz. Further along a sign indicating 'RIDING ACADEMY' told them to turn left.

The forest receded.

They went by several squat buildings that looked like barns, and Servaz saw some large rectangular enclosures scattered with jumps, a long, low stable, a paddock and a more imposing building that might be an indoor riding ring. A van from the gendarmerie was parked outside.

'A lovely place,' said Ziegler, climbing out of the car. She cast a gaze around the enclosures. 'Two outdoor schools, including one for showjumping and one for dressage, a cross-country course and, best of all, over there at the back, a galloping track.'

A gendarme came to meet them. Servaz and Ziegler followed him. They were greeted by nervous neighing and the sound of scraping hooves, as if the horses knew that something was going on. A cold sweat immediately trickled down Servaz's back. As a young man he had tried riding. A bitter failure. Horses frightened him. As did speed, height or even major crowds.

When they reached the far end of the stables, they came upon a yellow 'gendarmerie nationale' tape stretching along the side of the building roughly two metres from the wall. They had to walk through the snow to go round. Marchand and Captain Maillard were waiting for them at the back with two other gendarmes, outside the cordon. In the shade of the brick wall was a huge pile of snow. Servaz stared at it for a moment before he made out some brown spots. He shuddered when it dawned on him that two of the spots were a horse's ears, and the third one the lowered lid of its closed eye. Maillard and his men had done a good job: as soon as they had seen what they were about to uncover, they had roped off the surroundings without going any closer to the pile of snow. The snow was bound to have been disturbed before they got there, by the footprints of the person who'd found the head for a start, but they had avoided adding their own. The crime scene investigators hadn't arrived yet. No one was allowed into the area until they had finished their work.

'Who found it?' asked Ziegler.

'I did,' said Marchand. 'This morning, as I walked past the boxes, I noticed footprints in the snow around the building. I followed them and came upon this mound. I knew immediately what it was.'

'You *followed* them?' said Ziegler.

'Yes. But given the circumstances, I immediately thought of you, so I was careful not to trample them and to keep at a distance.'

Servaz suddenly focused his attention.

'Do you mean that these traces are intact, that no one has stepped on them?'

'I would not allow my colleagues to come anywhere near the area or to walk in the snow,' answered the steward. 'There are only two sorts of footsteps here: mine, and the ones belonging to the bastard who decapitated my horse.'

'If I dared, Monsieur Marchand, I would kiss you,' said Ziegler.

Servaz saw the old stable boss blush and he smiled. They retraced their steps and looked over the yellow tape.

'There,' said Marchand, pointing to the footprints that ran along the wall, sharp and clear, the dream of any crime scene investigator. 'Those are his prints; these are mine, there.'

Marchand had kept his footsteps a good metre away from his predecessor's. At no point did their paths cross. He had not, however, been able to resist the temptation of going over to the mound, as the path of his steps showed.

'You didn't touch the mound?' asked Ziegler when she saw where his footprints led.

He lowered his head.

'I did. I'm the one who brushed the snow off the ears and eye. As I already told your colleagues, I nearly went on to brush off all the snow, but then I realised what I was doing and stopped in time.'

'You did the right thing, Monsieur Marchand,' said Ziegler, congratulating him.

Marchand turned to them with a dazed expression, full of fear and bemusement.

'What sort of person could do this to a horse? Maybe you understand something about this society we live in – because I certainly don't. Are we all going mad?'

'Madness is contagious,' replied Servaz. 'Like the flu. That's something psychiatrists should have figured out a long time ago.'

'Contagious?' asked Marchand, disconcerted.

'It doesn't jump from one individual to the next the way flu does,' explained Servaz, 'but from one sector of the population to another. It contaminates an entire generation. The carrier of malaria is the mosquito. The carrier of madness, or at least its preferred carrier, is the media.'

Marchand and Ziegler looked at him, stunned. Servaz gave a little wave of the hand, as if to say, 'Don't mind me,' and walked away. Ziegler checked her watch. Nine forty-three. She looked at the sun blazing brilliantly above the trees.

'For God's sake! What are they doing? The snow is going to melt all this before long.'

The sun had turned and some of the footprints, which had been in the shade when they arrived, were now exposed to its rays. It was still cold enough to stop the snow from melting, but it would not stay that way for much longer. At last they heard the sound of a siren coming from the forest. The crime scene investigators' lab van pulled up in the courtyard one minute later.

A yellow plastic tab with a black number had been stuck into the snow next to every clue or print to be photographed. Squatting down by one of the prints, an investigator was taking pictures with a flash, enlarging or reducing the depth of field with each shot. A small, graduated black vinyl ruler lay on the snow next to the print. A

74

second man came over and opened a briefcase, which Servaz recognised as a footprint moulding kit. The first investigator came to lend him a hand, for they had to act quickly: the snow was already melting in several places. While they were busy, the third man was uncovering the horse's head. The back wall faced north so, unlike his colleagues, he could take his time. Servaz felt as if he were watching the patient labour of an archaeologist unearthing a particularly precious artefact. At last the entire head appeared. Servaz didn't know anything about horses, but he could have sworn that even a specialist would have said Freedom was a splendid specimen. The animal had his eyes closed, as if he were sleeping.

'It looks as if he were put to sleep before he was killed and beheaded,' remarked Marchand. 'If that's the case, at least he won't have suffered. And that would explain why no one heard anything.'

Servaz exchanged a glance with Ziegler: the toxicology test would confirm it, but this already went some way towards answering one of their questions. On the other side of the tape the investigators were taking their last samples with the help of tweezers, sealing them in tubes. Servaz knew that fewer than seven per cent of all criminal investigations were solved thanks to the material evidence found at the scene of the crime, but that in no way diminished his admiration for the men's patience and perseverance.

When they had finished, Servaz was the first to step over the tape, and he bent down over the footprints.

'Size forty-five or forty-six,' he reckoned. 'Ninety nine per cent sure it's a man.'

'According to the investigator, those are hiking boots,' said Ziegler. 'And the guy wearing them tends to lean a bit too much on the heel and the outside of his foot. Imperceptible, though. Except to a podiatrist. There are also some characteristic defects – there, there and there.'

Like fingerprints, the marks left by a pair of shoes were distinctive, not only because of the size and the pattern on the sole, but also due to an entire range of tiny telltale signs acquired through wear: everyday damage, tiny pieces of gravel embedded in the sole, gashes, holes and cuts caused by branches, nails, pieces of glass or metal or by sharp stones . . . Except that, unlike fingerprints, these signs had a limited lifespan. Only a rapid comparison with the original pair could ensure positive identification, before kilometres of walking, over all sorts of terrain, would erase these tiny defects and replace them with others.

'Have you informed Monsieur Lombard?' he asked Marchand.

'Yes, he's crushed. He is going to cut short his stay in the US to come back as soon as possible. He'll be on the plane tonight.'

'Are you the one who's in charge of the stables?'

'The riding academy, yes.'

'How many people work here?'

'It's not a very big academy. In the winter there are four of us. Between us we do everything, more or less. But let's say there's one groom, there's me, there's Hermine – she's the most distraught of all – who works mainly as a stablehand for Freedom and two other horses, and then there's a riding instructor. In the summer we hire additional staff: two instructors, guides for trekking, seasonal workers.'

'How many of you sleep on site?'

'Two of us: the groom and me.'

'Is everyone here today?'

Marchand looked at them in turn.

'The instructor is on holiday until the end of the week. Autumn is slack season. I don't know whether Hermine came in today. She's terribly upset. Follow me.'

They walked across the stable yard towards the tallest building. On entering, Servaz was overwhelmed by the smell of horse manure. A thin film of sweat formed at once on his face. They walked past the tack room and found themselves at the entrance to a large indoor riding ring. A horsewoman was exercising a white horse; the horse marked out each of his steps with an infinite grace. The rider and her horse seemed completely united. The animal's white coat was tinged with blue: from a distance, his chest and nose shone like porcelain. Servaz thought of a female centaur.

'Hermine!' called the manager of the stables.

The horsewoman turned her head and rode slowly towards them, came to a halt and dismounted. Servaz saw that her eyes were red and swollen.

'What is it?' she asked, patting the horse's neck and nose.

'Can you fetch Hector? The police want to interview you. You can go into my office.'

She nodded silently. No older than twenty. Smaller than average, quite pretty in a tomboyish way, with freckles, and hair the colour of wet straw. She gave Servaz a sorrowful look, then walked away, leading the horse behind her, head down.

'Hermine loves horses; she's an excellent rider and an excellent trainer. And a good kid, but she's got quite a personality. She just needs to grow up a bit. She's the one who looked after Freedom. Ever since he was born.'

'What did that involve?' asked Servaz.

'Getting up very early, grooming and caring for the horse, feeding, taking him out to the field to lunge him. The groom's job is both to exercise and take care of the horses. Hermine also has two other adult thoroughbreds she's responsible for. Show animals. It's not a profession where you count your hours. Of course, she wasn't going to start breaking Freedom in until next year. Monsieur Lombard and she were waiting impatiently. He was a very promising horse, with a fine pedigree. He was the mascot here, so to speak.'

'And Hector?'

'He's the oldest of us all. He's been working here for ever. He was here long before I arrived, before anyone.'

'How many horses are there?' asked Ziegler.

'Twenty-one. Thoroughbreds, French saddle horses, one Holsteiner. Fourteen of them belong to us; the rest are boarders. We provide boarding, foaling and coaching for outside customers.'

'How many boxes are there?'

'Thirty-two. And one foaling box that's forty metres square, with video surveillance. And exam rooms for pregnant mares, a dispensary, two stabling areas, an inseminating centre, two outdoor schools with professional showjumping obstacles, eight hectares of paddocks, pens and pathways, with wooden shelters and a galloping track.'

'It's a very fine academy,' confirmed Ziegler.

'At night there are only the two of you to keep an eye on everything?' asked Servaz.

'There's an alarm system, and all the boxes and buildings are locked: these horses are worth a great deal.'

'And you didn't hear anything?'

'No, nothing.'

'Do you take something to help you sleep?'

Marchand gave him a scornful look.

'We're not in town here. We sleep well. We live the way we were meant to live, to the rhythm of things.'

'Not the slightest odd noise? Anything unusual? That might have woken you up in the middle of the night? Try and remember.'

'I've already tried. If I had thought of something, I would have told you. There are always noises in a place like this: the horses move; the wood creaks. With the forest nearby, it's never silent. I haven't paid it any mind for a long time. And then there are Cisco and Enzo; they would have barked.'

'The dogs,' said Ziegler. 'What breed are they?'

'Cane corso.'

'I don't see them anywhere. Where are they?'

'We've locked them in.'

Two dogs and an alarm system. And two men on site . . .

How much did a horse weigh? He tried to remember what Ziegler had told him: roughly two hundred kilos. The visitors could not possibly have come and gone on foot. How could they have killed a horse, decapitated it, loaded it onto a vehicle and left again without anyone noticing, without waking up the dogs or the residents? Without setting off the alarm? Servaz didn't get it. Neither the men nor the dogs had been alerted – and the watchmen at the power plant had not heard a thing, either: it was simply impossible. He turned to Ziegler.

'Could we ask a vet to come and take a blood sample from the dogs? At night, are they free to roam or kept in the kennel?' he asked Marchand.

'They're outdoors, but attached to a long chain. No one can get to the boxes without walking within reach of their fangs. And their barking would have woken me. Do you think they were drugged, is that it? That would surprise me: they were wide awake yesterday morning, perfectly normal.'

'The toxicology test will confirm that,' replied Servaz, already wondering why the horse had been drugged and not the dogs.

Marchand's office was a cluttered little room between the tack room and the stables, its shelves crowded with trophies. The window looked out onto the forest and snow-covered fields bounded by a complex network of gates, enclosures and hedges. On his desk were a laptop computer, a lamp and a jumble of invoices, binders and books about horses.

During the previous half-hour Ziegler and Servaz had toured the facilities and examined Freedom's box, where the CSIs were already busy at work. The door to the box had been forced, and there was a great deal of blood on the ground. Clearly Freedom had been decapitated there and then, probably with a saw, probably after he had been put to sleep. Servaz turned to the groom.

'You didn't hear anything that night?'

'I was asleep,' replied Hector.

He hadn't shaved. He looked old enough to have taken retirement long ago. Grey hairs pricked his chin and hollow cheeks like the spines of a porcupine.

'Not a single sound? Nothing?'

'There's always some noise in a stable,' he said, echoing Marchand's words, but unlike the two watchmen's answers, this did not sound rehearsed.

'Have you been working for Monsieur Lombard for a long time?'

'I've always worked for him. And his father before him.'

His eyes were bloodshot, and tiny burst veins wove a fine purplish network over the thin skin of his nose and cheeks. Servaz would have wagered he didn't take sleeping tablets but always had another soporific to hand, of the liquid variety.

'What is he like to work for?'

The man stared at Servaz with his red eyes.

'We don't see him very often, but he's a good boss. And he loves the horses. Freedom was his favourite. Born right here. A royal pedigree. He was crazy about that horse. So was Hermine.'

The old man lowered his eyes. Servaz saw that, next to him, the young woman was trying to keep from crying.

'Do you think someone could have had a grievance against Monsieur Lombard?'

The man kept his head lowered.

'That's not for me to say.'

'But you've never heard that he'd been threatened in any way?'

'No.'

'Monsieur Lombard has a lot of enemies,' interrupted Marchand.

Servaz and Ziegler turned to look at the steward.

'What do you mean?'

'Just what I said.'

'Do you know any of them?'

'I'm not interested in Éric's business. Only his horses interest me.'

'You used the word "enemy" – you must have meant something by it.'

'Just a manner of speaking.'

'And what else?'

'Éric's business always causes a lot of tension.'

'That is clear as mud,' insisted Servaz. 'Is it involuntary or intentional?'

'Forget what I said,' answered the steward. 'It was just idle talk. I don't know anything about Monsieur Lombard's business.'

Servaz didn't believe it for a moment. But he thanked him. On leaving the building, he was dazzled by the blue sky, the snow melting in the sun's rays. Horses gazed out of their boxes into a stream of sunlight; others were already being ridden, taken over the jumps. Servaz stood there for a moment, clearing his mind, his face in the sun . . .

Two dogs and an alarm system. And two men on site.

And no one had seen or heard a thing. Here or over at the power plant. Impossible. Absurd.

The more details they unearthed about this horse business, the more space it seemed to fill in his thoughts. He felt as if he were a pathologist digging up first a finger, then a hand, then an arm, then the entire corpse. He was beginning to feel more and more uneasy. Everything about this business was extraordinary. And incomprehensible. Instinctively, like an animal, Servaz sensed danger. He was trembling, in spite of the sun.

7

Vincent Espérandieu raised an eyebrow when he saw a lobster-faced Servaz come into his office on the Boulevard Embouchure.

'You've got sunburn,' he pointed out.

'It's the reflection,' answered Servaz by way of a greeting. 'And I went for a helicopter ride.'

'You, in a helicopter?'

Espérandieu had known for a long time that his boss had no liking for speed or heights: drive any faster than 130 kilometres and he went all pale and sunk down into his seat.

'Have you got something for a headache?'

Vincent Espérandieu opened a drawer.

'Aspirin? Paracetamol? Ibuprofen?'

'Something fizzy.'

His assistant took out a bottle of mineral water and a glass and handed them to Servaz. He laid a fat, round tablet in front of him, then swallowed a capsule with a bit of water himself. Through the open door, someone let out the perfect imitation of a neigh; there was a smattering of laughter.

'Stupid bastards,' said Servaz.

'But you've got to admit they're right: the crime unit for a horse . . .'

'A horse that belongs to Éric Lombard.'

'Ah.'

'And if you'd seen it, you'd be wondering too whether the men who did it aren't capable of more.'

'Men? You think there are more than one?'

Servaz looked distractedly at the beautiful little fair-haired girl grinning on Espérandieu's computer screen, a large star painted round her left eye like a clown.

'Can you see yourself hauling two hundred kilos of meat all alone in the middle of the night and hanging it up three hundred metres from the ground?'

'That is a perfectly valid point,' his assistant conceded.

Servaz shrugged and looked around him. On one side of the room, the blinds were lowered against the grey sky and roofs of Toulouse, and on the other, over the glass partition that separated them from the corridor. The second desk, belonging to Samira Cheung, a new recruit, was empty.

'And the kids?' he asked.

'The eldest has been remanded in custody. As I told you, the other two went home.'

Servaz nodded.

'I spoke to the father of one of them,' Espérandieu added, 'an insurer. He doesn't get it. He's shattered. At the same time, when I mentioned the victim, he lost his temper: "He was a tramp. Drunk all God's hours! You're not going to put kids in prison because of some homeless tramp?"'

'He said that?'

'Word for word. He met me in his big office. The first thing he said was, "My son hasn't done a thing. That's not how he was brought up. It's the others. That boy Jérôme dragged him into it. His father is unemployed." He said it as if in his eyes being unemployed was the same thing as drug trafficking or paedophilia.'

'Which one is his son?'

'The boy called Clément.'

The ringleader, thought Servaz. *Like father like son. And the same disdain for others.*

'Their lawyer has contacted the examining magistrate,' continued Espérandieu. 'Obviously they've got their whole strategy worked out: they're going to charge the eldest one.'

'The son of the unemployed bloke.'

'Yes.'

'The weakest link.'

'Those people make me want to puke,' said Espérandieu.

He had a childish, drawling voice. Because of it, and his somewhat mannered air, some of his colleagues suspected him of being interested not only in women, even when they were as beautiful as his wife. Servaz had wondered as much himself when Espérandieu joined the department. The young man's taste in clothes also caused the hackles to rise among some of the Cro-Magnon men on the squad, the ones who thought that if you were a cop, you were duty bound to display nothing but virility and machismo triumphant.

Life had been kind to Espérandieu. At the age of thirty he'd made an excellent marriage and he had a very pretty little five-year-old girl, the one whose smile lit up his computer screen. Servaz had quickly befriended him, and his assistant had invited him round to dinner half a dozen times in the two years since he'd joined the squad. Every time, Servaz had been completely overwhelmed by the charm and wit of Madame and Mademoiselle Espérandieu: they looked as if they belonged in the pages of a magazine – in adverts for toothpaste, travel or family holidays.

But then there'd been an incident between the newcomer and the veterans on the squad, whose homicidal tendencies seemed to be aroused by the fact of sharing their everyday life with a young and potentially bisexual colleague. Servaz had had to get involved, with the end result that he'd made himself a few lasting enemies. There were two blokes in particular, two macho and narrow-minded rough-necks, who would never forgive him. One of them had got a bit of an earful during their argument. But Servaz had also earned Espérandieu's lasting recognition and respect: Charlène was pregnant again and they'd asked Servaz to be the godfather.

'A reporter from France TV3 called, and several journalists from the papers. They wanted to know if we had any proof regarding the kids. But above all they wanted to know if they'd been beaten. "Rumours of police brutality towards minors": that's the expression they used. As usual, they've spread the word. Copy and paste, that's all they know how to do. But someone must have started the rumour.'

Servaz frowned. If the journalists were on to something, the telephone would not stop ringing. There would be declarations, rebuttals, press conferences – and a minister would get on television and promise to 'get to the bottom of it'. And even once it had been proven that everything had been done according to the rules, if they managed to prove it, the suspicion would remain.

'Would you like a coffee?' asked his assistant.

Servaz nodded. Espérandieu got up and went out. Servaz looked at the computer screens blinking in the semi-darkness. He thought about those three teenage boys again – what had pushed them to commit such a senseless act.

Those kids were being sold dreams and lies all day long. *Sold*, not given. Cynical salesmen had made adolescent frustration their stock in trade. Mediocrity, pornography, violence, lies, hatred, alcohol, drugs

– everything was for sale in the flashy display windows of mass consumerism, and young people were a perfect target.

Espérandieu came back with the coffee.

'The kids' rooms?' asked Servaz.

Samira Cheung came in. That morning their latest recruit was wearing a short leather jacket that was too light for the season, a sweatshirt that proclaimed, 'I am an Anarchist,' a pair of black leather trousers and thigh-high red vinyl boots.

'Hey,' she said, her iPod earphones dangling over her jacket, a steaming mug in her hand.

Servaz returned her greeting, not without a mixture of fascination and bewilderment at the sight of her unbelievable get-up. Samira Cheung was Chinese on her father's side, and French-Moroccan on her mother's. She had told Espérandieu (who in turn had wasted no time in telling Servaz) that twenty-six years ago her mother, an interior decorator with an international reputation, had fallen madly in love with a client from Hong Kong – a man whose beauty and intelligence were absolutely exceptional, according to Samira – but that she had come back to Paris, pregnant, once she discovered that Samira's father was into hard drugs and visited prostitutes on an almost daily basis. It was weird: Samira Cheung combined a perfect body with one of the ugliest faces Servaz had ever seen. Protruding eyes accentuated by heavy eyeliner, a large mouth painted an aggressive red, and a pointed chin. One of the male chauvinists on the squad had summed up her look in one sentence: 'With her, every day is Halloween.' Samira Cheung had one feature, however, where her genes or education deserved full credit: her mind was sharp as a whip. And she did not hesitate to use it. She had quickly assimilated the basics of the profession and had proven her sense of initiative on more than one occasion. Servaz had entrusted her with increasingly complex tasks and she was not afraid to put in overtime to get them done.

Now she swung her boot heels up onto the edge of her desk and rocked back on her office chair before turning to look at them.

'We've searched the three boys' rooms,' she said, in answer to Servaz's question. 'On the whole we didn't find much – except for one detail.'

Servaz looked at her.

'The first two boys had very violent video games at their house. The sort of thing where you have to blow off your opponent's head to get a maximum number of points; or those ones where you have to bomb civilian populations or wipe out your enemies with all sorts of sophisticated weapons. Really gory stuff, you know, bloody as hell.'

Servaz recalled a recent debate in the press regarding these violent video games. The games' manufacturers took offence, stating that they were 'very aware of the issue of violence and mindful not to overstep the boundaries'. They considered that some of the accusations against them were 'unacceptable'. And went right on selling games where the player could commit torture, robberies and murder. At that point the psychiatrists got involved, learnedly affirming that there was no correlation between video games and violence among young people. But other studies had shown that, on the contrary, young people who indulged in such displayed greater indifference towards other people's suffering.

'In contrast, we didn't find any video games at the home of the one called Clément. And yet there was a console . . .'

'As if someone had cleaned up beforehand,' said Espérandieu.

'The father,' suggested Servaz.

'Right,' replied his assistant. 'We suspect he made all the games disappear to give us a cleaner image of his son. And the better to accuse the other two.'

'Did you put the rooms under seal?'

'Yes, but the family's lawyer has filed an appeal to have them removed, on the grounds that it's not the crime scene.'

'Have they got computers in their rooms?'

'Yes, we looked at them, but someone did a crack job of erasing the data. We've ordered the parents not to touch anything. We have to get back there with an investigator to go over their hard drives.'

'We can establish premeditation,' said Samira, 'if we can prove the kids planned the crime. That would reduce the notion of an accident to nothing.'

Servaz gave her a questioning look.

'What do you mean?'

'Well, up to now nothing proves they really wanted to kill him. The victim had a huge amount of alcohol in his blood. The lawyers for the defence might be able to cite drowning as the primary cause of death: it will depend on the results of the autopsy.'

'Drowning in fifty centimetres of water?'

'Why not? It's happened before.'

Servaz thought for a moment: Samira was right.

'And the prints?' he asked.

'We're waiting.'

She put her heels back down on the floor and stood up.

'I have to go. I've got an appointment with the magistrate.'

'A good recruit, right?' said Espérandieu when she had left the room.

Servaz nodded and smiled. 'You seem to like her.'

'She works hard, she's dependable, and she's eager to learn.'

Servaz agreed. He had not hesitated to entrust the bulk of the investigation into the homeless man's death to Vincent and Samira. They shared the same office, liked quite a few of the same things (particularly certain types of clothing), and they seemed to get along, in so far as one could expect two cops with strong characters to get along.

'We're having a little party on Saturday,' said Vincent. 'You're invited. Charlène insists.'

Servaz thought about his assistant's wife and her disturbing beauty. The last time he saw her, she was wearing a red party dress which enhanced her figure, while her long auburn hair danced in the light like flames, and he had felt his throat tighten. Charlène and Vincent had been perfect hosts, it had been a very enjoyable evening, but that did not mean he wanted to join their circle of friends. Now he declined the offer, on the pretext that he had promised to spend the evening with his daughter.

'I put the kids' file on your desk,' called Espérandieu just as he was going out the door.

Back in his office, Servaz connected his phone to the charger and switched on his computer. Two seconds later his mobile informed him he had a text message, and he unlocked it. Reluctantly. For Servaz mobile phones were the ultimate stage of technological alienation. But Margot had forced him to get one after he arrived half an hour late to one of their appointments.

dad its me can u get sat am off? kisses

What the hell sort of language is this? he wondered. Are we climbing back up the tree when it's taken us this long to get down it? He suddenly felt as if he had lost the key. That was the effect the modern world had on him these days: he felt as much a stranger here as if he had arrived straight from the eighteenth century in a time machine.

86

He retrieved her number from the memory and heard his daughter's voice explaining, in detail, that she would return the call if you left a message, to a background noise that led him to conclude that hell was peopled with bad musicians.

His gaze fell on the homeless guy's file. Logically he should get to work on it straight away. He owed it to that poor man whose cock-up of a life had ended in the stupidest way imaginable. But he didn't feel up to it.

Servaz had something else on his mind. He turned to his computer, went to Google and typed in a string of key words. The search engine provided no fewer than 20,800 results for 'Éric Lombard Group Enterprises'. Less than if he'd typed Obama or the Beatles, of course, but it was nevertheless a significant figure. No surprise, either: Éric Lombard was a charismatic figure much loved by the media, and he must have had the fifth or sixth biggest fortune in the country.

Servaz skimmed the first pages. Several sites offered biographies of Éric Lombard, of his father, Henri, and his grandfather, Édouard; there were also articles from the business pages, the gossip columns and even the sporting press – because Éric Lombard had built up a stable of champions in the making. There were a few pages devoted to his own sporting feats. The man was a dedicated athlete and adventurer – an experienced mountain climber, marathon and triathlon runner and rally driver; he had also taken part in expeditions to the North Pole and the Amazon. There were a few pictures showing him on his motorcycle in the desert or at the controls of a commercial airliner. Scattered among the articles were several English words whose meaning completely escaped Servaz: *free-ride, base-jump, kite-surf.*

There was one photograph, almost always the same one, that accompanied some of the articles. *A Viking.* That's what Servaz thought when he looked at him. Blond hair, blond beard, steel-blue gaze. Tanned. Healthy. Energetic. Virile. Sure of himself. Staring at the camera lens the way he must stare at everyone who came near him: with the impatience of someone who is expected and who has arrived.

A living advertisement for the Lombard Group.

Age: thirty-six.

From a legal point of view, the Lombard Group was an SCA, a limited joint-stock partnership, but the parent company – Lombard Enterprises – was a holding company.

The four main subsidiaries of the group were Lombard Media (books, press, distribution, audiovisual), Lombard Company (sporting equipment, clothing, travel and luxury products, fourth global purveyor of luxury items), Lombard Chemical (pharmaceuticals and chemicals) and AIR, specialising in aeronautics, defence and the space industry. The Lombard Group owned fifteen per cent of AIR, through the intermediary of the parent holding company, Lombard Enterprises. Éric Lombard himself was the CEO and managing partner of Lombard SCA, CEO of the Lombard Company and of Lombard Chemical, and chairman of the board of AIR. With a degree from a French business school and the London School of Economics, he began his career with one of the subsidiaries of the Lombard Company, a well-known sporting-goods manufacturer.

The group employed 78,000 people, spread over roughly 75 countries, and the previous year had a turnover of €17,928 million, for a gross receipt of €1,537 million and net profit of €677 million, while its financial debts totalled €3,458 million. Figures that would have dazed any normally constituted individual, but probably not specialists in international finance. As he read this, Servaz understood that if the group had hung on to the ageing little hydroelectric power plant, it could only be for historical and sentimental reasons. It was there, in the Pyrenees, that the Lombard empire had been born.

To string the horse up there was to target a symbol. The aim was to deal a blow to Éric Lombard where it would hurt: his family history and his consuming passion for horses.

For that is what stood out from all these articles: of all his passions, his love of horses came first. Éric Lombard owned stud farms in several countries – Argentina, France, Italy – but he was loyal to his first love: the riding academy where he had his start as a horseman, near the family chateau in the Comminges valley.

Servaz was suddenly convinced that the dramatic crime at the power plant was not the gesture of some lunatic who'd escaped from the Institute, but almost certainly a conscious, premeditated and planned act.

He paused to think. He hesitated to set off down a trail which would oblige him to take all of an industrial empire's skeletons out of the closet just to explain the death of a horse. On the other hand, the terrifying sight of the decapitated animal being brought out of the cable car remained, along with the shock he had felt at the time. What was it Marchand had said? 'Monsieur Lombard has a lot of enemies.'

The phone rang. Servaz picked up. It was d'Humières.

'The watchmen have disappeared.'

'Don't ever turn your back on them,' said Dr Xavier.

Beyond the huge picture windows the sun set the mountains ablaze, spreading a red lava of light into the room.

'Be attentive. Every second. You've got to get it right in here. You will learn soon enough to recognise the signals: a fleeting gaze, a snarl of a smile, breathing that's just a touch too rapid . . . Don't ever let your guard down. And don't ever turn your back on them.'

Diane nodded. A patient was walking towards them. One hand on his stomach.

'Where's the ambulance, Doctor?'

'The ambulance?' said Xavier, all smiles.

'The one that's supposed to take me to the maternity hospital. My waters have broken. It should be here by now.'

The patient was a man in his forties, well over six foot tall and weighing over twenty-three stone. Long hair, his face swallowed by a thick beard, tiny eyes shining feverishly. Next to him Xavier looked like a child. Yet he did not seem worried.

'It will be here soon,' he replied. 'Is it a girl or a boy?'

The little eyes stared at him.

'It's the Antichrist,' said the man.

He walked away. Diane noticed that a male nurse was watching his every move. There were fifteen or more patients in the ward.

'There are a fair number of gods and prophets here,' said Xavier, still smiling. 'Since time immemorial madness has drawn on religious and political sources. Not that long ago our residents saw communists everywhere. Now it's terrorists. Come.'

The psychiatrist went up to a round table where three men were playing cards. One of them resembled a convict, with muscular, tattooed arms; the other two looked normal.

'I'd like to introduce Antonio,' said Xavier, indicating the tattooed man. 'Antonio was in the French Foreign Legion. Unfortunately, he was convinced that the camp he'd been posted to was full of spies, and one night he ended up strangling one of them. Isn't that right, Antonio?'

Antonio nodded without taking his eyes from the cards.

'Mossad,' he said. 'They're everywhere.'

'As for Robert, he took it out on his parents. He didn't kill them, no, just messed them up rather badly. It must be said that his parents had been forcing him to slave away on the family farm since he was seven, feeding him on bread and milk, and making him sleep in the cellar. Robert is thirty-seven. They're the ones who should have been locked up, if you want my opinion.'

'It's the voices that told me to do it,' said Robert.

'And, finally, this is Greg. Possibly the most interesting case. Greg raped a dozen women in less than two years. He would spot them at the post office or the supermarket, follow them home and make a note of their address. Then he'd get into their place while they were asleep, hit them, tie them up and turn them on their stomach before he switched on the light. We'll pass on the details of what he put them through: just bear in mind that his victims have been marked for life. But he didn't kill them, no. Instead, he started writing to them. He was convinced that their . . . *intercourse* had made the women fall in love with him and that they were all carrying his child. So he left his name and address and it did not take the police long to track him down. Greg still goes on writing to them. Naturally we do not post the letters. I will show them to you. They are absolutely magnificent.'

Diane looked at Greg. An attractive man, in his thirties: dark hair, pale eyes – but when their eyes met, she shivered.

'Shall we continue?'

A long corridor ablaze with the setting sun.

A door with a small window on their left. Voices coming through the door. Nervous chatter, a rapid-fire delivery. She glanced through the window as they walked by and was taken aback. There was a man lying on an operating table, with an oxygen mask over his face and electrodes on his temples, with nurses standing round him.

'What is that?' she asked.

'Electroconvulsive therapy.'

Electroshock . . . Diane felt the hair rise on the back of her neck. Ever since it was first applied in psychiatry in the 1930s, the use of electric shock therapy had been controversial: its detractors believed it was inhumane, degrading, a form of torture. So much so that by the 1960s, with the arrival of antipsychotic drugs, the use of ECT had reduced considerably. Until a sudden resurgence in the mid-1980s in a number of countries, including France.

'You must understand,' said Xavier on seeing her mute surprise, 'ECT in the present day is not at all what it used to be. It is used on patients who have severe depression; they are placed under general anaesthesia and given a muscle relaxant. This treatment gets remarkable results: it is effective in over eighty-five per cent of cases of severe depression. A rate far higher than that of anti-depressants. It is painless, and thanks to today's methods there are no longer any orthopaedic complications or long-term effects on the skeleton.'

'But it does impact on memory and cognition. And the patient can remain in a state of confusion for several hours. And we still don't know exactly how ECT acts on the brain. Are there many depressives here?'

Xavier gave her a cautious look.

'No. Only ten per cent of our patients.'

'How many schizophrenics, psychopaths?'

'Roughly fifty per cent are schizos, twenty-five per cent are psycho-paths and thirty psychotics. Why do you ask?'

'I'm assuming you only use ECT on the patients with depression?'

She felt an infinitesimal displacement of air. Xavier stared at her.

'No, we also use it on the occupants of Unit A.'

She raised an eyebrow in surprise.

'I thought you had to have the patient's consent, or that of their legal guardian, in order to—'

'In this particular case, we do without.'

She looked hard at Xavier's impenetrable face. There was some-thing she was failing to grasp. She took a deep breath and tried to make her voice sound as neutral as possible.

'What is the purpose? It's not therapeutic . . . ECT is not known to be effective on pathologies besides depression, mania and certain very limited forms of schizophrenia, and—'

'For the purposes of law and order.'

Diane gave a slight frown.

'I don't understand.'

'And yet it is perfectly clear: it is a punishment.'

He had his back to her now, as he gazed at the orange sun

disappearing behind the black mountains. His shadow lengthened across the floor.

'Before you go into Unit A, there is one thing you must understand, Mademoiselle Berg: there is nothing left to frighten those seven men. Not even solitary confinement. They are in their own world; nothing can reach them. Get this into your head: you have never met patients like them. Ever. And of course corporal punishment is forbidden here, as elsewhere.'

He turned round and stared at her.

'They are afraid of only one thing: electroshock.'

'Do you mean,' said Diane hesitantly, 'that with them you apply it—'

'Without anaesthesia.'

8

As he drove down the motorway the next day, Servaz thought about the watchmen. According to Cathy d'Humières, they hadn't shown up for work the night before. After an hour had gone by, Morane, the power plant manager, had picked up the phone.

He'd called them on their mobiles. One after the other. No reply. So Morane had alerted the gendarmerie, who had sent some men over to their homes, twenty kilometres from Saint-Martin for one of them, forty or more for the other. The two men lived alone; they were not allowed to reside in the same *départements* as their former partners, whom they had repeatedly threatened to kill; one had even ended up in hospital. Servaz knew very well that in practice the police were not very diligent about enforcing such restrictions, for obvious reasons: it involved too much procedure, there were too many criminals, too many men on probation, too many sentences for everything to be enforced. One hundred thousand individuals sentenced to imprisonment without parole were actually at liberty, waiting their turn to serve their time – if they hadn't already made a run for it the moment they left the court, only too aware there was not much risk the French State would devote money and manpower to look for them, hoping they'd be forgotten by the time the statute of limitations kicked in.

After she'd told Servaz about the watchmen, the prosecutor had informed him that Éric Lombard was on his way back from the US and wanted to speak to the investigators without delay. Servaz had almost lost his temper. He had a murder on his hands; even if he wanted to find out who had killed the horse, even if he had a dread feeling that this business was a prelude to something worse, he was not at Éric Lombard's disposal.

'I don't know if I can,' he'd said curtly. 'There's a lot on, here, with the death of the homeless guy.'

'You'd do better to get down there,' insisted d'Humières. 'Apparently

93

Lombard called the Minister of Justice, who called the chief judge at the county court, who called me. And now I'm calling you. A regular chain reaction. And in any event it won't be long before Canter tells you the same thing; I'm sure Lombard also got hold of the Ministry of the Interior. Besides, I thought you found the culprits in that case.'

'The testimony we've got is a bit wobbly,' confessed Servaz, reluctantly, not wanting to go into details. 'And we're waiting to see what comes back from pathology. There were quite a few clues on site: fingerprints, footprints, blood—'

'It's not for nothing you're a Capricorn, am I right? Servaz, don't give me the line about the overworked policeman, I can't take it. I'm not about to beg you. Do me a favour. When can you go back down there? Éric Lombard will be expecting you at his chateau in Saint-Martin anytime after tomorrow. He'll be there over the weekend. Find the time.'

'Fine. But as soon as the interview is over I'm coming back here to wind up the case of the homeless man.'

On the motorway he stopped at a petrol station to fill up. The sun was shining; the clouds had fled elsewhere. He took a moment to call Ziegler. She had an appointment at nine o'clock at the stud farm in Tarbes for the horse's autopsy. She suggested he join her. Servaz agreed but said he'd rather wait for her in town.

'As you like,' she said, not hiding her surprise.

How could he explain to her he was afraid of horses? That walking through a stud farm full of the beasts was an unbearable ordeal for him? She gave him the name of a nearby bistro, on the avenue du Régiment-de-Bigorre. She would meet him there as soon as it was over.

When he got to Tarbes, an almost spring-like sunshine illuminated the town. At the edge of the Pyrenees National Park, tall buildings rose amid the greenery, against a background of immaculate white mountains. The sky was immensely pure, and the sparkling summits seemed light and airy enough to rise into the blue like balloons. *It's like a mental barrier*, thought Servaz on seeing them. Your mind collides with these peaks as if against a wall. You are left with the impression of a territory utterly unfamiliar to man, a terra incognita, a land's end, literally.

He went into the café Ziegler had told him about, sat down at a table near the window and ordered a white coffee and a croissant.

In a corner above the bar was a television showing the twenty-four-hour news channel. The volume was on full blast and Servaz couldn't think straight. He was about to ask them to turn it down a bit when he heard a reporter say the name Éric Lombard; the man was standing at the edge of Tarbes airfield holding a microphone. When Éric Lombard's face filled the screen, Servaz stood up and moved closer to the bar.

The billionaire was being interviewed as he stepped down from his plane. Behind him was a sparkling white jet with 'Lombard' printed in blue letters on the fuselage. Lombard wore the grave expression of someone who has just lost a loved one. The reporter was asking him whether this horse was particularly important to him?

'He was not just a horse,' answered the businessman, his voice a careful mixture of emotion and firmness. 'He was a companion, a friend, a partner. People who really love horses will know that they are more than mere animals. And Freedom was an exceptional horse. We had great hopes for him. But above all, it is the way he died that is unbearable. I will do my utmost to make sure the guilty party is found.'

Servaz watched as Éric Lombard's gaze moved to stare at the camera and, through it, at the television viewers – a gaze that went from pain to anger, defiance and intimidation.

'Whoever did this, I want them to know that they will not get away with it – *I am a man with a thirst for justice.*'

Servaz glanced around him. Everyone was staring at the television screen. *Not bad*, he thought. *Nice act.* Planned in advance, that much was obvious, but it nevertheless exuded a brutal sincerity. Servaz wondered how far a man like Éric Lombard was prepared to go to carry out his threat.

He spent the next two hours trying to take stock of what they knew and what they didn't know. Obviously at this point ignorance was greater than knowledge. When at last he saw Irène Ziegler on the pavement outside the café, he was left speechless: she was wearing a biker's suit, black leather with grey metal protective patches on the shoulders and the knees, and boots reinforced at the toe and the heel, and she was holding a full-face helmet in her hand. *An Amazon . . .* Once again he was struck by her beauty. He thought she was almost as beautiful as Charlène Espérandieu, but it was a different sort of beauty – more athletic, less sophisticated. Charlène was like a fashion plate, Irène Ziegler a surfing champion. Once again he was troubled. He recalled his reaction on seeing the ring in her nostril. Without a doubt, Irène Ziegler was an attractive woman.

Servaz looked at his watch. Eleven o'clock already.

'Well?' he said.

She explained that they hadn't found out much from the autopsy other than that the animal had been beheaded post mortem. Marchand had come along. The pathologist thought the horse had probably been drugged; the toxicology analysis would confirm this. When they left, the boss of the riding academy seemed relieved. In the end he agreed to send the animal to the abattoir. Except for the head, which his boss wanted to keep. According to Marchand he wanted to have it stuffed, to put it on the wall.

'Put it on the wall?' echoed Servaz, gobsmacked.

'Do you think they're guilty?' Ziegler asked.

'Who?'

'The watchmen.'

'I don't know.'

He took out his mobile and dialled the number at the chateau. A female voice answered.

'Commandant Servaz here, Toulouse crime unit. I would like to speak to Éric Lombard.'

'What did you say your name was?'

'Servaz.'

'Please hold.'

An endless ringing. Then the voice of a middle-aged man.

'Yes?'

'I would like to speak with Éric Lombard.'

'Who's calling?'

'Commandant Servaz, crime unit.'

'What is this regarding?'

Servaz felt his temper flaring.

'Listen, your boss is the one who asked to see me. I have enough on my plate without this. So I have no time to waste!'

'Spell your name clearly and tell me why you are calling,' said the man on the other end of the line, unflappable. 'Monsieur Lombard also has no time to waste.'

The man's arrogance left Servaz speechless. He almost hung up, but caught himself in time.

'Servaz, S-E-R-V-A-Z. I'm calling regarding his horse Freedom.'

'Could you not have said so earlier? Please hold.'

The man was back on the line twenty seconds later.

'Monsieur Lombard will be expecting you at three o'clock this afternoon.'

It was not an invitation; it was an order.

Driving into Éric Lombard's territory was like entering a fairy-tale land. They had left the car and motorcycle behind in the car park of the gendarmerie in Saint-Martin and borrowed a squad car. They took the same route as before, the one that led to the riding academy, but instead of turning left into the forest, they carried on straight ahead.

Then they drove through an open, hilly landscape planted with oaks, elms, linden and fir trees. The estate was vast, stretching as far as the eye could see. There were fences everywhere, horses in meadows and farm machinery by the roadside, ready for use. There were still patches of snow here and there, but the air was luminous and clear. Servaz was put in mind of a ranch in Montana or a hacienda in Argentina. They saw signs, 'PRIVATE PROPERTY DO NOT ENTER', nailed to tree trunks or fences round the fields. But there were no walls. Then five kilometres further along they saw the stone wall. It was four metres high and blocked off part of the landscape. Beyond it was woodland. They stopped the car outside the gate. There was a granite plaque on one of the pillars.

Servaz read 'Chateau-Blanc' in golden letters.

At the top of the pillar a camera was turning. They did not need to get out and speak into the intercom: the gates opened almost immediately.

They drove another kilometre or more along an avenue of centuries-old oak trees. The road, straight as a ruler and impeccably paved, traced a black line beneath the twisted branches of the great trees. Servaz saw the house gradually approaching at the end of the grounds. A few moments later they parked alongside a border of winter heather and pale pink camellias covered in snow. Servaz was disappointed: the chateau was not as big as he'd expected. But a second look immediately cancelled that impression: it was a building of childlike beauty, probably built at the end of the nineteenth century or the beginning of the twentieth, part Loire chateau, part English stately

97

home. A fairy-tale castle . . . Outside the ground-floor windows was a row of boxwood trees pruned in the shape of animals: an elephant, a horse, a giraffe and a stag stood out against the snow. On their left, to the east, Servaz saw a formal garden with ornamental basins and statues. A covered swimming pool and a tennis court. A vast orangery towards the back, with a host of strange antennas on the roof.

He recalled the figures he had seen online: Éric Lombard was one of the wealthiest men in France, and one of her most influential citizens. He was the head of an empire present in over seventy countries. In all likelihood the former orangery had been converted into an ultramodern communications centre. Ziegler slammed her door.

'Look.'

She was pointing to the trees. He looked. Counted thirty or more cameras fixed to the tree trunks, among the branches. They must cover the entire perimeter of the garden. There were no blind spots. Somewhere in the chateau they were being watched. They headed up a gravel path through the flowerbeds and passed two topiary crouching lions. Each one was five metres high. *Strange*, thought Servaz, *it's like a garden designed for the entertainment of very rich children.* But he had not read anywhere that Éric Lombard had children. On the contrary, most of the articles described a confirmed bachelor with numerous conquests. Or did these sculptures date back to his own childhood? Waiting at the top of the steps was a man in his sixties. Tall, dressed in black. He looked at them with a gaze as hard as ice. Although he was seeing him for the first time, Servaz immediately knew who it was – the man on the telephone – and he felt his anger welling up again. The man greeted them without a smile and asked them to follow, then turned on his heels. His tone indicated that once again, this was not a request but an order.

They crossed the threshold.

A long series of rooms led one into the other, vast, empty and echoing, all the way through the building; they could see the daylight at the far end, as if they were in a tunnel. The interior was monumental. The hall was two storeys high, the light coming in from windows far up the walls. The man in black led them along the hall and through a salon empty of any furniture before turning to a double door on their right. A library whose walls were covered in ancient books, with four high French doors giving out onto the forest. Éric Lombard was standing by one of them. Servaz recognised him at once, although he had his back to them. The businessman was talking into a headset.

'The police are here,' said the man in black, his tone half deferential, half scornful in referring to the visitors.

'Thank you, Otto.'

Otto left the room. Lombard finished his conversation in English, removed the headset and put it down on an oak table. His gaze lingered on them, Servaz first, then Ziegler, for longer, sparking briefly with surprise at her outfit. He gave a warm smile.

'Please excuse Otto. He's got the wrong era. He has an occasional tendency to treat me like a prince or a king, but I also know I can count on him under any circumstances.'

Servaz said nothing. He waited for what came next.

'I know you are very busy. And that you have no time to waste. Nor do I. I was very fond of that horse. A marvellous animal. I want to be sure that everything, absolutely everything, will be done in order to find the person who committed this abominable deed.'

Again he looked closely at them. There was sadness in his blue eyes, but also toughness and authority.

'Let me make this much clear, you can call me at any time of day or night, ask me any question you think might be useful, no matter how ridiculous it might seem. I asked you to come here so that I can insist that no stone be left unturned, that you'll do everything in your power to solve this. What I want is to get to the bottom of this case, and I have been assured that you are excellent investigators.' He smiled; then the smile faded. 'If it should prove otherwise, if you are negligent in any way, if you treat this matter in an offhand manner on the pretext that it's only a horse, I will be merciless.'

The threat was not even veiled. *What I want* . . . The man was direct. He had no time to lose and went straight to the point. Consequently Servaz found him almost likable. Along with his love for his horse.

But Irène Ziegler clearly didn't see it that way. Servaz noticed she had turned very pale.

'You won't get anywhere by threatening us,' she retorted, her anger cold.

Lombard stared at her. His features softened and his expression became one of sincere contrition.

'Forgive me. I am sure you are both perfectly competent and

conscientious. Your superiors cannot stop singing your praises. I am being foolish. These . . . *events* have been very upsetting. Please accept my apologies, Captain Ziegler. They are sincere.'

Ziegler nodded reluctantly but said nothing more.

'If you have no objection,' said Servaz, 'I'd like to start right away by asking you a few questions, since we are here.'

'Of course. Follow me. Let me offer you a coffee.'

Éric Lombard opened another door at the far end of the room. A drawing room. The sun spilled in through French windows onto two leather sofas and a coffee table, where a tray was waiting with three cups and a coffee pot. Servaz knew the coffee pot must be a priceless antique. Like the rest of the furnishings. Everything was already set out, including the sugar, some Danish pastries and a jug of milk.

'My first question,' said Servaz straight off, 'do you have any idea who could have committed this crime, or who at least would have a reason to commit it?'

Éric Lombard was pouring the coffee.

He paused in what he was doing to stare intensely at Servaz. His blond hair was reflected in the large mirror behind him. He was wearing an off-white rollneck jumper and grey woollen trousers. And he was very tanned.

He did not blink when he replied, 'Yes.'

Servaz shuddered. Next to him Ziegler too had reacted.

'And no,' he added at once. 'Those are two questions in one: yes, I know plenty of people who would have good reason to do it. No, I don't know anyone actually capable of doing it.'

'Could you be more specific?' said Zeigler, annoyed. 'Why would anyone want to kill the horse?'

'To hurt me, to get their revenge, to intimidate me. I suppose you know that in a profession like mine and with my fortune you are bound to make enemies: you arouse people's envy; you invade your rival's market; you reject people's offers; you drive people to ruin; you give hundreds the sack . . . If I had to make a list of everyone who despises me, it would be as thick as a telephone directory.'

'Could you be just a little more specific?'

'Unfortunately, no. I can see what you're getting at: someone has killed my favourite horse and stuck it up on top of a cable car that belongs to me. So they are trying to get at me. It all points to me, I couldn't agree with you more. But I don't have the slightest idea who could have done it.'

'You haven't received any written or verbal threats, any anonymous letters?'

'No.'

'Your group does business in over seventy-five countries,' said Servaz.

'Seventy-eight,' corrected Lombard.

'Does the group have any connections, even indirectly, with any local mafias or organised crime rings? I can imagine there are some countries where this type of . . . *contact* is more or less unavoidable.'

Once again, Lombard stared at Servaz, but without aggression this time. He even allowed himself a smile.

'You get straight to the point, Commandant. Maybe you are thinking of the horse's head in *The Godfather*? No, my group has no connections with organised crime. In any case, not that I know of. I'm not saying that there aren't a few countries where we have to turn a blind eye to certain behaviour, say in Africa or in Asia, but in those cases, let's be frank, we're dealing with dictatorships, not the mafia.'

'And that doesn't bother you?' asked Ziegler.

Lombard raised an eyebrow.

'Dealing with dictators,' she explained.

Lombard smiled again, indulgently, but the smile was that of a monarch hesitating between laughing at the impertinence of one of his subjects and having her beheaded on the spot.

'I don't think it will be much use to your investigation for me to answer that question,' he replied. 'You should also know that, contrary to appearances, I am not the only one in charge: there are many sectors where we have partners, including the French government. From time to time there are "political" aspects that I have no control over.'

Direct, but capable of coming out with the cant when he has to, thought Servaz.

'There is one thing I don't understand. How is it possible that nobody heard or saw anything, either at the riding academy or the power plant? You don't drag a dead horse around like that in the middle of the night.'

Lombard's face clouded over.

'You're right. That's something I've wondered myself. Someone, somewhere has got to be lying. *And I would like very much to find out who,*' he added, threateningly.

He put his cup back down so brusquely that they were startled.

'I summoned everyone – day and night staff of the power plant, employees at the stud farm. I questioned them all one by one as soon as I got here. It took me four hours. I'm sure you'll believe me when I tell you I put as much pressure on them as I possibly could. No one heard a thing that night. Of course it's impossible. I do not doubt the sincerity of Marchand or Hector: they have never hurt a single one of my horses, and they've been working for the family for a very long time. They are honest, competent men, and my dealings with them have always been excellent. They are part of the family, so to speak. So you can cross them off your list. And Hermine as well. She's a nice girl, and she adored Freedom. This has been devastating for her.'

'Did you know that the watchmen disappeared?' asked Servaz.

Lombard frowned.

'Yes. They are the only ones I didn't question.'

'There are two of them, and it would take at least two people to hang the horse up there. And they both have police records.'

'Two ideal suspects,' said Lombard dubiously.

'You don't seem convinced?'

'I don't know . . . Why would they go and hang Freedom up right where they work? What better way to attract suspicion?'

Servaz nodded in agreement.

'But they did run off, all the same,' he objected.

'Put yourself in their position. With their police records. Don't be offended, but they know perfectly well that when the police find a culprit, they rarely go looking any further.'

'Who hired them?' asked Ziegler. 'What do you know about them? I'll bet you've found out all about them since yesterday.'

'Exactly. Marc Morane, the manager of the power plant, hired them. Through a rehabilitation programme for ex-cons, from the prison in Lannemezan.'

'Have they ever caused any trouble at the power plant?'

'Morane assured me they hadn't.'

'Have any of the workers at the power plant or on your estate been let go over the last few years?'

Lombard looked at them in turn. With his hair, beard and blue eyes he really did have something of the irresistible Viking warrior about him. He looked just like his photographs.

'These are details. I have nothing to do with human resources management. Any more than I do with managing minor concerns like the power plant. But you will have full access to all the files regarding personnel, and my associates are at your disposal. They've all been given their orders in this regard. My secretary will send you a list of names and telephone numbers. Do not hesitate to contact anyone. If any of them gives you trouble, call me. I told you, as far as I'm concerned, this matter is of the highest priority, and I will be at your disposal twenty-four hours a day.' He took out a business card and handed it to Ziegler. 'Also, you've seen the hydroelectric plant: it's run-down, and not really profitable. We only keep it for historical and family reasons. Marc Morane,' he added, 'is someone I have known since childhood: we were at primary school together. But I hadn't seen him in years.'

Servaz understood that this last remark was meant to establish a hierarchy of all those involved. For the heir to the empire, the manager of the power plant was only one employee among others, all the way at the bottom of the ladder, at the same level, more or less, as his workers.

'How much time do you spend here in an average year, Monsieur Lombard?' asked Ziegler.

'That's a hard one: let me think . . . I suppose somewhere between six and eight weeks. Not more. Of course I'm more often based in Paris than in this old chateau. I also spend long periods in New York. And to be honest, half the time I'm travelling on business. But I love to come here, particularly during the skiing season and in the summer, to enjoy the horses. I have other stud farms, as you probably know. But this is where I spent most of my childhood, before my father sent me away to school. It may seem like a gloomy place to you, but to me it's home. I've had so many experiences here, both good and bad. But in time, even bad experiences end up seeming good: memory does its work . . .'

His voice grew slightly husky towards the end. Servaz stiffened, all his senses on alert. He waited for Lombard to speak, but he was silent.

'What do you mean by "good and bad" experiences?' asked Ziegler quietly.

Lombard brushed the question away with a wave of his hand.

'It's not important. It was all so long ago . . . It has nothing to do with the death of my horse.'

'That is up to us to determine,' replied Ziegler.

Lombard hesitated.

'Let's just say that people might think it was an idyllic place for a little boy like me to grow up in, but in fact it was anything but.'

'Really?' said the gendarme.

Servaz saw the businessman throw her a cautious glance.

'Listen, I don't think that—'

'That what?'

'Let's drop it. It's of no interest.'

Servaz heard Ziegler sigh.

'Monsieur Lombard,' said the gendarme, 'you have put a certain pressure on us, saying that if we take this affair too lightly we'll be sorry. And you have urged us not to neglect any lead, even the most far-fetched. We are detectives, not soothsayers or fortune tellers. We need to know everything we can about the context of this investigation. Who knows, perhaps the motive for this bloody deed has something to do with the past?'

'It is our job to find connections and motives,' insisted Servaz.

Lombard stared at them one after the other, and they knew he must be weighing the pros and cons in his mind. Neither Ziegler nor Servaz moved. The businessman hesitated a moment longer, then shrugged.

'Let me tell you about Henri and Édouard Lombard, my father and grandfather,' he said suddenly. 'It is a rather edifying story. I'll tell you who Henri Lombard really was. A man as cold as ice, hard as stone, absolutely rigid. Violent and selfish as well. And fanatic about order, like his father before him.'

Ziegler's face was a portrait of stupefaction; as for Servaz, he was holding his breath. Lombard paused again and sat looking at them for a moment. The two investigators waited for him to continue, in what seemed like an endless silence.

'As you may know, the Lombard enterprise really began to prosper during the Second World War. Actually, my father and grandfather didn't mind the presence of the Germans. My father had only just turned twenty, and my grandfather was running the company, here and in Paris. One of the most prosperous periods in its history – they did some very good business with their Nazi clients.'

He leaned forward. His movement was reversed in the mirror behind his back, as if the copy wanted nothing to do with what the original was about to say.

'When the Liberation came, my grandfather was tried as a collaborator, sentenced to death and then eventually pardoned. He was released in 1952 and died a year later of a heart attack. In the meantime, his son, Henri, had taken over. He set about expanding the family business, diversifying and modernising. Unlike his father, my father – in spite of, or perhaps because of, his young age – had felt the wind turning in 1943 and, unbeknown to my grandfather, forged closer ties with the Resistance and the Gaullists. Hardly through any sense of idealism, it was purely opportunistic. He was a brilliant man, with a great deal of foresight. After Stalingrad, he understood that the Third Reich's days were numbered, and he made the most of both worlds: the Germans on one side, the Resistance on the other. It was my father who made the Lombard Group what it is. After the war he further developed his contacts among the former Resistance fighters, now in key positions of power. He was a great captain of industry, an empire builder, a visionary – but at home he was a tyrant. Physically, he was very imposing: tall, slender, always dressed in black. The people in Saint-Martin either respected or despised him, but everyone feared him. He was a man who had great love for himself and nothing left to give others. Not even his wife or children . . .'

Éric Lombard got to his feet. Servaz and Ziegler watched as he went over to a sideboard. He picked up a framed photograph and handed it to Servaz. A tall man with a severe face, the burning eyes of a bird of prey, a long, strong nose and white hair, wearing a dark suit and an immaculate white shirt. Henri Lombard did not look at all like his son, but rather like an evangelist, some fanatical preacher. Servaz could not help but think of his own father, a slim, distinguished man whose face refused to fix in his memory.

'Both at home and work my father imposed a reign of terror. He was psychologically and even physically violent with his staff, his wife and his children.' Servaz discerned a catch in Lombard's voice. The adventurer of modern times, the magazine icon, had given way to someone else. 'My mother died of cancer aged forty-nine. She was his third wife. During the nineteen years she was married to my father she was the constant victim of his tyranny, his fits of anger – and his blows. He also sacked a number of servants and employees.

I belong to a new era where it is a virtue to be hard. But my father's hardness went beyond what was acceptable. His mind was devoured by shadows.'

Servaz and Ziegler exchanged a glance. Both of them were aware that this was an incredible story the heir to the empire was dishing up to them: what wouldn't the press give for such a story? Apparently Éric Lombard had decided to trust them. And why? Suddenly Servaz understood. In the course of the last twenty-four hours the tycoon must have made dozens of phone calls. Servaz recalled the dizzying figures he had seen on the web and he felt an unpleasant sense of unease. Éric Lombard had enough money and power to obtain all the information he wanted. The policeman wondered whether he had launched a parallel inquiry, an investigation within the investigation – to deal not only with the death of his horse, but also to keep close tabs on the official investigators. It was obvious. Lombard surely knew as much about them as they knew about him.

'This is important information,' Ziegler said at last. 'You were right to share it with us.'

'Do you think so? I wonder. All this business has been buried for so long. Naturally everything I have just told you is strictly confidential.'

'If what you say is true,' said Servaz, 'we have a motive: hatred, revenge. On the part of a former employee, for example, some former connection, an old enemy of your father's.'

Lombard shook his head, sceptical.

'If that were the case, why would they wait so long? My father has been dead for eleven years.'

He was about to add something when Irène Ziegler's mobile phone vibrated. She checked the number, then looked at them.

'Excuse me.'

The gendarme got up and went over to a corner of the room.

'Your father was born in 1920, if I'm not mistaken,' continued Servaz. 'And you were born in 1972. The least one can say is that he had you quite late. Did he have other children?'

'My sister, Maud. She was born in 1976. Both of us were from his last marriage. He had no children from his previous ones. Why, I don't know. The official version is that he met my mother in Paris, at the theatre where she was an actress . . .'

Once again, Lombard seemed to be wondering just how much he

could trust them. He probed Servaz, looking him straight in the eye, then made up his mind.

'My mother was actually a fairly good actress, but the truth is she never set foot on stage, nor was she ever on a movie set. Her talent consisted, instead, of putting on an act for one person at a time: wealthy older men who were prepared to pay a great deal for her company. It would seem she had a loyal clientele of rich businessmen. She was very much in demand. My father was one of the most persistent. He must have become jealous very quickly. He wanted her all to himself. As with everything else, he had to be first, and he had to get rid of his rivals one way or another. So he married her. Or rather, the way he saw it, he bought her. After a fashion. He never stopped thinking of her as a . . . *whore*, even after they were married. When my father married her, he was fifty-one; she was thirty. As for her, she must have been thinking that her "career" was winding down, and that it was time to think of getting into something else. But she had no clue that the man she was about to marry was violent. She had a rough time.'

Éric Lombard became gloomy all of a sudden. *He has never forgiven his father.* Servaz realised with a start that there was a close parallel between Lombard and himself: for both of them, family memories were a mixed bag of joy and suffering, moments of light and others of horror. He watched Ziegler out of the corner of his eye. She was still on the telephone at the far end of the room, her back to the two men.

She turned round abruptly and her gaze met Servaz's.

He was instantly on the alert: whatever the phone call was about was unsettling her.

'How did you learn all this about your parents?'

Lombard gave a joyless laugh.

'I hired a journalist a few years ago, to dig around in our family history.' He hesitated briefly. 'For a long time I had wanted to know more about my father and mother, and I was well positioned to know that their marriage had not been a harmonious one, to say the least. But I did not expect these revelations. After that, I bought the journalist's silence. It cost me. But it was worth it.'

'And since then, have any other journalists come sniffing around?'

Lombard stared at Servaz. He was once again the uncompromising businessman.

'Of course they have. I've bought them all. One by one. I've spent a fortune . . . but above a certain limit, everyone is for sale . . .'

He stared at Servaz and the cop got the message: even you. Servaz felt a surge of anger. So much arrogance was exasperating. But at the same time he knew that the man sitting opposite him was right. Perhaps he, Servaz, would have had the strength to refuse, in the name of the code of ethics he had adopted on joining the force. But suppose he had been one of those journalists, and the man offered to improve his daughter's lot – the best schools, with the best teachers, then the best universities and later on a guaranteed position in the profession of her dreams: would he have had the courage to turn down such a future for Margot? Lombard was right: above a certain limit, everyone was for sale. The father had bought the wife; the son was buying the journalists – and politicians, too, no doubt: Éric Lombard was more like his father than he knew.

Servaz had no more questions.

He put down his empty cup. Ziegler came and joined them. He gave her a sidelong glance. She looked tense and worried.

'Well, and now,' said Lombard coldly, 'I would like to know if you have any leads.'

The liking Servaz felt for him only a moment ago disappeared instantly. Once again the man was speaking to them as if they were his servants.

'I'm sorry,' he said hurriedly with his best tax auditor's smile. 'At this point we prefer to avoid commenting on the investigation with anyone who is involved.'

Lombard gave him a long stare. Servaz saw clearly that he was hesitating between two options: threaten them again, or retreat for the time being. He opted for the latter.

'I understand. In any case, I know where to go to find out. Thank you for coming, and for your time.'

He stood up. The interview was over.

They went back the way they had come. Night was falling as they walked back through the series of rooms. Outside, the wind had picked up and the trees were swaying and groaning. Servaz thought it might snow again. He looked at his watch. Twenty minutes to five. With the setting sun, the long shadows of the topiary animals length-ened over the ground. He glanced behind him at the chateau and saw Éric Lombard in one of the many windows on the first floor, watching them, motionless. He had two people with him, one of them the man called Otto. Servaz recalled his hypothesis: the investigators were themselves the subject of an investigation. In the dark rectangle of the window Lombard and his henchmen looked like reflections in a mirror. Every bit as strange, silent and frightening. As soon as they were back in the car, Servaz turned to Ziegler.

'What's going on?'

'That was Rosny-sous-Bois on the line. They've got the DNA back.'

He looked at her, incredulous. The swabs had been taken no more than forty-eight hours ago. DNA analyses simply were not completed in so little time: the labs were swamped! Someone very high up must have had the case moved to the top of the pile.

'Most of the DNA traces found in the cabin – hair, saliva, nails – match the workers from the power plant. But they also found a trace of saliva on one of the windows. A trace belonging to someone outside the power plant, with a profile in the FNAEG. *Someone who should never have been there . . .'*

Servaz stiffened. The FNAEG was the national DNA database. A controversial thing: it contained the DNA profiles not only of rapists, murderers and paedophiles, but also of people who had committed all sorts of minor crimes, everything from shoplifting to the possession of a few grams of cannabis. Consequently, the previous year the number of profiles in the database had reached 470,492. The database may well have been under the most stringent control of any in France, but such excess was a legitimate source of concern to lawyers and magistrates. At the same time, the tendency for the FNAEG to go beyond its natural bounds had already enabled investigators to make some significant arrests, because criminality often spilled over beyond the neat categories used to define it: a 'nonce' – the term for a paedophile in prison slang – might also be a cat burglar or a robber. And DNA traces found on the site of a burglary had led to the arrest of more than one serial sex offender.

'Who is it?' he asked.

Ziegler gave him a disconcerted look.

'Have you ever heard of Julian Hirtmann?'

A few snowflakes had begun to fall again. A sudden smell of madness in the car. *It can't be,* cried his brain.

Servaz remembered reading several articles in *La Dépêche du Midi* when the notorious Swiss serial killer was being transferred to the Pyrenees. Articles that described at length the exceptional security measures being taken for the transfer. How could Hirtmann have managed to scale the walls of the Institute, commit such an insane act and then return to his cell?

'It can't be,' whispered Ziegler, echoing his thoughts.

He gazed at her, still just as incredulous. Then he looked through the windscreen at the snow.

'*Credo quia absurdum*,' he said at last.

'Latin again,' she said. 'And it means?'

'"I believe it because it's absurd."'

9

Diane had been sitting at her desk for an hour when suddenly her door opened and closed. She looked up, wondering who would come in like that without knocking: she expected to see Xavier or Lisa Ferney standing there.

No one.

She gazed at the closed door, puzzled. Footsteps echoed in the room, but the room was empty . . . The blue-grey light coming through the frosted window illuminated nothing but the faded wallpaper and a metal filing cabinet. The footsteps stopped and someone pulled out a chair. More steps – a woman's heels this time – stopped in turn.

'How are our residents doing today?' asked a voice.

She stared at the wall. It was Xavier. The sounds were coming from his room next door. Yet there was a very thick wall between the two offices. It took her a moment to understand. Her gaze landed on the air vent in a corner beneath the ceiling: that was why she could hear the voices.

'Nervous,' answered Lisa Ferney. 'All anyone can talk about is this horse business. It's getting them all excited, by the looks of it.'

The strange acoustic phenomenon made every word, every syllable the head nurse said perfectly audible.

'Increase their doses if need be,' said Xavier.

'I have already.'

'Very good.'

Diane could grasp the slightest nuance, the slightest inflection, even when their voices were hardly above a murmur. She wondered whether Xavier was aware of this. He had probably never noticed. There had never been anyone in this room before Diane, and she didn't make much noise. Perhaps the sound only travelled in one direction. Her office was a small, dusty space, two metres by four, which had been used as a storage room: there were still some boxes of archives piled up in a corner. It smelled of dust and something else, an indefinable but unpleasant odour. Despite the fact that, in something of a rush, they had set up a desk, computer and an armchair for her, she nevertheless felt as if her office was in the place where the rubbish bins were kept.

'What do you think of the new woman?' asked Élisabeth Ferney.

Diane sat up straight, straining to hear.

'And you, what do you think?'

'I don't know, that's the problem. Do you suppose the police will come here because of that horse?'

'And if they do?'

'They'll go sticking their noses everywhere. You're not afraid?'

'Afraid of what?' said Xavier.

A silence.

'Why should I be afraid? I have nothing to hide.'

But the psychiatrist's voice, even through an air vent, implied just the opposite. Diane suddenly felt very ill at ease. She was eavesdropping in spite of herself on a conversation that would take an extremely embarrassing turn if she were caught. She took her mobile phone from her lab coat and hurriedly switched it off, although it was unlikely that anyone would call her there.

'If I were you, I would fix it so that they see as little as possible,' said Lisa Ferney. 'Do you plan on showing them Julian?'

'Only if they ask.'

'Perhaps I should go pay him a little visit, in that case.'

'Yes.'

Diane could hear the rustling of Lisa Ferney's lab coat. Then silence once again.

'Stop it,' said Xavier after a moment, 'this is not the right time.'

'You are too tense. I could help you.'

The nurse's voice had become coaxing, caressing.

'Oh dear Lord, Lisa . . . what if someone comes . . .?'

'You dirty little pig, it doesn't take much to get you going.'

'Lisa, Lisa, please . . . not here . . . *Oh God, Lisa* . . .'

Diane felt her cheeks blush bright red. How long had Xavier and Lisa been lovers? The psychiatrist had only been at the Institute for six months. But then, hadn't she and Spitzner . . . Yet she couldn't place what she was hearing on the same level. Perhaps it was because of the asylum itself, all the impulses, hatred, psychoses, anger and mania stewing together like some filthy gruel: there was something distinctly unsavoury about their conversation.

'You want me to stop, is that it?' whispered Lisa Ferney from the other side of the wall. 'Say it. Say it and I'll stop.'

'Noooo . . .'

'Let's get going. We're being watched.'

Night had fallen. Ziegler turned her head and also saw Lombard at the window. On his own now.

She turned the ignition and backed round in the lane. As before, the gates opened in front of them. Servaz glanced in the rear-view mirror. He thought he could see Lombard pull away from the window as it too receded behind them.

'What about the fingerprints and the other swabs?' he asked.

'Nothing conclusive for the moment. But they've still got quite a way to go. There are hundreds of fingerprints and traces. It will take days. Up to now everything seems to belong to the staff. Our suspect used gloves, that's obvious.'

'But he did leave some saliva on the window.'

'Do you think it's some sort of message on his part?'

For a moment she took her eyes from the road to look at him.

'A challenge . . . Who knows?' he said. 'We can't rule anything out.'

'Or it might have been simply accidental. It happens more often than you'd think; all he had to do was sneeze next to the window.'

'What do you know about this Hirtmann?'

Ziegler started the windscreen wipers: the snow was coming down faster, thick in the dark sky.

'He's an organised killer. Not the psychotic, delirious type, like some of the inmates at the Institute; he's a major psychopathic pervert, a particularly intelligent and formidable social predator. He was convicted for the murder, in atrocious circumstances, of his wife and her lover, but he is also suspected of the murder of over forty people. All women. In Switzerland, Savoie, northern Italy, Austria . . . five countries altogether. The trouble is, he has never confessed. And they've never been able to prove anything. Even in the case of his wife, he would never have been caught were it not for a combination of chance events.'

'You seem well acquainted with the case.'

'I took something of an interest sixteen months ago, in my spare time, when he was transferred to the Wargnier Institute. There was a lot of talk in the papers. But I never saw him.'

'Whatever the case, this changes everything. From now on we have to base things on the assumption that Hirtmann is the man we are after. Even if, at first glance, it seems impossible. What do we know about him? What are the conditions of his detention at the Institute? We have to start with that.'

She nodded, her eyes on the road.

'We also have to think about what we're going to say,' added Servaz. 'About the questions we're going to ask him. We'll have to prepare the visit. I don't know the case as well as you do, but it's obvious that Hirtmann is no ordinary killer.'

'There's also the question of whether he had any accomplices inside the Institute,' Ziegler pointed out. 'And whether there were any breaches in security.'

Servaz nodded.

'We'll organise a preparatory meeting. Things are clearer, but more complicated. We have to picture every possible aspect of the problem before we go there.'

Ziegler agreed. The Institute was now top priority, but they did not have all the necessary resources; they did not yet hold all the cards.

'The shrink is supposed to get here from Paris on Monday,' she said. 'And I have to give a press conference in Bordeaux tomorrow. I'm not about to cancel because of a horse. I suggest we wait until Monday to go to the Institute.'

'On the other hand,' said Servaz, 'if Hirtmann really is behind this, and he was able to get out of the Institute, we must make sure at all costs that the other inmates cannot do likewise.'

'I've asked for reinforcements from the regional unit at Saint-Gaudens. They're on their way.'

'We'll have to set up checkpoints at all the entrances to the Institute, search all the cars that go in and out, even the ones belonging to staff. And have surveillance teams posted on the mountain to keep an eye on the surrounding area.'

Ziegler nodded.

'The reinforcements will take over tonight. I also asked for some night-vision goggles and infrared scanners. And permission to double our resources on the ground, but I'd be surprised if we get it. We're also adding two canine units to the operation. Anyway, some of the mountains around the Institute are impassable without equipment. The only real way in there is along the road or the valley. This time, even if Hirtmann manages to get past the Institute's security system, he won't get past us.'

It's no longer just about a horse, he thought. *It's suddenly a lot more serious.*

'There's another issue we'll have to deal with.'

She looked at him questioningly.

'What is the connection between Hirtmann and Lombard? Why the devil did he go after that horse?'

At midnight Servaz still wasn't asleep. He switched off his PC and his desk lamp – the computer was a dinosaur of a machine that still ran on Windows 98, which he had inherited in the divorce – before closing the door behind him. He walked through the living room, opened the glass door and went out onto the balcony. Three floors down, the street was deserted. Except for a solitary car, which from time to time made its way through the double row of vehicles parked bumper to bumper. Like most cities, this one had an acute sense of the limited space it had. And like most cities, even when its inhabitants were asleep, the city itself was never really sleeping. At all hours, it purred and vibrated like a machine. From a restaurant kitchen below rose the clatter of dishes. There were echoes of a conversation from somewhere, or rather an argument, between a man and a woman. A man in the street let his dog pee against a car. Servaz went back into the sitting room, rummaged through his CDs and put on Mahler's Eighth Symphony, Bernstein conducting, at a respectable volume. At this time of night his downstairs neighbours, always early to bed, would be fast asleep: even the terrible hammer blows of the Sixth, or the major discordant chord of the Tenth would not rouse them from their sleep.

Julian Hirtmann . . .

The name resonating, yet again. Ever since Irène Ziegler had uttered it several hours earlier in the car, it had been in the air. Over these last few hours Servaz had been trying to find out as much as possible about the inmate at the Wargnier Institute. It was not without some surprise that he learned that Julian Hirtmann, like himself, was partial to Mahler. That was something they had in common. He spent several hours on the Internet, taking notes. As with Éric Lombard, but for other reasons, there were hundreds of web pages devoted to Hirtmann.

The uneasy premonition Servaz had felt right from the start was spreading like a toxic cloud. Up until now they had merely been dealing with a strange affair – the death of a horse in unusual circumstances – which would never have taken on such proportions if the horse's owner had been a local farmer rather than a billionaire. And now the case was connected – although he could not understand how or why – with one of the most formidable killers in recent history. Servaz suddenly felt as if he were in a long corridor full of closed doors. Behind each door another unsuspected and frightening aspect of the investigation awaited. He dreaded walking down that corridor, opening those doors. In his mind, the corridor was strangely lit by a red lamp – red like blood, red like fury, red like a beating heart. He retreated back inside. While he was splashing his face with cold water, a knot of anxiety in his guts, he became certain that many other doors would open soon, to reveal a series of rooms each one more obscure and sinister than the next. *And this was just the beginning* . . .

Julian Alois Hirtmann had been detained for nearly sixteen months in Unit A of the Wargnier Institute, the unit reserved for the most dangerous social predators, with only seven inmates in all. But Hirtmann differed from the other six in more ways than one:

1. He was intelligent, in control, and the long series of suspected murders had never been proven.
2. He had once occupied – rare but not totally exceptional among serial criminals – an elevated social rank, since at the time of his arrest he had been a prosecutor at the Geneva High Court.
3. His arrest – following the unfortunate events Ziegler had mentioned – and trial had led to a political and criminal tangle unprecedented in Switzerland's legal history.

The combination of circumstances Ziegler had referred to was a story that beggared belief, one that might have seemed merely lurid had it not been incredibly sordid and, above all, tragic. On 21 June 2004, while a violent storm was raging over Lake Geneva, Julian Hirtmann, in a gesture of grandiose indulgence, invited his wife's lover to dinner at his lakeside estate. The purpose of his invitation:

he wanted to 'clarify things and conclude a gentlemanly arrangement for Alexia's departure'.

His ravishing wife had already informed him that she wished to leave him for her lover, like Hirtmann a magistrate at the Geneva Court. At the end of the meal, during which time they listened to Mahler's sublime *Kindertotenlieder* and discussed the terms and practicalities of the divorce (Servaz paused, dumbfounded for a moment on reading this information, wondering which zealous investigator had noted that 'these "Songs for Dead Children" were one of his favourite pieces of music'), Hirtmann pulled out a gun and forced the couple to go down to the cellar. Hirtmann and his wife had transformed it into a 'cavern of sadomasochistic delights' where they held orgies with friends from Geneva's high society. Hirtmann, it seemed, liked to see his very beautiful wife penetrated and beaten by several men at a time, and subjected to all sorts of refined torture – handcuffed, chained, whipped and attached to strange machines that were sold in specialist shops in Germany and the Netherlands. He had nevertheless gone mad with jealousy when he found out she wanted to leave him for someone else. One aggravating circumstance: he held his wife's lover to be a perfectly stupid and insipid individual.

One of the many articles Servaz looked at showed Hirtmann and his future victim pictured at the Geneva High Court.

The fellow seemed short next to Hirtmann, who was tall and thin. Judging by the photograph, Servaz would have said he was in his forties. The giant had laid a friendly hand on the lover-colleague's shoulder, and was gazing warmly at him the way a tiger gazes at its prey. With hindsight, Servaz wondered whether Hirtmann knew then that he was going to kill him. The caption said, '*Prosecutor Hirtmann with his future victim, the judge Adalbert Berger, posing in the hall in their magistrates' gowns.*'

On the night of 21 June Hirtmann forced his wife and her lover down into the cellar, then made them undress, lie down and drink champagne until they were both drunk. Then he ordered the lover to empty a magnum over Alexia's body where she lay trembling on the bed, while he in turn splattered champagne over her lover. Once these libations were finished, he handed the lover one of the gadgets that were lying around the place: the object resembled a big electric drill, with the drill bit replaced by a dildo. Such items, however strange they may seem to ordinary mortals, are not hard to find, and the guests at the Hirtmanns' lakeside parties occasionally made use of them. During the afternoon, Hirtmann had carefully fiddled with the instrument, so that if a suspicious expert examined the bare electric wires, it would look like a purely accidental defect. He had also replaced the perfectly functional circuit-breaker in his fuse box with a totally inefficient one. Once the wife's lover had placed the dripping dildo into his mistress's vagina, Hirtmann, wearing an insulating rubber glove, plugged it in. The effect was immediate, the champagne clearly a good conductor. And Hirtmann would no doubt have taken immense pleasure from the spectacle of the two bodies rattling with uncontrollable trembling, their hair standing on end like iron shavings on a magnet, had there not been at that moment the 'combination of circumstances' that Ziegler had referred to.

Because of the defective circuit-breaker, cutting the power would not have saved the two lovers from electrocution, but the voltage surge nevertheless had a consequence that Hirtmann had not foreseen: it set off the house alarm system. By the time Hirtmann regained his self-control, the diligent Swiss police, alerted by the shrieking siren and by the neighbours, were at his door.

Still, the prosecutor did not completely lose his sangfroid for all that. As he had planned to do in any event, but somewhat later that evening, he stated his personal particulars and his position as a magistrate and, confused and distraught, informed the police that a tragic accident had just occurred in the cellar. Ashamed and overwhelmed, he invited the police officers to follow him downstairs. This is when the second circumstance came into play: in order to turn off the alarm, and make it look as if he had tried to help the lovers, Hirtmann had been obliged to switch off the power altogether; the gendarme Christian Gander, from the Geneva cantonal police, swore that when he and his colleague entered the gloomy cellar, one of the victims was still alive. Hirtmann's wife, Alexia. In the gleam of their torches, she suddenly came to, and had just time enough to point to her executioner with a terrified look before collapsing once and for all. The two gendarmes then trained their guns at Hirtmann and handcuffed him, heedless of his protests and threats. They made two phone calls, the first to the emergency services, the second to the Geneva crime unit. Reinforcements arrived on the premises fifteen minutes later and undertook a thorough search, which, fairly quickly, led to the discovery of an automatic pistol – loaded and with the safety catch off – thrust under a piece of furniture. Hirtmann was taken away and a CSI team was brought in. Analysis of the leftovers from dinner showed that the prosecutor-murderer had also drugged his victims.

It was the documents and newspaper cuttings found somewhat later in Hirtmann's office that established a link with the unsolved disappearances of twenty or more young women over the last fifteen years. Suddenly the case took on another dimension: a crime of passion pointing the way to a serial killer. A search through a safe deposit box revealed several binders filled with newspaper cuttings concerning other disappearances, spread over five countries: the French Alps, the Dolomites, Bavaria, Austria and Switzerland. Altogether forty or more cases in twenty-five years. None of these cases had ever been solved. Hirtmann claimed he was interested in them from a purely professional point of view, even showing a certain sense of humour when he declared that he suspected the young women must have all been the victims of a single killer. Nevertheless, no legal connection could be established between the disappearances and the murder of his wife, as they differed both in motive and in the nature of the crime.

At the hearing Hirtmann revealed his true nature at last. Far from seeking to play down his proclivities, he flaunted them with a self-satisfied smirk. A series of spectacular scandals erupted during the trial, for it turned out that several members of the court and of Genevan high society had attended his soirées. Hirtmann served up their names with relish, ruining untold reputations. The case became an unprecedented political and criminal cataclysm, mixing sex, drugs, money, justice and the media. A number of photographs had survived from the time, originally displayed in the world press with captions such as *The house of horror* (where you could see the big lakeside residence with its ivy-covered façade), *The monster leaving court* (where Hirtmann appeared wearing a bullet-proof jacket, a good head taller than the policemen who surrounded him), *Geneva in turmoil, So-and-so accused of taking part in Hirtmann's orgies* and so on.

In the course of his virtual wanderings Servaz noticed that there was a veritable cult around Hirtmann among some online denizens. There were numerous sites devoted to him, most of them portraying him not as an insane criminal, but rather as an emblem of sadomasochism or – all joking aside – of the *will to power*, like *an incandescent star of the Satanic galaxy* or even a *Nietzschean rock superman*. Forums were even worse. Even Servaz, a policeman, could never have imagined there were so many lunatics at large. Individuals with pseudonyms as grotesque as 6-Borg, Sympathy for the Devil or Goddess Kali expounded theories as woolly-minded as their counterfeit identities. All these alternative worlds depressed him, these forums and websites. He told himself that in the old days these crazies would have assumed they were the only ones of their kind, and kept well hidden. Nowadays, thanks to modern means of communication, which start by spreading idiocy and madness and – more rarely – knowledge, they were discovering they were not alone; they could get in touch and reinforce their madness. Servaz recalled what he had said to Marchand, and made a mental correction: insanity was indeed an epidemic, but its two preferred carriers were the media and the Internet.

He suddenly remembered the message from his daughter asking him if he could get Saturday off. He looked at his watch: 1.07 a.m. It was already Saturday. Servaz hesitated. Then he dialled the number to leave a message on her voicemail.

'Hello?'

He made a face. She had picked up immediately, her voice so very different from normal, and he wondered if he had called the wrong number.

'Margot?'

'Is that you, Dad?' she exclaimed in a murmur. 'Have you seen the time?'

He instantly guessed she had been expecting another call. She must leave her mobile on all night, taking her calls hidden under her duvet, unbeknown to her mother and stepfather. What sort of boyfriend would call at such a time? Then he remembered it was Friday, a night out for students.

'Did I wake you up?'

'What do you think?'

'I just wanted to tell you that I got your message,' he said. 'I'll try to get off this afternoon. Is five o'clock OK with you?'

'Are you sure you're all right, Dad? You sound weird . . .'

'I'm fine, sweetheart. It's just that . . . I have a lot of work at the moment.'

'You always say that.'

'Because it's true. You know, don't go thinking that it's only people who earn a lot of money who work a lot. Pack of lies.'

'I know, Dad.'

'Don't ever believe a politician either,' he said without thinking. 'They're all liars.'

'Dad, do you know what time it is? Can we talk about this some other time?'

'You're right. Besides, parents shouldn't try and manipulate their children, even if they think what they're saying is true. They should try and teach them to think for themselves. Even if their children don't think the way they do . . .'

A long speech for such a late hour.

'You're not manipulating me, Dad. It's called a conversation – and I'm quite capable of thinking for myself.'

Servaz suddenly felt ridiculous. But it made him smile.

'I have a marvellous daughter,' he said.

She gave a quiet laugh.

'You sound pretty good actually.'

'I feel great and it's a quarter past one in the morning. Life is beautiful. And so is my daughter. Goodnight, kid. See you tomorrow.'

'Goodnight, Dad.'

He went back out onto the balcony. The moon was shining above the steeple of Saint-Sernin. Students went by in the street, shoving one another. A cavalcade of shouts and sniggers, until the merry band melted into the night and their laughter lingered like a faraway echo from his youth. At around two o'clock, Servaz lay down on his bed and fell asleep at last.

The next morning, Saturday, 13 December, Servaz got part of his team together to go over the murder of the homeless man. Samira Cheung was wearing knee socks with horizontal red and white stripes, leather shorts as tight-fitting as they come, and boots with six-inch heels and a whole row of metal buckles down the back. Servaz reckoned she wouldn't even have to wear a disguise if she had to infiltrate a local prostitution ring, then thought that this was exactly the type of remark someone like Pujol or Simeoni would make, the two narrow-minded machos on the squad who had given his assistant such a hard time. As for Espérandieu, he was wearing a striped jersey that made him look even younger, not at all like a policeman. In a moment of sheer metaphysical anxiety, Servaz wondered whether he were in charge of an investigation or whether he had been teleported to a literature class at university. Both Samira and Vincent had taken out their laptops. As usual, the young woman had her MP3 player round her neck, and Espérandieu was swiping his finger over his iPhone as if he were turning the pages of a book. At Servaz's request, Samira again pointed out one of the weak points of the case: they had no proof that the three young boys were directly involved in the death of the homeless man. The autopsy had established that the victim died of drowning in fifty centimetres of water after losing conscious-ness, in all probability due to a series of blows, including one very violent one to the head. This 'in all probability' made things extremely awkward. Because the homeless man also had a blood alcohol content of over 100 milligrams at the time of the incident, Servaz and Espérandieu were perfectly aware that the autopsy report would be used by the defence in an attempt to redefine the facts as 'deliberate violence unintentionally leading to death', or even to cast doubt upon the fact that the blows were the cause of the drowning, which could be attributed to the victim's intoxication – but they had carefully avoided broaching the subject until now.

'That will be for the judge to decide,' said Servaz in the end. 'Stick to what you know, not to what you suppose.'

That same Saturday he looked, bewildered, at the list his daughter had handed to him.

'What's this?'

'My Christmas list.'

'All this?'

'It's a list, Dad. You don't have to buy everything,' she teased him.

He looked at her. The fine silver ring was still in place on her lower lip, as was the ruby-coloured loop on her left eyebrow, but a fifth ring had come to join the four others on her left ear. Servaz was reminded of his teammate on the current investigation. He also noticed that Margot had bumped into something, because she had a bruise on her right cheekbone. Then he went over the list again: an iPod, a digital photo frame (this was a frame, she explained, where photographs stored in memory could be displayed on a screen), a Nintendo DS Lite game console ('with Dr Kawashima's Brain

Training'), a compact camera (with, if possible, a 7-megapixel sensor, a 3x zoom lens, a 2.5-inch screen and image stabilisation), a laptop computer with a 17-inch screen (preferably an Intel Core 2 Duo with 2 GHz, 2 GB of RAM, a 250-GB hard drive and a CD-DVD burner). She had hesitated over an iPhone, but then decided that, at the end of the day, it might be 'a bit expensive'. Servaz had no idea what these things cost nor what '2 GB of RAM', for example, might mean. But he did know one thing: *there were no innocent technologies.* In their interconnected technological world, moments of freedom and authentic thought were becoming increasingly rare. What did it all mean, this frenetic buying, this fascination with the most superfluous gadgets? Why did a member of a tribe in New Guinea now seem to him wiser and healthier than most of the people he spent his time with? Was it just him or was he, like the old philosopher in his barrel, gazing at a world that had lost its reason? He slipped the list into his pocket and kissed her on her forehead.

'I'll think about it.'

In the course of the afternoon the weather had changed. It was raining, there was a strong wind, and they had taken shelter under a flapping canvas awning in front of one of the many brilliantly lit window displays in the town centre. The streets were full of people, cars and Christmas decorations.

What was the weather like up there? he suddenly wondered. Was it snowing at the Institute? Servaz pictured Julian Hirtmann in his cell, unfolding his long body to watch the snow falling silently outside his window. Ever since the previous day and Captain Ziegler's revelations in the car, the thought of Hirtmann had rarely left him.

'Dad, are you listening to me?'

'Yes, of course.'

'You won't forget my list, will you?'

He reassured her on that point. Then he suggested they go for a drink in a café on the Place du Capitole. To his great surprise, she ordered a beer. Until now she had always ordered Diet Coke. Servaz became brutally aware of the fact that his daughter was seventeen and that he still saw her, despite all evidence to the contrary, as if she were five years younger. Perhaps it was because of this short-sightedness that he hadn't known how to behave with her for some time now. His gaze fell again upon the bruise on her cheek. He studied her for a moment. She had shadows under her eyes, and as she looked down at her glass of beer her expression was sad. Suddenly the questions came pouring in. What was making her sad? Whose phone call had she been waiting for at one o'clock in the morning? What was that mark on her cheek? *A cop's questions*, he thought. *No: a father's questions* . . .

'How did you get that bruise?' he asked.

She looked up.

'What?'

'That bruise on your cheekbone . . . where did it come from?'

'Uh . . . I bumped into something. Why?'

'Where?'

'Does it matter?'

Her tone was biting. He could not help but blush. Easier to question a suspect than his own daughter.

'No,' he said.

'Mum says your problem is that you see evil everywhere. That you've been conditioned by your job.'

'She's probably right.'

It was his turn to look down at his beer.

'I got up during the night to go to the loo and I walked into a door. Is that a good enough answer?'

He looked at her closely, wondering whether to believe her. It was a plausible explanation; he himself had cut his forehead that way, in the middle of the night. However, there was something about the aggressive tone of her response that made him uncomfortable. Or was he just imagining things? Why could he, as a rule, see so clearly into the people he was interrogating, while his own daughter remained so impenetrable? And, more generally, why was he like a fish in water when he was on a case and so useless when it came to relationships? He knew what a shrink would have said. He would have talked to him about his childhood . . .

'Let's go see a film,' he said.

That night, after he had put a ready meal in the microwave and gulped down a coffee (he saw too late that he'd run out, and had to use an old jar of instant easily past the sell-by date), he reimmersed himself in the biography of Julian Alois Hirtmann. Night had fallen over Toulouse. Outside, there was a gusty wind and it was raining, but his study was filled with the strains of Gustav Mahler (Sixth

Symphony) wafting through the room, and his intense concentration was aided by the late hour and a semi-darkness troubled only by a little desk lamp and the luminous computer screen. Servaz had got out his notebook and started adding to it. His notes already covered several pages. While the sound of violins rose from the sitting room, he returned to the career of the serial killer. The judge in Switzerland had requested a psychiatric evaluation to establish criminal responsibility, and the appointed experts concurred, after a long series of interviews, that the suspect was 'fully irresponsible', invoking his fits of delirium, his hallucinations – intensive drug use having altered the subject's judgement and reinforced his schizophrenia – and a total absence of empathy. This final point was indisputable, even Servaz agreed on that. According to the reports, their patient did not have 'the psychological means to control his acts, nor the degree of inner freedom that would enable him to make choices and decisions'.

According to certain Swiss forensic psychiatry websites, the appointed experts were nostalgic for a scientific method that left little room for personal interpretation: they had subjected Hirtmann to a battery of standard tests based on the DSM-IV, the *Diagnostic and Statistical Manual of Mental Disorders*. Servaz wondered whether Hirtmann were not already as well acquainted with the manual as the appointed experts were.

Still, well aware of their subject's dangerousness, they had recommended a detention order and internment in a specialised establishment 'for an indeterminate period'. Hirtmann had stayed in two Swiss psychiatric hospitals before landing at the Wargnier Institute. He was not the only inmate in Unit A who had come from abroad, for the Institute, unique in Europe, was an initial venture into psychiatric detention as part of a potential Europe-wide legal framework. Servaz frowned as he read this: what could that mean, when European legal systems were all so different in their laws, the length of sentences and the size of their budgets – where France spent half as much per head of population as Germany, the Netherlands or even Great Britain?

He got up to get a beer, and it occurred to him that there was a clear contradiction between Hirtmann's socially integrated and professionally recognised personality as described by the press, and the dark portrait established by the experts of a man prey to pathological jealousy and uncontrollable fantasies of murder. Jekyll and Hyde? Or had Hirtmann managed, thanks to his talent as a manipulator, to avoid a prison sentence? Servaz was ready to bet on this second hypothesis. He was convinced that when Hirtmann first appeared before them, he knew exactly how to behave and what to say to the experts. Did this mean that Servaz and his team, in turn, would be confronted with a peerless actor and manipulator? How could they see through him? Would the psychologist sent by the gendarmerie succeed where three Swiss specialists had been taken for a ride?

Then Servaz wondered what the link between Hirtmann and Lombard could be. The only obvious one was geography. Could Hirtmann have gone after the horse purely by chance? Had he hit upon the idea as he went by the riding academy? The stud farm was well off the main roads. There was no reason for Hirtmann to be there. And if he was the one who had killed the horse, why hadn't the dogs sensed his presence? And why hadn't he used the opportunity to escape? How could he have outsmarted the security system at the Institute? Every question led to a new one.

Servaz's mind suddenly switched gears: *his daughter had shadows under her eyes and a sad gaze*. Why? Why did she look so sad and tired? She had answered the phone at one o'clock in the morning. Whose call was she expecting? And that bruise on her cheek: he was far from convinced by Margot's explanation. He would talk about it with her mother.

Servaz went on digging into Julian Hirtmann's past life until the early hours of the morning. When he went to lie down, that Sunday, 14 December, it was with the impression that he was holding the pieces of two separate puzzles in his hands: they just didn't fit.

His daughter had shadows under her eyes and a sad gaze. And she had a bruise on her cheekbone. What did it mean?

That same night, Diane Berg was thinking about her parents. Her father was a secretive man, middle class, a rigid, distant Calvinist of the sort Switzerland produced with the same regularity as chocolate and safes. Her mother lived in her own world, a secret, imaginary one where she heard the music of angels, a world where she was the centre of everything – her mood constantly vacillating between depression and euphoria. A mother who was far too self-absorbed to lavish on her children anything other than leftover crumbs of affection, and Diane had learned very early on that the bizarre world of her parents was not for her.

She had run away for the first time at fourteen. She didn't get very far. The Geneva police brought her home after she'd been caught red-handed stealing a Led Zeppelin CD together with a boy her own age whom she'd met two hours earlier. In such a 'harmonious' environment rebellion was inevitable and Diane went through her 'grunge', 'neo-punk' and 'Goth' phases before heading off to the psychology department of the university, where she learned to know herself and to know her parents, even if she could not understand them.

Her encounter with Spitzner had been decisive. Diane had not had many lovers before him, even though, from the outside, she gave the impression of a young woman who was forthcoming and sure of herself. But not to Spitzner. He had seen through her very quickly. Right from the start she had suspected that she was hardly his first conquest among his students, something he went on to confirm, but she didn't care. Just as she didn't care about the age difference or the fact he was married and the father of seven children. If she had had to apply her talents as a psychologist to her own case, she would have seen their relationship as pure cliché: Pierre Spitzner represented everything her parents were not. And everything they hated.

She recalled the long and very serious conversation they had once had.

'I'm not your father,' he had said at the end. 'Or your mother. Don't ask me for things I will never be able to give you.'

He was stretched out on the sofa in the little bachelor studio the university put at his disposal, a glass of Jack Daniels in his hand. He was unshaven and bare-chested, displaying not without a certain vanity a body that was remarkably fit for a man his age.

'Such as?'

'To be faithful.'

'Are you sleeping with other women at the moment?'

'Yes, my wife.'

'I mean, *other* women.'

'No, not at the moment. Satisfied?'

'I don't care.'

'You're lying.'

'Oh, all right, I do care.'

'Well, I don't give a damn who you sleep with,' he had replied.

But there was one thing that neither he nor anyone else had noticed: Diane had grown up with her mother's secrets in a house

127

where there were closed doors, and rooms she was told 'you mustn't go in', all of which had merely served to stimulate her overactive curiosity. A trait that was useful to her in her profession, but it had sometimes ended up getting her into uncomfortable situations. Diane emerged from her thoughts and watched the moon slipping behind clouds torn like shreds of gauze. It reappeared a few seconds later in a new tear in the clouds, then disappeared again. Near her window, for a brief moment the branch of a fir tree flocked with snow seemed phosphorescent in the white falling from the sky; then everything returned to darkness.

She turned away from the deep, narrow window. The red numbers on her clock radio shone in the obscurity. Twenty-five minutes past midnight. Everywhere was still. There must be one or two guards awake upstairs, that much she knew, but they were probably sprawling in their armchairs watching television at the far end of the building.

In this wing of the Institute reigned silence and sleep.

But not for everyone . . .

She went over to the door of her room. Because there was a gap of a few millimetres beneath the door itself, she had switched off the light. A caress of icy air brushed against her bare feet and she immediately began to shiver. Because of the cold, but also because of the adrenaline rush in her veins. Something had aroused her curiosity.

Half past midnight.

The sound was so faint she almost failed to hear it.

Like the night before. And the other nights.

A door opening. Very slowly. Then nothing more. Someone who did not want to be caught.

Silence again.

Like her, the person was waiting.

The clicking of a switch, then a ray of light beneath her door. Footsteps in the corridor. So muffled they were almost drowned by the pounding of her heart. For a moment a shadow blocked the light filtering into her room. She hesitated. Then she suddenly made up her mind and opened it. Too late. The shadow had disappeared.

Silence fell once again; the light went out.

She sat on the edge of the bed in the darkness, freezing despite her winter pyjamas and hooded dressing gown. Once again she wondered who could be walking around the Institute every night. Above all, for what purpose? It was clearly something that must remain discreet, because they took a great many precautions to avoid being heard.

The first night, Diane had thought it must be one of the auxiliaries or a nurse with a sudden hunger who didn't want anyone to know that he or she was on a midnight raid of the refrigerator. But her insomnia had kept her awake, and the light in the corridor had passed by again a full two hours later. The following night, exhausted, she had fallen asleep. But last night, the same thing again: her insomnia was back, and with it the infinitesimal creaking of the door, the light in the corridor and the shadow sliding furtively towards the stairway.

Vanquished by fatigue, she nevertheless fell asleep before their return. She slipped under her duvet and looked in the pale rectangle of the window at the reflection of her icy little room with its bathroom and toilet. She had to get some sleep. The next day was Sunday; she'd be off duty. She'd use the time to go over her notes; then she'd go down into Saint-Martin. But Monday was an important day: Dr Xavier had informed her that on Monday he would take her to visit Unit A . . .

She had to get some sleep.

Four days . . . She had been at the Institute for four days and it seemed to her that in this short period of time her senses had been sharpened. Was it possible to change in so little time? If so, what would it be like a year from now, when she left to go back home? She scolded herself. She had to stop thinking about that. She had months ahead of her.

She still could not understand why they had locked criminal madmen away somewhere like this, undoubtedly the most sinister and uncommon place she had ever been.

But this will be your home for a year, girl.

With that thought, all desire for sleep evaporated.

She sat at the head of her bed and switched on her bedside lamp. Then she plugged in her computer, opened it and waited for it to boot up so that she could check her inbox. Fortunately, the Institute had wireless Internet connection.

You have no new messages.

She had mixed feelings. Had she really expected him to write? After what had happened? She was the one who had taken the decision to end it, even though it had devastated her. He had accepted with his usual stoicism and she had felt wounded. The depths of her distress had surprised even her.

She hesitated for a moment before tapping away on the keyboard.

She knew he would not understand her silence. She had promised to give him details and write to him soon. Like any expert in forensic psychiatry, Pierre Spitzner was dying to find out everything he could about the Wargnier Institute. When he had heard that Diane's application had been accepted, not only had he seen this as a chance for her, but also as an opportunity for him to learn more about the place that was the source of so many rumours.

She typed the first few words:

> *Dear Pierre,*
> *I'm doing fine. This place—*

Her hand stopped.

An image had suddenly appeared . . . A clear, sharp flash, like ice . . .

Spitzner's place overlooking the lake, the room in the half-light, the silence of the empty house. Pierre and herself in the big bed. They had only come to pick up a file he had forgotten. His wife was at the airport, waiting for her flight to Paris, where she would be giving a talk entitled Characters and Points of View. *(Spitzner's wife was the author of a dozen complicated, bloody crime thrillers with a heavy sexual component that had met with a certain success.) Pierre had taken the opportunity to show her his home. When they arrived outside the couple's bedroom, he had opened the door and taken Diane by the hand. At first she had refused to make love there, but he had insisted in that childlike manner of his that always broke down her resistance. He had also insisted that Diane put on his wife's underwear. Underwear from the most expensive boutiques in Geneva . . . Diane had hesitated. But the transgressive atmosphere, the spice of the taboo were too tempting for her to obey her scruples for long. She had noticed that she wore the same size as her lover's wife. She lay under him, her eyes closed, their bodies perfectly bonded and in tune, Pierre's scarlet face above her, when a voice – detached, sharp, biting – came from the threshold of the room:*

'Get your whore out of here.'

She closed the computer; any desire to write had fled. She turned her head to switch off the light. And shuddered. The shadow was beneath her door . . . motionless . . . She held her breath, unable to move even an inch. Then curiosity and irritation got the better of her and she leapt towards the door.

But the shadow had disappeared once again.

PART 2

Welcome to Hell

10

On Sunday, 14 December, at a quarter to eight in the morning, Damien Ryck, known as Rico, twenty-eight years old, left his house for a solitary hike on the mountain. The sky was grey, and he already knew the sun wouldn't come out that day. As soon as he woke up, he went out on the big terrace and saw a thick fog had enveloped the roofs and streets of Saint-Martin; above the town, the clouds wrapped sooty scrolls round the peaks.

Given the weather forecast, he decided on a simple stroll to clear his mind, and took a path he knew by heart. The night before, or, to be more precise, a few hours earlier, he had unsteadily made his way home after a party where he had smoked several joints, and he had gone to sleep with all his clothes on. Once he was awake, after a shower, a mug of black coffee and another joint, he decided that the pure upland air would do him the world of good. It was Rico's intention to finish inking in a plate sometime later that morning, a delicate task which required a steady hand.

Rico was an author of graphic novels.

A marvellous profession which allowed him to work at home and make a living doing what he loved. His very dark works had found an appreciative audience among connoisseurs, and his renown was growing in the small world of independent graphic novels. As he was a great enthusiast of off-piste skiing, mountain climbing, paragliding, mountain biking and world travel in general, he had discovered that Saint-Martin was an ideal place to come home to. His profession, combined with modern technology, meant that he didn't need to live in Paris, where the offices of his publisher, Éditions d'Enfer, were located and which he visited half a dozen times a year. In the beginning, the inhabitants of Saint-Martin had some difficulty getting used to his caricature alter-globalisation look, with his black and yellow dreadlocks, bandana, orange poncho, numerous piercings and pink beard. In the summertime they could also admire the dozen

135

or more tattoos on his quasi-anorexic body: his shoulders, arms, back, neck, calves and thighs were covered with veritable works of art. Yet it was worth the effort to get to know Rico: not only was he a talented artist, he was also a charming man with a deadpan sense of humour, extremely considerate towards children and old people and all his neighbours.

That morning Rico put on his special lightweight walking boots, and a hat with ear flaps of the kind worn by peasants in the High Andean plateaus. Then he set off at an easy trot towards the hiking trail, which started just beyond the supermarket 200 metres below his house.

The fog had not lifted. He made a loop round the rows of abandoned shopping trolleys in the deserted supermarket car park, and lengthened his stride once he reached the path. Behind him, the church bells rang eight o'clock. Their tolling seemed to reach him through several layers of cotton.

He had to be careful not to twist an ankle on the uneven ground scattered with roots and big stones. He ran two kilometres over deceptively flat terrain, to the roar of a torrent, which he crossed and recrossed over solid little bridges made of fir bark boards. Then the slope grew steeper and he could feel his hamstrings working. The mist had lifted slightly. He saw the metal bridge that crossed the water a short way up, just before it fell in a roaring tumult. This was the toughest part of the trail. Once he was up there, the ground would be nearly flat again. He raised his head, pacing himself, and noticed that there was something hanging below the bridge. Some large bag or other object, fixed to the metal structure.

He lowered his head as he covered the last bends in the trail and only lifted it again when he reached the bridge. His heart was beating 150. But when he looked up, it raced: that was no bag hanging from the bridge! Rico froze. The violent shock, together with the climb, had taken his breath away. With his mouth wide open, he stared at the body; he walked the last few metres, his hands on his hips.

Fuck, what the hell is that?

At first, Rico simply could not understand what he was seeing. He wondered if he wasn't hallucinating, given his lack of restraint the night before, but he knew at once that this was no vision. It was too real, too terrifying. It had nothing to do with the horror films he liked to watch. What he saw before his eyes was a man . . . *a man who was dead, and naked, and hanging from a bridge!*

Fucking hell!

A polar chill ran through his veins.

He glanced round. The man had not died all on his own; this was no suicide: in addition to the strap round his neck he was bound to the metallic structure of the bridge and someone had placed a hood over his head – a hood made of black waterproof cloth, which hid his face and belonged to the cape hanging down his back.

Fuck, fuck, fuck!

Rico was overwhelmed with terror. He had never seen anything like it. The sight filled his veins with a venomous panic. He was all alone on the mountain, four kilometres from the nearest dwelling, and there was only one path to get here, the one he had taken.

The path the murderer had taken.

He wondered if the murder had just been committed. Was the killer still nearby? Rico gazed apprehensively at the rocks and the mist. Then he took two deep breaths and turned on his heels. Two seconds later, he was hurtling down the path towards Saint-Martin.

Servaz had never been one for sports. To be honest, he hated them. In any shape or form. In a stadium or on television. He disliked watching sports as much as he did playing any himself. One of the reasons he did not have a television was that they showed too much sport for his liking and, more and more, at any time of day or night.

In the old days, that is, during the fifteen years he was married, he had nevertheless forced himself to do a minimum of physical activity, which meant thirty-five minutes, and not a minute more, of jogging on a Sunday morning. In spite of, or perhaps thanks to this minimal activity, he had not gained a single pound since the age of eighteen, and he still bought the same size trousers. He knew the reason for this miracle: he had his father's genes, and the old man had stayed as thin and dashing as a greyhound all his life – except towards the end, when drink and depression had left him all skin and bone.

But since his divorce Servaz had forsworn any activity that remotely resembled exercise.

If he had suddenly decided to start up again that Sunday morning, it was because of what Margot had said the day before: 'Dad, I've decided we should spend the summer holidays together. The two of us. All alone. A long way away from Toulouse.' She had talked about Croatia, the small inlets, the mountainous islands, the monuments and sunshine. She wanted a holiday that would be both playful and sporty, which meant jogging and swimming in the morning, wandering and sightseeing in the afternoon, and in the evening he would take her dancing or they'd go for a walk by the sea. She had it all planned. In other words, Servaz had better be in shape.

So he put on a pair of old shorts, a shapeless T-shirt and some running shoes, and set off along the banks of the Garonne. It was a grey day, with a little bit of mist. Ordinarily he never set foot outdoors before noon when he was off duty, but now he was experiencing an astonishingly peaceful atmosphere in the pale pink city, as if on Sunday mornings even fools and bastards took time off.

As he ran at a moderately good pace, he thought back to what his daughter had said. *A long way away from Toulouse* . . . Why a long way from Toulouse? Once again he saw her sad, tired expression and his worry returned. Was there something in Toulouse that she wanted to get away from? Something or *someone*? He thought again of the bruise on her cheek and suddenly had a dark premonition.

A second later, he ground to a halt, wheezing, gasping for breath.

He'd set off at far too brisk a pace.

He stooped with his hands on his knees, his lungs on fire. His T-shirt was drenched in sweat. He looked at his watch. Ten minutes! He'd lasted ten minutes! Yet he felt like he'd been running for half an hour! *For Christ's sake, he was shattered. Only just turned forty and I'm limping around like an old man*, he moaned, and at that very moment his telephone began to vibrate deep in his pocket.

'Servaz,' he croaked.

'What's wrong?' asked Cathy d'Humières. 'Don't you feel well?'

'I was jogging,' he barked.

'I get the impression you need it. Sorry to disturb you on a Sunday. Something's come up. This time, I'm afraid, it's not a horse.'

'What do you mean?'

'We've got a dead body – in Saint-Martin.'

He stood up straight.

'A . . . dead body?' He was still trying to catch his breath. 'What sort of dead body? Have you got an ID?'

'Not yet.'

'No documents on him?'

'No. He was naked – except for his boots and a black windbreaker.'

Servaz felt as if he just been kicked by a horse. He listened to d'Humières telling him what she knew: the young guy who'd set off to run round the lake, the metal bridge above the torrent, the body hanging underneath . . .

'If he was hanging from a bridge, it might have been suicide,' he ventured, not altogether convinced – who would want to make their exit in such a ridiculous outfit?

'According to the initial report, it looks more like murder. I don't have any more details. I'd like you to meet me there.'

Servaz felt an icy hand caressing the back of his neck. What he'd been dreading had happened. First there had been Hirtmann's DNA, and now this. What did it mean? Was it the first of a series? This time, Hirtmann could not possibly have left the Institute. In that case, who had killed the man under the bridge?

'All right,' he answered. 'I'll let Espérandieu know.'

She told him where to go, then hung up. There was a nearby bench and Servaz went and sat down. He was in the park, the Prairie aux Filtres, lawns sloping gently down towards the Garonne, at the foot of the Pont-Neuf. There were lots of joggers running along the river.

'Espérandieu,' said Espérandieu.

'We've got a dead body in Saint-Martin.'

There was a silence. Then Servaz heard Espérandieu talking to someone. His assistant's voice was muffled by his hand on the receiver. Servaz wondered if he was still in bed with Charlène.

'OK, I'll get ready.'

'I'll come by for you in twenty minutes.'

He hung up, then thought, too late, that would be impossible: he had taken ten minutes to get here at a run and, in his state, he wouldn't be able to make his way home as quickly. He rang Espérandieu back.

'Yes?'

'Take your time. I won't be there for at least half an hour.'

'You're not at home?' asked Espérandieu, surprised.

'I was getting some exercise.'

'Exercise? What kind of exercise?'

His assistant's tone made it clear he didn't believe it for a moment.

'Jogging.'

'You, jogging?'

'It was my first session,' said Servaz righteously, annoyed.

He supposed Espérandieu must be smiling at the other end of the line. Maybe even Charlène Espérandieu was smiling, lying there next to her husband. Did they ever make fun of him and his divorcee ways when they were on their own? But there was one thing he was sure of: Vincent admired him. His assistant had been absurdly proud when Servaz agreed to act as godfather to the child they were expecting.

By the time he reached his car at the Cours Dillon car park he was limping, a stitch in his side like a nail. Once he got to his flat, he took a shower, shaved and changed. Then he headed back out towards the suburbs.

A recently built detached house, set back from an unfenced lawn, with a semicircular paved driveway leading to the garage and front door, American-style. Servaz got out of the car. A neighbour was standing at the top of a ladder attaching a Father Christmas to the edge of the roof; a bit further down the street children were playing ball; a tall, thin couple in their fifties jogged by on the pavement in fluorescent running clothes. Servaz went up the driveway and rang the bell.

He turned to watch the neighbour's perilous struggle with his fairy lights and Father Christmas at the top of the ladder.

When he turned back, he nearly jumped: Charlène Espérandieu had opened the door without making a sound and was standing there before him, smiling. She was wearing a hooded jersey cardigan open over a lilac T-shirt and a pair of maternity jeans. She was barefoot. You could not fail to see her round belly. And her beauty. Everything about Charlène Espérandieu was lightness, delicacy and spirit. It was as if even pregnancy could not weigh her down or take away her sense of humour and her artist's wings. Charlène ran an art gallery in the centre of Toulouse; Servaz had been invited to a few private views, and had discovered artwork that was strange, disturbing and sometimes fascinating. For a moment, he stood there without moving. Then he regained his composure and smiled at her, a smile that paid homage to her.

'Come in. Vincent is almost ready. Would you like a coffee?'

He remembered he hadn't had a thing since he got up. He followed her into the kitchen.

'Vincent told me you've started jogging,' she said, sliding a cup over to him.

Her playful tone was not lost on him. He was grateful to her for lightening the atmosphere.

'Just a try. A fairly pathetic one, I have to admit.'

'Keep at it. Don't give up.'

'*Labor omnia vincit*. "Hard work conquers all,"' he translated, with a nod.

She smiled.

'Vincent told me you often quote things in Latin.'

'Just a little trick to get attention at important moments.'

For an instant he was tempted to talk to her about his father. He'd never told anyone about him, but if there was one person he could have confided in, it would be Charlène: he had sensed this from the very first evening, when she had subjected him to a veritable interrogation – but it was a friendly interrogation, even tender at times. She approved with a nod of her head, then went on to say, 'Vincent admires you so much. I've noticed there are times when he tries to copy you, to act or respond the way he thinks you would act or respond. In the beginning I couldn't understand where these changes in him were coming from, but by observing you I figured it out.'

'I hope he only copies the good parts.'

'I hope so, too.'

He remained silent. Espérandieu burst into the kitchen, putting on a silvery jacket that Servaz almost found inappropriate, under the circumstances.

'I'm ready!'

He put one hand on his wife's round belly.

'Take care of yourselves.'

'How far along is she?' asked Servaz in the car.

'Seven months. Start preparing yourself to be a godfather. Now, why don't you give me the rundown.'

Servaz told him the little he knew.

An hour and thirty minutes later they left the car in the supermarket car park, which had been invaded by motorcycles and vehicles from the gendarmerie. One way or another, the news had got out. The fog had lifted slightly, was nothing more than a veil – it was like looking at their surroundings through a misted windowpane. Servaz saw several press vehicles, including one from the local television station. Journalists and curious onlookers had gathered at the foot of the concrete ramp out of the car park; halfway up, the yellow tape of the gendarmerie blocked any further access. Servaz got out his card and lifted the tape. One of the junior officers pointed them in the direction of the path. They left the furore behind them and walked silently, their tension growing. They met no one until they reached the first bends in the path – but the further they went, the thicker the mist became.

Halfway up the slope, Servaz felt the stitch in his side return. He slowed down to catch his breath before attacking the final bend and then he looked up. He could see a number of figures coming and going in the fog above them. And a great burst of light, as if a truck were parked there with all its headlights on.

He climbed the last hundred metres with the growing certainty that the killer had chosen these surroundings deliberately. Like the first time.

He was leaving nothing to chance.

He knew the area.

Something doesn't fit, thought Servaz. Could Hirtmann ever have been here, before he'd been transferred to the Institute? Could it be he knew the region? These were all questions they would have to answer. He remembered what he'd thought the moment d'Humières rang: this time there was no way Hirtmann could have left the Institute. And that being the case, who had killed the man beneath the bridge?

Through the mist Servaz could see Captain Ziegler and Captain Maillard. Ziegler was having an animated conversation with a suntanned little man with a white lion's mane of hair, someone Servaz recalled having seen before. Then it came back to him: Chaperon, the mayor of Saint-Martin – he'd been at the power plant. The gendarme said a few more words to the mayor, then headed their way. Servaz introduced her to Espérandieu. She pointed to the steel bridge, and below it in the halo of white light they could just make out a vague figure.

'It's dreadful!' she shouted above the roar of the water.

'What have you got so far?' he shouted in turn.

Ziegler pointed to a young man sitting on a rock wearing an orange poncho, and summed up the situation: the young man out jogging, the body dangling under the bridge, Captain Maillard cordoning off

142

the area and confiscating the mobile of their only witness and, despite all that, word had got out to the media.

'What is the mayor doing here?' Servaz wanted to know.

'We asked him to come and identify the body, in case it was a local. Perhaps he told the press. Politicians, even small-timers, always need journalists.'

She made an about-turn and headed towards the crime scene.

'It seems we've identified the victim. According to the mayor and Maillard, it's a man called Gilles Grimm, a chemist in Saint-Martin. Maillard says his wife called the gendarmerie to report his disappearance.'

'Disappearance?'

'According to the wife, Grimm left last night for his Saturday-evening poker game and should have been home by midnight. She called to say he hadn't returned and she'd had no news from him.'

'When did she call?'

'Eight o'clock. When she woke up this morning, she was surprised not to find him at home, and his bed was cold.'

'*His* bed?'

'They sleep in separate rooms,' she confirmed.

They went closer. Servaz steeled himself. Powerful spotlights lit both sides of the bridge. The mist swirling before them was not unlike the smoke of cannons on a battlefield. In the blinding light of the projectors, everything was vapour, fog, foam. Even the stream seemed to be smoking, as did the rocks, which were as sharp and shiny as knife blades. Servaz went closer. The roaring waters filled his ears, mingled with the roaring of his blood.

The body was naked.

Fat.

White.

Because of the humidity, the skin shone in the blinding halo of light as if it had been oiled. Servaz's first thought was that the chemist was fat – even very fat. His attention was drawn to the nest of black hair and tiny genitals shrinking against the massive thighs with their folds of flab. Then his gaze travelled up the bulging torso, hairless and white, as flabby as his thighs. Then on up to the throat squeezed by a strap embedded so deep in his flesh that it almost disappeared. And, finally, the hood drawn over his face, and the large black water-proof cape down his back.

143

'Why would anyone put a windbreaker over the victim's head and then hang him up stark naked?' said Espérandieu, his voice altered, hoarse and shrill at the same time.

'Because the windbreaker must mean something,' said Servaz. 'As will the nudity.'

'What a fucking show,' added his assistant.

Servaz turned to look at him. He pointed to the young man in the orange poncho seated a bit further down.

'Borrow a car and take him back to the gendarmerie to get his statement.'

'Right,' said Espérandieu, then went quickly on his way.

Two investigators wearing white overalls and surgical masks were bending over the metal railing. One of them had taken out a pen light and was casting its beam over the body below him.

Ziegler pointed at him.

'The pathologist thinks the cause of death is strangling. Do you see those straps?'

She pointed to the vertical strap circling the dead man's throat, and the two straps binding his wrists and connecting them to the bridge above him, his arms raised and spread in a V.

'It would seem that the murderer gradually lowered the body into the void by adjusting the length of the straps on either side. The more slack he gave, the more the central strap tightened round his victim's neck until eventually it strangled him. It must have taken a very long time to die.'

'A horrible death,' said someone behind them.

They turned round. Cathy d'Humières was staring at the dead body. She looked older, drained.

'My husband wants to sell his shares in his company and open a diving club in Corsica. He wants me to quit my job. On mornings like this I'd be inclined to listen to him.'

Servaz knew she would do no such thing. He could easily picture her as the guerrilla wife, valiant little soldier of the social circuit, finding it no trouble after an exhausting day at work to play hostess to her friends, laugh with them, put up with life's vagaries without batting an eyelid, as if they were no more significant than a glass of wine spilled on the table.

'Do we know who the victim is?'

Ziegler repeated what she had told Servaz.

'Do you know the pathologist's name?' asked Servaz.

Ziegler went over to the investigator, then came back with the information. Servaz nodded his head, satisfied. When he had first started in the job, he'd had a run-in with a pathologist who had refused to report to a crime scene for an investigation Servaz was handling. Servaz had gone to the Toulouse University Hospital and flown into a terrible rage. But the doctor had stood her ground, never losing her composure. Later on, he learned that the same person had hit the headlines in the matter of a famous serial killer – a killer whose murders of young women in the region had been taken as suicides, due to her incredible negligence.

'They're about to lift up the corpse,' said Ziegler.

It was much colder and damper than down at the car park. Servaz pulled his scarf tight round his neck, then thought about the strap buried deep in the victim's neck and hastened to loosen it again.

All of a sudden he noticed two details which he had overlooked in the horror of the initial discovery.

The first of these was the victim's only remaining item of clothing, other than the cape: a pair of leather boots that seemed curiously small for such a big fellow.

The second was his right hand.

There was a finger missing.

The ring finger.

It had been cut off.

'Let's go,' said d'Humières, once the investigators had got the body onto the bridge.

The metal walkway vibrated beneath their feet, and Servaz had an instant of pure panic when he saw the void into which the water was hurtling below. Crouched around the dead body, the investigators were painstakingly removing the hood. There was a moment when everyone watching suddenly recoiled. Beneath the hood the victim had been gagged with silver duct tape. Servaz could easily imagine the screams of terror and pain muffled by the adhesive tape: his eyes were popping out of his sockets. On closer inspection he understood Grimm's eyes were not wide open for natural reasons: the murderer had peeled back his eyelids, pulled on them – no doubt with the help of a pair of tweezers – then stapled them to his eyebrows and cheeks. *He had forced him to watch* . . . In addition, the murderer had so badly mutilated his victim's face, probably with a heavy object like a hammer or mallet, that he had practically torn off his nose, for it was only held in place by a thin strip of flesh and cartilage. Finally, Servaz noticed that there were traces of mud in the chemist's hair.

For a moment no one spoke. Then Ziegler turned towards the bank of the racing stream. She signalled to Maillard, who took the mayor by the arm. Servaz watched as they came closer. Chaperon looked terrified.

'That's him all right,' he stammered. 'It's Grimm. Oh my God! What have they done to him?'

Ziegler gently nudged the mayor over to Maillard, who led him away from the dead body.

'Last night he was playing poker with Grimm and a friend of theirs,' she explained. 'They were the last people to have seen him alive.'

'I think that this time we have a problem,' said d'Humières, pulling herself upright.

Servaz and Ziegler glanced at each other.

'We're going to have the honour of being in the papers. All over the front page. And not just the local press.'

Servaz knew what she was getting at: they were going to be in the eye of the hurricane, at the centre of a media storm: the dailies, the weeklies, all the television newscasts. It was not the best way to progress with an investigation, but they would not be given any choice in the matter. Then he noticed a detail that he had missed until now: Cathy d'Humières was very elegant this morning. Not strikingly so, it was almost imperceptible, because the prosecutor was always impeccably turned out anyway, but this morning she had made an extra effort. Her blouse, suit, coat, necklace and earrings: everything matched perfectly, right down to her make-up, which enhanced her austere yet pleasing face. She was very sober, but she must have spent a long time in front of her mirror to achieve such sobriety.

She knew the press would be getting involved so she prepared herself accordingly.

Unlike Servaz, who hadn't even combed his hair. At least he had remembered to shave.

And yet there was something she could not have foreseen: the effect the sight of the dead body would have on her. To a certain degree it had ruined her effort and she now looked weary, run-down and old, despite her attempt to stay in control. Servaz went over to the CSI who was taking shot after shot of the corpse, flash popping.

'I'm counting on you not to let any of these photographs go astray,' he said. 'Don't leave anything lying around.'

The CSI nodded. Had he got the message? If any of those pictures made it into the paper, Servaz would hold him personally responsible.

'Did the pathologist have a look at the right hand?' he asked Ziegler.

'Yes. He thinks the finger was severed with a sharp instrument, like pliers or pruning shears. A closer examination will confirm it.'

'The ring finger on the right hand,' said Servaz.

'Yet his wedding ring and other fingers haven't been touched,' observed Ziegler.

'Are you thinking the same thing?'

'A signet ring, or some other ring.'

'Did the murderer want to steal it, take it as a trophy, or make sure no one else saw it?'

Ziegler looked at him with surprise.

'Why would he want to hide it? Besides, all he had to do was take it off.'

'Perhaps he couldn't. Grimm has fat fingers.'

On his way back down, Servaz saw the crowd and felt like fleeing. But the concrete ramp behind the supermarket was the only way out, unless he were to trek all over the mountain. He assumed a suitable expression and was preparing to confront the crowd when a hand stopped him.

'Let me.'

Cathy d'Humières had regained her composure. Servaz stood back and admired her performance, the way she evaded the issue while giving the impression she was letting them in on things. She answered all the journalists' questions, looking them straight in the eye, gravely, punctuating her responses with a knowing yet restrained little smile, which nevertheless kept the horror of the situation in focus.

It was great art.

He wove his way to his car through the journalists and didn't wait to hear the end of her speech. The Cherokee was parked on the far side of the car park, beyond the rows of shopping trolleys. He could hardly see it through the mist. Stung by gusts of wind, he raised the collar of his jacket, thinking of the artist who had composed that gruesome picture up there. *If it's the same person who killed the horse, he likes his peaks, his high places.*

Servaz walked over to the Jeep and suddenly sensed that there was something not right. He stared at the car until he understood. The tyres sagged down to the asphalt like deflated balloons. They'd been punctured. All four of them . . . and the metalwork had been scratched.

Welcome to Saint-Martin, he thought.

11

Sunday morning at the Institute. A strange calm reigned. For Diane it was as if the place had been deserted by all its inhabitants. Not a sound. She emerged from under her duvet and headed towards the tiny, icy bathroom. A quick shower; she washed her hair, dried it, then brushed her teeth as hastily as she could because of the cold.

When she came back, she glanced out of the window. Fog. Like a ghostly presence which had used the dark of night to settle in. It drifted above the thick layer of snow, drowned the white fir trees. The Institute was wrapped in it; only ten metres away the view was blocked by a wall of vaporous whiteness. She pulled her dressing gown tighter.

Her plan was to drive down and explore Saint-Martin. She dressed quickly and left the room. The ground-floor cafeteria was empty, apart from the server on duty; she asked for a cappuccino and a croissant, and went to sit by the picture window. She had not been sitting there for more than two minutes when a man in his thirties wearing a white lab coat came into the room. She watched him discreetly as he ordered a large café au lait, an orange juice and two croissants; then he walked over to her with his tray.

'Good morning. May I sit down?'

She nodded with a smile.

'Diane Berg,' she said, holding out her hand. 'I'm—'

'I know. Alex. I'm one of the psychiatric nurses. So, are you settling in?'

'I only just got here . . .'

'It's not easy, is it? When I first arrived here and saw the place, I nearly got back in my car to run away,' he said with a laugh. 'And I don't even sleep here.'

'Do you live in Saint-Martin?'

'No, I don't live in the valley.'

He said it as if it were the last thing he would ever want to do.

149

'Do you know if it's always so cold in the bedrooms in winter?' she asked.

He looked at her with a smile. He had a rather pleasant, open face, with warm brown eyes and curly hair. He also had a large mole in the middle of his forehead, which made him look as if he had a third eye. For a moment, her gaze was unpleasantly drawn to the mole and she blushed when she saw he had noticed.

'Yes, I'm afraid so,' he said. 'The top floor is very draughty, and the heating system is pretty ancient.'

Beyond the big window, the landscape of snow and fir trees was magnificent, and very near. It was strange to be sitting there drinking coffee in a warm place, separated from all that whiteness by a simple pane of glass. Diane felt as if she were looking at a film set.

'What is your role exactly?' she asked, determined to seize the chance to find out as much as she could.

'You mean, what is the role of a nurse here?'

'Yes.'

'Well . . . the psychiatric nurses prepare and distribute the medication, we make sure the patients take it the way they're supposed to, and that there are no adverse reactions post treatment . . . We keep an eye on the residents, too, of course . . . But we also organise activities, we talk to them, we make ourselves available, we're there to listen . . . But not too much, either. The nurse's job is to be neither too present nor too absent. Neither indifferent nor systematically helpful. We have to know our place. Especially here. With these—'

'The treatment,' she asked, trying to avoid staring at the mole on his forehead, 'is it aggressive?'

He gave her a cautious glance.

'Yes . . . The dosage here goes far beyond recommended norms. It's sort of the nuclear option, as far as the medication goes. We're not particular about details. But look, that doesn't mean we knock them out either. You've seen them, they're not zombies. The thing is, most of these . . . *individuals* . . . have become resistant to drugs. So we juggle with mixtures of tranquillisers and antipsychotics, enough to stun an ox, four times a day instead of three; then there is electroshock, the straitjacket, and when nothing else works, we resort to a miracle drug: clozapine . . .'

Diane had heard of it: clozapine was an atypical antipsychotic used with cases of schizophrenia that were resistant to other forms of treatment. As with most medicines used in psychiatry, the side effects could be dreadful: incontinence, hypersalivation, blurred vision, weight gain, convulsions and thrombosis, among others.

'What you have to understand,' he added with a faint smile that froze into a grimace, 'is that here, violence is never far away, nor is danger . . .'

She thought she was hearing Xavier: 'Intelligence can only be developed where there is change – *and where there is danger.*'

'At the same time,' he amended, with a short laugh, 'it's safer here than in a lot of inner-city neighbourhoods.'

He shook his head.

'Just between us, not that long ago psychiatry was in the stone age, and patients were used in incredibly barbaric experiments. Just as bad as the Inquisition or the Nazi doctors . . . Things have progressed, but there's still a long way to go . . . There's never talk of cures here. It's always stabilisation, decompression . . .'

'Do you have other responsibilities?' she asked.

'Yes. There's all the administrative stuff: lots of paperwork, procedures . . .'

He glanced outside.

'Then there are the psychiatric interviews prescribed by Dr Xavier and the head nurse.'

'What do they consist of?'

'It's all structured. The techniques are proven, the interviews follow the same course, the questions are more or less standard, but there's some improvisation as well . . . You have to adopt as neutral an attitude as possible, and not give any signs of being too invasive, so as to keep the anxiety level down . . . respect the silences, have breaks . . . Otherwise, you risk running into trouble very quickly . . .'

'Do Xavier and Ferney do interviews as well?'

'Yes, of course.'

'What's the difference between your interviews and theirs?'

'There isn't really any difference. Except that some patients will confide in us, when they won't confide in them. Because they're closer to us on a daily basis, and we've been trying to create a relationship of trust between caregiver and patient, while keeping our therapeutic distance . . . The rest of the time, it's Xavier and Élisabeth who decide on the treatments and protocols . . .'

His voice went strange as he said the last sentence. Diane frowned slightly.

'You sound as if you don't always approve of their decisions.'

She was surprised by the time it took him to answer.

'You're new here, Diane . . . you'll see . . .'

'What will I see?'

He didn't reply. He looked somewhat shifty. Clearly he had no desire to go down that path. But she waited, her gaze questioning.

'How can I explain it? This place, don't forget, is like nowhere else . . . We're dealing with patients none of the other establishments could treat. What goes on here just isn't like what goes on elsewhere.'

'Electroshock without anaesthesia for the patients in Unit A, for example?'

She was immediately sorry she had said it. His expression had turned frosty.

'Who told you about that?'

'Xavier.'

'Just forget it.'

He gazed down at his café au lait, frowning. He seemed sorry he had let himself get caught up in this discussion.

'I'm not even sure that's legal,' she insisted. 'Does French law allow such things?'

He looked up.

'French law? Do you know how many cases of people being forcibly sectioned there are every year in this country? *Fifty thousand* . . . In a modern democracy, hospitalisation without a patient's consent is the exception. But not here . . . Mental patients, and even people who are simply presumed to be mentally ill, have fewer rights than normal citizens. You want to arrest a criminal? You have to wait until six o'clock in the morning. But if it's a guy accused of insanity by a neighbour who has signed a third-party request for hospitalisation, the police can show up day or night. The law only gets involved once the individual has already been deprived of his liberty. And even then only if that person is aware of his rights and knows how to make sure they are respected. That's what psychiatry is about in this country. That, and a lack of resources, and the abusive use of drugs, and shoddy treatment. Our psychiatric hospitals are a no-go area. And this one even more so than the rest.'

He had delivered this long tirade in a bitter tone, the smile gone from his face. Now he stood up and pushed back his chair.

'Have a good look round and make up your own mind,' he advised.

'My own mind about what?'

'About what's going on here.'

'Because there's something going on?'

'What does it matter? You're the one who wanted to learn more about the place.'

She watched him return his tray and leave the room.

The first thing Servaz did was to lower the blinds and turn on the lights. He wanted to make sure no journalists could be stalking them with a telephoto lens. The young author of graphic novels had gone home. In the incident room, Espérandieu and Ziegler had taken out their laptops and were typing away. Cathy d'Humières was standing in the corner talking on the telephone. She snapped her phone shut and came to sit down. Servaz observed them for a moment, then turned round.

There was a whiteboard in a corner by the window. He pulled it out into the light, picked up a marker and drew two columns:

HORSE	GRIMM
dismembered	naked
decapitated	strangled, finger cut off, boots, cape
killed at night?	killed at night?
Hirtmann's DNA	Hirtmann's DNA?

'Do we have enough to go on to assume that the same people are responsible for both crimes?' he asked.

'There are similarities, and there are differences,' answered Ziegler.

'Still, two crimes committed four days apart in the same town,' said Espérandieu.

'Exactly. The hypothesis of a second criminal is highly unlikely. It's bound to be the same person.'

'Or persons,' specified Servaz. 'Don't forget what we talked about in the helicopter.'

'I haven't forgotten. In any case, there is one thing that would establish a definite connection between the two crimes—'

'Hirtmann's DNA.'

'Hirtmann's DNA,' she confirmed.

Servaz lifted the slats of the blinds. He peered outside, then let go with an abrupt snap.

'Do you really think he could have got out of the Institute and given your men the slip?' he asked, turning back to them.

'No, that's impossible. I checked our set-up myself. There's no way he could have slipped through the net.'

'In that case, it's not Hirtmann.'

'Or at least, not this time.'

'If it's not Hirtmann this time, conceivably, it might not have been him the previous time either,' suggested Espérandieu.

Everyone turned to look at him.

'Hirtmann never went up to the top of the cable car. Someone else did. Someone who is in contact with him at the Institute and who, voluntarily or not, had a hair belonging to Hirtmann on him.'

Ziegler turned to Servaz with a questioning look. She understood that he hadn't told his assistant everything.

'Except that it wasn't a hair they found in the cable-car cabin,' she said, 'it was saliva.'

Espérandieu looked at her. Then he trained his gaze in turn at Servaz, who nodded his head apologetically.

'I don't see the logic in any of this,' said Servaz. 'Why would they kill the horse first and then the man? Why hang the animal up at the top of the cable car? And the man below a bridge? What is the point?'

'Both of them were hanged, after a fashion,' said Ziegler.

Servaz looked at her.

'That's true.'

He went over to the whiteboard, wiped out some of his notes and wrote:

HORSE	GRIMM
hanging from cable car	hanging from metal bridge
isolated place	isolated place
cut up	naked
decapitated	strangled, finger cut off, boots, cape
killed at night?	killed at night?
Hirtmann's DNA	Hirtmann's DNA?

'Fair enough. Why take it out on an animal?'

'To get at Éric Lombard,' said Ziegler once again. 'The power plant and the horse lead to him.'

'OK. Let's suppose Lombard was the target. What does the chemist have to do with anything? Moreover, the horse was decapitated and half flayed, whereas the chemist was naked except for a cape. What's the connection between the two?'

'Partly skinning an animal is a way of making it naked,' ventured Espérandieu.

'And the horse had two large pieces of skin hanging on either side,' said Ziegler. 'We thought they were meant to represent wings – but maybe they were the imitation of a cape . . .'

'It's possible,' said Servaz, not fully convinced. 'But why chop off its head? And why the cape and the boots: what do they stand for?'

No one had an answer.

He went on: 'And we always come up against the same puzzle: what could Hirtmann have to do with all this?'

'He's setting you a challenge!' called a voice from the doorway.

They turned round. A man was standing at the entrance to the room.

Servaz's first thought was that he must be a journalist, and was about to throw him out. The man was in his forties, with long light brown hair, a curly beard and little round glasses, which he removed in order to wipe off the mist that had formed when he came into the warmth from the cold, then put back on to gaze at everyone with his pale eyes. He was wearing a heavy jumper and thick corduroy trousers. He looked like a teacher of social sciences, or a union activist, or someone who was nostalgic for the 1960s.

'Who are you?' asked Servaz curtly.

'Are you the person in charge of the investigation?'

The visitor came closer.

'Simon Propp. I'm the psychologist. I was supposed to come tomorrow, but the gendarmerie called me and told me what happened. So here I am.'

He went round the table and shook everyone's hand. Then he stopped to look at the empty chairs. He chose one on Servaz's left. Servaz was sure he chose it for a particular reason and felt vaguely irritated, as if he were trying to manipulate him.

Simon Propp looked at the whiteboard.

'Interesting,' he said.

'Really?' Servaz's tone was involuntarily sarcastic. 'What sort of thoughts does it inspire in you?'

'I'd rather you went on as if I wasn't here, if you don't mind,' answered the shrink. 'I'm sorry I interrupted. I'm not here to judge your work methods.' Servaz watched him flap his hand. 'And besides, it's not something I could do. I'm only here to assist you when the time comes to discuss Julian Hirtmann's personality, or when you need to draw up a clinical profile on the basis of the clues found at the crime scene.'

'You said when you came in that he's setting us a challenge?' said Servaz.

He saw the shrink narrow his little yellow eyes behind his glasses. Beneath his shining beard, which made him look like a clever leprechaun, he had round cheeks, ruddy with the cold. Servaz got the unpleasant sensation he was being mentally dissected. He nevertheless held the newcomer's gaze.

'Right,' said Propp. 'I did my homework yesterday. I studied Hirtmann's file when I heard his DNA had been found in the cable car cabin. It's obvious he's a manipulator, a sociopath and a very smart man. But it goes further than that: Hirtmann is a special case even as far as organised killers go. Sooner or later the personality disorders they suffer from are bound to affect their intellectual faculties and their social life, one way or the other. And sooner or later the people around them will become aware of their monstrous nature. That is why they often need an accomplice, generally a wife who is as much of a monster as they are, to help them maintain their façade. But Hirtmann, when he was at liberty, managed perfectly to disconnect the part of himself that was prey to rage and madness from his social life. He was an expert at putting others off the scent. Other sociopaths have managed to do something similar before him, but none of them were in a profession as prominent as his.'

Propp stood up and slowly began to circle the table. With increasing irritation, Servaz surmised that this must be one of the shrink's conjuring tricks.

'He is suspected of the murder of over forty young women in twenty-five years. Forty murders and not the slightest clue, not a single lead to connect them with the perpetrator! If it weren't for the newspaper cuttings and files that were found at his home and in his safe deposit box, the crimes would never have been traced to him.'

He stopped behind Servaz, who refused to turn his head, and merely looked at Irène Ziegler on the other side of the table.

'And suddenly, he leaves a trace – an obvious, vulgar, ordinary trace.'

'You're forgetting one detail,' said Ziegler.

Propp sat back down.

'At the time he committed most of his crimes, DNA analysis either did not yet exist or was far less conclusive than it is today.'

'That's true, but—'

'So you're thinking that what we have today doesn't look anything like the Hirtmann we know, is that it?' said Ziegler, staring right into the shrink's eyes.

Propp blinked and nodded his head.

'So, in your opinion, despite his DNA, he did not kill the horse?'

'I didn't say that.'

'I don't understand.'

'Don't forget he's been locked up for several years. His circumstances have changed. Hirtmann has been in prison for a long time and he's dying of boredom. He's slowly wasting away – and this is a man who used to be incredibly active. He wants to play. Think about it: until he got caught for that stupid crime of passion, he had an intense, stimulating, demanding social life. He was held in high professional regard. He had a beautiful wife, and the orgies he hosted were attended by the cream of Geneva high society. At the same time he was kidnapping, torturing, raping and killing young women in the utmost secrecy. In other words, for a monster like him, a dream life. He certainly did not want it to end. Which is why he was so careful to ensure his victims disappeared.'

Propp joined his fingers beneath his chin.

'Nowadays he has no reason to hide. On the contrary: he wants people to know it's him; he wants to be talked about, attract attention.'

'But he could have escaped outright and started up again in complete liberty,' objected Servaz. 'Why would he go back to his cell? It doesn't make sense.'

Propp scratched his beard.

'I confess that is the question that has been nagging me, too, since yesterday. Why would he go back to the Institute? With the obvious chance that he couldn't get out again if security was tightened. Why run such a risk? What would be the point? You're right: it doesn't make sense.'

'Unless we suppose that to him the game is more exciting than his freedom,' said Ziegler. '*Or that he is certain of being able to get out again.*'

'How could that be?' said Espérandieu, astonished.

'I thought it was impossible for Hirtmann to have committed the second murder,' insisted Servaz. 'Given the extent of the police security. That's what we just agreed, isn't it?'

The shrink looked at them one after the other, still thoughtfully stroking his beard. Behind his glasses his yellow eyes looked like two overripe grapes.

'I think you are grossly underestimating this man,' he said. 'I think you absolutely do not realise what you are dealing with.'

'The watchmen,' said Cathy d'Humières suddenly. 'What's the latest on them?'

'Nothing,' said Servaz. 'I don't think they're guilty. In spite of the fact they ran away. It's too subtle for them. Up to now they've never shown themselves to be capable of anything but the kind of violence that's too ordinary for words. A painter and decorator doesn't turn into Michelangelo overnight. The swabs we took will tell us whether they were present at the crime scene or not, but I don't think so. But they are hiding something, that's obvious.'

'I agree,' said Propp. 'I had a look at the interview transcripts. They just don't have the profile. But I'll check all the same to see whether they have any psychiatric history. Petty delinquents have been known to turn overnight into monsters of unbelievable cruelty. The human spirit can conceal a great many mysteries. Let's not rule anything out.'

Servaz shook his head with a frown.

'Then there's the poker game last night. Let's try and determine whether there was a quarrel. Maybe Grimm had debts . . .'

'There is another issue we have to settle quickly,' said the prosecutor. 'Before, all we had was a dead horse, which meant we could take our time. Now we've got a human victim. And it won't take long for the media to make the connection with the Institute. If, perish the thought, the news gets out about finding Hirtmann's DNA, they'll be all over us. Have you seen the number of journalists outside? The two essential questions are these: were the security measures at the Wargnier Institute at fault in any way? Are our roadblocks and cordons enough? The sooner we have answers, the better. I suggest we go and visit the Institute right now.'

'But if we do that,' objected Ziegler, 'those journalists camped outside could easily tail us. There's surely no point in luring them over there.'

The prosecutor paused for a moment to think.

'True, we'll have to put off the visit until tomorrow. In the meantime I'll organise a press conference to distract the journalists' attention. Martin, what is your take on things?'

'Captain Ziegler, Dr Propp and I will go to the Institute first thing tomorrow while you give your press conference, and Lieutenant Espérandieu will attend the autopsy. Today we can interview the chemist's widow.'

'Fine, let's do that. But let's not lose sight of our two priorities: a) to find out whether Hirtmann could have got out of the Institute, and b) find the connection between the two crimes.'

'There's one angle of attack we didn't consider,' declared Simon Propp once they had left the meeting.

'And what is that?' asked Servaz.

They were in the little car park at the rear of the building, out of sight of the media. Servaz aimed his remote-control key at the car, which a mechanic had dropped off after replacing the tyres. A few snowflakes were fluttering in the cold air, and the sky above was a relentless grey: it would start snowing again soon.

'Pride,' answered the shrink. 'Someone in this valley is playing God. He thinks he's above mankind, above the law, and he's manipulating us poor mortals. That takes boundless pride. And one way or another an ego like that will show on the person who has it – unless he hides it beneath extreme false modesty.'

Servaz stopped short and looked at Propp.

'That's a description that fits Hirtmann,' he said. 'Apart from the false modesty.'

'And plenty of other people as well,' Propp corrected him. 'Pride is not hard to come by, believe me, Commandant.'

*

The chemist's house was the last one on the street. A street which, in fact, was more like a track barely wide enough for vehicles. When he saw the house, Servaz was reminded of Sweden or Finland, a Scandinavian sort of place: it was covered in faded blue shingles, with a large wooden terrace that took up part of the first floor beneath the roof. Birch and beech trees grew all around.

Servaz and Ziegler got out of the car. On the other side of the track, warmly wrapped children were making a snowman. Servaz pulled up his collar and watched them scraping the last layer of snow from the grass. In a sign of the times, they had armed their creation with a plastic gun. For a brief moment Servaz was glad to see, in spite of the warlike pose they'd given their snowman, that children could still enjoy simple pleasures, instead of staying cloistered in their bedrooms, glued to their computers and game consoles.

Then his blood froze. A little boy had just gone over to one of the large dustbins along the street. Servaz saw him stand on tiptoes to open it. Before the eyes of the astounded policeman, the boy plunged his arm inside and pulled out a dead cat. He took hold of the little corpse by the scruff of its neck, crossed the snowy ground and dropped his trophy two metres from the snowman.

The scene was amazingly true to life: it looked exactly as if the snowman had just shot the cat.

'Dear Lord,' said Servaz, petrified.

'According to child psychiatrists,' said Irène Ziegler next to him, 'it has nothing to do with the influence of television and the media. They know what's real and what isn't.'

'Well, sure,' said Servaz. 'I used to play Tarzan when I was a kid, but I never believed for a moment I could really confront a gorilla or swing from tree to tree.'

'And yet they're bombarded with violent games and images and ideas from early childhood.'

'All we can hope is that the psychiatrists are right,' he said with a sad irony in his tone.

'Why do I suspect that they aren't?'

'Because you're a cop.'

A woman was waiting for them in the doorway, smoking a cigarette. Narrowing her eyes behind the ribbon of smoke, she watched them walk towards her. Although the gendarmerie had informed her only three hours earlier of her husband's murder, she did not seem terribly upset.

'Hello, Nadine,' said Chaperon. Captain Ziegler had asked him to come along. Now he said, 'Please accept my sincere condolences. You know how fond I was of Gilles . . . This is terrible . . . what has happened . . .'

The mayor's words were halting; he was still having trouble talking about it. The woman gave him a half-hearted kiss, but when he went to put his arms around her, she held him firmly at a distance, directing her attention to the newcomers. She was in her fifties, tall and lean, with a long horsy face and grey hair. Servaz also offered his condolences. The handshake he received in return was surprisingly strong. He immediately felt the hostility in the air. What had Chaperon told them? That she worked in charity.

'The police would like to ask you a few questions,' continued the mayor. 'They promised me they'd ask you only the most urgent ones and keep the others for later. May we come in?'

Without a word, the woman turned on her heels and led them inside. Servaz saw that the house was entirely made of wood. There was a tiny hall, with a shaded lamp on a shelf on the right, next to a stuffed fox with a crow in its mouth. It made Servaz think of a hunting lodge. There was also a coat rack, but Nadine Grimm did not offer to take their coats. She disappeared up a steep staircase that led to the first-floor terrace. Still not making the slightest sound, she pointed to a wicker sofa full of worn cushions that faced out onto the fields and forests. She herself collapsed into a rocking chair near the railing and pulled a blanket over her lap.

'Thank you,' said Servaz. 'My first question,' he added after a moment of hesitation, 'is, do you have any idea who could have killed your husband?'

Nadine Grimm breathed out smoke and looked deep into Servaz's eyes. Her nostrils quivered as if she had just smelled something unpleasant.

'No. My husband was a chemist, not a gangster.'

'Had he ever received any strange or threatening phone calls?'

'No.'

'Visits from drug addicts at the pharmacy? Was he ever burgled?'

'No.'

'Did he distribute methadone?'

The look she gave them was one of impatience mixed with exasperation.

'Do you have many more questions like this? My husband had nothing to do with drug addicts, he had no enemies, and he wasn't mixed up in any shady business. He was just an imbecile and a drunk.'

Chaperon went pale. Ziegler and Servaz exchanged a glance.

'What do you mean?'

She looked at them, her disgust even more apparent.

'Nothing, just what I said. What has happened is revolting. I don't know who could have done such a thing. Even less, why. I can only see one explanation: one of those crazies locked away up there managed to escape. You'd do better doing something about that, rather than wasting your time here,' she added bitterly. 'But if you were expecting to find a weeping widow, you could have spared yourself the trouble. My husband did not like me very much, and I didn't like him either. I had nothing but scorn for him. For a long time, our marriage has been nothing than a sort of . . . modus vivendi. But I didn't kill him for all that.'

Distracted, Servaz thought he had heard a confession, until he understood that she was saying just the opposite: she hadn't killed him, although she had reason to do so. He had rarely seen so much coldness and hostility concentrated in a single person. Such arrogance and detachment was disconcerting. For a moment he did not know quite how to behave. They would have to dig further into the life of the Grimms – but he wondered if now was the right time.

'Why did you feel scorn for him?' he asked finally.

'I just told you.'

'You said your husband was an imbecile. What gives you the right to say that?'

'I ought to know, of all people, don't you think?'

'Please be more exact.'

She was on the verge of saying something unpleasant. But then her gaze met Servaz's and she thought better of it. She exhaled more smoke, and then with a gesture of mute defiance said, 'My husband studied to become a chemist because he was too lazy and stupid to be a doctor. He bought the pharmacy thanks to his parents, who had a prosperous business. It's a good location, right in the centre of Saint-Martin. And yet, because of his laziness, because he simply didn't have what it takes, he never managed to make the shop turn a profit. There are six pharmacies in Saint-Martin. His had the fewest customers by far; people only went there as a last resort, or by chance:

tourists who were walking by and needed something. Even I didn't trust him when I needed medicine.'

'Then why didn't you get a divorce?'

She sniggered.

'Can you see me starting life over at my age? This house is big enough for two. We each had our own territory, and we avoided getting in each other's way as much as possible. Besides, I'm often away for work. That makes . . . made things easier.'

Servaz thought of a legal expression in Latin: *Consensus non concubitus facit nuptias*. 'Consent, not consummation, makes the marriage.'

'Every Saturday evening he had his poker games,' he said, turning to the mayor. 'Who else took part?'

'It was me and a few friends,' answered Chaperon, 'as I already told the captain.'

'Who was there yesterday evening?'

'Serge Perrault, Gilles and me.'

'Are they your usual partners?'

'Yes.'

'Did you play for money?'

'Yes, small amounts. Or for restaurant meals. He never signed any IOUs, if that's what you're thinking. And anyway, Gilles often won: he was a very good player,' he added, looking in the widow's direction.

'Did anything in particular happen during that game?'

'Such as?'

'I don't know. An argument . . .'

'No.'

'Where were you playing?'

'At Perrault's place.'

'And afterwards?'

'Gilles and I left together, as usual. Then Gilles went on his way and I went home to bed.'

'You didn't notice anything on the way back? You didn't run into anyone?'

'No, not that I can recall.'

'Your husband didn't mention anything out of the ordinary recently?' Ziegler asked Nadine Grimm.

'No.'

'Did he seem worried, anxious?'

'No.'

'Did your husband have anything to do with Éric Lombard?'

She looked at them, not understanding. Then there was a brief spark in her eyes. She crushed her cigarette against the railing and smiled.

'You think there's a connection between my husband's murder and that horse business? That's absurd!'

'You didn't answer my question.'

She sniggered again.

'Why would someone like Lombard waste his time with a loser like my husband? No. Not that I know of.'

'Do you have a photograph of your husband?'

'What for?'

Servaz nearly lost it, forgetting that she had only been a widow for a few hours. But he restrained himself.

'I need a photograph for the investigation,' he replied. 'If you have several, that would be even better. As recent as possible.'

He met Ziegler's gaze briefly and she understood: *the severed finger.* Servaz hoped that the signet ring would be visible in one of the photographs.

'I don't have any recent photographs. And I don't know where he put the older ones. I'll have a look through his things. Anything else?'

'Not for the moment,' said Servaz, getting to his feet.

He felt chilled to the bone, and wanted simply to get out of there as fast as possible. He wondered if that was why the widow Grimm had seated them out on the terrace, to encourage them to leave. Anxiety and cold were twisting his guts, for he had noticed something that pricked him like a needle, a detail he alone had seen: when Nadine Grimm reached out to crush her cigarette on the railing, the sleeve of her jumper had slid up . . . Gaping, Servaz had clearly seen the little white ridges of several scars on her bony wrist: the woman had tried to end it all.

As soon as they were in the car he turned to the mayor. A thought had occurred to him while he was listening to the widow.

'Did Grimm have a mistress?'

'No,' said Chaperon without hesitating.

'Are you sure?'

The mayor gave him a strange look.

'You can never be one hundred per cent sure. But as far as Grimm is concerned, I'd stake my life on it. He wasn't the sort with anything to hide.'

Servaz thought for a moment about what the mayor had just said.

'If there is one thing we do learn in this job,' he said, 'it is that people are rarely what they seem. And that everyone has something to hide.'

As he was saying this, he looked into his rear-view mirror, and again witnessed something quite unexpected: Chaperon had gone very pale, and his eyes had filled with pure terror.

Diane came out of the Institute and the icy wind hit her. Fortunately she had put on her down jacket, a rollneck jumper and fur-lined boots. She took out her keys as she walked towards her Lancia. She was relieved to be able to get out of that place for a while. She sat behind the wheel, turned the ignition and heard the click of the starter. The indicator lights came on, then went out again almost at once. Nothing else happened. *Shit!* She tried again. Same thing. *Oh, no!* She tried again and again, turning the key over and over. Nothing . . .

The battery, she thought. *It's dead.*

Or else it's the cold.

She wondered if anyone at the Institute could help her, but a wave of discouragement swept over her. She sat motionless behind the wheel, looking at the buildings through the windscreen. Her heart was pounding for no particular reason. Suddenly she felt very far from home.

12

That night, Servaz got a phone call from Alexandra, his ex-wife. It was about Margot. Servaz instantly felt worried. Alexandra told him that their daughter had decided to drop her piano and karate, two things she'd been doing since she was small. She gave no valid reason for her decision, merely said that she would not change her mind.

Alexandra was distraught. Margot had been different lately. Her mother got the impression that she was hiding something. She was no longer able to talk to her the way she used to. Servaz let his ex-wife vent her feelings, wondering all the while if she hadn't already unburdened herself to Margot's stepfather – or had he stayed well out of it? Perfectly aware that he was being petty, Servaz found himself hoping his second idea was correct. 'Does she have a boyfriend?' he asked.

'I think she does. But she refuses to talk about it. Which is not like her.'

Then he asked Alexandra if she had gone through Margot's belongings. He knew her well enough to know she must have. And as he expected, she had. But she hadn't found anything.

'Nowadays with all these emails and texts, you can't see who they're talking to,' Alexandra admitted regretfully. 'I'm worried, Martin. See if you can get more out of her. Perhaps she'll confide in you.'

'Don't worry. I'll speak to her. I'm sure it's nothing.'

But he remembered his daughter's sad gaze. The shadows under her eyes. And, above all, the bruise on her cheek. He felt the knot in his guts again.

'Thanks, Martin. And how are you doing?'

He avoided the question and spoke to her about the current investigation, without going into detail. Back when they were married, Alexandra had occasionally had some surprisingly good hunches, or given a new perspective on things.

'A horse and a naked man? That's really odd. Do you think there will be more?'

'That's what I'm afraid of,' he confessed. 'But don't mention it to anyone. Not even your cat burglar,' he added, refusing, as always, to call the wife-thieving airline pilot by name.

'It makes you think those people must have done something really ugly,' she said, when he had told her about Lombard and Grimm. 'And that they did it together. Everyone has something to hide.'

Servaz nodded in silence. *You know what you're talking about, don't you?* They'd been married for fifteen years. For how many years had she been cheating on him with her pilot? How many times had they used a layover in order to get laid – an appropriate expression for air hostess and captain? And after every flight she came home and went on with her family life as if nothing had happened, and always brought a little present for each of them. Until the day she finally made her decision. To justify herself, she told Servaz that Phil didn't have nightmares, that he didn't suffer from insomnia – and that 'he didn't live surrounded by dead bodies.'

'Why a horse?' he asked. 'What's the connection?'

'I don't know,' she replied indifferently, and he knew what that meant: the time for exchanging ideas about his investigations was in the past. 'You're the cop,' she added. 'Right, I have to go. Try and talk to Margot.'

She hung up. When had things started going wrong? When had their paths diverged? Was it when he began spending more and more time at the office and less and less at home? Or was it before that? They had met at university, and were married barely six months later, against her parents' advice. In those days, when they were still students, Servaz wanted to teach literature and Latin like his father, and write the 'great contemporary novel'; Alexandra, more modestly, was studying to work in the tourist industry. Then he joined the police force. Officially on a whim, but in truth because of his past.

It makes you think those people must have done something really terrible. And that they did it together.

With her quick, non-police mind, Alexandra had put her finger on an essential point. But could Lombard and Grimm have joined forces to commit an act that was likely to incite revenge? It seemed completely improbable to him. And if they had, where did Hirtmann fit in?

Suddenly something else permeated his thoughts: Margot – was she in some sort of danger? The tightness in his stomach would not go away. He grabbed his jacket and left the room. Down at reception he asked if they had a computer and webcam available somewhere. The receptionist told him they did, and took him to a little meeting room. Servaz thanked her and opened his mobile phone.

'Dad?' said his daughter.

'Hook up to your webcam,' he said.

'Right now?'

'Yes, right now.'

He sat down and got online. After five minutes his daughter had still not contacted him and Servaz was beginning to get impatient, when the notice 'Margot is connected' appeared onscreen. Servaz immediately turned on the video and a splinter of blue light flashed above the camera.

Margot was in her bedroom, a steaming cup in her hand, and she gave him a curious, cautious look. Behind her on the wall was a huge poster for a film called *The Mummy*, a character with a gun against a background of a desert, sunset and pyramids.

'What's up?' she asked.

'I should be asking you.'

'Pardon?'

'You dropped your piano and karate lessons – why?'

He realised, a bit late, that his voice was far too curt and his approach too abrupt. It was because he'd been made to wait, obviously, he knew that. He hated waiting. But he should have handled it differently, should have started with a topic that was less urgent, should have made her smile with their usual jokes. A few elementary principles of manipulation – even with his own daughter.

'Oh! So Mum called you . . .'

'Yes.'

'And what else did she tell you?'

'That's all . . . Well?'

'Well, it's very simple: I'll only ever be a mediocre pianist, so what's the point going on with it? It's just not my thing, that's all.'

'And the karate?'

'I'm sick of it.'

'Sick of it?'

'Yes.'

'Mm-hmm. Just like that, all of a sudden?'

'No, not all of a sudden: I took my time to think it over.'

'And what do you intend to do instead?'

'I have no idea. Do I have to do something? It seems to me I've reached an age where I can decide for myself, right?'

'You could say that,' he acknowledged, forcing himself to smile.

But at the other end, his daughter was not smiling. She was staring at the camera and at him, darkly. The lamp next to her lit her face from one side and the bruise on her cheek was even more visible. The piercing in her eyebrow glittered like a real ruby.

'What is it with all these questions? What are you and Mum trying to do to me?' asked Margot, her voice shriller and shriller. 'Why do I feel like I'm in the middle of some sort of fucking police interview?'

'Margot, I only asked . . . and you're not obliged to—'

'Oh, no? You know what, Dad? If this is the way you go about interrogating your suspects, you must not get too many results.'

She pounded her fist on the side of the desk and the noise resounded in the loudspeaker and made him jump.

'Shit, bloody fucking hell!'

He abruptly felt cold inside. Alexandra was right: this was not their daughter's usual behaviour. What remained to be seen was whether this change was temporary, owing to some circumstances he knew nothing about, or whether it was due to someone else's influence.

'I'm sorry, sweetheart,' he said. 'I'm a bit on edge because of this investigation. Can you forgive me?'

'Mm-hmm.'

'I'll see you in two weeks' time, all right?'

'Will you call me again before then?'

He smiled to himself. That was more like the Margot he knew.

'Of course I will. Goodnight, sweetheart.'

'Goodnight, Dad.'

He went back up to his room, tossed his jacket on the bed and took a miniature of Scotch from the minibar. Then he went out onto the balcony. It was almost dark; the sky was clear, somewhat lighter to the west than the east, above the black mass of mountains. A few stars were beginning to come out, as bright as if they'd been scrubbed. Servaz told himself that it was going to get very cold. The Christmas lights formed a flow of glistening lava in the streets, but all this hustle and bustle seemed trivial beneath the eternal gaze of the Pyrenees. Even the most atrocious crimes became insignificant, meaningless, in the presence of the mountains. Scarcely more than an insect crushed on a windscreen.

Servaz leaned against the railing, and opened his phone again.

'Espérandieu,' replied his assistant.

'I need to ask you for a favour.'

'What's going on? Is there anything new?'

'No. It has nothing to do with the investigation.'

'Oh, I see.'

Servaz struggled with his words.

'I'd like you to tail Margot after school once or twice a week. For, let's say, two or three weeks. I can't do it myself: she'd see me.'

'What?'

'You heard me.'

At the other end of the line, the silence was endless. Servaz could hear noise in the background. His assistant was obviously in a bar.

Espérandieu sighed.

'Martin, I can't do that.'

'Why not?'

'It's against all the—'

'I'm asking you a favour, as a friend,' interrupted Servaz. 'Just once or twice a week for three weeks. Follow her either on foot or by car. Nothing more. You're the only person I can ask.'

Another sigh.

'Why?' said Espérandieu.

'I think she may be hanging out with the wrong sort of people.'

'And that's all?'

'And that her boyfriend is hitting her.'

'Shit!'

'Exactly,' said Servaz. 'Now just imagine if it were Méghan, and you had to ask me. Besides, you may have to someday.'

'All right, all right, I'll do it. But once or twice a week, no more, agreed? And three weeks from now I quit, even if I haven't found anything.'

'You have my word,' said Servaz, relieved.

'What will you do if your suspicions are confirmed?'

'We haven't got there yet. For the time being, I just want to find out what's going on.'

'OK, but supposing what you think is true, and she's shacked up with some violent, twisted little jerk, then what will you do?'

'Am I in the habit of acting impulsively?' said Servaz.

'On occasion.'

'I just want to find out what's going on.'

He thanked his assistant and hung up. He was still thinking about his daughter. About her outfits, her tattoos, her piercings . . . Then he let his thoughts take him to the Institute. He pictured the buildings up there drifting slowly off to sleep in the snow. What did those monsters dream about at night in their cells? What slippery creatures, what fantasies fed their sleep? He wondered if any of them stayed awake, their eyes looking into a macabre inner world, summoning the memory of their victims.

High above the mountains an aeroplane flew by, on its way from Spain to France. A tiny silver shaving, a shooting star, a metallic comet, its landing lights twinkling in the night sky, and Servaz once again sensed how isolated this valley was, far away from everything.

He went back to his room and switched on the light.

Then he took a book out of his suitcase and sat at the head of the bed. Horace, the *Odes*.

When he awoke the following morning, Servaz saw that it had snowed: the streets and rooftops were white, the cold air striking his chest. He hurried back from the balcony into his room, took a shower and got dressed. Then he went down for breakfast.

Espérandieu was already sitting out on the spacious art deco veranda. He had finished breakfast and was reading. Servaz observed him from a distance: his assistant was completely absorbed in his book. Servaz sat down and peered at the book's cover with curiosity: *A Wild Sheep Chase,* by a certain Haruki Murakami. Japanese. An author he had never heard of. Servaz sometimes felt, in Espérandieu's company, as if they did not speak the same language, as if they came from two countries that were far apart, each with its own customs and traditions. His assistant's interests were as numerous as they were different from his own: graphic novels, Japanese culture, science, contemporary music, photography . . .

Espérandieu looked up, his expression like a child at the breakfast table, and he checked his watch.

'The autopsy is at eight o'clock,' he said, closing the book. 'I'd better get going.'

Servaz nodded, without adding a thing. His assistant knew his job. Servaz took a gulp of coffee and could tell at once that his throat was irritated.

Ten minutes later, he too was walking through the snowy streets. He was to meet Ziegler and Propp at Cathy d'Humières's office before they went on to visit the Institute. The prosecutor wanted to introduce them to the examining magistrate she was putting on the case. As he walked, he followed his train of thought from the previous day. When had Lombard and Grimm been singled out as victims? What was the connection between them? According to Chaperon and the widow, Lombard and Grimm were not acquainted. Lombard might have stopped in at the pharmacy once or twice, but nothing could be certain: there were five other chemists in Saint-Martin – and Éric Lombard would surely send someone in his place on that type of errand.

That was as far as his thoughts had got when he suddenly tensed. There was something, a vague feeling, that had thrown him onto high alert. The unpleasant sensation that he was being followed . . . He turned round abruptly and peered down the street behind him. Nothing. Only a couple who were stamping their feet in the snow, laughing, and an old woman who went round the corner, a shopping bag on her arm.

Shit, this valley is making me paranoid.

Five minutes later he went through the gate to the law courts. Lawyers were talking on the steps, smoking one cigarette after another; defendants' relations were biting their fingernails, waiting for sessions to resume. Servaz walked across the hall and headed towards the grand staircase on the left. Just as he reached the first landing, a small man emerged from behind a marble column and rushed down the stairs.

'Commandant!'

Servaz stopped. He studied the person who had come up to him.

'Ah,' said the man, 'so you are the cop who's here from Toulouse.'

'Do we know one another?'

'I saw you yesterday morning at the crime scene, together with Catherine,' answered the man, holding out his hand. 'She told me your name. She seems to think you're the right man for the job.'

Catherine . . . Servaz shook his outstretched hand.

'And you are—?'

'Gabriel Saint-Cyr, honorary examining magistrate, retired. I've been conducting investigations for these law courts for nearly thirty-five years.' He took in the spacious hall with an all-embracing gesture. 'I know their every cupboard. Just as I know every inhabitant of this town, or near as dammit.'

Servaz looked at him closely. He was short, but he had a wrestler's build, a good-natured smile and an accent that indicated he had been born or grown up not far away. Servaz also caught the sharp spark in his eyes, and he understood that behind the jovial exterior the former magistrate hid a penetrating mind – just the opposite of so many people who wore a mask of cynicism and irony to hide a total absence of ideas.

'And are you offering your services?' said Servaz cheerfully.

The magistrate burst out laughing. A clear, resounding laugh.

'Well, goodness, if you're a judge for a day, you're a judge for ever. I won't hide the fact that I'm sorry I retired, when I see what's going on these days. We've never had anything like this before. A crime of passion from time to time, some neighbours quarrelling and ending up shooting one another: the usual displays of human stupidity. But if you feel like talking about the case over a drink, I'm your man.'

'Have you already forgotten professional secrecy, m'lud?' joked Servaz.

Saint-Cyr winked at him.

'Oh, you wouldn't have to tell me everything. But you won't find anyone who knows the secrets of these valleys better than I do, Commandant. Think about it.'

Servaz was already thinking about it. The man's proposal might well be a good one: a contact among the local inhabitants. Someone who had spent almost his entire life in Saint-Martin, and whose profession had let him in on a number of secrets.

'You must be missing work.'

'I would be lying if I claimed otherwise,' confessed Saint-Cyr. 'I retired two years ago, for my health. And ever since, I've been feeling like the living dead. Do you think it was Hirtmann who did it?'

Servaz was startled.

'What do you mean?'

'Oh, come on! You know perfectly well, the DNA they found in the cable car.'

'Who told you about that?'

The little judge gave out another resounding laugh as they went down the steps.

'I already told you: I know everything that goes on in this town. See you soon, Commandant! And happy hunting!'

Servaz watched him disappear through the big double doors into a whirlwind of snow.

'Martin, I'd like to introduce examining magistrate Martial Confiant. I've entrusted him with the preliminary investigation I started yesterday.'

Servaz shook the young magistrate's hand. In his early thirties, tall and thin, very dark skin, elegant rectangular glasses with a thin frame. His handshake was solid, his smile warm.

'Contrary to appearances,' said Cathy d'Humières, 'Martial is a local boy. He was born and grew up twenty kilometres from here.'

'Before you got here, Madame d'Humières was telling me how much she admires you, Commandant.'

His voice had the smooth warmth of a tropical island, with just a touch of the local accent. Servaz smiled.

'We're going to the Institute this morning,' he said. 'Would you like to join us?'

He was having trouble talking; his throat was sore.

'Have you notified Dr Xavier?'

'No. Captain Ziegler and I have decided to make this a little surprise visit.'

Confiant nodded.

'All right, I'll come along,' he said. 'But just this once: I don't want to impose. I make it a principle to let the police get on with their work. Every man to his trade,' he added.

Servaz agreed in silence. This would be excellent news, if his declaration of principle turned out to be practice as well.

'Where is Captain Ziegler?' asked d'Humières.

He checked his watch.

'She won't be long. She might be having trouble getting here because of the snow.'

Cathy d'Humières turned towards the window, as if in a hurry.

'Right, I have a press conference to give. Anyway, I wouldn't have gone with you. Such a sinister place in this sort of weather – brrr, not for me!'

13

'A lack of oxygen to the brain,' said Delmas, washing his hands and forearms with antibacterial soap, then rinsing them under the tap.

The hospital in Saint-Martin was a large red-brick building which stood out against the snow-covered lawns. As is often the case, the entry to the morgue was located well away from the main entrance, at the bottom of a concrete ramp. Staff members called this place 'Hell'. When he had arrived thirty minutes earlier, listening to the Gutter Twins singing 'Idle Hands' on his iPod, Espérandieu had seen a coffin waiting on trestles against the back wall. In the hall he came upon Dr Delmas, the pathologist from Toulouse, and Dr Cavalier, a surgeon at the Saint-Martin hospital, as they were putting on short-sleeved shirts and plastic-coated protective aprons. Delmas was describing to Cavalier how they had found the body. Espérandieu had begun to get changed; then he popped a menthol pastille in his mouth and took out a jar of camphor-based cream.

'You should avoid using that,' Delmas immediately told him. 'It's very corrosive.'

'I'm sorry, Doctor, but I have sensitive nostrils,' replied Vincent, before fitting a surgical mask over his nose and mouth.

Since joining the squad, Espérandieu had been called on several times to attend autopsies, and he knew there was always a moment, when the coroner opened the stomach and took samples from the viscera – liver, spleen, pancreas, intestines – when a stench would spread through the room that was unbearable for anyone with a normal sense of smell.

Grimm's remains were waiting for them on a slightly tilted autopsy table, equipped with a plughole and a drain. A fairly rudimentary set-up compared with the large elevating tables Espérandieu had seen at the University Hospital in Toulouse. The body, moreover, had been propped up with the help of several metal crossbars to keep it from bathing in its own fluids.

'For a start, there are the usual signs of mechanical asphyxia . . .' Delmas said straight away, manoeuvring the mobile arm of the lamp above the body.

He pointed to the chemist's blue lips, then to the tips of his ears, which had also turned blue: '. . . the bluish colour of the mucous membranes and the integuments . . .'

He showed them the inside of the victim's stapled eyelids: 'Conjunctival hyperaemia . . .'

He pointed to the chemist's swollen, purple face: 'Congestion gives us this purplish colour. Unfortunately, the signs are difficult to detect given the state of the face,' he said to Cavalier, who was finding it hard to look at the bloody pulp with its two eyes staring out of their sockets. 'We also have petechiae on the surface of the lungs and heart. These are classic symptoms. They're simply proof we're dealing with a non-specific asphyxial syndrome: the victim clearly did die of mechanical asphyxia, but it took a very long time. However, these symptoms don't provide any additional information regarding the cause of death.'

Delmas removed his glasses to give them a wipe, then put them back on. He was not wearing a surgical mask. He smelled of eau de cologne and antibacterial soap.

'Whoever did this clearly had some medical or at least anatomical knowledge,' he declared. 'He opted for a procedure that would be as long and painful as possible.'

Delmas pointed with his chubby finger to the groove left by the strap in the chemist's neck.

'From a physiopathological point of view, there are three mechanisms that can cause death by hanging. The first is vascular, which means that the blood is prevented from reaching the brain by a simultaneous occlusion of the two carotid arteries. That's what happens when the slipknot is found at the back, on the nape of the neck. In this case, cerebral hypoxia is direct, and loss of consciousness is almost instantaneous, followed by rapid death. Anyone who wants to commit suicide by hanging cannot be told too strongly about the importance of placing the knot at the back of the neck,' he added.

Espérandieu had stopped taking notes. He had a hard time, as a rule, with pathologists' sense of humour. As for Cavalier, he was almost feasting on his colleague's words.

'Then there is the neurological mechanism: if our culprit had pushed the chemist into the void instead of lowering him progressively by playing with the straps attached to his wrists, the bulbar and medullary lesions caused by the shock, that is, the lesions to the medulla oblongata and the spinal cord,' he added, for Espérandieu's sake, gently lifting what had once been Grimm's skull, 'would have caused almost instantaneous death. But that is not what he did . . .'

Behind his glasses, his pale blue eyes were seeking out Espérandieu's.

'Oh, no, young man! *That is not what he did* . . . Our culprit is a clever sod: he was careful to place the slipknot to one side. That way he maintained blood flow to the brain along at least one of the two arteries: the one opposite the knot. As for the straps attached to his wrists, they prevented any traumatic shock to the spinal cord. He knew damned well what he was up to, believe me. The victim will have died a very long and painful death.'

His chubby, impeccably clean finger wandered over the groove again.

'In any case, we're dealing with a hanging. Look: the groove is high up, just under the jaw, and it curves up to the point where the body was suspended. Also, it is incomplete, which means there couldn't have been prior strangulation with the rope, which normally leaves a low, regular groove round the entire neck.'

He gave Espérandieu a wink.

'You know: the husband strangles his wife with a rope, then tries to make us believe she hanged herself.'

'You read too many crime novels, Doctor,' said Espérandieu.

Delmas stifled a little laugh, then once again became as serious as a pope when the time for the blessing has come. He brought the lamp down level with the shredded nose, the swollen face and the stapled eyelids.

'This is really one of the most disgusting things I've ever been called on to witness,' he said. 'There's a rage and fury here, almost too much to bear.'

The psychologist had joined them. He sat in the back together with the examining magistrate. Ziegler was driving the 4x4 with the ease and confidence of a rally driver. Servaz admired the way she drove. Just as he had admired her skill with the helicopter. In the back, Confiant had asked Propp to fill him in on Hirtmann. The judge had been stunned by what he heard, and now he was as grimly silent as the rest of them. The morbid atmosphere in the valley only served to increase their unease.

The road wound its way beneath the dark sky through tall, snow-topped fir trees. The snow plough had been through there, leaving high drifts on either side of the road. They drove past the last farm imprisoned by cold; the fences round the fields had almost disappeared beneath the blanket white, and a scroll of smoke rose from the chimney. Then came the implacable reign of silence and winter.

Further along they caught up with the snow plough and overtook it; its spinning headlight cast a bright orange beam onto the white fir trees, and after that the road became tricky.

They drove through a petrified landscape of forests and frozen peat bogs encircled by the meandering river. Above them, grey and formidable, were the wooded slopes of the mountain. Then the valley became even narrower. The forest overlooked the road, which overlooked the river, while with each bend they could see the thick roots of beech trees that had been laid bare by the work to build the embankment. They went round another bend and saw several buildings with rows of windows in the upper storeys and large picture windows on the ground floor. A track led over a rusty bridge across the torrent, then through a white meadow to the buildings. Servaz read the crumbling sign as they went past: 'LES ISARDS HOLIDAY CAMP.' The buildings looked dilapidated and deserted.

He wondered who would want to stick a holiday camp in such a gloomy place. He felt a blast of cold air down his spine just thinking about the surroundings of the Institute. But given how abandoned it looked, in all likelihood the camp had closed long before the Wargnier Institute had ever opened its doors.

The valley was devastatingly beautiful; Servaz was transfixed.

The atmosphere of a fairy tale.

Yes, that's what it was, a modern, grown-up version of the sinister fairy tales he remembered from childhood. For at the end of this valley and this white forest, thought Servaz with a shudder, ogres really were waiting for them.

'Good morning, may I sit down?'

She looked up and saw the psychiatric nurse who had left so rudely the day before – what was his name again? Alex – standing by her table. The cafeteria was crowded now. It was Monday morning and all the staff were there. The place was a hubbub of conversation.

'Of course,' she said, clenching her teeth.

She was all alone at her table. Obviously no one had felt like inviting her to join them. From time to time she caught people looking her way. Once again she wondered what Dr Xavier had said about her.

'Uh, I'd like to say sorry about yesterday,' said Alex, sitting down. 'I was probably a little abrupt. I don't know why. You had the right to ask those questions, after all. Please accept my apologies.'

She eyed him. He seemed genuinely contrite. She nodded uncomfortably. She didn't want to discuss it any more. Or even hear him apologise.

'No problem. I'd already forgotten about it.'

'So much the better. You must think I'm odd.'

'Not at all. My questions were actually fairly . . . impertinent.'

'That's true,' he said with a laugh. 'You were never at a loss for words.'

He bit deep into his croissant.

'What happened down in the valley yesterday?' she asked, to change the subject. 'I overheard some conversation; apparently something terrible happened.'

'A man was found dead, a chemist from Saint-Martin.'

'How did he die?'

'They found him hanging underneath a bridge.'

'Oh! I see . . .'

'Mmm,' he went, his mouth full.

'What a horrible way for someone to kill himself!'

He looked up and swallowed the mouthful he was chewing on.

'It wasn't suicide.'

'It wasn't?'

He looked deep into her eyes.

'Murder.'

She wondered if he were joking. She studied his expression with a smile. Apparently not. Her smile vanished. She felt a chill between her shoulder blades.

'That's horrible! Are they sure?'

'Yes,' he said, leaning towards her in order to be heard without raising his voice, despite all the noise around them. 'And that's not everything . . .'

He leaned even closer. She thought his face was a bit too near. She withdrew slightly, not wanting to cause rumours when she had only just arrived.

'According to what I heard, he was naked, except for a cape and a pair of boots. And he'd been beaten, tortured. Rico found him. He's a writer, he does graphic novels, and every morning he goes running.'

Diane digested the information in silence. A murder in the valley, an insane crime, only a few kilometres from the Institute . . .

'I know what you're thinking,' he said.

'Oh, really?'

'You're thinking it sounds mad, and this place is full of crazy murderers.'

'Yes.'

'It's impossible to get out of here.'

'Really?'

'Yes.'

'No one has ever escaped?'

'No.' He swallowed another mouthful. 'And anyway, there's no one missing.'

She took a sip of her cappuccino and wiped the chocolate from her lips with a paper napkin.

'Well, that makes me feel better already,' she said jokingly.

This time, Alex gave a hearty laugh.

'Yes, I know it must be depressing enough under normal circumstances to be here when you're new. So to have a horrible event like this on top of everything else . . . It's not the sort of thing that will help you relax, is it? I'm sorry to have been the bearer of bad news.'

'Just as long as you're not the one who killed him.'

He laughed even louder, so loud that a few people turned to look.

'Is that Swiss humour? I love it!'

She smiled. Between the way he had stalked out the day before and his good mood today, she still did not know what to make of him. But on the whole he seemed likable enough. With a nod of her head, she pointed to the people around them.

'I was rather hoping that Dr Xavier would introduce me to all the staff. So far he's done no such thing. It won't be easy to fit in if no one extends a hand.'

He enfolded her with a friendly look and slowly nodded his head.

'I understand. Listen, here's what I suggest: I can't do it this morning, I have a staff meeting with my therapeutic team. But a bit later on I'll take you round and introduce you to the rest of the team.'

'That would be very kind of you.'

'It's only right. I don't even understand why Xavier or Lisa haven't done it.'

Good question, indeed, she thought.

The pathologist and Dr Cavalier were cutting off one of the boots with the help of post-mortem rib shears and a sharp hook retractor.

'By the look of it, these boots did not belong to the victim,' announced Delmas. 'At least three sizes too small. They were rammed on by force. I don't know how long the poor man wore them, but it must have been quite painful. Although not as bad as what was coming.'

Espérandieu looked at him, his notebook in his hand.

'Why would they make him wear boots that were too small?' he asked.

'That's for you to find out. Perhaps they simply wanted to make him wear boots and didn't have any others available.'

'But then why strip him, remove his shoes and then put on the boots?'

The pathologist shrugged and turned his back in order to place the cut-up boot on a work surface. He then picked up a magnifying glass and a pair of pliers and painstakingly removed the tiny gravel and blades of grass which were sticking to the mud and rubber. He dropped the samples into a series of little cylindrical boxes. After that, he picked up the boots and hesitated conspicuously between a black bin liner and a large brown paper bag. In the end, he opted for the paper bag. Espérandieu shot him a questioning look.

'Why have I chosen this one? Because the mud on the boots may look dry, but it probably isn't completely. Damp exhibits must never be kept in plastic bags: the humidity could cause mould to form that would destroy biological evidence.'

Delmas walked round the autopsy table. He went closer to the severed finger with the magnifying glass in his hand.

'It's been cut with a sharp, rusty tool: shears or secateurs. And it was cut while the victim was still alive. Hand me those pliers, and a bag,' he said to Espérandieu.

Espérandieu complied. Delmas labelled the bag, threw the last scraps into one of the bins lined up against the wall, then removed his gloves with a loud snap.

'We've finished. There's no doubt it was mechanical asphyxia which killed Grimm – hanging, in other words. I will forward these samples to the gendarmerie's lab in Rosny-sous-Bois, as Captain Ziegler requested.'

'What are the odds, in your opinion, that two heavies could have been behind the whole gruesome thing?'

The pathologist stared at Espérandieu.

'I don't like guesswork,' he said. 'I work with facts. Speculation is your department. What sort of heavies?'

'Night watchmen. Two blokes who've already been convicted of assault and petty trafficking. Thugs with no imagination, no brains and a tank full to overflowing of male hormones.'

'If they're like that, I would say about as much chance as seeing all the macho idiots in this country suddenly twig that cars are more dangerous than firearms. But I'll say it again, it's up to you to draw your own conclusions.'

The heavy snow made it seem like they were driving into an enormous cream cake. As if with the wave of a magic wand, the winter had transformed the thick vegetation, turning the end of the valley into a filigree of tightly woven spiders' webs of ice. The stream ran between two folds of snow.

Dug into the very rock, protected by a solid safety barrier, the road embraced the contours of the mountain and was so narrow that Servaz wondered what they would do if they met an oncoming truck.

Ziegler suddenly slowed down and pulled over to the other side of the road, into a layby with a parapet over the frozen slopes.

'What's going on?' asked Confiant.

Without replying she opened her door and got out. She went over to the edge and the other three joined her.

'Look,' she said.

They turned their gaze in the direction she was pointing and saw the buildings in the distance.

'My goodness, it's creepy,' exclaimed Propp. 'It looks like a medieval prison.'

The part of the valley where they were standing was still immersed in the blue shadow of the mountain, while higher up the buildings were drenched in yellow morning light flowing from the peaks like a glacier. It was an incredibly wild and solitary place, but also so beautiful that Servaz was left speechless. That same titanic architecture he had found at the power plant: he wondered what the buildings had been used for before the Wargnier Institute took them over. Because it was obvious that they dated from the same glorious era as the plant and its underground facility, an era when walls and structures were built to last for centuries. When less thought was given to immediate gain than to a job well done; when a company was judged less for its financial prowess than for the grandeur of its accomplishments.

'I am finding it harder and harder to believe that someone could escape from that place and want to go back,' added the psychologist.

Servaz turned to him. He had just had the same thought. Then he looked for Confiant and saw him a few metres away, talking into his mobile. Servaz wondered whom he needed to call at such a time.

The young magistrate closed his mobile and walked over.

'Let's go,' he said.

A kilometre further along, after yet another tunnel, they left the valley road for one that was even narrower, and which crossed the torrent before it climbed up through the first trees. Beneath the heavy layer of snow it was hard to tell the new road from the drifts on the verge, but several vehicles had left their tracks. Servaz counted up to ten, then stopped counting. He wondered if the road led anywhere else besides the Institute, and he had his answer two kilometres further along, when they came out in front of the buildings: the road went no further.

They slammed their doors and silence fell once again. As if they were in the grip of a respectful fear, they remained. It was very cold and Servaz burrowed further into his jacket.

Built on the flattest part of the slope, the Institute dominated the upper sector of the valley. The narrow windows looked onto the mountain across the way, with its immense wooded slopes, crowned with dizzying cliffs of rock and snow.

Then he saw, several hundred metres higher up the mountain, the gendarmes in their winter cloaks, talking into walkie-talkies while staring back down at them through their binoculars.

A little man in a white lab coat burst out of the Institute and came to meet them. Servaz glanced at his companions in surprise. Confiant made a gesture of apology.

'I took it upon myself to notify Dr Xavier,' said the examining magistrate. 'He's a friend.'

14

Dr Xavier seemed delighted to have visitors. He walked across the little snow-covered path, his arms spread wide.

'You've come at an awkward time. We're in the middle of a staff meeting. Every Monday I convene one meeting after the other with the different therapeutic teams from the care units: all the doctors, nurses, auxiliaries and social workers.'

But his broad smile seemed to imply that he was not sorry he'd had to put an abrupt end to one of the boring meetings. He shook the magistrate's hand with particular warmth.

'It's taken this terrible incident for you to come at last to see me at work.'

Dr Xavier was a little man, still young, impeccably turned out. Servaz noticed the trendy necktie under his lab coat. He could not stop smiling, gazing indulgently at the two detectives, his expression both kindly and sparkling with humour. Servaz was immediately on the alert: he was instinctively wary of elegant people who smiled too much.

He looked up at the high walls. The Institute consisted of two huge four-storey buildings that formed a T shape – a T where the horizontal bar was three times as long as the vertical one. He studied the rows of narrow windows in the grey stone walls – so thick they could probably withstand the attack of a rocket launcher. One thing was certain: it was unlikely the residents could escape by tunnelling through the walls.

'We've come in order to determine the odds that one of your residents might have got out,' said Confiant to the psychiatrist.

'That's completely impossible,' replied Xavier without a shadow of hesitation. 'And besides, there is no one missing.'

'We know,' said Servaz.

'I don't understand,' said the psychiatrist, disconcerted. 'If that's the case, then why are you here?'

'We suspect that one of your residents was able to get out, kill Éric Lombard's horse, then get back into his cell,' said Ziegler.

The psychiatrist's eyes narrowed.

'You can't be serious?'

'That's just what I thought,' Confiant hastened to say, giving the two investigators a harsh look. 'It's totally absurd. But they want to make sure, all the same.'

Servaz felt as if he had been given an electric shock: not only had the young judge alerted Xavier without telling them, but now he had just criticised their work in front of him too.

'Were you thinking of anyone in particular?' asked Xavier.

'Julian Hirtmann,' replied Servaz tonelessly.

The psychiatrist looked at him, but this time he said nothing. He merely shrugged and turned on his heels.

'Follow me.'

The entrance was a triple-glass door at the top of three steps.

'Every visitor who comes here, and all staff members, go through this entrance,' explained Xavier as he went up the steps. 'There are four emergency exits on the ground floor and one in the basement: two on the side at either end of the central corridor, one by the kitchen, another in the annexe after the gym room – but it is impossible to open them from the outside, and from the inside you need a special key. They do unlock automatically, however, in the case of a major fire. And only then.'

'Who has these keys?' asked Servaz.

'Twenty people or so,' said Xavier, walking through the glass doors. 'The staff members in charge of the care units, the three supervisors on the ground floor, the head nurse, the head chef, myself . . . But if one of those doors were unbolted, it would immediately set off an alarm in the control room.'

'We need the list of everyone who has keys,' said Ziegler.

'Is there always someone on duty in the control room?' asked Servaz.

'Yes. You'll see, it's just here.'

They had entered a large foyer. To the right they could see what looked like a waiting room, with green pot plants and a row of plastic seats. Directly opposite was a semicircular glassed-in cubicle of the kind found in banks or reception areas. There was no one there. To the left was a vast space whose glossy white walls were decorated with drawings and paintings. Tortured faces baring teeth as sharp as knives; twisted bodies; garish colours. Servaz knew this must be the residents' artwork.

Then his gaze went from the drawings to a steel door with a small round window. The control room. Xavier crossed the foyer to the room. He took one of the keys hanging on a chain from his belt, inserted it and pushed open the armoured door. There were two guards inside, watching dozens of screens. They wore orange boiler suits over white T-shirts. Handcuffs and rings full of keys jangled from their belts whenever they moved. Servaz also noticed canisters of tear gas hanging on the wall. But no firearms.

The screens displayed long, deserted corridors, stairways, common rooms and a cafeteria. The two men looked at them indifferently; their expressions were as blank as the watchmen's had been.

'The Institute is equipped with forty-eight cameras,' explained Xavier. 'Forty-two on the inside, six on the outside, and all of them, obviously, set in strategic places.'

He pointed to the two men.

'There is always at least one person on duty at night. Two during the day.'

'One person to keep an eye on over forty screens,' said Servaz emphatically.

'We don't only have cameras,' replied Xavier. 'The establishment is divided into several sectors, each of which has a greater or lesser level of security, depending on how dangerous the occupants are. Unauthorised passage from one sector to another will automatically set off an alarm.'

He pointed to a row of little red lamps above the screens.

'Appropriate biometric measures also correspond to each level of security. In order to have access to Unit A, where the most dangerous residents are, one must go through a door which has a twenty-four-hour security guard.'

'Do all staff members have access to Unit A?' asked Ziegler.

'Of course not. Only the therapeutic team in charge of Unit A has access, along with the head nurse, the two guards from the fourth floor, our physician, the chaplain and myself. And more recently, a psychologist from Switzerland.'

'We will need that list as well,' said Ziegler. 'With each person's job description and relevant skills.'

'Is it all computerised?' asked Servaz.

'Yes.'

'Who installed the system?'

'A private security firm.'

'And who takes care of the maintenance?'

'The same firm.'

'Do you have plans somewhere?'

The psychiatrist seemed disconcerted.

'What sort of plans?'

'Showing the building's installations, cables, biometric devices . . .'

'I suppose the security company must have them,' ventured Xavier.

'We'll need their address, business name and phone number. Do they send someone to do regular checks on the equipment?'

'They check everything remotely. If something breaks down or there's a glitch somewhere, their computers inform them immediately.'

'Don't you think that's dangerous? That the security locks can be controlled from outside by someone you don't know?'

Xavier frowned.

'They have no way of unbolting the doors. Or of disabling the security systems. All they can do is observe what is going on and check whether everything is working properly.'

'What about the guards?' asked Servaz, looking at the two men. 'Are they sent by the same company?'

'Yes,' said Xavier, leaving the control room. 'But they don't intervene in the event of a crisis with any of the patients; that would be the auxiliaries' job. As you know, the trend everywhere is towards "outsourcing", as they say in the ministries.'

He stopped in the middle of the hall to look at them.

'Like everyone else, we make do with what we have available – and we seem to have less and less of everything. In the last twenty years each successive government has discreetly done away with over fifty thousand beds in psychiatry units and cut thousands of jobs. And yet on the outside, in the name of economic imperatives and the free market, the pressure on individuals has never been greater; there are more crazy, psychotic, paranoid, schizophrenic people wandering around than ever.'

He headed towards a long corridor at the end of the hall. The endless corridor seemed to run the entire length of the building, but from time to time they had to stop at a metal gate, which, Servaz supposed, would be locked at nightfall. He also saw doors with copper plates displaying the doctors' names, including one with Xavier's own name, then another which said, 'Élisabeth Ferney, Head Nurse.'

'But I suppose we should consider ourselves lucky, all the same,' added Xavier as he ushered them through another metal door. 'To compensate for the lack of personnel, we are fortunate to have the most sophisticated security and surveillance systems possible. That is far from being the case elsewhere. In France, when someone wants to hide the fact that budgets are tight and the workforce has been slashed, they come up with the most preposterous concepts: pure semantic fraud, as someone recently pointed out, expressions such as "quality progress", or "annual performance projects", or "nursing diagnosis". Do you know what a nursing diagnosis is? It consists in making nurses think they are capable of offering a diagnosis in the doctor's place, which, obviously, allows for fewer hospital doctors. For example, one of my colleagues witnessed a case where nurses sent a patient to psychiatry after labelling him a "dangerous paranoid", on the grounds that he was very irritable and in open conflict with his employer, and he was threatening to take him to court! Fortunately for the poor man, my colleague, who was present at the time of admission, immediately reversed the diagnosis and sent him straight home.'

Dr Xavier stopped right in the middle of the corridor and gave them a surprisingly grave look.

'We are in the midst of an era of unprecedented political mendacity and institutionalised violence towards the weakest in society,' he said ominously. 'Our current governments and their minions are all pursuing a dual purpose: social control and the commodification of individuals.'

Servaz looked at the psychiatrist. His own conclusions were not that different. But he wondered, nevertheless, whether back in the days when they were all-powerful, psychiatrists had not pulled the rug from under their own feet by indulging in all sorts of experiments whose foundations were more ideological than scientific – often with destructive consequences, where human beings were used as guinea pigs.

As they went past, Servaz noticed two more orange-clad guards in their glass cubicle.

Then on the right was the cafeteria they had glimpsed on the screens.

'The staff cafeteria,' explained Xavier.

Tall picture windows looked out onto a snowy landscape, and the walls were painted with warm colours. A handful of people sat chatting and drinking coffee. They then went into a room with a high ceiling and salmon-coloured walls. Cheap, comfy armchairs were set about here and there, creating quiet, cosy nooks.

'This is the visitors' room,' said the psychiatrist, 'where families can speak in private with their relatives. Of course, this facility is only available to the least dangerous residents, which does not mean a great deal, here. There is constant camera surveillance, and the auxiliaries are never far away.'

'And the others?' asked Propp, opening his mouth for the first time.

Xavier looked closely and cautiously at the psychologist.

'Most of them never receive any visits,' he replied. 'This is neither a psychiatric hospital nor your usual model prison. This is a pilot establishment, unique in Europe. We get patients from all over. And all of them are very violent individuals: abuse, rape, torture, murder. Committed on their families or on strangers. All repeat offenders. All on a knife's edge. We have only the crème de la crème here,' added Xavier with a curious smile. 'Not many people care to remember that our patients exist. Perhaps that is why the establishment is located in such an isolated place. We are their final family.'

Servaz found this last sentence a touch melodramatic, like everything else about Dr Xavier, in fact.

'How many security levels are there?'

'Three. Depending on the dangerousness of the clientele: low, medium and high, which determines not only the intensity of the security systems and the number of guards, but also the nature of the treatment and the relationships between the staff and the residents.'

'Who determines how dangerous a newcomer is?'

'Our teams. We combine clinical interviews, questionnaires and the case files our colleagues send us with a revolutionary new method imported from my country. Actually, we have a newcomer who is being evaluated at this very moment. Follow me.'

He led them towards a stairway of wide concrete steps. Once they reached the first floor, they found themselves outside a door reinforced by fine metal mesh.

This time, in addition to the code he typed on a little keyboard, Xavier had to place his hand on a biometric sensor.

A sign above the door informed them: 'Sector C: Low-level danger – Restricted to Personnel Categories C, B and A.'

'Is this the only access to this zone?' asked Ziegler.

'No, there is a second security door at the end of the corridor that provides access from this zone to the next one – medium security – an area which, consequently, is reserved only for staff members authorised for levels B and A.'

He led them along another corridor. Then he stopped outside a door labelled 'Evaluation', and opened it.

Xavier stood back to let them go past.

A windowless room, so narrow that they had to squeeze together inside. Two people were seated in front of a computer screen, a man and a woman. The screen showed both an image from a video camera and several other windows where diagrams and lines of information were scrolling past. The camera was filming a young man sitting on a stool in another windowless room hardly bigger than a broom closet. Servaz saw that the man was wearing a virtual-reality helmet. Then his gaze was drawn further down and he gave a slight shudder: the man's trousers were pulled down onto his thighs, and a strange tube connected to electric wires had been placed round his penis.

'This new method for evaluating sexual deviancy is based on virtual reality, using a system of oculomotor observation and penile plethysmography,' explained the psychiatrist. 'That is the device you can see attached to his genitals: it allows us to measure the physiological proportion of excitement in response to various stimuli – his erection, in other words. In conjunction with the erectile response, the movements of the subject's eye muscles are measured with the help of an infrared tracking device which determines how long the images coming from the virtual-reality mask are observed, as well as the exact spot in each scene where his attention is focused.'

The psychiatrist bent down and pointed at one of the windows on the screen. Servaz saw coloured lines going up and down. Beneath each line the category of stimulus was indicated: 'male adult', 'female adult', 'male child' and so on.

'The stimuli that are sent into the mask alternate between an adult man, an adult woman, a nine-year-old girl, a little boy the same age and finally a control character that is sexless and neutral. Each short film lasts three minutes. Each time, we measure the physical response.'

He stood up straight.

'It must be said that the majority of our clientele is made up of sex abusers. We have eighty-eight beds altogether: fifty-three in Sector C, twenty-eight in B and the seven residents in Unit A.'

Servaz leaned against the wall. He was sweating, and shivers were running through him. His throat was on fire. It was the vision of that man sitting in a position both humiliating and surreal while his deviant fantasies were aroused in order to be measured: it was making him feel physically unwell.

'How many of them are murderers?' he asked in an unsteady voice.

Xavier gave him an intense stare.

'Thirty-five. The entire contingent of patients in Sectors B and A.'

Diane watched them cross the huge foyer and take the corridor to the service stairway. Three men and a woman. Xavier was talking to them, but he looked tense, on the defensive. The man and the woman who were on either side of him were bombarding him with questions. She waited until they were gone; then she went over to the glass doors. A 4x4 was parked in the snow a dozen metres from there.

The word 'gendarmerie' was painted on it.

Diane remembered the conversation she had had with Alex about the murdered chemist: apparently the police had also made the connection with the Institute.

Then something else occurred to her: the air vent in her office, the conversation she'd overheard between Lisa and Xavier. And that strange business with the horse. Even then, Lisa Ferney had mentioned the possibility the police might call. Could there be a connection between the two events? The police must be wondering the same thing. Then her thoughts returned to the air vent.

She turned away from the glass doors and hurried across the foyer.

'Do you have something for a cold?'

The psychiatrist stared again at Servaz, then opened his desk drawer.

'Of course.' He handed him a yellow tube. 'Here, take this:

paracetamol with ephedrine. It works fairly well, as a rule. You are really very pale. You don't want me to call a doctor?'

'No, thank you. I'll be all right.'

Xavier walked over to a small fridge in the corner of the room and came back with a bottle of mineral water and a glass. His office was unpretentious, with metal filing cabinets, the fridge, a little bookshelf filled with professional titles, a few pot plants on the windowsill, and a table that was empty except for telephone, computer and lamp.

'Just take one at a time. Four a day maximum. You can keep the tube.'

'Thank you.'

For a moment Servaz lost himself in contemplation of the tablet dissolving in the glass. A headache was boring into his skull behind his eyes. The cold water felt good on his throat. He was soaked in sweat; beneath his jacket his shirt was sticking to his back. He must have a fever. It was cold, too – but it was an internal cold: the thermostat by the door indicated 23 degrees. Once again he saw the picture on the computer screen – the rapist being raped in turn by machines, probes, electronic instruments – and once again he felt the bile rising in his throat.

'We're going to have to visit Unit A,' he said, after he put his glass down.

He had wanted his voice to sound firm, but the fire in his throat had reduced it to a scratchy croak. Across from him, the doctor's cheery expression suddenly soured. Servaz imagined a cloud passing in front of the sun and transforming a spring-like landscape into something far more sinister.

'Will that really be necessary?'

The psychiatrist cast a discreet yet imploring look at the judge sitting to the left of the two investigators.

'Yes,' said Confiant immediately, turning to them. 'Do we really need to—'

'I believe we do,' interrupted Servaz. 'I am going to tell you something that must stay between us,' he said, leaning towards Xavier. 'But perhaps you already know.'

He had turned to look at the young judge. For a brief moment the two men gauged each other in silence. Then Servaz looked from Confiant to Ziegler and he could clearly read the silent message she was sending him: *go easy.*

'What are you talking about?' asked Xavier.

Servaz cleared his throat. The medication would not begin to work for several minutes. His temples were squeezed in a vice.

'We found the DNA of one of your residents . . . in the place where Éric Lombard's horse was killed: at the top of the cable car. DNA belonging to Julian Hirtmann.'

Xavier opened his eyes wide.

'Dear God! That's impossible!'

'Do you understand what this means?'

The psychiatrist gave Confiant a distraught look and lowered his head. His stupor was not feigned. *He didn't know.*

'What this means,' continued Servaz implacably, 'is that there are two possibilities. Either Hirtmann himself was up there that night, or someone who could get close enough to him to obtain his saliva was up there. Which means that, whether it was Hirtmann or not, someone in your establishment is mixed up in this business, Dr Xavier.'

15

'My God, this is a nightmare,' said Xavier.

He gave them a desperate look.

'My predecessor, Dr Wargnier, fought very hard to found this place. There was no lack of opposition to the project, as you can imagine. And there still is, just waiting for a chance to re-emerge. There are people who think these criminals should be in prison. People who've never accepted their presence in the valley. If word of this gets out, the very existence of the Institute will be under threat.'

Xavier took off his extravagant red glasses. He took a small cloth from his pocket and began to wipe the lenses.

'The people who end up here have nowhere else to go. We are their last refuge: after us, there's nothing. Ordinary psychiatric hospitals and prisons won't have them. There are only five facilities for difficult patients in France, and this institute is the only one of its kind. Every year we receive dozens of requests for admission. Either for the perpetrators of horrific crimes who have been judged mentally incapable or for convicts who have personality disorders so serious they can no longer be kept in prison, or psychotics who are so dangerous they cannot be treated in a traditional unit. Where will these people go if we close our doors?'

His fingers on the lenses were moving in ever quicker circles.

'As I told you, for over thirty years now, in the name of ideology, profitability and budget priorities, psychiatric care in this country has been devastated. This establishment costs the taxpayers a great deal. Unlike ordinary units for difficult patients, this one is part of an experiment on a European level, financed in part by the EU. But only in part. And in Brussels, too, there are quite a few people who take a dim view of this experiment.'

'We have no intention of letting this information get out,' said Servaz.

The psychiatrist looked at him doubtfully.

'It will get out, sooner or later. How will you conduct your investigation without word getting out?'

Servaz knew he was right.

'There is only one solution,' said Confiant. 'We must get to the bottom of the matter as quickly as possible if we want to make sure the media don't get hold of it and start spreading crazy rumours. If we manage to find out who was involved in this before the media hear about the DNA, at least we will have proven that no one could have got out of here.'

The psychiatrist agreed with a nod of his head.

'I'll conduct my own little investigation,' he said. 'And I will do everything I possibly can to help you.'

'In the meantime, may we see Unit A?' said Servaz.

Xavier stood up.

'I'll take you there.'

She was sitting at her desk. Motionless. Holding her breath.

She heard every sound, every word as clearly as if they were speaking in her own office. The cop's voice, for example: he sounded both exhausted and under enormous stress. Far too much pressure. He was dealing with it, but for how long? Every word he said had been branded on Diane's brain. She didn't follow the business about a dead horse, but she had clearly understood that they'd found Hirtmann's DNA at the scene of a crime. And that the police suspected someone in the Institute was mixed up in it.

A dead horse . . . A murdered chemist . . . The Institute under suspicion . . .

She was afraid, but now something else was taking shape: irrepressible curiosity. The memory of the shadow passing by her door at night was there again.

When she was a student, Diane had overheard a man intimidating and threatening the girl who slept in the room next door. He had come several nights in a row, just as Diane was about to fall asleep, and every time she had heard the same threats, in a low, growling voice, threats that he would kill her, mutilate her, make her life hell; then the door slammed and the footsteps faded along the corridor. After that, all that remained in the silence were her neighbour's muffled sobs, like the sad echo of thousands of other solitudes, thousands of other sorrows locked away in the silence of cities.

She did not know who the man was – she didn't recognise his voice – nor did she really know the girl next door; she'd only ever said hello and good evening to her, or shared vague, unimportant chitchat in passing. All she knew was that her name was Ottilie and she was studying for a Master's in economics; she had been seen going out with a bearded, bespectacled student, but most of the time she was on her own. No group of friends, no phone calls to parents.

Diane shouldn't have got involved, it was none of her business, but one night she couldn't help following the man when he left the girl's room. That is how she found out that he lived in a pretty little house, and through the window she saw a woman. She could have left it at that. But she'd gone on watching him when she had the free time. One thing led to another and she found out a lot about him: he was a manager at a supermarket, he had two children aged five and seven, he bet on the races, and quietly did his shopping at Globus, a rival chain. She eventually found out that he'd got to know her neighbour at a time when the girl was paying for her studies by working at the supermarket, and he'd got her pregnant. Which was why he was intimidating her, threatening her. He wanted her to have an abortion. He also had another mistress: a checkout assistant who wore too much make-up and stood noisily chewing her gum while she looked the customers up and down. *'I'm in love with the queen of the supermarket'*, as Bruce Springsteen sang. One evening Diane wrote an anonymous letter on her computer and slipped it under her neighbour's door. All the letter said was, 'He will never leave his wife.' One month later she found out that her neighbour had had an abortion in the twelfth week, only a few days before the legal limit in Switzerland.

Now she wondered once again if this need of hers to get involved in other people's lives was due to the fact that she'd been raised in a family where silence, secrets and things left unsaid were far more common than moments of sharing. She also wondered whether her strict Calvinist father had ever been unfaithful to her mother. She knew very well that the opposite had occurred, that the discreet men who visited her mother included several who took advantage of her over-active imagination, in order to feed on her eternally disappointed hopes.

Diane squirmed on her chair. What was going on here? She felt increasingly uncomfortable as she tried to connect the few elements she had.

The worst was the business in Saint-Martin. A terrible crime; the fact that it might be connected in some way to the Institute only served to increase the unease she'd felt ever since she arrived. She was sorry she had no one to confide in, no one with whom she could share her doubts. A friend, or Pierre.

Then there was that cop; she knew nothing about him except for the inflection and the tone of his voice. And one other thing, most definitely: that he was under stress. There was tension, worry. But at the same time strength and determination. And a lively curiosity. Someone who was rational and sure of himself: the policeman had displayed a character much like her own.

'Allow me to introduce Élisabeth Ferney, our head nurse.'

Servaz saw a tall woman coming towards them, her heels clacking on the tiles in the corridor. She wore her hair loose to her shoulders, although it was not as long as Charlène Espérandieu's. She greeted them with a nod, not saying a word, not smiling, either, and her gaze lingered a bit longer than necessary on Irène Ziegler.

Servaz saw the young gendarme lower her eyes.

Élisabeth Ferney had an abrupt, authoritarian air about her. Servaz thought she must be in her forties, but he also knew that she could as easily be thirty-five or fifty, because her lab coat and strict demeanour made it impossible to determine her age. He suspected she was highly energetic, with an iron will. *And what if the second man were a woman?* he suddenly wondered. Then he saw that this notion was proof of how distraught he was: if everyone became a suspect, it meant that no one was. They had no solid leads.

'Lisa is the soul of our establishment,' said Xavier. 'She knows it better than anyone – and there's not a single therapeutic or practical aspect with which she isn't familiar. She's also acquainted with every one of our eighty-eight residents. Even the psychiatrists have to submit their work to her.'

No trace of a smile graced the head nurse's face. She motioned to Xavier, who immediately interrupted what he was saying to listen to her. She murmured something in his ear. Servaz wondered whether he had just been introduced to the person who was really in charge. Xavier replied to her in similar fashion, while the others waited in silence for the end of their little private consultation. Finally she consented, acknowledged the visitors with a brief nod and left the room.

'Let's continue,' said the psychiatrist.

As they were heading off in the opposite direction, Servaz stopped and turned right round to watch Lisa Ferney walk away, her lab coat stretched tight over her broad shoulders, her high heels clicking. At the end of the corridor, before disappearing round the corner, she turned back too and their gazes met. Servaz thought he saw her smile.

'The important thing,' said Xavier, 'is to avoid any attitude that might cause conflict.'

They were standing outside the last security door, the one that led to Unit A. No more glossy paint on the walls, only bare stone and the impression of being in a medieval fortress, were it not for the armoured steel doors, the pale neon lights and the concrete floors.

Xavier raised his head to a camera above the door. An LED light went from red to green and locks clicked in the thick armour plating. He pulled open the heavy door and ushered them into the narrow space between the two armoured doors. They waited for the first one to shut slowly on its own and lock with a click, then for the locks of the second door to pull back in turn, making just as much noise. It was like being in the engine room of a ship, in an obscurity broken only by the light filtering through the portholes. The smell of metal. Xavier looked solemnly at each of them in turn and Servaz suspected he had a little catchphrase ready, something he must serve up to every visitor who went through this door:

'*Welcome to hell,*' he declared with a smile.

A glass cubicle. Inside, a guard. A corridor to one side. Servaz moved forward and saw a white hallway, thick blue pile carpets, a row of doors with small windows on the left and lights on the right.

The guard put down the magazine he was reading and came out of the cubicle. Xavier shook his hand ceremoniously. He was a huge man, well over six foot tall.

'I'd like to introduce Mr Atlas,' said Xavier, 'as our residents in Unit A have christened him.'

Mr Atlas laughed. He shook their hands. A handshake as light as a feather, as if he were afraid he might break their bones.

'How are they this morning?'

'Calm,' said Mr Atlas. 'It will be a good day.'

'It might not,' said Xavier, eyeing the visitors.

'The main thing is not to provoke them,' explained Mr Atlas, echoing what the psychiatrist had said. 'Keep your distance. There is a limit you have to respect. Go beyond and they might feel they're being attacked and react violently.'

'I'm afraid these people are here precisely to go beyond the limit,' said Xavier. 'They're from the police.'

Mr Atlas's expression hardened. He shrugged his shoulders and went back into his cubicle.

'Follow me,' said Xavier.

They went down the corridor, the sound of their footsteps absorbed by the thick blue carpet. The psychiatrist pointed to the first door.

'Andreas came here from Germany. He killed his father and mother in their sleep with two shots from a rifle. Then because he was afraid to be alone, he cut off their heads and put them in the freezer. He took them out every night so he could watch television with them, placing the heads on decapitated dummies, which sat next to him on the sofa.'

Servaz was listening attentively. He visualised the scene with a shudder: he had just thought of the horse's head found behind the riding academy.

'One day the family doctor showed up to ask after his parents, because he was surprised they hadn't shown up at his surgery, and Andreas killed him with a hammer. Then he cut his head off, too. Wasn't it wonderful, he said, that his parents had company now, because the doctor was such a nice man, such a good conversationalist. Of course, the police began to look into the doctor's disappearance. When they came to question Andreas and his parents, who were on the list of the doctor's patients, Andreas let the men in and said, "Here they are." And indeed, there they were: the three heads, in the freezer, waiting to be taken out for the evening.'

'Charming,' said Confiant.

'The problem,' continued Xavier, 'was that at the psychiatric hospital where he was interned, Andreas tried to decapitate one of the night nurses. The poor woman didn't die, but she'll never be able to speak properly again, and all her life she will have to wear scarves and polo necks to hide the terrible scar left by Andreas's paper knife.'

Servaz met Ziegler's eyes. He saw the gendarme was thinking the same thing. Here was someone who, clearly, made a habit of cutting off heads. And his cell was not far from Hirtmann's. Servaz looked through the small window. Andreas was a giant who must have weighed nearly 24 stone, with a 42-inch waist and a shoe size of 11 or 12; his enormous head was rammed into his shoulders as if he had no neck, and his face wore a scowl.

Xavier then pointed to the second door.

'Dr Jaime Esteban has come to us from Spain. He killed three couples over two summers on the other side of the border, in the national parks of Aigüestortes and Ordesa y Monte Perdido. Before that he had been a model citizen, a bachelor but very respectful of the women who came to his surgery; in his village he was a local councillor and he always had a kind word for everyone.'

He went up to the small window, then stepped aside and motioned to the others to come near.

'We still don't know why he did it. He went after hikers. Always couples, always young. First he would crush the man's skull with a stone or a stick; then he raped and strangled the women before throwing their bodies into a ravine. Oh, and he drank their blood. Nowadays he thinks he's a vampire. In the Spanish hospital where he was held he bit two male nurses in the neck.'

Servaz went up to the window. He saw a thin man with a neatly trimmed black beard sitting on a bed; he wore a short-sleeved white boiler suit, and his hair shone with brilliantine. Above the bed a television was switched on.

'And now, for our most famous resident,' announced Xavier, like a collector presenting his finest piece.

He typed a code on the box next to the door.

'Good morning, Julian,' said Xavier as he went in.

No answer. Servaz followed him in.

He was surprised by the size of the room. It seemed much larger than the previous cells. Other than that, the walls and floor were white, like the others. At the far side of the room was a bed, and against the wall were a small table and two chairs; two doors on the left looked as if they might lead to a shower and a cupboard, and a window looked out onto the mountains.

Servaz was also surprised by how bare the room was. He wondered if this were by choice, or whether the situation had been imposed upon the Swiss inmate. According to his file, Hirtmann was a curious, intelligent, sociable man, and no doubt he had been a great reader and consumer of all sorts of culture in his former life as a free man and murderer. Here there was nothing, apart from a cheap CD player set on the table. However, unlike in the previous cells, the furniture was not fastened to the ground or sheathed in plastic. It was as if they did not consider Hirtmann to be a danger either to himself or to others.

Servaz started when he recognised the music coming from the CD player. Gustav Mahler's Fourth Symphony.

Hirtmann had his eyes down. He was reading the newspaper. Servaz leaned slightly forward. He noticed that he had lost weight compared to the photographs in the file. His skin was milkier, almost transparent, in contrast with his short, dark, wiry hair, interspersed with a few grey strands. He hadn't shaved, and black stubble shadowed his chin, but he had preserved a veneer of breeding – which he would have had even dressed like a tramp and living under a bridge in Paris – and that rather strict face with frowning brows, which must have intimidated people in court. He was wearing a boiler suit and a white T-shirt going grey from washing.

He had aged somewhat too, in comparison with the photographs.

'Allow me to introduce Commandant Servaz,' said Xavier, 'Monsieur Confiant, the judge, Captain Ziegler and Professor Propp.'

In the back-light from the window, Hirtmann looked up and for the first time Servaz could see how bright his eyes were. They did not reflect the outside world; they were burning with an internal fire. The effect lasted only a second. Then it vanished and he became once again the former prosecutor from Geneva – urbane, polite and smiling.

He pushed back his chair and unfolded his tall frame. He was even taller than in the photos. Nearly six foot three, Servaz guessed.

'Hello,' he said.

He looked straight at Servaz. For a moment the two men observed each other in silence. Then Hirtmann did something strange: he abruptly held his hand out to Servaz, who nearly jumped and recoiled. He seized the cop's hand with his own and shook it vigorously. Servaz could not help but give a shudder. The Swiss man's hand was cold and slightly damp, like a fish – perhaps it was the effect of his medication.

'Mahler,' said the policeman, to give an impression of composure.

Hirtmann looked up at him, astonished.

'Do you like Mahler?'

'Yes. The Fourth, first movement,' added Servaz.

'*Bedächtig . . . nicht eilen . . . Recht gemächlich . . .*'

'Moderately, not rushed. Leisurely moving,' translated Servaz.

Hirtmann seemed surprised but delighted.

'Adorno likened this movement to the "once upon a time" of a fairy tale.'

Servaz fell silent, listening to the strings.

'Mahler wrote it under very difficult circumstances,' continued Hirtmann. 'Did you know that?'

I most certainly do.

'Yes,' answered Servaz.

'He was on holiday. A nightmare of a holiday, terrible weather—'

'Constantly disturbed by the sound of the village brass band.'

Hirtmann smiled.

'What a symbol, no? A musical genius being disturbed by a village brass band.'

His voice was deep and poised. Pleasant. The voice of an actor, an orator. There was something feminine about his features, particularly his mouth, which was wide and thin, and his eyes. His nose, on the other hand, was fleshy, and he had a high forehead.

'As you can see,' said Xavier, walking over to the window, 'it is impossible to escape from here unless your name is Superman. There are fourteen metres between the window and the ground. And the window is reinforced and sealed.'

'Who has the combination to the door?' asked Ziegler.

'Well, I do, and Élisabeth Ferney, and the two Unit A guards.'

'Does he get a lot of visits?'

'Julian?' said Xavier, turning to face him.

'Yes?'

'Do you get a lot of visits?'

Hirtmann smiled.

'You, Doctor, and Mademoiselle Ferney, Mr Atlas, the barber, the chaplain, the therapy team, Dr Lepage . . .'

'He's our consultant physician,' explained Xavier.

'Does he ever leave this room?'

'He's left his room once in sixteen months. To have a cavity treated. We use a dentist from Saint-Martin, but we have all the necessary materials at our disposal here.'

'And those two doors?' asked Ziegler.

Xavier opened them: a closet with a few piles of underwear and a supply of white boiler suits on hangers, and a small windowless bathroom.

Servaz observed Hirtmann on the sly. Something indisputably charismatic emanated from him; he had never seen someone who looked so little like a serial killer. Hirtmann resembled the man he had been back in the days when he was free: an uncompromising prosecutor, a well-mannered man and also someone who enjoyed life to the fullest: you could tell from his mouth and chin. The only thing that was not quite right was his gaze. Dark. Staring. Irises that shone with a clever brilliance, his eyelids narrowed but not blinking. A gaze as electric as a Taser. Servaz had met other criminals with that sort of gaze. And yet he had never felt like this, that he was in the presence of a radiant, ambiguous personality. In another era, he thought, a man like Hirtmann would have been burned for sorcery. Nowadays he was studied; people tried to understand him. But Servaz was experienced enough to know that evil was in no way quantifiable, nor could it be reduced to a scientific principle or a psychological theory, or to biological considerations. So-called free-thinkers claimed that evil did not exist; they made it into a sort of superstition, an irrational belief for weak minds. But that was simply because they had never been tortured to death in the depths of a cellar; they had never watched videos on the Internet of children being abused; they had never been abducted from their family and been broken, drugged and raped by dozens of men for weeks at a time before they were made to walk the pavements of some major European city; nor had they ever been brainwashed into blowing themselves up in the middle of a crowd. *And they had never, at the age of ten, heard their mother screaming on the other side of the door . . .*

Servaz shook himself. He felt the hair on his neck standing on end when he saw that Hirtmann was watching him.

'Do you like it here?' asked Propp.

'I think so. I'm treated well.'

'But you would rather be outside?'

Hirtmann's smile, indisputably, was meant to be sarcastic.

'That's a strange question,' he replied.

'Indeed it is,' agreed Propp. 'You don't mind if we talk about it a bit?'

'I see no objection,' replied Hirtmann, looking out of the window.

'How do you spend your days?'

'How do you?' he answered with a wink as he turned round.

'You haven't answered my question.'

'I read the newspaper, I listen to music, I chat with the staff, I look at the view, I sleep, I dream . . .'

'What do you dream about?'

'What do any of us dream about?' he echoed, as if it were a philosophical question.

For a good quarter of an hour Servaz listened to Propp bombarding Hirtmann with questions. The patient answered quickly, calmly, with a smile. At the end, Propp thanked him and Hirtmann inclined his head as if to say, 'Not at all.' Then it was Confiant's turn. Obviously he had prepared his questions in advance. *The judge has done his homework*, thought Servaz, who favoured more spontaneous methods. He hardly listened to the dialogue that followed.

'Have you heard about what happened outside?'

'I read the papers.'

'And what do you think?'

'What do you mean?'

'Do you have any idea what sort of person could have done a thing like that?'

'Are you implying . . . that it could have been someone like me?'

'Is that what you think?'

'No, that's what *you* think.'

'And what do you think about it?'

'I don't know. I don't think anything. It might be someone from here . . .'

'What makes you say that?'

'There are plenty of people who could do it, correct?'

'People like you?'

'People like me.'

'And you think someone could have got out of here to commit the murder?'

'I don't know. What do you think?'

'Do you know Éric Lombard?'

'He's the owner of the horse that was killed.'

'And Grimm, the chemist?'

'Ah, I understand.'

'What do you understand?'

'You found something there that is connected to me.'

'What makes you say that?'

'What is it? A message that says, "I'm the one who killed him," signed Julian Alois Hirtmann?'

'Why would someone want you to take the rap?'

'It's obvious, isn't it?'

'Would you care to expand on that?'

'Any one of the residents in this establishment is the ideal culprit.'

'Do you think so?'

'Why don't you say the word?'

'What word?'

'The word you are thinking.'

'What word?'

'Insane.'

(Confiant was silent.)

'Deranged.'

(Confiant was silent.)

'Demented, bonkers, loopy, barmy, crackers, bananas—'

'All right, I think that's enough,' interrupted Dr Xavier. 'If you don't have any other questions, I'd like you to leave my patient alone now.'

'One moment, if you don't mind.'

They turned round. Hirtmann had not raised his voice, but his tone had changed.

'I have something to tell you, too.'

They looked at one another and stared at him questioningly. He wasn't smiling anymore. There was a solemn expression on his face.

'You have come here to examine me from every angle. You wonder if I have something to do with what's going on outside – obviously, that is absurd. You feel pure, honest, cleansed of all your sins because you are in the presence of a monster. That too is absurd.'

Servaz and Ziegler exchanged a surprised look. He saw that Xavier was puzzled. Confiant and Propp were waiting for whatever came next, unflinching.

'Do you think my crimes make your evil deeds less blameworthy? Your vices and your petty behaviour less hideous? You think there are murderers, rapists and criminals on one side, while you're on the other? This is what you have to understand: there is no barrier preventing evil from circulating. There are not two types of humanity. When you lie to your wife and your children, when you send your aged mother to a retirement home so that you can have the freedom to do as you please, when you get rich on the back of other people, when you baulk at donating even a penny of your salary to those who have nothing, when because of your selfishness or indifference you make others suffer, then you are not so different from me. Basically, you are much more like me and the other residents than you think. It's a question of degree, not of nature. We have the same nature: it's shared by all of humanity.'

He leaned over and pulled a big book out from under his pillow. A Bible.

'The chaplain gave this to me. He thinks it will save me.' He gave a short, shrill laugh. 'It's absurd! There's nothing wrong with me as an individual. The only thing that can save us is a nuclear holocaust.'

His voice was strong and persuasive now, and Servaz could easily imagine the effect it used to have in court. His severe expression commanded contrition, submission. Suddenly they were the sinners, and he was the apostle. They were completely disoriented. Even Xavier seemed surprised.

'I'd like to have a few words with the commandant in private,' said Hirtmann suddenly, his tone more subdued.

Xavier turned to Servaz, who shrugged. Looking ill at ease, the psychiatrist frowned.

'Commandant?' he said.

Servaz nodded.

'Very well,' said Xavier, heading for the door.

Propp shrugged in turn, no doubt annoyed that Hirtmann had not asked to talk to him; Confiant's expression clearly conveyed his disapproval. Yet they all trooped out behind the psychiatrist. Ziegler was the last to go out, casting an icy glance in Hirtmann's direction.

'Pretty girl,' said Hirtmann, once she had closed the door behind her.

Servaz remained silent. He looked around nervously.

'I can't offer you anything to drink, tea or coffee. I don't have anything like that here. But it's the thought that counts.'

Servaz felt like telling him to stop acting and get to the point, but refrained.

'Which is your favourite symphony?'

'I don't have any preference,' replied Servaz curtly.

'Everyone has a preference.'

'Then let's say the Fourth, the Fifth and the Sixth.'

'Which versions?'

'Bernstein, of course. After that, Inbal is excellent. And Haitink for the Fourth, Wien for the Sixth . . . Listen—'

'Mmm . . . Good choices. At the same time, it doesn't much matter, here,' added Hirtmann, pointing to his cheap CD player.

Servaz could not deny that the sound coming from the stereo was mediocre. It occurred to him that Hirtmann was the one who'd been leading the conversation from the start, even when the others were bombarding him with questions.

'I'm sorry to say this,' he said, straight out, 'but your moralising little lecture just now did not convince me, Hirtmann. I have nothing in common with you, let's make that clear.'

'You're free to think that if you like. But what you just said is wrong: we have Mahler in common, at least.'

'What did you want to talk to me about?'

'Have you spoken to Chaperon?' asked Hirtmann, changing his tone once again, staring at Servaz, focused on his every reaction.

Servaz felt a tremor run down his spine. *He knows the name of the mayor in Saint-Martin . . .*

'Yes,' he replied cautiously.

'Chaperon was friends with that . . . Grimm fellow, did you know that?'

Servaz stared at Hirtmann, flabbergasted. How did he know? Where did he get his information?

'Yes,' answered the cop. 'Yes. He told me. And you, how—'

'So ask the mayor to tell you about the suicides.'

'The what?'

'The suicides, Commandant. Ask him about the suicides!'

16

'Suicides? What's that about?'

'I have no idea. But apparently Chaperon knows.'

Ziegler gave him a puzzled look.

'It was Hirtmann who told you that?'

'Yes.'

'And you believed him?'

'I'll have to see.'

'That man is quite mad.'

'Could be.'

'And he didn't say anything else?'

'No.'

'Why did he want to speak to you?'

Servaz smiled.

'Because of Mahler, I suppose.'

'What?'

'Music . . . *Gustav Mahler*: that's what we have in common.'

For a moment Ziegler took her eyes from the road to give him a look that suggested that not all madmen were locked up at the Institute. But Servaz's thoughts were already elsewhere. The impression that he was confronting something new and terrifying was stronger than ever.

'It's very clever, what he's trying to do,' said Propp a little later, as they were heading back down to Saint-Martin.

All around, the fir trees were rushing by. Servaz looked through the window, lost in thought.

'I don't know how he does it, but he immediately sensed there was a dividing line in the group, and he's trying to split us up by arousing the sympathy of one of our members.'

Servaz turned abruptly to look deep into the psychiatrist's eyes.

'"The sympathy of one of our members,"' he echoed. 'Nicely put.

What do you mean by that, Propp? Do you think I've forgotten who he is?'

'That's not what I meant, Commandant,' said the shrink, uncomfortable.

'You're right, Doctor,' added Confiant. 'We have to remain united and come up with a coherent and credible strategy.'

His words cut Ziegler and Servaz like a knife. Servaz felt the anger boiling up in him again.

'United, you say? Yet you've criticised our work in front of another person twice! Is that what you call *united*? I thought you said you were in the habit of letting the police get on with their job.'

Unflinching, Confiant held the cop's gaze.

'Not when I see that my investigators are clearly headed down the wrong path,' he answered, in a stern voice.

'In that case you should talk to Cathy d'Humières. "A coherent and credible strategy." And what, in your opinion, would that be, your honour?'

'In any event, not one leading to the Institute.'

'We could not be certain until we came here,' protested Irène Ziegler, so calmly that Servaz was surprised.

'One way or the other,' he insisted, 'Hirtmann's DNA got out of that place. And that is no hypothesis, it's fact: once we find out how, we'll be close to catching the guilty party.'

'I'll grant you that,' said Confiant. 'Someone at the Institute has something to do with the horse's death. But it could not possibly be Hirtmann, you said so yourself. And we could have acted more discreetly. If any of this gets out, the very existence of the Institute could be in jeopardy.'

'That's as may be,' said Servaz coldly. 'But it's not my problem. And until we've examined the plans of the entire security system, we cannot rule out any hypothesis. Ask any prison director: there is no infallible system. Some individuals are very gifted at finding the weak links. And there is always the theory of complicity among the staff.'

Confiant looked stunned.

'Are you still thinking that Hirtmann could have got out of there?'

'No,' said Servaz reluctantly, 'it seems increasingly unlikely. But it's too soon to rule it out for good. And, in any case, we have to find the answer to another question that's just as important: who could have got hold of Hirtmann's saliva and left it in the cable car? Above all, *for what purpose?* Because there can be no doubt that the two crimes are connected.'

'The possibility of the two watchmen murdering the chemist is very slim,' declared Espérandieu in the incident room, his laptop open in front of him. 'According to Delmas, whoever did it is intelligent, underhanded, sadistic and has some sound notions of anatomy.'

Reading from his notes on the screen, he relayed the pathologist's conclusions about the position of the slipknot.

'That confirms our initial impression,' said Ziegler, looking around the room. 'Grimm took a long time to die. And he suffered.'

'According to Delmas, his finger was severed before he died.'

A heavy silence fell over the room.

'By the looks of it, the hanging, nudity, cape and severed finger are connected,' said Propp. 'You can't have one without the others. There's some sort of significance to the way it was done. And it's up to us to find it. Everything seems to point to a carefully laid out plan. They had to prepare the equipment, and choose the time and place. Nothing was left to chance. Any more than in the horse's murder.'

'Who's in charge of finding out about the straps?' asked Servaz.

'I am,' answered Ziegler, raising her pen. 'The lab identified the make and model. I have to call the manufacturer.'

'Good. And the cape?'

'Our men are working on it. We've got to have a closer look at the victim's house, too,' said Ziegler.

Servaz thought again about the Grimm widow, the look she'd given him, the scars on her wrist. He felt a spasm run through him.

'I'll take care of it,' he said. 'Who's in charge of the watchmen?'

'Our men are,' said Ziegler once again.

'Right.'

He turned to Espérandieu.

'I want you to go back to Toulouse and gather as much information as you can on Lombard. It's fairly urgent. We have to find the link between him and the chemist at all costs. Ask Samira to give a hand if need be. And get an official search going on the watchmen, on the police side.'

Servaz was referring to the fact that the police and the gendarmerie

213

still had separate databases – something that made everyone's job harder. But the French administration was not known to be partial to simplicity. Espérandieu got up and checked his watch. He closed his laptop.

'As usual, everything is urgent. If you don't need me, I'll be on my way.'

Servaz glanced at the clock on the wall.

'Fine. We all have something to do. As for me, I've got a little visit to make. I think it's time to ask Chaperon a few questions.'

Diane left the Institute bundled up in a rollneck jumper, ski trousers, her winter down jacket and fur-lined boots. She was wearing a second pair of socks over the first, and had put on some protective lip balm. The path started to the east of the buildings and led deep into the trees in the general direction of the valley.

Very quickly her boots sank into the layer of fresh snow, but she went calmly on her way at a good pace. Her breath made small clouds of condensation. She needed some fresh air. Ever since she had overheard the conversation through the air vent, the atmosphere in the Institute had become stifling. Dear Lord! How would she ever last a year in this place?

Walking had always helped her clear her mind. And the icy air stimulated her neurons. The more she thought about it, the more she felt that nothing at the Institute was going the way she had planned.

And then there were all these outside events that apparently had something to do with the place . . .

Diane was puzzled. Had anyone else noticed the nocturnal wanderings? It probably had no connection to the rest, but she wondered whether she should speak to Xavier just in case. A raven suddenly cawed above her head before flying off in a flutter of wings, and her heart leapt in her chest. Then silence fell once again. It was a pity she had no one to speak to. But she was alone here, and only she could make the right decisions.

The solitude of the mountains oppressed her. The light and the silence falling from the treetops had something funereal about them. The high rock faces surrounding the valley never disappeared from sight completely, any more than the walls of a prison disappear from a prisoner's view. It was nothing like the vibrant, airy landscape of her native Switzerland around Lake Geneva.

The path had begun to turn into a steep slope and she had to be careful where she put her feet. She eventually made her way through the undergrowth and found herself at the edge of the forest facing a large clearing with several buildings in the middle. She recognised them at once: the holiday camp, further down the valley, which she had passed on her way to the Institute. The three buildings looked just as sinister and dilapidated as they had the first time she'd seen them. One of them, right on the edge of the forest, was practically overgrown. The other two were nothing but cracks, broken windows and empty porches, the concrete green with moss and black from bad weather. The wind whistled through the openings, the sound now deep, now shrill, a lugubrious *lamento*. Dead leaves, curling and sodden, lay in piles at the foot of the concrete walls, partly buried beneath the snow and giving off a smell of decomposition.

She went in slowly through an opening. The halls and corridors on the ground floor were covered with the same scourge that blooms on the walls of the poorer neighbourhoods: graffiti promising to 'fuck the police' or 'screw the cops', laying claim to their territory, although no one would have dreamt of fighting with them over it; primitive, obscene drawings . . . everywhere. She concluded that Saint-Martin must also have its share of budding artists.

Her steps echoed in the void of the hallways. Icy currents caressed her, making her shiver. She could easily imagine the hordes of kids running and shoving here and there, and the good-natured monitors like sheepdogs gathering them into the fold. Still, without knowing why, she could not shake off the impression that this place was more redolent of sadness and duress than the joys of summer holidays. She recalled a credibility evaluation she had carried out on an eleven-year-old boy when she was working in private practice in forensic psychology in Geneva: the child had been raped by an activity-camp monitor. She was well positioned to know that the world did not resemble *Heidi*. Perhaps it was because she found herself in an unfamiliar place, perhaps it was because of recent events, but she could not help but think of the seemingly countless incidents of rape, murder, torture and physical and psychological brutality, all the time, no matter where, at all God's hours – a thought almost as unbearable as staring into the sun – and some lines by Baudelaire came back to her:

Among the jackals, the panthers, the hounds,
The apes, the scorpions, the vultures and snakes,
The yelping, howling, growling, crawling monsters,
In the vile menagerie of our vice.

Suddenly she froze. There was the sound of an engine outside. A car slowed and came to a halt. Tyres crunched. Motionless in the hallway, she listened carefully. She heard a door slam. Someone was coming. Was it the budding artists, returning to finish their Sistine Chapel? If so, she wasn't sure whether it would be a good idea to find herself alone with them in this place. She turned round and was already heading soundlessly towards the back of the building when she realised that she had taken a wrong turn, that this corridor was a cul-de-sac. *Shit!* Her pulse began to beat faster. She was already retracing her steps when she heard the visitor's footfall, as furtive as leaves blowing in the wind, crossing the concrete at the entrance. She started. He was already there! She had no reason to hide, but that didn't mean she should show herself. Particularly as the person was walking so cautiously, and had now stopped. She did not make another sound. She leaned against the cold concrete and felt her fear cause tiny drops of sweat to pearl at the roots of her hair. Who could possibly want to hang about such a place? The fact the visitor was proceeding so cautiously made her think instinctively that he or she must have a reason too shameful to mention. But what would happen if she suddenly burst out and called, 'Hello'?

The visitor began to walk decisively in her direction. Diane went into a panic. Not for long, however: the visitor stopped again and she heard him turn round and head back the other way. She took a chance to peer round the corner that was hiding her from him. What she saw did nothing to reassure her: a long black cape with a hood flapping against his back like a bat's wing. A cape for the rain, its stiff waterproof fabric rustling with every step.

Viewed from behind, with such a loose garment, Diane could not say whether it was a man or a woman . . . Yet there was something so stealthy about the way the figure was moving, so shifty, that it was as if someone were running a cold finger over her neck.

She seized her chance to come out of her hiding place when the visitor began to head the other way, but the toe of her boot struck something metallic, making a loud scraping noise against the concrete.

Diane plunged back into the shadows, her heart pounding. She could hear the footsteps stop again.

'Is anyone there?'

A man. A high, reedy voice, but it was a man's.

Diane felt as if her neck were swelling and deflating, so wildly was her terrified heart pumping the blood through her arteries. A minute went by.

'*Is someone there?*' shouted the man, even more loudly.

There was something unusual about his voice. A touch of something menacing, but also a plaintive note, fragile and tormented. Inexplicably, Diane thought of the way a frightened cat will arch its back.

It was not a voice she recognised, in any case.

The silence seemed endless. The man didn't move; nor did she. Somewhere nearby, water was dripping into a puddle. The slightest sound resonated ominously in the bubble of silence. A car passed by on the road, but she hardly noticed it. Then she gave a sudden start when the man let out a long, croaking wail which bounced against the walls like a squash ball.

'Bastards, bastards, baaastards!' she heard him sob. 'Scum! Vermin! I hope you all die! That you'll burn in hell!'

This was followed by a terrible cry.

Diane hardly dared breathe. She was covered in goosebumps. The man burst into tears. She could hear his cape rustling as he fell to his knees. He cried and moaned for a long time and she ventured another glance, but there was no way to see his face beneath the hood. Then suddenly he got up and left at a run. A moment later she heard the car door slam, the engine started, and the vehicle took off down the road. She came out of her hiding place and forced herself to breathe normally. She had no idea what she had just seen and heard. Did the man come here often? Had something happened in this place that might explain his behaviour? The sort of behaviour she would have expected to find at the Institute . . .

In any event, he had scared her half to death. She decided to go home and cook something hot in the staff kitchenette. It would calm her nerves. Once she had left the buildings behind, the wind became even chillier and she began to shake uncontrollably. She knew it wasn't only from the cold.

★

Servaz went straight to the town hall. It sat in a long rectangular square by the river, French and European Union flags hanging listlessly from its balcony. Servaz left his car in a little car park between the square and the river, which flowed wide and fast past the foot of a concrete embankment.

He skirted the flowerbeds and threaded his way past the cars parked by the cafés before he entered the town hall. When he reached the first floor, he learned that the mayor was not in, and could probably be found at the mineral-water bottling plant he managed. The secretary gave him a hard time before agreeing to give Servaz the mayor's mobile number, but when Servaz called, it went straight to voicemail. He suddenly felt hungry and looked at his watch. Twenty-nine minutes past three. They had spent more than five hours at the Institute.

On leaving the town hall he sat down in the first café he found, facing the square. Nearby, teenagers were heading home from college, schoolbags on backs; others went by on mopeds with deafening exhaust pipes.

The waiter came over. Servaz looked up. Tall, dark, just short of thirty, he must be popular with the women, with his stubble and dark eyes. Servaz ordered an omelette and a beer.

'Have you lived around here for long?' he asked the waiter.

The waiter regarded him warily. An amused wariness. Servaz suddenly understood that the man was wondering if he was making a pass. It probably wouldn't be the first time.

'I was born twenty kilometres from here,' he replied.

'The suicides – does that mean anything to you?'

This time, wariness won out over amusement.

'What are you? A journalist?'

Servaz showed him his warrant card.

'Crime unit. I'm investigating the murder of the chemist, Grimm. You must have heard about it?'

The waiter nodded cautiously.

'So? The suicides – does that mean anything to you?'

'Same thing as to everyone else round here.'

His words made Servaz sit up straight.

'Which is?'

'It's an old story. I don't know much about it.'

'Tell me the not much you do know.'

The waiter was looking more and more uncomfortable, casting a nervous glance around the terrace.

'It happened a long time ago . . .'

'When?'

'About fifteen years ago.'

'"It happened" . . . What happened?'

'Well . . . the series of suicides.'

Servaz looked at him, not understanding.

'What series of suicides?' he said, annoyed. 'Make yourself clear, for God's sake!'

'There were several suicides . . . teenagers. Boys and girls between the ages of fourteen and eighteen, I think.'

'Here in Saint-Martin?'

'Yes. And in the villages in the valley.'

'There were several suicides? How many?'

'How am I supposed to know? I was eleven at the time! Maybe five. Or six. Or seven. No more than ten, anyway.'

'And did they all die at the same time?' asked Servaz, stunned.

'No. But close together. It lasted for several months.'

'What do you mean by that? Two months? Three? Twelve?'

'More like twelve. Yes. Maybe a year. I don't know . . .'

No Einstein, our Sunday playboy, thought Servaz. *Or else he had no desire to cooperate.*

'And does anyone know why they did it?'

'I don't think so. No.'

'They didn't leave a note?'

The waiter shrugged.

'Listen, I was a kid. You're bound to find older people who could tell you about it. That's all I know. Sorry.'

Servaz watched him walk away through the tables and disappear inside. He didn't try to stop him. Through the glass he saw him speaking to a fat man who must be the proprietor. The man glanced darkly in Servaz's direction, then shrugged and went back to his till.

Servaz could have gone over and questioned him in turn, but he didn't believe this was the place to get reliable information. A series of adolescent suicides fifteen years earlier . . . He thought furiously. What an unbelievable story! What could have driven several teens in the valley to kill themselves? And fifteen years later, a murder and a dead horse . . . Could there be any connection between the two series of events? Servaz narrowed his eyes at the peaks at the end of the valley.

When Espérandieu rushed into the department at 26, boulevard Embouchure, a stentorian voice could be heard shouting from one of the offices.

'Hey, here comes the boss's little sweetheart!'

Espérandieu decided to ignore the insult. Pujol was a moron with a big mouth, two things that generally went together. A tall, sturdy man with greying hair, medieval views on life and a repertory of jokes that were funny only to his mate and alter ego, Ange Simeoni – the two inseparable 'tenors of stupidity', as the Aznavour song went. Martin had brought them in line, and they would never have dared come out with something like that in his presence. But Martin wasn't there.

Espérandieu went along the row of offices until he reached his own at the end of the corridor, next to the boss's. He closed the door behind him. Samira had left a note on his desk: *I entered the watchmen into the FPR the way you asked me to.* The FPR was the missing persons record. He crumpled up the bit of paper, threw it in the basket, put TV on the Radio's 'Family Tree' on his iPhone, then checked his messages. Martin had asked him to get as much information as he could about Éric Lombard, and Espérandieu knew where to go to get it. He had one advantage over most of his colleagues – with the exception of Samira – he was *modern*. He belonged to the generation of multimedia, cyberculture, social networks, forums. And provided you knew where to look, you often came across interesting people. But he did not particularly want Martin or anyone else to know just how he obtained his information.

'Sorry, he hasn't been in today.'

The assistant manager of the bottling plant gave Servaz an impatient look.

'Do you know where I can find him?'

The big man shrugged.

'No. I tried to reach him, but he hasn't got his mobile on. Normally he should be in work by now. Did you try his home? Perhaps he's ill.'

Servaz thanked him and went back out of the little factory. It was surrounded by a high chain-link fence topped with a spiral of barbed wire. Servaz was lost in thought as he unlocked the Jeep. He had already called Chaperon at home, in vain: there was no answer. Servaz felt a knot of anxiety forming in his belly.

He climbed back in the car and sat behind the wheel.

Once again he recalled Chaperon's terrified look when he saw Grimm's body. What was it Hirtmann had said? *Ask the mayor to tell you about the suicides.* What did Hirtmann know that they didn't? And how the devil did he know?

Then another thought came to him. He grabbed his mobile and dialled a number he had jotted down in his notebook. A woman answered.

'Servaz, crime unit,' he said. 'Did your husband have a private room – a study, a place where he kept his papers?'

There was a brief silence, then the sound of someone exhaling cigarette smoke near the telephone.

'Yes.'

'Would you mind if I come and have a look?'

'Do I really have any choice?'

She had blurted out the question, but without any real acrimony.

'You can refuse. In that case I will be obliged to ask for a warrant, and I will get it, and your refusal to cooperate will no doubt attract the attention of the magistrate in charge of the investigation.'

'When do you want to come?' she asked curtly.

'Right away, if you don't mind.'

The snowman was still there, but the children had disappeared. As had the cat's carcass. Night was beginning to fall. The sky had filled with dark, threatening clouds, and only a single orange-pink streak remained above the mountains.

As on the previous occasion, the widow Grimm was waiting at the front door with a cigarette in her hand, a mask of absolute indifference on her face. She stepped back to let him in.

'At the end of the corridor, the door on the right. I haven't touched a thing.'

Servaz went down a corridor cluttered with furniture, paintings, chairs, knick-knacks and stuffed animals that seemed to be watching him go by. He opened the last door on the right just past a bookshelf. The shutters were closed; the room was bathed in darkness. It smelled stuffy. Servaz opened the window. A little office of nine square metres that looked out onto the woods at the back of the house. An indescribable mess. He had difficulty making his way to the middle of the room. Grimm must have spent most of his time in this study when he was at home. There was even a miniature television opposite an old sagging sofa piled high with binders, files, hunting and fishing magazines, a portable stereo and a microwave oven.

For a few moments he stood in the middle of the room and gazed speechlessly at the chaos of cardboard boxes, furniture, binders, dust.

A burrow, a den . . .

A *kennel*.

Servaz shuddered. Grimm had been living a dog's life with his ice-cold wife.

On the walls were postcards, a calendar and posters depicting mountain lakes and rivers. On top of the wardrobes there were more stuffed animals: a squirrel, several owls, a mallard and even a wild cat. In one corner, Servaz saw a pair of ankle boots. On one of the dressers there were several fishing reels. Had Grimm been a nature lover? An amateur taxidermist? Servaz tried for a moment to put himself in the shoes of the fat man who had locked himself away in this room, his only company a menagerie whose eyes stared glassily into the shadowy light. He could imagine him stuffing himself with leftovers in front of his little television before falling asleep on the sofa, banished to the end of the corridor by the dragon lady he had married thirty years earlier. Servaz began to open the drawers, methodically. In the first one he found pens, bills, lists of medicines, bank statements, credit-card receipts. In the next one there was a pair of binoculars, playing cards still in their original wrapping and several ordnance survey maps.

Then his fingers closed around something at the bottom of the drawer: keys. He took them out into the light. There was one big key for a door lock and two smaller ones for padlocks. Servaz slipped them into his pocket.

In the third drawer he found a collection of fishing flies, hooks and line – and a photograph.

Servaz took it over to the window.

Grimm, Chaperon and two other people.

The photograph was old: Grimm was almost thin, and Chaperon looked fifteen years younger. The four men were sitting on rocks round a campfire, smiling into the lens. Behind them, on the left-hand side of the picture, were two tents, in a clearing surrounded by an autumnal forest; a gently sloping meadow, a lake and mountains were on the right. It was taken at dusk: long shadows stretched from the tall trees to the lake. The smoke from the campfire rose in a spiral in the evening light. A bucolic atmosphere.

An impression of simple happiness and camaraderie. Men who enjoyed getting together to go camping in the mountains, one last time before winter.

Servaz suddenly understood how Grimm had managed to put up with a reclusive life and a wife who despised him: thanks to these moments when he could escape into nature in the company of friends. He had been mistaken: this room was neither a prison nor a kennel; on the contrary, it was a tunnel that led to the outside world. The stuffed animals, the posters, the fishing gear, the magazines: everything was there to remind him of those moments of absolute freedom that must have formed the heart of his existence.

In the photograph the four men were wearing the sort of checked shirts, cardigans and trousers that were in fashion in the 1990s. One of them was holding up a flask that might well contain something besides water; another was looking into the lens with a faint, absent smile, as if his mind were elsewhere, as if this little ceremony did not concern him.

Servaz looked closely at the other two hikers. One was a bearded, jovial giant of a man, the other a tall, fairly thin fellow with a head of thick brown hair and large glasses.

He compared the lake in the photo with the one on the poster on the wall, but could not decide whether it was the same lake from two different angles, or two different lakes.

He turned the photograph over.

Lake Oule, October 1993.

Small, precise handwriting.

He was right. It was fifteen years old. The men would have been roughly his age then. Approaching forty. Did they still have dreams then, or had they already taken stock of their lives? And were their conclusions positive or negative?

They were smiling in the photo, their eyes shining in the soft light of an autumn evening, their faces lined with deep shadows.

But which way lay the truth? Everyone, or almost everyone, smiles for pictures. *Everyone plays a part, nowadays*, thought Servaz; *everyone is influenced by the banal conventions of the global media*. There were even plenty of people who *overacted*, as if they were on stage. Appearances and kitsch had become the norm.

Fascinated, Servaz scrutinised the photograph. Was it important? A vague yet familiar little sign told him it was.

He hesitated, then slid the picture into his pocket.

As he was doing this, he got the feeling he had missed something. A powerful feeling. The impression that his brain had unconsciously noticed something and was now ringing an alarm bell.

He took the photograph back out. Studied each detail. The four smiling men. The tender evening light. The lake. The autumn colours. No, that wasn't it. And yet the feeling was there – distinct, indisputable. Without realising it, he had *seen* something.

And suddenly he understood.

Their hands.

The hands of three of the four men were visible: each of them was wearing a large gold signet ring on his ring finger.

The picture had been taken from too far away to be sure, but Servaz could have sworn that it was the same ring each time.

The ring that should have been on Grimm's severed finger.

He left the room. Music filled the house. Jazz. Servaz went back up the corridor towards the source of the music, and came out into an equally cluttered sitting room. The widow was sitting in an armchair, reading. She raised her head and gave him a supremely hostile look. Servaz dangled the keys before her.

'Do you know what these open?'

She hesitated for a moment, as if wondering what she risked if she said nothing.

'We have a cabin in the Sospel valley,' she said finally. 'Ten kilometres from here. To the south of Saint-Martin . . . Not far from the

Spanish border. But we only went there . . . rather, my husband only went there on weekends, starting in the spring.'

'Your husband? And you?'

'It's a gloomy place. I never set foot there. My husband went there to be alone, to rest, meditate, go fishing.'

To rest, thought Servaz. *Since when do chemists need to rest? Don't they have their assistants to do all the drudgery?* Then he thought he was being mean-spirited: what did he know, in the end, about that profession? One thing was certain: he had to visit the chalet.

Espérandieu got an answer to his message thirty-eight minutes later. Fine rain was streaking the windowpanes. Night had fallen over Toulouse, and the blurry lights beyond the streaming window looked like a screensaver.

Vincent had sent the following message:

From vincent.esperandieu@hotmail.com to kleim162@lematin.fr, 16:33:54:
Do you know anything about Éric Lombard?

From kleim162@lematin.fr to vincent.esperandieu@hotmail.com, 17:12:44:
What do you want to know?

Espérandieu smiled and typed the following message:

Whether there are any skeletons in the closet, scandals that have been hushed up, lawsuits pending against the Lombard Group in France or abroad. Any rumours about him. Any nasty old rumour.

From kleim162@lematin.fr to vincent.esperandieu@hotmail.com, 17:25:06:
Is that all! Can you log on to msn?

The valley was buried in shadows and Servaz had switched on his headlights. The road was deserted. No one would be wandering around here at this time of year. There were twenty or so chalets and houses along the twelve kilometres of river, summer houses whose shutters were open from May to September, and, more rarely, at Christmas. At this time of day, they were nothing more than low shapes hunched down at the side of the road, almost merging with the huge black mass of the mountain.

Suddenly after a wide bend, Servaz saw the beginning of the track the widow had told him about. He slowed down, turned into it and found himself bouncing along the road, clinging to the steering wheel, going fifteen kilometres an hour. Night had fallen and the black trees stood out against a sky that was only slightly lighter. Servaz went a few hundred metres further; then the chalet appeared.

He turned off the engine, left the lights on and got out. The sound of the nearby river immediately filled the darkness. There wasn't a single light for miles.

He walked up to the cabin in the blaze of his headlights, which projected his shadow ahead of him as if a giant made of darkness were leading the way. Then he climbed the steps to the veranda and took out the key ring. There were indeed three locks: the central lock corresponded to the biggest key, and the two smaller ones were for the locks above and below. It took him a moment to figure out which key went where, particularly as the small ones were the same size, and the top lock had been put on backwards. Then he shoved open the door, which resisted before yielding with a groan. Servaz groped around for the light switch near the doorway. He found it on the left. He switched it on and the light poured from the ceiling.

For a few seconds he stood motionless on the threshold, transfixed by what he saw.

The inside of the cabin was nothing more than a countertop running along one wall, with what might be a kitchenette behind, a sofa bed at the back and a wooden table and two chairs. But hanging on the wall on the left was a cape made of black waterproof cloth. *He was getting closer.*

Espérandieu opened his instant messaging service. He waited three minutes before a message accompanied by an icon of a cartoon dog sniffing something popped up in the lower right-hand corner of the screen:

kleim162 has just logged on

A dialogue box with the same icon opened three seconds later.

kleim162 said:
why are you interested in Éric Lombard?

vince.esp said:
sorry can't tell you just now

kleim162 said:
I just dug around a bit before logging on. Someone killed his horse. The info was reported in several papers. Any connection?

vince.esp said:
no comment

kleim162 said:
vince you're in the crime unit. Don't tell me you're investigating the death of a horse!!!!

vince.esp said:
will you help me or not???

kleim162 said:
what's in it for me?

vince.esp said:
a friend's affection

kleim162 said:
we'll talk about cuddles some other time. And besides that?

vince.esp said:
you'll be the first to hear what the investigation turns up

kleim162 said:
so there is an investigation. That all?

vince.esp said:
the first to hear if this business is hiding something more important

kleim162 said:
ok I'll have a look

Espérandieu logged out with a smile.

'Kleim162' was the user name of an investigative journalist who worked freelance for several major weekly magazines. A veritable ferret who loved to stick his nose where it was not welcome. Espérandieu had met him in rather unusual circumstances, and he had never spoken of this 'contact' with anyone, not even Martin. Officially, he was like the other members of the squad: wary of the press. But his secret opinion was that cops, like politicians, could only gain – significantly – by having one or two journalists up their sleeve.

Sitting at the wheel of his Jeep, Servaz dialled Ziegler's mobile. He got her voicemail and hung up. Then he called Espérandieu.

'I found a photograph at Grimm's place,' he said. 'I'd like you to rework it.'

The squad had image-processing software, but Espérandieu and Samira were the only ones who knew how to use it.

'What kind of photograph? Digital or analogue?'

'Paper. An old print showing a group of men. One of them is Grimm, and another is Chaperon, the mayor of Saint-Martin. It looks as if all the men are wearing the same signet ring. It's slightly blurry, but there's something engraved on it. I'd like you to try and see what it is.'

'You think it might be some sort of club, like the Rotary or the Freemasons?'

'I don't know, but—'

'*The severed ring finger,*' his assistant suddenly remembered.

'Exactly.'

'Right, can you scan it and send it to me from the gendarmerie? I'll take a look. But the software is primarily for dealing with digital photos. It's not as efficient with old ones.'

Servaz thanked him. He was about to drive off when his mobile rang. It was Ziegler.

'Did you call?'

'I found something,' he said straight out. 'In a cabin belonging to Grimm.'

'A cabin?'

'The widow told me about it. I found the keys in Grimm's desk. Evidently, she never went there. You have to see it . . .'

'What do you mean?'

'There is a cape, just like the one that was found on Grimm's corpse. And boots. It's late; I'm going to lock the door and give the keys to Maillard. I want a CSI team to go over the place with a fine-tooth comb, first thing tomorrow morning.'

Silence at the end of the line. Outside the Cherokee, the wind was howling.

'And you, how far have you got?' he said.

'The straps are a common make,' she replied. 'Mass-produced, sold all over western and southern France. There's a serial number on each strap. They're going to get back to the manufacturer to try and find out who stocks them.'

Servaz paused to think for a moment. Just outside the halo from the headlights, an owl had landed on a branch and was watching him. Servaz thought about Hirtmann's gaze.

'If we can find the shop, we might be able to get our hands on the video surveillance tapes,' he said.

He could hear the scepticism in Ziegler's voice when she replied.

'Even if they keep the tapes, they have to destroy them within a month. Which means the straps would need to have been bought very recently.'

Servaz was almost certain that Grimm's killer must have been preparing his crime for months. Did he buy the straps at the last minute, or did he already have them?

'Fine,' he said. 'See you tomorrow.'

He drove back down the forest track towards the main road. Black clouds slipped in front of the moon. The valley was now little more than a lake of dark shadows. Servaz stopped, looked right and left, then pulled out onto the main road.

Out of habit, he checked the rear-view mirror.

For a split second his heart stopped beating: a pair of headlights had just come on behind him . . . A car parked on the verge, in the dark, not far from where he had left the track. In the mirror he saw the headlights move away from the hard shoulder and begin to follow him. Judging by the size and height of the vehicle, it was a 4x4. The hairs on his neck began to prickle. It was obvious that the 4x4 was there for him. Why else would it be there, at the end of this deserted valley? He wondered who was behind the wheel. One of Lombard's henchmen? But why, if they were keeping an eye on him, would Lombard's men choose to show themselves like this?

He was beginning to feel nervous.

He was squeezing the steering wheel too tightly. He took a deep breath. Stay calm. Don't panic. *There's a car following you, so what?* A feeling very close to fear overwhelmed him, however, when it occurred to him that it might be the killer. By opening the door to that chalet, he had strayed too close to the truth . . . Someone had decided he was in the way. Servaz looked into the mirror again. He had just come out of a wide bend; his pursuer's headlights had disappeared behind the tall trees along the road.

Then he saw them once again – and Servaz's heart leapt in his chest at the same time as a blinding light flooded the Jeep. On full beam! He was soaked in sweat. He blinked, blinded like an animal trapped in headlights, like the owl just before. His heart was in his mouth.

The 4x4 was closer now. Very close. Right behind him.

Servaz stepped on the accelerator, his fear of speed vanquished by his fear of whoever was behind him, and his pursuer let him get some distance. He tried to breathe deeply and evenly, but his heart was leaping like a wild goat in his chest and the sweat was streaming from his face like water. Every time he looked back, the white light exploded in his face, and dark spots danced before his eyes.

Suddenly the 4x4 accelerated. *Fuck, this guy's crazy! He's going to crash into me!*

Before he could even try anything, the black vehicle had overtaken him. In a moment of sheer panic, Servaz thought the other car was going to drive him off the road, but the four-wheel drive continued to accelerate along the straight stretch of road, then pulled away, its lights melting quickly into the night. Servaz saw the brake lights flash briefly just before the next bend; then the car disappeared. He slowed down and pulled over to the verge with a jolt, leaned over to take his weapon from the glove box and got out, his legs shaking. The cold night air felt good. He wanted to check the gun chamber, but his hand was trembling so violently that it took him several seconds.

But the warning was as clear as the night was dark: someone, in this valley, did not want his investigation to go any further. Someone did not want him to find out the truth.

But what truth was that?

17

The next day, Servaz and Ziegler attended Grimm's funeral among the fir trees and gravestones at the little cemetery on top of the hill.

Behind the mourners congregated around the grave, the trees seemed to be wearing mourning, too. The wind made the branches rustle in a murmured prayer. The wreaths and the grave stood out against the snow. The town lay spread across the valley below them. Servaz reflected that here, indeed, they were closer to the sky.

He had slept badly. He had awoken several times with a start, his forehead bathed in sweat. He could not help but mull over what had happened that night. He had not mentioned it to Irène yet; oddly, he was afraid that if he spoke about it, he might be sidelined, that someone else would be entrusted with the investigation. Were they in danger here? *One thing was certain: they didn't like strangers nosing about in this valley.*

He tried to regain his calm. It must be pleasant here in the summer, on this luxuriant green hillside, which seemed to be advancing through space like the prow of the ship above the valley. A round, gentle hill, like a woman's body. The mountains were no longer as threatening from this perspective; even the weather seemed more pleasant.

As they were on their way out of the cemetery, Ziegler gave him a nudge with her elbow. He looked to where she was pointing: Chaperon had reappeared. He was talking with Cathy d'Humières and other notables. Suddenly Servaz's mobile vibrated in his pocket. He answered. Someone from the general director's office in Paris. Servaz immediately recognised the patrician accent, the worldly tone, as if the fellow gargled every morning with treacle.

'How are you doing with the horse?'

'Who wants to know?'

'The office of the General Director of the Police Nationale is following this matter closely, Commandant.'

'Do they know that a man has been killed?'

'Yes, a chemist called Grimm, we are aware of that,' replied the bureaucrat, as if he knew the case inside out, which was unlikely.

'Therefore you must realise that Monsieur Lombard's horse is not my priority.'

'Commandant, Catherine d'Humières has assured me that you are an asset to the force.'

Servaz felt his temper flaring. *Clearly more of an asset than you are,* he thought. He didn't spend his time shaking hands in corridors, or disparaging his little friends, or sitting in meetings acting as if he were up on all the cases.

'Do you have a lead?'

'Not a single one.'

'And the two night watchmen?'

Well, well, he did take the trouble to read the reports. Probably in great haste, just before calling, like a student hurrying to finish his homework before class.

'It's not them.'

'How can you be so sure?'

Because I spend my time among victims and murderers while you sit there on your arse all day long.

'They're not the right profile. But if you would like to make sure for yourself, you are very welcome to come down and join us.'

'Please, Commandant, do remain calm. No one is questioning your competence,' said the man soothingly. 'Conduct your investigation as you see fit, but don't lose sight of the fact that we want to find out who killed the horse.'

The message was clear: it was perfectly all right to murder a man and hang him naked from a bridge – but you could not go beheading a horse belonging to one of the most powerful men in France.

'Very well,' said Servaz.

'We'll talk soon, Commandant,' said the man, before hanging up.

Servaz could imagine him at his desk, in his bespoke suit and tie, his fancy eau de toilette, smiling at the power he wielded over his little provincial employees, writing up reports of no real importance but full of grand-sounding words, then trotting along to relieve his bladder and admire himself in the mirror before going down to remake the world in the cafeteria with his acolytes.

'A lovely ceremony in a lovely place,' said someone next to him.

He turned his head. Gabriel Saint-Cyr was smiling at him. Servaz shook the former magistrate's hand. A solid, informal handshake, not the least bit intimidating, like the man himself.

'I was just thinking that it is indeed a lovely place to spend eternity,' said Servaz.

The retired judge approved with a nod of his head.

'And that is precisely what I intend to do. I will probably get here before you, but if you feel so inclined, I am sure you would be good company in death: my spot is over there.'

Saint-Cyr pointed to a corner of the cemetery. Servaz burst out laughing and lit a cigarette.

'How do you know?'

'Know what?'

'That I would be good company in death.'

'At my age, and with my experience, you can assess people quite quickly.'

'And you're never mistaken?'

'Rarely. Besides, I trust Catherine's judgement.'

'Did she ask you your sign?'

Now it was Saint-Cyr's turn to laugh.

'Of the zodiac? It's the first thing she did when we were introduced! My family has a tomb here,' he added. 'Three years ago I bought a plot at the opposite end of the cemetery, as far away as possible.'

'Why?'

'I was terrified at the thought of having certain relatives as neighbours for all eternity.'

'Were you acquainted with Grimm?'

'So you've decided to make use of my services?'

'Perhaps.'

'He was a very secretive sort. You should ask Chaperon,' said Saint-Cyr, pointing at the mayor, who was walking away from them. 'They knew each other well.'

Servaz remembered what Hirtmann had said.

'That's what I thought,' he said. 'Grimm, Chaperon and Perrault, right? The Saturday-night poker game . . .'

'Yes. And Mourrenx. The same foursome for forty years. Inseparable since their days at the lycée.'

Servaz remembered the photograph in his jacket pocket. He showed it to the judge.

'Is this them?'

Gabriel Saint-Cyr pulled out a pair of glasses and put them on before leaning over the picture. Servaz noticed that his index finger was deformed by arthritis and that it shook when he pointed at the four men: Parkinson's, perhaps.

'Yes. This is Grimm . . . And that's Chaperon . . .'

His finger moved.

'This one here is Perrault.' The tall, thin fellow with thick hair and heavy glasses. He runs a sports shop in Saint-Martin. He's also a mountain guide.'

Then his finger moved to the bearded giant who was holding his flask up to the camera lens, laughing in the autumn light.

'Gilbert Mourrenx. He used to work at the paper mill in Saint-Gaudens. He died of stomach cancer two years ago.'

'You say the four of them were inseparable?'

'They were,' replied Saint-Cyr, putting his glasses away. 'Inseparable, yes . . . you could say that . . .'

Servaz stared at the judge. *Something in his voice* . . . The old man didn't take his eyes off him. He was sending him a message, as subtly as could be.

'Did they ever get into any sort of trouble?'

Saint-Cyr returned Servaz's intense gaze. Servaz held his breath.

'More like rumours . . . Once, about thirty years ago, there was a complaint . . . filed by a family in Saint-Martin. A modest family: the father was a worker at the power plant; the mother was unemployed.'

The power plant: Servaz's senses were immediately on the alert.

'They filed a complaint?'

'Yes. For blackmail. Something like that . . .'

The old man frowned, trying to summon his memories.

'If I remember rightly, there were a few Polaroids. The poor couple's daughter, a seventeen-year-old kid. In the pictures she was naked and visibly drunk. And in another one she was . . . with several men, I think. Apparently the men were threatening to go public with the photographs if the girl didn't do certain things for them. But she ended up going to pieces and telling her parents everything.'

'And then what happened?'

'Nothing. The parents withdrew their complaint before the gendarmes were even able to question the four young men. They must have settled it on the quiet: drop the charges and in exchange

235

no more blackmail. The parents wouldn't have wanted those photos to get out . . .'

Servaz frowned.

'That's strange. Maillard didn't mention it to me.'

'He probably didn't know anything about it. He wasn't in the job yet.'

'But you were.'

'Yes.'

'And did you believe it?'

Saint-Cyr looked doubtful. 'You're a cop, you know as well as I do that everyone has secrets. And that they're usually not very nice secrets. Why should the girl's parents lie?'

'To extort money from the boys' families.'

'And let their daughter's reputation be ruined for ever? No. I knew her father: he had done a few odd jobs at my place when he was unemployed. An upstanding fellow, old school. I'd venture that wasn't their style.'

Servaz thought of the cabin and what he had found there.

'You just said that everyone has secrets.'

Saint-Cyr looked at him attentively.

'Yes. What's your secret, Commandant?'

Servaz gave him his enigmatic rabbit-like smile.

'The suicides,' he said. 'Does that mean anything to you?'

This time he saw real surprise in the judge's eyes.

'Who told you about that?'

'You wouldn't believe me if I told you.'

'Try me.'

'Julian Hirtmann.'

Gabriel Saint-Cyr stared at him for a long time. He seemed puzzled.

'Are you serious?'

'Absolutely.'

For a split second the old judge was speechless. Then he said, 'What are you doing at around eight o'clock tonight?'

'I have nothing planned.'

'Well, in that case, come to dinner. If I'm to believe what my guests tell me, I'm a veritable cordon bleu chef. Number six, impasse du Torrent. You can't miss it, it's an old mill, all the way at the end of the street, just before the forest. See you this evening.'

★

'I hope everything is all right,' said Servaz.

Chaperon turned round with an awkward gesture. He already had his hand on the car door. He looked tense and preoccupied. When he saw it was Servaz, he blushed.

'Why do you ask?'

'I tried to reach you all day yesterday,' said Servaz, with a friendly smile. 'With no luck.'

For a fraction of a second the mayor of Saint-Martin looked flustered. He was trying to keep his composure, but could not manage altogether.

'I've been terribly shaken by Gilles's death. Such a horrible murder . . . To go to such extremes . . . it's dreadful . . . I needed to get away, to be alone. I went for a hike on the mountain.'

'Alone on the mountain? And you weren't afraid?'

The mayor baulked at his question.

'Why should I be afraid?'

As he looked more closely at the suntanned little man, Servaz became absolutely certain that he was not merely afraid, he was terrified. Servaz wondered if he should ask him about the suicides now, but decided that it would be better to hold back some of his cards. He'd know more about it tonight after his dinner with Saint-Cyr. Nevertheless, he took the picture from his pocket.

'Does this remind you of anything?'

'Where did you get that?'

'At Grimm's place.'

'It's an old photo,' said Chaperon, avoiding his gaze.

'Yes, October 1993,' said Servaz.

Chaperon waved his right hand, as if to say it was all so long ago. For a brief moment his bronzed hand, covered with little brown spots, fluttered before Servaz's eyes, time enough for him to freeze with surprise. The mayor was no longer wearing the signet ring, but he must have removed it recently: a narrow band of lighter skin ran all round his ring finger.

In no time Servaz was filled with questions.

Grimm's finger had been cut; Chaperon had taken off his ring – the signet ring the four men on the photograph were wearing. What did it mean? The killer, obviously, knew the answer. Did the two other men in the photograph have anything to do with the chemist's death? And if they did, how did Hirtmann find out about it?

'Did you know them well?' asked Servaz.

'Yes, fairly well. Although Perrault and I saw each other more frequently back then than we do now.'

'They were also your poker partners.'

'Yes. And we went hiking together. But I don't see what—'

'Thank you,' interrupted Servaz. 'I don't have any more questions just now.'

'Who's that?' asked Ziegler in the car, pointing to a man who was walking carefully towards a Peugeot 405 that was almost as worn out as he was.

'Gabriel Saint-Cyr, honorary examining magistrate, retired. I met him yesterday at the courts.'

'What did you talk about?'

'Grimm, Chaperon, Perrault and a certain Mourrenx.'

'The three poker players . . . and who is Mourrenx?'

'The fourth member of the group. He died two years ago of cancer. According to Saint-Cyr, thirty years ago they were accused of blackmail. They got a girl drunk, then made her pose naked for a photograph. Then they threatened to go public with the photograph if—'

'—if she didn't do certain things . . .'

'Exactly.'

Servaz caught a fleeting light in Ziegler's eyes.

'That could be a lead,' she said.

'What connection would there be with Lombard's horse? And Hirtmann?'

'I don't know.'

'It was thirty years ago. Four drunk young men and a girl who was drunk as well. So what? They were young; they did something stupid. Where does that leave us?'

'Perhaps it's merely the tip of the iceberg.'

Servaz looked at her.

'What do you mean?'

'Well, there may be more "stupid" things, of the same type. Maybe they didn't stop there. Maybe one of those stupid things ended badly.'

'That's a lot of maybes,' said Servaz. 'And there's something else: Chaperon had taken off his signet ring.'

'What?'

Servaz described what he had just seen. Ziegler frowned.

'What do you think it means?'

'No idea. In the meantime, I have something to show you.'

'The cabin?'

'Yes. Shall we go?'

At five o'clock that morning, the alarm on the night table rang and Diane dragged herself to the bathroom. As on every other morning, the shower began with a scorching jet before ending up a trickle of cold water, and she hurried to dry herself off and get dressed. She spent the following hour reviewing her notes before going down to the cafeteria on the ground floor.

The place was deserted. But she now knew where to find the coffeemaker, and she slipped behind the counter to make herself an espresso. She went back to reading her notes until she heard the sound of footsteps in the corridor. Dr Xavier came into the room, gave her a little nod, then went in turn behind the counter to make a coffee. After that, with his cup in his hand, he came over to her.

'Good morning, Diane. You're up early.'

'Good morning, sir. An old habit . . .'

She noticed he seemed to be in a good mood. He sipped his coffee, still looking at her with a smile.

'Are you ready, Diane? I have good news. This morning we will go and visit the residents in Unit A.'

She made an effort to hide her excitement and keep her tone professional.

'That's excellent, sir.'

'Please, do call me Francis.'

'Very well, Francis.'

'I hope I didn't frighten you too much last time. I simply wanted to warn you. You'll see, everything will be fine.'

'I feel completely ready.'

He cast her a look that clearly indicated he was not so sure.

'Who are we going to see?'

'Julian Hirtmann.'

The White Stripes were singing 'Seven Nation Army' in his headphones when the office door opened. Espérandieu looked up from the screen.

'Hey,' said Samira. 'How was the autopsy?'

'Yucky,' said Espérandieu, pulling off his headphones.

She walked round Vincent's desk to her workspace. As she passed, Espérandieu caught a whiff of a fresh, pleasant perfume, with a background of shower gel. The moment she had set foot in his department, Vincent had felt an affinity with Samira Cheung. Like him, she was the butt of sarcasm and barely concealed gibes from certain members of the squad. But the young woman knew how to hold her own. She had put the old bastards in their place more than once. Which made them hate her even more.

Samira Cheung grabbed some mineral water and drank it straight from the bottle. That morning she was wearing a short leather coat over a denim jacket and a hoodie, camo trousers, boots with three-inch heels and a peaked ski cap.

She peered at her computer screen with her extraordinarily ugly face. Her make-up didn't help matters. Even Espérandieu had felt like laughing the first time he saw her, but he had eventually got used to her. Now he even thought she had a strange charm.

'Where were you?' he asked.

'At the courts.'

He knew this meant she had been talking to the magistrate in charge of the case of the three boys. He wondered, with a smile, what sort of effect she had had on him.

'Any headway?'

'It would seem that the arguments of the opposing party have found a sympathetic ear in the person of His Honour . . .'

'What do you mean?'

'Well, that the drowning hypothesis is gaining ground.'

'Shit!'

'Did you notice anything when you got here?' she asked.

'What sort of thing?'

'Pujol and Simeoni.'

Espérandieu winced. It was something he did not like to talk about.

'Sure, they seem in fine form,' he said lugubriously.

'They've been like that since yesterday,' said Samira. 'I get the feeling that Martin's absence has given them wings. You should be on your guard.'

'Why me?'

'You know very well.'

'No, I don't, explain.'

240

'They hate you. They think you're gay. Which, for them, is about the same as being a paedophile or buggering goats.'

'They hate you too,' Espérandieu pointed out, choosing not to dwell on Samira's choice of words.

'Less than you. They don't like me because I'm half Chink, half Arab. All that's missing is a little black blood. Basically, I'm the enemy. With you it's different. They have a thousand reasons to hate you: your mannerisms, your clothes, Martin's support, your wife—'

'My *wife*?'

Samira could not help but smile.

'Yes. They cannot understand how a guy like you could be married to a woman like her.'

It was Espérandieu's turn to smile. He appreciated Samira's outspokenness, but there were times when a bit of diplomacy would have done her no harm.

'They're Neanderthals,' he said.

'Primates,' Samira agreed. 'But I'd watch it if I were you. I'm sure they have something nasty up their sleeves.'

When he climbed out of the car outside Grimm's cabin, Servaz wondered if he hadn't had a hallucination the night before. The valley no longer seemed the least bit dark and haunted. As he was closing the car door, he realised his throat was irritated again. He had forgotten to take his medicine that morning.

'You wouldn't have any water on you?' he asked.

'There's a bottle of mineral water in the glove compartment,' said Ziegler.

They began walking towards the cabin. They could see the stream sparkling through the trees, weaving a web of crystal-clear voices. A few beech trees stood out on the grey slopes of the mountain among the spruces and firs. There was an illegal dump somewhat further along, by the water. Servaz could see rusty cans, black bin bags, a filthy mattress, a refrigerator and even an old computer dragging its cables behind it, like a dead octopus's tentacles. Even here in this wild valley man could not help but deface everything he touched.

He went up the steps onto the veranda. A thick tape marked 'Gendarmerie Nationale – Do Not Enter' was blocking the door. Servaz lifted it up, unlocked the door and gave it a firm shove. He stood aside to let Ziegler go in.

'The wall on the left,' he said.

She took a step inside – and stopped at once.

'Shit!'

Servaz followed her in. The kitchenette counter and cupboards on the right, the sofa bed covered in cushions at the back, the bookshelves, the fishing equipment – rods, net, boots – in a corner: everything had been painstakingly covered with an assortment of powder: aluminium, cerise, black magnetic powder, pink fluorescent powder . . . All used for dusting latent prints. In some places, large blue zones indicated that the investigators had used Bluestar: they'd been looking for traces of blood, apparently to no avail. Numbered cards were still pinned here and there. Scraps of fabric had even been cut out of the carpet.

He stole a glance at Ziegler.

She looked stunned. She was staring at the wall on the left: hanging from a peg by its hood, like a sleeping bat, was the large cape, its black moiré folds contrasting sharply with the pale wood of the wall. Below it on the rough pine floor was a pair of boots. Traces of powder also shone on the cloth and boots.

'I don't know why that thing gives me goosebumps,' said Ziegler. 'It's only a rain cape and a pair of boots, after all.'

Servaz glanced out of the open door. Outside, everything was silent. But the image of the headlights flashing onto his rear-view mirror was burned onto his retina. He tried to listen for an engine, but all he could hear was the babbling of the stream. Once again he felt the instinctive fear that had overwhelmed him last night. A brute fear, entirely raw.

'What's the matter?' asked Ziegler, noticing his expression.

'I was followed, yesterday, on this road . . . A car was waiting for me as I pulled out from the forest track . . .'

Ziegler studied his expression. A worried look came over her face.

'Are you sure?'

'Yes.'

There was a moment of crushing silence.

'You have to tell d'Humières.'

'No. I'd rather we kept it to ourselves. For the time being, anyway.'

'Why?'

'I don't know . . . Confiant would be perfectly capable of using it as a pretext to take me off the case. On the grounds that it's for my own protection, naturally,' he added, with a weary smile.

'Who do you think it was?'

'Might have been Éric Lombard's henchmen.'

'Or the killers?'

She was staring at him, wide-eyed. He understood that she was wondering how she would react if it happened to her. *Fear is a contagious disease,* he thought. There was an element of such absolute darkness in this investigation, a deeply sinister critical mass that formed the heart of the matter, and now they were drawing perilously close to it. For the second time he wondered if they were putting their own lives at risk.

'It's time to have a little chat with the mayor,' he said suddenly.

'Don't worry, everything will be fine.'

Diane looked at Mr Atlas's tall form, imagining the powerful muscles beneath his boiler suit. He must spend hours working out. He gave her a friendly wink and she nodded her head.

Contrary to what all these men seemed to think, she wasn't particularly apprehensive. She felt, instead, an intense professional curiosity.

Then they were in a neon-lit corridor. Blue carpeting absorbing their footsteps. White walls . . .

Piped music was playing quietly in the background – like in a supermarket. Some New Age thing, harp and piano, as impalpable as a whisper.

The doors . . .

She went past them without stopping at the little windows. Xavier was striding ahead. She followed obediently.

Not a sound. They must all be asleep. It was like being in a five-star hotel, of the modern sort, minimalist, clean lines. She remembered the long, sinister scream she'd heard from the other side of the security door the first time she'd come near this place. Had they been drugged for the occasion? No, Alex had been clear on that score: most of them were resistant to medication.

At the last door Xavier stopped in front of her; he typed a code into the box and then turned the handle.

'Good morning, Julian.'

'Good morning, Doctor.'

A deep, composed, worldly voice. Diane heard him before she saw him.

'I've brought you a visitor, our new psychologist: Diane Berg. She is *Swiss*, like you.'

She stepped forward. Julian Hirtmann was standing by the window. He turned away from the landscape and let his gaze fall on her. He was over six foot tall and Dr Xavier looked like a child next to him. In his forties, short brown hair, firm, regular features. Sure of himself. Rather good-looking, she thought, if you're into the uptight sort. A high forehead, pursed lips, square jaw.

But it was his eyes that struck her. Piercing. Black. Intense. Irises shining with a wily, unflinching brilliance. He narrowed his lids and she felt his gaze enveloping her.

'Good morning, Julian,' she said.

'Good morning to you. Psychologist, huh?' he said.

She saw Xavier smile. Hirtmann's lips formed a dreamy smile as well.

'Where in Geneva do you live?'

'Cologny,' she replied.

He nodded and came away from the window.

'I had a beautiful house on the lake. Now there are some *nouveau riche* people living there. The type who are all computers and mobile phones and not a single book in the house. Good Lord! Percy Bysshe Shelley lived in that house when he was in Switzerland, can you imagine?'

He was staring at her with his dark, shining eyes. He was waiting for her to respond.

'You like to read?' she said awkwardly.

He shrugged, clearly disappointed.

'Dr Berg would like to have regular consultations with you,' interrupted Xavier.

He turned to look at her again.

'Really? What is in it for me? Other than the pleasure of your company?'

'Nothing,' she replied, honestly. 'Absolutely nothing. I make no claim to relieve your suffering in any way. Besides, you're not suffering. I have nothing to sell you other than, as you say, the pleasure of my company. But I will be grateful if you agree.'

No fawning, no lies – she thought she was managing rather well. He gave her an intense stare.

'Hmm, you are frank.' His gaze went from Diane to Xavier. 'A

244

rare virtue in this place. And if I were to accept, what would our . . . *meetings* consist of? I hope you do not intend to try and analyse me. Let me tell you right away: it won't work. Not with me.'

'No, I mean real conversations. We can talk about all sorts of topics, anything you like.'

'It remains to be seen if we have anything in common,' he said ironically.

She did not react.

'Tell me about yourself,' he said. 'About your career so far.'

She told him. She mentioned the Faculty of Psychology and Educational Sciences at Geneva, the Institute of Forensic Psychology, the private practice where she had worked and the Champ-Dollon prison where she had interned.

He nodded gravely, one finger on his lower lip, as if he were an examiner. She refrained from smiling at his pose. She reminded herself of what he had done to young women her age and any desire to smile vanished.

'I suppose that since you've been here,' he said, 'in this environment that is so new and unusual, you must feel a certain apprehension.'

He was testing her. He wanted to find out if there would be any reciprocity. He did not want one-sided meetings where he would do all the talking and she would merely listen.

'Yes, the apprehension of being in a new position, in a new place, with new responsibilities,' she said. 'Professional stress. I see it as something positive, which will allow me to progress.'

He nodded.

'If you say so. As you know, groups of people who are shut away together have a tendency to regress. Here it's not only the residents, but the staff as well, and even the psychiatrists. You'll see. There are three levels of confinement, nested one in the other: the confinement of this asylum, then of the valley and finally of the town down there – all those brutes corrupted by centuries of inbreeding, incest and violence. You'll see. After a few days or weeks, you'll begin to feel childish, like a little girl again; you'll want to start sucking your thumb . . .'

In his cold eyes she could read his desire to say something obscene, but he controlled himself. He had had a strict upbringing, after all. It came to her that Hirtmann made her think of her father, with his stern demeanour, the grey strands in his brown hair, his appearance of a carefully groomed, ageing beau.

The same firm line of mouth and jaw, the same longish nose, the same intense gaze gauging her, judging her. She knew that if she did not banish these thoughts, she would lose control.

She would wonder, later, how this same man could have organised those notoriously violent orgies. Hirtmann was a man of multiple personalities.

'What are you thinking about?' he said.

He did not miss a thing. She would have to bear that in mind. She decided to be as frank as she could, while always maintaining a professional distance.

'I was thinking that you remind me in a way of my father,' she said.

For the first time, he seemed unsettled. She saw him smile. She noticed that the smile completely changed his appearance.

'Really?' he said, clearly surprised.

'I can sense you have had the same typically Swiss bourgeois upbringing, the same reserve, the same strictness. You have Protestant written all over you, even if you thought you got rid of it along the way. All those upper-class Swiss people who go about like a locked safe. I was just wondering if he had any shameful secrets, like you.'

Xavier gave her an astonished look. Hirtmann's smile grew wider.

'I believe we will get along quite well after all,' he said. 'When do we begin? I'm eager to continue this conversation.'

'Nowhere to be found,' said Ziegler, closing her mobile phone. 'He's not at the town hall; he's not at home; he's not at his factory. It looks like he's done a bunk.'

Servaz looked at her, then stared through the windscreen at the stream.

'We're going to have to take better care of our mayor. Once he reappears. In the meantime, let's try Perrault.'

The sales assistant, a young woman in her twenties, was chewing her gum so vigorously that it was as if she had a personal score to settle with it.

She didn't look particularly sporty. More the type to eat too many sweets and sit for hours in front of the telly or computer. Servaz mused that if he had been in Perrault's place, he would have thought twice about entrusting her with the till. He looked around him at the rows of skis and snowboards, the shelves full of hiking boots, the fluorescent jumpsuits, fleece jumpers and fashion accessories. He wondered what criteria Perrault had for hiring her. Perhaps she was the only candidate who had agreed to work for the salary he was offering.

'Did he seem worried?' he asked.

'Yup.'

Servaz turned to look at Ziegler. They had just tried ringing the bell at the studio Perrault rented above the shop. No answer. The salesgirl told them that she hadn't seen him since the previous day. Monday morning he had shown up and said that he had to go away for a few days – a family emergency, he explained. She had told him not to worry, that she would mind the shop in the meantime.

'In what way did he seem worried?' asked Ziegler.

She chewed briskly for a moment or two before answering.

'He looked a right mess, like someone who hasn't had any sleep. And he couldn't keep still.'

'Did he seem frightened?'

'Yep. I just told you.'

She almost blew a bubble but then thought better of it.

'Do you have a number where we can reach him?'

The young woman opened a drawer and rummaged among the papers. She pulled out a business card and handed it to the gendarme. Ziegler glanced at the logo representing a skier zigzagging down a mountain through the snow; beneath it, in fancy print, was written 'Sport & Nature.'

'This Perrault, what's he like to work for?' she asked.

The assistant gave her a wary look.

'Dead stingy,' she said finally.

Sufjan Stevens was singing 'Come On! Feel the Illinoise' on his headphones when Espérandieu glanced suddenly at his computer. On the screen, the image-processing software had just completed its task.

'Come and have a look at this,' he said to Samira.

She got up. Her hoodie was unzipped, and when she leaned over him, he could see the start of her breasts just beneath his nose.

'What is it?'

It was a close-up of the ring. Not completely sharp, but the gold signet ring could be clearly seen, magnified two thousand times; at the top, against a red background, were two golden letters.

'This is the ring that was on Grimm's severed finger,' he said, with a dry throat.

'Huh? How do you know – since his finger was chopped off?'

'It would take too long to explain. What do you see?'

'It looks like two characters, two letters,' said Samira.

Espérandieu forced himself to keep his eyes on the computer screen.

'Two Cs?' he said.

'Or a C and an E . . .'

'Or a C and a D . . .'

'Or an O and a C . . .'

'Hang on a sec.'

He opened several windows on the right-hand side of the screen, changed a few parameters, moved his cursor, then launched the process again. They waited in silence for the results. Samira was still leaning over his shoulder. Espérandieu conjured up a vision of two full breasts, soft and firm. There was a beauty spot on the left one.

'What do you think they're doing in there?' came a mocking voice from the corridor.

The computer told them that the task was completed. The image immediately reappeared. Sharp. The two letters stood out clearly against the red background: 'C S.'

Servaz found the place, as indicated, at the end of an impasse that led to a stream and a copse. He saw the lights before he could make out the black shape of the mill; its three lit windows were reflected in the stream. Up above were the mountains, the black fir trees and a sky full of stars. He got out of the car. It was a cold night, but warmer than before.

He felt frustrated. After trying in vain to find Chaperon and Perrault, they had also failed to find Chaperon's ex-wife. She had moved somewhere near Bordeaux, and their daughter lived in the Paris region. Serge Perrault had never married. Add to that the strange armed peace which reigned between Grimm and his dragon lady and you were left with the conclusion that family life really wasn't their thing, those three.

248

Servaz walked across the little humpbacked bridge that connected the mill to the road. Nearby, a paddlewheel turned in the darkness; he could hear the sound of water splashing along the blades.

He banged the door knocker. A low, very old, heavy door. It opened almost immediately. Gabriel Saint-Cyr stood there, wearing a white shirt, a cardigan and an impeccable bow tie. Strains of familiar music came from within. A string quartet: Schubert, *Death and the Maiden*.

'Come in.'

Servaz noticed that the retired judge had said *tu* to him, but he didn't respond. A pleasant smell from the kitchen teased his nostrils the moment he entered and his stomach reacted at once. He was famished; all he had eaten since morning was an omelette. Walking down the steps into the sitting room on the right, Servaz could not help but raise an eyebrow: the judge had gone all out. The tablecloth was so white it almost shone, and two candles flickered in silver candlesticks.

'I'm a widower,' explained Saint-Cyr on seeing Servaz's look. 'My work was my entire life. I wasn't prepared to stop. Whether I live ten more years or thirty, it won't change a thing. Old age is nothing but a long, useless wait. So, while I'm waiting, I keep busy. I wonder whether, all things considered, I shouldn't open a restaurant.'

Servaz smiled. The judge was clearly not the sort who could sit around doing nothing.

'But you can be sure of one thing – you don't mind if I say *tu* to you, at my age? – I don't think about death. And I make the most of the short time remaining to cook and cultivate my garden. I make things. Read. Travel . . .'

'And stop in at the courts from time to time to keep up with what's going on.'

There was a brief twinkle in Saint-Cyr's eyes.

'Exactly!'

He motioned to him to sit down, then went behind the kitchen counter which faced onto the room. Martin saw him tie a chef's apron round his waist. The fire was crackling in the hearth, casting a glow onto the ceiling beams. The sitting room was full of old furniture, probably unearthed at antique markets; there were paintings, large and small.

'"To cook one must have a light head, a generous spirit and a warm heart": Paul Gauguin. I hope you don't mind if we skip the aperitif?'

'Not at all,' replied Servaz. 'I'm starving.'

Saint-Cyr came back with two plates and a bottle of wine, displaying the ease of a professional waiter.

'*Feuilleté de ris de veau aux truffes*,' he announced, placing a large steaming plate before Servaz.

It smelled wonderful. Servaz stabbed his fork into the food and lifted a mouthful to his lips. It burned his tongue, but rarely had he eaten anything quite so delicious.

'Well?'

'If you were as good a judge as you are a chef, the courts in Saint-Martin have suffered a great loss.'

Saint-Cyr took the flattery for what it was. He was sufficiently aware of his talent as a chef to know that behind the exaggerated compliment there was sincere praise. He tilted a bottle of white wine towards Servaz's glass.

'Have a taste of that.'

Servaz raised the glass to his eyes before drinking. In the light from the candles the wine was the colour of pale gold. Servaz was no great connoisseur, but from the very first sip he knew beyond a doubt that the wine he had just been served was truly exceptional.

'It's wonderful. Really. Even if I'm no expert.'

Saint-Cyr nodded.

'Bâtard-Montrachet 2001.'

He winked at Servaz and clicked his tongue.

By the second sip, Servaz felt his head begin to spin. He shouldn't have started on an empty stomach.

'Are you hoping this will loosen my tongue?' he asked.

Saint-Cyr laughed.

'It's a pleasure to see you relishing your food like that. You look as if you haven't eaten in ten days. What do you think of Confiant?' asked the judge, suddenly changing tack.

His question caught Servaz off guard. He hesitated.

'I don't know. It's a bit too soon to say.'

Once again, the wily twinkle in the judge's eye.

'Of course it's not. You already have an opinion. And it's negative. That's why you don't want to talk about him.'

Servaz was thrown by his comment. The judge was never at a loss for words.

'Confiant's name doesn't suit him,' continued Saint-Cyr, without waiting for an answer. 'He shows no confidence in anyone, and one shouldn't show him any, either. As you may already have noticed.'

Touché. Once again, Servaz thought that this man would prove useful. When they had finished, Saint-Cyr cleared the plates.

'Rabbit in a mustard sauce,' he said when he came back. 'Will that do you?'

He had brought another bottle. Red, this time. Half an hour later, after an apple dessert accompanied by a glass of Sauternes, they were sitting in the armchairs by the fireplace. Servaz felt well fed and slightly tipsy, suffused with a feeling of well-being he had not known for a long time. Saint-Cyr served him some cognac in a balloon glass and poured himself an Armagnac.

Then he shot him a keen look and Servaz understood that the time had come to get down to business.

'You're also in charge of that incident with the dead horse,' declared the judge, after the first sip. 'Do you think there is any connection with the chemist?'

'Could be.'

'Two dreadful crimes in the space of a few days and only a few miles apart.'

'Yes.'

'What did you think of Éric Lombard?'

'Arrogant.'

'Don't get on the wrong side of him. He has a long arm and he could be useful to you. But don't let him run the investigation for you either.'

Servaz smiled once again. The judge might be retired, but he hadn't lost his touch.

'You were going to tell me about the suicides.'

Saint-Cyr raised his glass to his lips.

'Why would anyone become a cop these days?' he asked, without answering Servaz's question. 'Corruption is rife, and all anyone thinks about is filling their own pockets. How do you know what matters? Hasn't it become terribly complicated?'

'Oh, no, the opposite: it's very simple,' said Servaz. 'There are two sorts of people: bastards and everyone else. And everyone has to choose sides. If you haven't chosen, it means you're already on the side of the bastards.'

'Do you really think so? Things are that simple: good guys and bad guys? You're very fortunate. What if, for example, you have the choice at an election between three candidates: the first one is half paralysed by polio, suffers from high blood pressure and anaemia and numerous other serious illnesses, has been known to lie, consults an astrologist, cheats on his wife, is a chain-smoker and drinks too many martinis; the second one is obese, has already lost three elections, is going through a depression and has had two heart attacks, smokes cigars and in the evening glugs champagne, port, brandy and whisky before taking two sleeping tablets; and the third one is a decorated war hero who respects women, loves animals, might drink a beer from time to time and doesn't smoke. Which one would you choose?'

Servaz grinned.

'I suppose you expect me to say the third one?'

'Well done, you've just rejected Roosevelt and Churchill and elected Adolf Hitler. You see, things are never what they seem.'

Servaz burst out laughing. He really did like this man. Very hard to catch him napping, and his mind was as clear as the stream that flowed past his mill.

'And that's what's wrong with the media nowadays,' the judge continued. 'They latch on to details that are totally unimportant and blow them out of all proportion. With the end result that if today's media had existed back then, Roosevelt and Churchill would probably not have been elected. Trust your intuition, Martin. Don't trust appearances.'

'The suicides,' said Servaz again.

'I'm getting there.'

The judge poured himself another Armagnac, then gave Servaz a hard look.

'I was the examining magistrate on the case. The most difficult one of my entire career. It lasted for over a year. From May 1993 to July 1994, to be exact. Seven suicides. Teenagers between the ages of fifteen and eighteen. I remember it as if it were yesterday.'

Servaz held his breath. The judge's voice had changed, was filled now with infinite solemnity and sadness.

'The first one to die was a child from a neighbouring village, Alice Ferrand, sixteen and a half. A brilliant kid, top marks at school. She came from an educated background: her father was a literature professor, her mother a schoolteacher. Alice was considered an easy

252

child. She had friends her own age; she liked drawing and music; everyone thought highly of her. They found her hanging in a barn on the morning of 2 May 1993.'

Hanging ... Servaz's throat tightened, but his attention grew sharper.

'I know what you're thinking,' said Saint-Cyr, meeting Servaz's gaze, 'but I can assure you that she hanged herself, there was no doubt. The pathologist was categorical. It was Delmas, you know him, he's a competent fellow. And they found a clue in the girl's desk drawer: a sketch she had made of the barn, which even included the exact length of the rope she needed to be sure that her little feet would not touch the ground.'

The judge choked on these last words. Servaz could see he was on the verge of tears.

'A heartbreaking affair. She was such a sweet child. When a seventeen-year-old boy took his life five weeks later, on 7 June, everyone thought it was just a terrible coincidence. But by the third one, at the end of the month, people were beginning to wonder.'

He finished his Armagnac and put the glass down on the coffee table.

'I remember that one, too, as if it were yesterday. That summer there was a heatwave in June and July, magnificent weather, endless warm evenings. People lingered in their gardens, by the river or in the outdoor cafés, just to find some cool air. It was too hot if you lived in a flat. They didn't have air-conditioning back in those days – or mobile phones, either. That evening, 29 June, I was in a café with Cathy d'Humières's predecessor and a deputy prosecutor. The café owner came looking for me. He pointed to the telephone on the counter. It was a call for me. The gendarmerie. "They've found another one," they said. I immediately understood what that meant.'

Servaz was feeling colder and colder.

'The boy hanged himself too. In a ruined barn at the end of a field of wheat. I remember every detail: the summer evening, the ripe wheat and the day that seemed to go on and on, the heat baking the stone even at ten o'clock in the evening, the flies, the body in the shadow of the barn. I came over faint. They had to take me to hospital. Then I went on with the case. As I said, I've never had a more difficult matter to deal with: a terrible ordeal. The grief of the families, the incomprehension, the fear it might happen again . . .'

'Does anyone know why they did it? Did they leave any explanation?'

The judge looked at Servaz with an expression that, even now, was bewildered.

'Not the slightest idea. We never found out what had been going through their heads. Not a single one left an explanation. Obviously everyone was traumatised. You would get up in the morning afraid you would find out about another suicide. No one ever understood why it happened here, in our part of the world. And of course parents were terrified. They tried as best they could to keep an eye on their children, without the kids knowing – or they simply didn't allow them to go out. It lasted for more than a year. Seven in all. *Seven!* And then, one fine day, it stopped.'

'What an incredible story,' said Servaz.

'Not really all that incredible. Since then, I've heard of similar events in other countries – Wales, Quebec, Japan. Suicide pacts among teenagers. Nowadays, it's worse: they can contact each other over the Internet; they send each other messages through forums: "My life has no meaning, seek partner to die with." I'm not exaggerating. In the case of the suicides in Wales, they found other notes among the letters of condolence and the poems, messages that said, "I'll be with you soon" . . . Who could imagine such a thing was possible?'

'I think that in the world we live in now, everything is possible,' said Servaz. 'Particularly the worst.'

An image came to his mind: a boy walking through a wheatfield with a heavy step, the setting sun at his back and a rope in his hand. All around him the birds were singing, the long summer evening was bursting with life – but in his mind there was already nothing but darkness.

The judge looked gloomily at Servaz. 'Yes, that's also my opinion. As regards our young people, they didn't leave any explanation for what they'd done, but we do have proof that they encouraged each other to go through with it.'

'What do you mean?'

'The gendarmerie found batches of letters in the homes of several of the suicide victims. They'd all written to each other. In their letters they spoke about their plans, how they would go about it, even their eagerness for it. The problem was that the letters were not sent by post, and they all used pseudonyms. When they were found, we decided to take the fingerprints of all the adolescents in the area between the ages of thirteen and nineteen, and compare them with the prints found on the letters. We also used a graphologist. A long, painstaking job. An entire team of investigators were on it twenty-four hours a day. Some of the letters had been written by children who had already died. But we were able to identify three new candidates. Incredible, I know. We put them under constant surveillance and had them work with a team of psychologists. One of them still managed to electrocute himself in his bathtub with a hair dryer. He was the seventh victim . . . The other two never went through with it.'

'And the letters?'

'I kept them. Do you really think there could be any connection between this business and the chemist's murder and Lombard's horse?'

'Grimm was found hanging . . .' suggested Servaz cautiously.

'And the horse, too, after a fashion . . .'

Servaz felt a familiar tingling: the feeling that a decisive step had been taken. But towards what? The judge stood up. He left the room and then came back a few minutes later with a heavy box filled to overflowing with documents and binders.

'It's all here. The letters, a copy of the case file, expert evaluations. Please, don't open it here.'

Servaz nodded as he looked at the box.

'Did they have anything in common? Other than the suicides and the letters? Did they belong to a gang, a group?'

'Oh, you can be sure we checked into that, followed up on every lead, moved heaven and earth. No luck. The youngest one was fifteen and a half years old, the oldest eighteen; they weren't in the same class, they didn't like the same things, and they didn't take part in the same activities. Some of them knew each other well, others hardly at all. The only thing they had in common was their social background, and even then . . . they all came from modest or middle-class families. None of them belonged to the wealthy bourgeoisie of Saint-Martin.'

Servaz could tell how frustrated the judge must be. He could imagine the hundreds of hours he had spent following the most insignificant leads, the tiniest clues, trying to understand something so incomprehensible. The case had mattered a great deal in the life of Gabriel Saint-Cyr. Perhaps it had even been the cause of his health problems and his premature retirement. He knew the judge would take his questions with him to the grave. He would never stop wondering.

'Are there any theories that are not in this box but that you considered?' Servaz asked suddenly, now beginning to say *tu* to the judge as well, as if his story had brought them closer together. 'A hunch you gave up on for lack of proof?'

The judge seemed to hesitate.

'Of course we had a great number of theories,' he said cautiously. 'But not one had even an inkling of proof. Not one was substantial. It is the greatest mystery of my entire career. I suppose that all examining magistrates and investigators have at least one such puzzle – the case they didn't solve. The one that will haunt them until the end of their days. A case that has left them with a permanent aftertaste of frustration – and which seems to cancel out all the successes.'

'That's true,' said Servaz. 'Everyone has their unsolved mystery. And in those cases there is always one lead that is more significant than the others. A vague idea that hasn't panned out, but we go on feeling that it might have led somewhere, if only we'd been lucky, or if the investigation had turned out differently. So there was nothing like that, really? Something that isn't in the box?'

The judge took a deep breath and looked Servaz straight in the eye. Once again he seemed to hesitate. He brought his bushy brows together, then said, 'Yes, there was one hypothesis I particularly liked. But I couldn't find a single thing, no testimony to support it. So it stayed in here,' he added, tapping his skull with his index finger.

'Les Isards Holiday Camp,' said Saint-Cyr. 'Maybe you've heard of it?'

Servaz allowed the words to wander through his brain until the memory pinged like a coin dropped in a piggy bank: the abandoned buildings, the rusty sign on the road to the Institute. He recalled his reaction at the sight of that sinister place.

'We went by it on our way to the Institute. It's all boarded up, right?'

'Exactly. But the camp was in operation for several decades.

It was opened after the war, and only stopped taking in children at the end of the 1990s.'

He paused.

'Les Isards was set up for children from Saint-Martin and the surrounding area who couldn't afford real summer holidays. It was run partly by the municipality, a director was appointed, and they took in kids between eight and fifteen. The usual activities: hiking on the mountain, ball games, physical exercise, swimming in the nearby lakes . . .'

The judge grimaced, as if he had a toothache coming on.

'What got me interested in the place was the fact that five of the suicide victims had been at the camp. And it was within the two years preceding their suicide. In fact, that was almost the only thing they had in common. When I took a closer look, I found they had all been there for two consecutive summers. And that the director of the camp had changed the year before the first summer.'

Servaz was rapt with attention. He could guess where the judge was heading.

'So, I began to look into the background of the director – a young man in his thirties – but I couldn't find anything. He was married, had a little girl and a little boy, an uneventful life . . .'

'And do you know where he is now?' asked Servaz.

'In the cemetery. He had a motorcycle accident, collided with an artic ten years ago or so. But I couldn't find anything anywhere suggesting that the teenagers might have been sexually abused. And besides, two of the suicide victims hadn't even been to the camp. Moreover, given the number of local kids who went there, it's not at all surprising several of them would have that in common. So I finally gave up on that lead . . .'

'But you go on thinking you might have been on to something?'

Saint-Cyr looked up. His eyes were sparkling.

'Yes.'

'You mentioned the complaint filed against Grimm and the other three that was almost immediately withdrawn – I suppose you questioned them, too, during the investigation into the suicides, no?'

'Why should I? There was no connection.'

'You're sure you didn't think about them at any point?' asked Servaz.

Saint-Cyr seemed to hesitate yet again.

257

'No, of course I did . . .'

'Can you explain?'

'This business with the sexual blackmail wasn't the first rumour to go round about those four. There were others, both before and after. But never anything that led to an official complaint, other than that one time.'

'What sort of rumours?'

'Rumours implying that other girls had been subjected to the same sort of treatment – and that for some of them it ended badly, that the boys had a tendency to drink, and once they were drunk they became violent – that sort of thing. But the girls in question were all of age, or almost. Whereas the suicide victims were children. So I rejected that theory. And besides, there was no shortage of rumours in those days.'

'And was it true? About Grimm and the others?'

'Perhaps it was . . . but I wouldn't bank on it: things are the same here as anywhere else. There are untold numbers of self-proclaimed gossips and nosy-parkers who are prepared to spread terrible stories about their neighbours just to pass the time of day. And they'll make them up if need be. It proves nothing. There is an element of truth in there, I'm convinced, but the rumour was probably exaggerated every time someone new got hold of it.'

Servaz nodded.

'But you're right to wonder whether the chemist's murder is connected in some way with this ancient history,' continued the judge. 'Everything that happens in this valley has its roots in the past. If you want to find out the truth, you must leave no stone unturned – and look carefully at what you find underneath.'

'And what about Hirtmann's role in all this?'

The judge gave him a thoughtful look.

'That is what, back in my working days, I would call the "detail that doesn't fit". There was always one in every case: an element that obstinately refused to fit into the puzzle. Rule it out and everything made sense. But it was still there. It refused to go away. It meant that something, somewhere had escaped us. Sometimes it was important. Sometimes it wasn't. Some judges and cops decide outright to ignore it; that's often the way a judicial error is born. As for me, I never overlooked that detail. But I didn't allow myself to become obsessed by it, either.'

Servaz looked at his watch and got to his feet.

'It's a pity you and I are not on this case together,' he said. 'I'd much rather be working with you than with Confiant.'

'Thank you,' said Saint-Cyr, getting up in turn. 'I think we would have made a good team.'

He gestured at the table, the kitchen and the empty glasses on the coffee table.

'Allow me to make a suggestion. Whenever you have to stay overnight in Saint-Martin, you will be my guest for dinner. That way you won't be obliged to eat that disgusting hotel food or go to bed on an empty stomach.'

Servaz smiled.

'If it's always this generous, before long I won't be able to conduct any more investigations.'

Gabriel Saint-Cyr gave a hearty laugh, banishing the tension that had lingered from his story.

'Let's say that was an inaugural meal. I wanted to impress you with my culinary talents. The next one will be more frugal, I promise. We have to keep the commandant in shape.'

'In that case, I accept.'

'At the same time,' added the judge with a wink, 'we'll be able to discuss how you're getting on with the investigation. Within the limits of what you can tell me, naturally. Or shall we say, from a theoretical rather than practical point of view. It never hurts to have to justify your conclusions to another person.'

Servaz knew the judge was right. He had no intention of telling him everything. But he was aware of the fact that Saint-Cyr, with his sharp mind and professional logic, could prove very useful. And if there were a connection with the suicides, the former judge would have a lot to tell him.

They shook hands warmly, and Servaz went back out into the night. When he reached the little bridge, he saw it was snowing again. He took a deep breath of night air to sober up a little, and felt the wet snowflakes on his cheeks. He had nearly reached the car when the phone in his pocket vibrated.

'Something's come up,' said Ziegler.

Servaz stiffened. He looked at the mill on the other side of the stream. The judge's silhouette went by the window, carrying plates and cutlery.

259

'We found some blood at the crime scene that didn't belong to Grimm. The DNA has just been identified.'

Servaz felt as if an abyss had just opened at his feet. He swallowed. He knew what she was going to say.

'It's Hirtmann's.'

It was past midnight at the Institute when Diane heard the tiny creak. She was not asleep, but in bed with her eyes open – fully clothed. She turned her head and saw the ray of light under her door. Then she heard the muffled steps.

She got up.

Why was she doing this? She didn't have to. She opened the door a crack.

The corridor was dark again, but the stairway at the end was lit. She glanced in the other direction, then went out. She was wearing jeans, a jumper and slippers. How would she justify her presence in the corridors at this time of night if she ran into someone? She reached the stairs. Listened again. The echo of furtive footsteps going down. They did not stop on either the third or the second floor. Finally on the first floor the footsteps came to a halt. Diane froze, without daring to lean over the banister.

A click.

Whoever she was following had just entered the access code to the first floor. There was one security box per floor, except the top floor, where the staff sleeping quarters were. She heard the door to the first floor give a buzz, open, then close again. Was she really doing this, tailing someone in the dead of night?

She went as far as the security door, where she hesitated, then counted up to ten. She was about to put in the code when something occurred to her.

The cameras.

Surveillance cameras were installed wherever the patients slept or could move about. At every strategic spot, on the ground floor as well as the first, second and third floors. There were no cameras, however, in the service stairs, which were off limits to the residents, or around the staff quarters. Everywhere else the cameras kept a close watch. If she carried on following the night wanderer, she would find herself recorded at some point or another . . .

So the person ahead of her was not afraid of being filmed. But if the cameras were to capture Diane's passage in their wake, she would be the one to look suspicious.

She had got no further with her deliberations when she heard footsteps on the other side of the door. She barely had the time to hurry to the stairway and hide before the biometric security lock buzzed again.

For a split second fear gripped her heart. But instead of going back up to the staff quarters, her quarry continued downstairs. Diane hesitated only a second.

You're insane!

When she got to the door on the ground floor, she stopped. There was no one in sight. Where were they? If they had gone into the common rooms, Diane would have heard the security lock buzz again. She almost failed to notice the door to the basement, on her left at the bottom of a final flight of stairs: the door was slowly closing . . . There was only a fixed doorknob on this side, so it could not be opened without a key. Diane rushed forward and slipped her hand into the space, just in time to stop the heavy metal door from clicking shut.

She struggled to swing it open.

Beyond, she could see more steps, concrete this time. They led into the dark depths of the basement. A dozen or so steps to a landing, then down again in the opposite direction. A steep staircase, peeling walls.

She hesitated.

It was one thing to follow someone along the corridors of the Institute; if she were caught, she could always say she'd stayed late in her office and lost her way. But it was another thing altogether to follow that same person into the basement.

She heard the footsteps continue.

Diane made up her mind, and let the heavy door close behind her. On the basement side, the metal door could be opened thanks to a horizontal safety bolt. It made a slight click as it locked. A damp chill enfolded her, along with a dank smell. She began to go down the steps. She had reached the second flight when all of a sudden the light went out. Her foot missed the next step. She lost her balance and with a little cry fell hard against the wall. Wincing with pain, she lifted her hand to her shoulder. Then she held her breath. The footsteps had stopped! Fear – which until now had been no more than a vague presence at the edge of her mind – overwhelmed her. Her heart was pounding in her chest; all she could hear was the blood throbbing in her eardrums. She was about to turn round when the footsteps started again. They were receding . . . Diane looked down. It was not completely dark: a faint, ghostly glow came up the stairway and spread against the walls like a fine layer of yellow paint. She continued on her way down, placing each foot cautiously, and eventually she came to a long, poorly lit corridor.

Pipes and bundles of electric wiring beneath the ceiling; rust streaks and black mouldy stains on the walls.

The basement . . . Not a place many of the staff members were likely to have visited.

The stale air, the terrible chill and damp made her think of a tomb.

The sounds – the fading footsteps, water dripping from the ceiling, the hum of a faraway ventilation system: it was all terrifyingly real.

She shivered, as if an icy hand were caressing her spine. Should she go on or not? The place was like a labyrinth, with its intersections and corridors. Mastering her emotion, she tried to determine which direction the footsteps had gone. They were becoming fainter and fainter, and the light, too, was dimming: she had to hurry. She reached the next corner and peered round it. *There was a silhouette at the end* . . . She barely had time to catch a glimpse of it before it disappeared to the right.

Diane could now see that the wavering, irregular light in the corridor had come from an electric torch.

Her throat tight, she rushed onwards, not to be alone in the dark. She was trembling, from cold or fear. *This is madness! What am I doing here?* She had absolutely nothing with which to defend herself. She also had to be careful where she put her feet: here and there the corridors, even though they were wide, were almost completely blocked by piles of old things: bed bases and mattresses propped up against the walls, chipped sinks, broken chairs, boxes, defunct computers and televisions. What was more, the silhouette continually swerved left and right, going ever deeper into the bowels of the Institute, and it was only thanks to the trembling light left in the night visitor's wake that Diane was able to guess where her quarry had gone. She was tempted to give up and go back the way she had come, but she knew it was already too late. She would never find her way out in the darkness! She wondered what would happen if she pressed a light switch, whether all these underground passages would suddenly be lit. The person would know they were being followed. How would they react? Would they retrace their steps? Diane had no other option but to follow the glimmering light. All around her, in almost total darkness, there was the sound of tiny claws scraping the ground. *Rats!* They scurried out of her way. Diane felt the weight of darkness on her shoulders.

It was increasingly obvious that she was being reckless. Why hadn't she stayed in her room?

Suddenly she heard the creak of a metal door; then it closed again and she found herself in complete darkness. As if she had suddenly been blinded. She was completely disoriented. She could not see her body, or her feet, or her hands . . . nothing but black on black. An impenetrable obscurity. The blood was pounding in her ears, and she tried to swallow, but her mouth was dry. She turned this way and that, in vain. There was still a dull hum from the ventilation, and water running somewhere, but these sounds seemed as far away and useless to her as a foghorn to a ship sinking on a stormy night. Then she remembered that she always kept her phone in her jeans pocket. She reached for it with a trembling hand. The light from the screen was even dimmer than she had feared. It hardly lit her fingertips. She started moving until the pitiful halo found something else to light besides her own hand: a wall. Or at least a few square centimetres of concrete. She followed the wall slowly for several minutes, until she saw a light switch. The neon lights flickered, then spread electric daylight through the basement, and she rushed towards the place where she had heard the door slam. It was identical to the one she had come through earlier. She pulled back the security bolt, then paused to consider the fact that once she was on the other side there would be no way for her to go back. She took several steps back until she found a board lying among the scrap, and wedged it in the door once she had gone through.

A stairway and a window. She recognised them at once. She had already been here. She went up the first few steps, then stopped. There was no need to go any further. At the top there was a camera that she knew. And a thick armoured security door, with a window.

Someone was going into Unit A every night.

Someone was using the service stairs and basement to avoid the cameras. Except for the one above the armoured door . . . Diane's palms were damp, her guts tied in a knot. She knew what this meant: whoever it was had an accomplice among the guards in Unit A.

Then she told herself that perhaps it was nothing. Perhaps there were staff members who, instead of sleeping, were playing poker unbeknown to everyone else; perhaps one of the staff was having a clandestine affair with Mr Atlas. But deep down she knew it was something else altogether. She had heard too much. She was in a place where death and madness reigned. Except that neither one was under control the way she had expected: inexplicably, they had managed to escape from their box. Something sinister was going on here, and whether she liked it or not, by coming to the Institute, she had entered the game.

18

By the time Servaz parked outside the gendarmerie the snow was falling thick and fast. The officer at the duty desk was dozing. They had already lowered the shutters and he had to raise them again to let Servaz in. Holding the heavy box out in front of him, Servaz headed for the incident room; the corridors were silent and deserted. It was almost midnight.

'In here,' said a voice just as he was walking past a door.

He stopped and looked through the open door. Irène Ziegler was sitting at a little desk in the half-light. Only one lamp was lit. Ziegler yawned and stretched. She must have fallen asleep while waiting for him. She looked at the box, then smiled. At this late hour, he found her smile charming.

'What's all that?'

'A box.'

'I can see that. What's in it?'

'Everything about the suicides.'

There was a gleam of surprise and interest in her green eyes.

'Saint-Cyr gave it to you?'

'Want a coffee?' he asked, putting the heavy box on the nearest desk.

'Espresso, with sugar. Thanks.'

He went out to the coffee machine at the end of the corridor, and came back with two polystyrene cups.

'Here, Irène,' he said.

She looked at him, surprised.

'I think it's time we called each other by our first names, no?' he said, by way of an apology, thinking of how informal the judge had been with him. Why the devil shouldn't he be the same? Was it the late hour, or the smile she had just given him that had suddenly prompted him to take the initiative?

He saw Ziegler smile again.

'All right. So, how was dinner? Informative, it seems.'

'You go first.'

'No, you go first.'

He perched on the edge of the desk and saw she'd been playing patience on the computer. Then he began his story. Ziegler listened with interest, without interrupting.

'What an incredible story,' she said when he had finished.

'I'm surprised you've never heard about it.'

She frowned and blinked.

'It does sound vaguely familiar. A few articles in the papers, perhaps. Or conversations between my parents at dinner. May I remind you that I hadn't joined the gendarmerie yet. In fact, at the time I was probably about the same age as the victims.'

It suddenly occurred to him that he knew nothing about her. Not even where she lived. And that she knew nothing about him, either. For a week now, all their conversations had been about the investigation.

'But you live not far from here,' he insisted.

'My parents lived fifteen kilometres or so from Saint-Martin, in another valley. I didn't go to school here. When you were young, if you were from another valley, it was like being from another world. Fifteen kilometres for a kid is like a thousand for an adult: every teenager has his or her territory. At the time of the events I was taking the school bus twenty kilometres further west – I went to the lycée in Lannemezan, forty kilometres from here. Then I studied law in Pau. Now that you mention it, I do remember schoolyard gossip about these suicides. I suppose I blocked it out.'

He sensed that she didn't like talking about her youth and he wondered why.

'It would be interesting to get Propp's opinion,' he said.

'His opinion about what?'

'About why your memory blocked it.'

She gave him a wry look.

'And this business with the suicides: is there any connection with Grimm?'

'There might not be any, no.'

'So why is it of interest?'

'Grimm's murder seems like revenge, and something or someone drove those children to put an end to their lives. There were charges brought years ago against Grimm, Perrault and Chaperon for some business involving sexual blackmail . . . If we put the pieces together, what do we get?'

Servaz suddenly felt something like an electric charge go through him: *they were on to something.* It was there, within reach. The dark heart of the story, the critical mass – from which everything radiated. Somewhere, hidden behind a blind spot . . . He felt the adrenaline rushing through his veins.

'I suggest we start by having a look at what's in this box,' he said with a slight tremor in his voice.

'Shall we get going?' she asked, but it was hardly a question.

He saw the same hope and excitement on her face. He checked his watch; it was almost one o'clock in the morning.

'All right. And the blood,' he added, abruptly changing the subject, 'where exactly did they find it?'

She looked troubled.

'On the bridge, not far from where the chemist was strung up.'

They sat for a few moments without speaking.

'Blood,' he said again. 'It seems impossible.'

'The lab is categorical.'

'Blood . . . as if—'

'As if Hirtmann had hurt himself while hanging up Grimm's body.'

Ziegler took over. She rummaged about in the box full of folders, binders, notepads and administrative correspondence until she unearthed a file entitled *Summary*. Obviously, it had been written by Saint-Cyr himself; the judge had legible, fine, quick handwriting, the very opposite of a doctor's scribble. Servaz saw that he had summed up the various stages of the investigation with remarkable clarity. Ziegler used the summary in order to find her way through the jumble. She began by removing the different elements and spreading them into small piles: autopsy reports, summaries of hearings, interviews with parents, the list of exhibits, letters found in the adolescents' homes. Saint-Cyr had photocopied all the documents relative to the case, for his personal use. In addition to the photocopies there were press cuttings, Post-its, loose pages, for each adolescent a map indicating where the suicide had been committed, but also mysterious itineraries made of arrows and red circles, school reports, class photos, notes scribbled on scraps of paper, toll receipts.

Servaz was dumbfounded. Clearly the old judge had made this case into a personal crusade. Like other investigators before him, he had allowed himself to become completely obsessed by the mystery. Did he really hope to uncover the true story in his home, when he would have nothing else to do and could devote all his time to it?

Then they found another even more troubling document: the list of the seven victims, with their photographs and the dates of their suicides.

2 May 1993: Alice Ferrand, 16
17 June 1993: Michaël Lehmann, 17
29 June 1993: Ludovic Asselin, 16
5 September 1993: Marion Dutilleul, 15
24 December 1993: Séverine Guérin, 18
16 April 1994: Damien Llaume, 16
9 July 1994: Florian Vanloot, 17

'Sweet Jesus.'

His hand was trembling when he spread them out on the desk in the halo of light: seven photographs stapled to seven little index cards that Ziegler had handed to him. Seven smiling faces. Some were facing the camera; others were looking away. He glanced over at his colleague. Standing next to him, she seemed distraught. Servaz focused again on the faces before him. He could feel his throat tighten.

Ziegler handed him half of the autopsy reports and immersed herself in the other half. For a while they read in silence. Unsurprisingly, the reports concluded that the cause of death was hanging, except in the case of one victim, who threw herself from the top of a mountain, and that of the boy who was under surveillance yet managed to electrocute himself in the bath. The pathologists had not discovered anything unusual, no grey areas; the 'crime' scenes were perfectly straightforward; everything confirmed that each teenager had gone alone to the place of death and had acted alone. Four of the autopsies had been carried out by Delmas and the rest by another pathologist whom Servaz knew and who was equally competent. After the autopsies, they went on to the house-to-house enquiries. The purpose had been to learn more about the victims' personalities, independent of the parents' testimonies. As always, there were a few examples of sordid or malicious gossip, but, on the whole, the portraits they drew were of typical adolescents, except in the case of one difficult boy,

Ludovic Asselin, who had been known to be violent with friends and rebellious towards authority. The most moving testimonies were those regarding Alice Ferrand, the first victim, whom everyone seemed to adore. Servaz looked at her photograph: curly hair the colour of ripe wheat, porcelain skin, staring at the camera with lovely, serious eyes. A very pretty face, where every detail seemed to have been sculpted with precision; the face of a lovely young girl of sixteen – but her expression was that of a much older person. A gaze full of intelligence. There was something else there, too . . . or was it his imagination?

By three o'clock in the morning they were showing the strain. Servaz decided to take a break. He went down the corridor and into the toilets, and splashed some cold water over his face. Then he stood up straight and looked at himself in the mirror; one of the neon lights was flickering and crackling, casting a gloomy light onto the row of doors behind him. He had had too much to eat and drink at Saint-Cyr's; he was exhausted and it was obvious. He went into one of the stalls, relieved himself, rinsed his hands and dried them. On his way back he stopped at the vending machine.

'Want a coffee?' he shouted down the deserted corridor.

His voice echoed in the silence. The answer came to him through the open door at the far end.

'Espresso! With sugar, thanks!'

He wondered if there was anyone else in the building, apart from the two of them and the officer at the duty desk. He knew the gendarmes had their lodgings in another wing. He carried the coffee across the dark cafeteria, weaving his way among the round tables painted yellow, red and blue. Beyond the picture window protected by a diamond-shaped metal grille the snow was falling silently into a little garden. Neatly trimmed hedges, a sandbox and a plastic slide for the children of the gendarmes who lived there. Past the garden there were white fields, and in the distance, stark against the black sky, the mountains. Once again he thought of the Institute and its inmates. And Hirtmann . . . *his blood on the bridge.* What did it mean? 'There is always one detail that doesn't fit,' Saint-Cyr had said. Sometimes it was important, sometimes not . . .

It was five thirty in the morning when Servaz leaned back in his office chair and declared that that was enough. Ziegler looked exhausted. The frustration was legible on her face. Nothing. There was absolutely nothing in the file to give credence to the theory of sexual abuse. Not the slightest embryo of a clue. In his final report, Saint-Cyr had reached the same conclusion. In the margin, in pencil, he had written: *'Sexual abuse? No proof.'* But all the same he had underlined the question, twice. At one point Servaz had been tempted to mention the holiday camp to Ziegler, but he'd given up on the idea. He was too tired; he simply didn't have the strength.

Ziegler checked her watch.

'I don't think we're going to get anywhere tonight. We should go and get some sleep.'

'Fine by me. I'm going back to the hotel. Meet you in the incident room at ten o'clock. Where are you staying?'

'Here. They've lent me a flat belonging to a gendarme who's on leave. It saves the administration money.'

Servaz nodded.

'These days you can't be too thrifty, right?'

'I don't think I've ever been on an investigation like this,' said Ziegler, getting to her feet. 'First a dead horse, then a chemist hanging under a bridge. And only one thing to connect the two: the DNA of a serial killer . . . And now, teenagers killing themselves one after the other. It's like a bad dream. There's no logic, no vital lead. Perhaps I'll wake up and find out none of it ever existed.'

'There will be an awakening,' said Servaz firmly. 'But not for us: for the culprit, or culprits. And before much more time goes by.'

He went out with a brisk stride.

That night he dreamt about his father. In his dream Servaz was a little boy, ten years old. Everything was bathed in the warm, pleasant glow of a summer evening, and his father was just a silhouette, like the two people he was talking to outside the house. On drawing nearer, the young Servaz saw two very old men wearing long white togas. Both of them were bearded. Servaz slipped in among them and looked up, but the three men paid no attention to him. On listening more closely, he realised they were speaking Latin. A very animated but friendly discussion. At one point his father laughed, then became serious again. There was music coming from the house, familiar music that Servaz couldn't recognise.

Then in the night there came the sound, from the road, of a motor in the distance, and the three men suddenly fell silent.

'They're coming,' said one of the old men finally.

His tone was funereal and, in his dream, Servaz began to tremble.

Servaz got to the gendarmerie ten minutes late. He'd had his big mug of black coffee, two cigarettes and a scorching shower to banish the fatigue that was threatening to do him in. His throat was still burning. Ziegler was already there. Once again she was wearing the leather and titanium jumpsuit that made him think of a modern suit of armour, and he recalled seeing her motorcycle outside the gendarmerie. They arranged to visit the parents of the suicide victims and divided the addresses up. Three for Servaz, four for Ziegler. Servaz decided to start with the first one on the list: Alice Ferrand. The house wasn't in Saint-Martin but in a neighbouring village. He expected to find a modest home, elderly parents broken by sorrow. So he was amazed to find himself face to face with a smiling, vigorous man still in the prime of life, who greeted him barefoot and barechested, wearing nothing but a pair of off-white linen trousers that were held up by a drawstring.

Servaz was so disconcerted that when it came time to introduce himself and explain the reason for his visit, he mumbled incoherently.

Alice's father immediately grew suspicious.

'Do you have a card?'

'Here.'

The man examined it carefully. Then he relaxed and handed it back.

'I just wanted to make sure you weren't one of those newspaper hacks who occasionally drag up the story when they've run out of copy,' he apologised. 'Come in.'

Gaspard Ferrand stood to one side to let Servaz go by. He was tall and thin. The cop couldn't help but notice his suntanned torso: not an ounce of fat, just a few strands of grey hair on his sternum; the skin was burnished and taut over his ribcage like the canvas of an awning. Ferrand intercepted his gaze.

'Please forgive my appearance, I was doing a bit of yoga. Yoga has helped me a lot since Alice died – as has Buddhism.'

Initially surprised, Servaz then recalled that Alice's father was not an office worker or a labourer like the other parents, but a literature professor. He immediately pictured a man who must enjoy extensive holidays and was fond of exotic destinations: Bali, Phuket, the Caribbean, Rio de Janeiro or the Maldives.

'I'm surprised the police are still interested in the case.'

'I'm actually investigating the murder of the chemist, Grimm.'

Ferrand turned round. Servaz saw he looked puzzled.

'And you think there is some sort of connection between Grimm's death and the suicide of my daughter and the other young people?'

'That is what I'm trying to find out.'

Gaspard Ferrand studied him closely.

'At first glance, there doesn't seem to be any obvious connection. Why do you think there might be one?'

An astute remark. Servaz hesitated to reply. Gaspard Ferrand must have seen how awkward his visitor felt – and also that they stood facing each other in a narrow corridor, that he was bare-chested and his visitor was bundled up for winter weather. He pointed to the door open to the sitting room.

'Tea, coffee?'

'Coffee, if it's no bother.'

'Not at all. I'll have tea myself. Please have a seat while I get it ready,' he said, disappearing into the kitchen on the other side of the corridor. 'Make yourself at home.'

Servaz had not expected such a warm welcome. Clearly, Alice's father liked having visits, even from a cop who had come to question him about his long-dead daughter. He looked around. The sitting room was a mess. Just like at his place, there were books and magazines piled everywhere: on the coffee table, the armchairs, the furniture. And the dust . . . Did he live alone? Was Gaspard Ferrand a widower, or divorced? That might explain his eagerness to entertain a visitor. There was an envelope from Action Against Hunger lying on a dresser; Servaz recognised the blue logo and the grey recycled paper: he too donated to the charity. In a frame were several pictures of Alice's father in the company of people who looked like Latin American or Asian peasants, against a background of jungle or rice paddies. Servaz suspected that Gaspard Ferrand's travels did not consist solely of deep-sea diving, daiquiris or soaking up the sun on Caribbean beaches.

He relaxed into the sofa. Nearby there was a pile of books on a fine elephant stool made of dark wood. Servaz tried to remember the African name for the stool: *esono dwa* . . .

The smell of coffee wafted down the corridor. Ferrand reappeared carrying a tray with two steaming mugs, sugar, sugar tongs and a photograph album, which he handed to Servaz after he had set the tray down on the coffee table.

'Here.'

Servaz opened the album. As he expected, it was full of photos of Alice: Alice at the age of four in a pedal car; Alice watering the flowers with a watering can nearly as big as she was; Alice and her mother, a slender, dreamy woman with a large nose like Virginia Woolf; Alice at the age of ten, in shorts, playing football with boys her age, rushing with the ball at her feet towards the opposite goal with a determined look . . . A regular tomboy. And a charming, luminous little girl. Gaspard Ferrand sank into the sofa next to him. He had put on a shirt with a Mao collar, the same off-white colour as his trousers.

'Alice was a wonderful child. So easy to get along with, always cheerful and helpful. She was our ray of sunshine.'

Ferrand continued to smile, as if recalling Alice's memory were pleasant, not painful.

'She was also a very intelligent child. Talented at so many things: drawing, music, languages, sports, writing . . . She devoured books. At the age of twelve she already knew what she wanted to do with her life: become a millionaire, then redistribute her money to the people who needed it the most.'

Gaspard Ferrand let out a strange, shrill laugh.

'We have never understood why she did it.'

This time the crack was there. But Ferrand pulled himself together.

'Why does life take away the best thing we have, then make us live with the loss? I've been asking myself that question for fifteen years; now I've found the answer.'

Ferrand gave him a look that was so strange that for a moment Servaz wondered whether Alice's father had lost his reason.

'But it's an answer that each of us has to find inside. What I mean is, no one can teach it to you or answer for you.'

Gaspard Ferrand probed him with a sharp gaze to see if he had understood. Servaz felt extremely ill at ease.

'But I'm putting you on the spot,' said his host. 'Forgive me. This is what happens when you live alone. My wife died of cancer, very abruptly, two years after Alice left us. So, you're interested in this spate of suicides from fifteen years ago, even though you're investigating the chemist's murder. Why is that?'

Without answering, Servaz said, 'Did none of the children leave a note?'

'No. But that doesn't mean there wasn't one. An explanation, I mean. There was a reason for all those suicides; those kids killed themselves for a very precise reason. It wasn't simply that they thought life wasn't worth living.'

Servaz wondered whether he had heard the rumours about Grimm, Perrault, Chaperon and Mourrenx.

'Had Alice changed in any way in the time leading up to her suicide?'

Ferrand nodded.

'Yes. We didn't realise right away. We noticed the changes gradually: she didn't laugh as much as she used to; she got angry more often; she spent more time in her bedroom . . . things like that. One day she wanted to stop playing the piano. She didn't talk to us about her plans the way she used to.'

Servaz felt as if ice were flowing through his veins. He remembered the call he had got from Alexandra. And saw again the bruise on Margot's cheek.

'And you don't know exactly when it began?'

Ferrand hesitated. Servaz got the strange feeling that Alice's father had a very precise idea of when it had started, but was reluctant to talk about it.

'It was several months before the suicide, I'd say. My wife put the changes down to puberty.'

'And you? Was that also your opinion? That the changes were natural?'

Ferrand shot him another strange look.

'No,' he replied firmly after a moment.

'What happened to her, do you think?'

Alice's father was silent for so long that Servaz nearly reached out to grab his arm and shake him.

'I don't know,' he said without taking his eyes from Servaz, 'but I am sure something happened. Someone in this valley knows why our children committed suicide.'

Something about his reply, and the tone he had adopted, was so enigmatic that it immediately got Servaz thinking. He was just about to ask his host to be more precise when his mobile vibrated in his pocket.

'Please excuse me,' said Servaz, getting to his feet.

It was Maillard. He sounded tense.

'We've just had a very strange phone call. Someone disguising his voice. He wanted to speak to you. He said it was very urgent, that he had information about Grimm's murder. But he would only speak to you. We get calls like this now and again, of course, but . . . I don't know . . . This one seemed serious. He sounded afraid.'

Servaz gave a violent start.

'Afraid? What you mean by "afraid"? Are you sure?'

'Yes. I'd bet my right arm.'

'Did you give him my number?'

'Yes. Should I not have?'

'No, no, you did right. Do you have his number?'

'It was a mobile. He hung up as soon as we gave him your number. We tried to call back, but we only got his voicemail.'

'Were you able to identify him?'

'No, not yet. We'll have to go through the operator.'

'Call Confiant and Captain Ziegler! Explain the situation; we have to get the man's identity. Do it right away!'

'Right. He's bound to ring you,' said the gendarme.

'How long ago did you get the call?'

'Less than five minutes ago.'

'Good. I'll probably hear from him in the next few minutes. In the meantime, get hold of Confiant. And Ziegler! He may not want to tell me who he is, and it might be a nuisance call. But we've got to find out who he is!'

Servaz hung up, coiled tight as a spring. What was going on? Who was trying to reach him? Was it Chaperon, or someone else? Someone who was afraid . . .

Someone who was frightened, too, that the gendarmes in Saint-Martin would recognise him. So he disguised his voice.

'Trouble?' asked Ferrand.

'Questions, more like,' replied Servaz absently. 'And perhaps answers.'

'You have a difficult job.'

Servaz could not help but smile.

'First time I've ever heard a professor tell me that.'

'I didn't say an honourable job.'

Servaz was staggered by the insinuation.

'And why shouldn't it be?'

'You serve the people in power.'

Servaz felt his anger returning.

'There are thousands of men and women who have no interest in power, as you call it, and who sacrifice their family life, their weekends and their sleep to be the last barrier, the last bulwark against—'

'Barbarity?' suggested Ferrand.

'Yes. You may despise them, criticise them or look down on them, but you cannot do without them.'

'No more than we can do without those teachers we criticise, despise or look down on,' said Ferrand with a smile. 'Point taken.'

'I'd like to visit her room.'

Ferrand unfolded his long, tanned body.

'Follow me.'

Servaz noticed the bits of fluff in the stairway, and the railing that had not been waxed in a long time. A man alone. Like himself. Or Gabriel Saint-Cyr. Like Chaperon. Or Perrault . . .

Alice's room was not off the first-floor landing but all the way at the top of the house, under the eaves.

'It's there,' said Ferrand, pointing to a white door with a brass handle.

'Have you . . . Did you throw out her things and redo the room since?'

This time Gaspard Ferrand's smile was replaced by a despairing grimace.

'We haven't touched a thing.'

He turned his back and went downstairs. Servaz stood for a long time on the tiny second-floor landing. He heard a clatter of dishes from downstairs in the kitchen. The narrow landing was lit from above through a skylight. When he looked up, Servaz saw that a fine film of snow was clinging to the glass. He took a deep breath and went in.

The first thing that struck him was the silence.

No doubt it was accentuated by the falling snow as it muffled all sound. But there was a special quality to this silence. The second thing he noticed was how cold it was. The heat had been turned off. He could not help but tremble in this room that was as silent and

276

icy as a tomb. Because it was obvious someone had lived here once. A young girl, typical for her age.

Photos on the walls. A desk, shelves, a wardrobe. A dresser with a big mirror. The bed and two night tables. The furniture looked as if it had been found at a flea market, then repainted in bright colours, with orange and yellow dominating, in contrast to the purple walls and white carpet.

The shades on the little lamps were orange; the bed and desk were orange; the dresser and the frame around the mirror were yellow. On one of the walls was a large poster of a blond singer with 'Kurt' written in large letters. A scarf, boots, magazines, books and CDs were scattered across the white carpet. For a long while, all he could do was soak in the chaos. Where was this impression of a rarefied atmosphere coming from? No doubt from the fact that everything was exactly as it had been, as if suspended in time. Everything except the dust. No one had bothered to put away even the tiniest object; it was as if her parents had wanted to stop time – they had turned the room into a museum, a mausoleum. Even after all these years, Alice's room gave the impression that she was about to come in at any moment and ask Servaz what he was doing there. How often over the years had Alice's father come in here and felt the same thing? Servaz thought that he would have gone mad in his shoes, knowing that this room remained untouched, confronting the daily temptation to go up the stairs and open the door once again – for the last time . . . He went over to the window and looked out. The street was turning white before his eyes. Then he took another breath, turned round and began his search.

Piled loose on the desk: schoolbooks, hairbands, a pair of scissors, several jars full of pencils, tissues, packets of sweets and a pink Post-it where Servaz read the following message: '*Library, 12.30*'; the ink had faded over time. A diary held closed with an elastic band, a calculator, a lamp. He opened the diary. On 25 April, one week before her death, Alice had written: '*Give Emma back her book.*' On the 29th, '*Charlotte.*' On the 30th, three days before hanging herself, '*Maths test.*' Neat round handwriting. Her hand did not tremble. Servaz turned the pages. For 11 August, she had written, '*Emma birthday.*' By then, Alice would have been dead for over three months. A date written long in advance . . . Where was Emma today? What had she become? He worked out that she would be in her thirties. Even after all these years, she must think back from time to time to that terrible year, 1993. All those deaths.

Above the desk, pinned to the wall, were a weekly timetable and a calendar. The school holidays had been highlighted with a yellow marker. Servaz's gaze paused on the fateful day: 2 May. Nothing to set it apart it from the other days. Still higher up was a wooden shelf with books, a cassette deck and judo trophies that showed that she had excelled at the sport.

He turned to the night tables. In addition to the two lamps, he saw an alarm clock, some more tissues, a Game Boy, a hair clip, nail varnish and a paperback novel with a bookmark. He opened the drawers. Fancy stationery, a little box with costume jewellery, a pack of chewing gum, a bottle of perfume, a stick of deodorant and batteries.

He groped underneath the bottom of the drawers.

Nothing.

In the desk there were binders, notebooks and schoolbooks, masses of pens, markers and paper clips. In the middle drawer, a spiral notebook full of sketches. Servaz opened it: he could see that Alice was genuinely talented. Her drawings in pencil or felt tip showed she had a sure hand and a sharp eye, even if most of them still suffered from a certain caution. In the bottom drawer, more elastic bands, a nail clipper, several lipsticks and a hairbrush to which a few blonde hairs still clung, but also a tube of aspirin, menthol cigarettes and a transparent cigarette lighter. Servaz opened the binders and notebooks from the top drawer: homework, essays, rough drafts. He put them to one side and went over to the little stereo on the floor in a corner. It was both a CD player and a radio, and was also covered in a thick layer of dust. Servaz blew on it, stirring up a grey cloud; then he opened the compartments one by one. Nothing. He went over to the big mirror and the wall of photographs. Some of them had been taken so close up that their subjects seemed to be sticking their nose into the camera lens. In others he could see landscapes behind the people in the photograph: mountains, a beach, even the columns of the Parthenon. Girls Alice's age, most of the time. Always the same faces. Occasionally one or two boys joined the group. But the photographer did not seem to have singled out any particular face. Were these school trips? Servaz took a long time studying the prints. They had all turned yellow and curled with age.

What exactly was he looking for? His gaze lingered on one of the photographs. A dozen or so young people, including Alice, standing next to a rusty sign. Les Isards Holiday Camp . . . *Alice was one of those who had stayed at the camp.* He also noticed that on the photographs where she appeared, Alice was always in the centre. The prettiest girl, the most luminous – the centre of attention.

The mirror.

It was cracked.

Someone had thrown something at it, and the projectile had left a crazed impact with a long crack. Was it Alice? Or her father, in a moment of despair?

There were yellowed postcards stuck between the frame and the mirror, sent from destinations like the Île de Ré, Venice, Greece or Barcelona. Over time, some had fallen onto the dresser or the carpet. One of them drew his attention. '*Rotten weather, I miss you.*' Signed Emma. A Palestinian scarf on the dresser, along with trinkets, round cotton make-up pads and a blue shoebox. Servaz opened it. Letters . . . A tremor went through him as he remembered the letters from the suicide victims that were in Saint-Cyr's box. He examined them one by one. Naive or funny letters written in purple or violet ink. Always the same signatures. He could not find the slightest reference to what was about to happen. He would have to compare the handwriting with that of the letters in the box; then he told himself it must have been done already. Now for the dresser drawers. He lifted up piles of T-shirts, underwear, sheets and blankets. Then he knelt on the carpet and looked under the bed. Huge dustballs, enough to stuff an entire quilt, and a guitar case.

He pulled the case out into the light and opened it. There were scratches on the finish of the instrument, and the B string was broken. Servaz glanced inside it: nothing. A quilt made of coloured lozenges covered the bed. He lingered over the CDs scattered on top: Guns N' Roses, Nirvana, U2. The room was like a museum devoted to the 1990s. No Internet, no computer, no mobile phone. *The world is changing too quickly now for a single lifespan,* he thought. He lifted the pillows, sheets and bedspread, and ran his hand under the mattress. No perfume, no particular scent emanated from the bed, other than the dust that covered it and drifted to the ceiling.

There was a little Voltaire chair next to the bed. Someone (Alice?) had painted it orange as well. An old military jacket lay over the back. He patted under the seat but did not manage to disturb anything other than a new cloud of dust; then he sat down and looked around him, trying to let his thoughts wander.

What did he see?

A young girl's bedroom; a young girl who was typical for her time but also mature for her age.

Among the books, Servaz had noticed *The Possessed* and *Crime and Punishment,* as well as Marcuse's *One-Dimensional Man.* Who had recommended these books to her? Surely not her little classmates with their chubby faces. Then he remembered that her father was a literature professor. Once again he looked around.

The dominant feature in this room, he thought, *is the* texts, *the* words. The words in the books, on the postcards, in the letters . . . All written by other people. Where were Alice's words? Would a girl who expressed herself through her guitar and her drawings, who devoured books really never have felt the need to express herself in words as well? Alice's life had ended on 2 May, and there was no trace anywhere of the final days of her life. *It's impossible,* he thought. No diary, nothing: something didn't fit. How could a curious, intelligent girl that age, who must have had an almost inexhaustible reserve of profound questions, particularly if she were desperate enough to put an end to her life, not have kept some sort of journal? Surely she would have recorded her thoughts somewhere? These days teenagers had blogs, noticeboards and pages on social networks, but in the old days only paper and ink could provide a space for their questioning, their doubts and their secrets.

He stood up and went through all Alice's notebooks and drawers one by one. Nothing but schoolwork. He glanced at her essays. Nothing but the highest marks, 15–19 out of 20. The teachers' comments were as full of praise as the marks themselves. *But there were no personal words.*

Had Alice's father gone through and cleaned up?

He had welcomed Servaz quite spontaneously, and told him that he was convinced the children had put an end to it all for a specific reason. Why would he hide anything that might have helped them to discover the truth? Servaz had found no mention of any diaries in the official papers, either. There was nothing to show that Alice had even kept one. But in spite of that, the impression was stronger than ever: something, in this room, was missing.

A hiding place . . . All young girls had one, didn't they? Where was Alice's?

Servaz got up and opened the wardrobe. On the hangers were coats, dresses, jackets, jeans and a white judo outfit with a brown belt. He spread them apart, one by one, and went through all the pockets. A row of shoes and boots along the bottom: Servaz checked inside with the beam of his little pocket torch. Above the hangers was a shelf with several suitcases and a backpack. He set them down on the carpet, freeing up a veritable tornado of dust, then searched them methodically.

Nothing. He paused to think.

The room must have been gone over by crack investigators – perhaps by Alice's parents themselves. Could it be they hadn't found a hiding place, if there was one? Had they even looked for one? Everyone had agreed, Alice was a brilliant girl. Had she devised the ultimate undetectable hiding place? Or was he headed down the wrong path?

What did he really know about the thoughts and dreams of a sixteen-year-old girl? His own daughter had turned seventeen a few months earlier, and he would have been at a loss to describe her room – for the simple reason that he had never set foot in it. The very thought made him feel queasy. At the edge of his brain something was tickling him, an itch. There was something he had missed while exploring the room. Or there was something that should have been here and wasn't. *Think!* It was there, so close, he could feel it. His instinct told him that something was missing. What? What? He looked all around the room again. He went over every single possibility. He had examined everything, including the skirting boards and the slats of the parquet floor underneath the white carpet. There was nothing. Yet his unconscious had sensed something, of that he was sure – even if he couldn't put his finger on it.

He sneezed from all the dust floating in the air, and pulled out a tissue.

Then Servaz remembered his mobile.

There had been no calls! An hour had gone by and not a single call. He felt his stomach form a knot. Damn it, what the fuck was the strange caller doing? Why hadn't he rung?

Servaz took his mobile out of his pocket and looked at it. He stifled a sense of panic: the stupid thing was switched off. He tried to turn it on: no battery! Shit!

He rushed out of the room and hurried noisily down the stairs.

Gaspard Ferrand peered out of the kitchen as Servaz bolted past him in the corridor.

'I'll be back!' he shouted, opening the front door without stopping.

Outside a blizzard was raging. The wind had picked up. The pavement was white and the snowflakes were whirling.

He hurried to unlock the Jeep, and rummaged in the glove compartment for the charger. Then he ran back to the house.

'It's nothing!' he said to a stunned Ferrand.

He hunted for a socket, found one in the corridor and plugged in the charger.

He waited five seconds and switched on the phone. Four messages!

He was about to read the first one when the telephone rang.

'Servaz!' he shouted.

'Where have you been, for fuck's sake!'

A voice in a total panic, almost as panicked as his own. His ears were buzzing with the blood pounding in his temples. The man wasn't disguising his voice, this time – but he didn't recognise it.

'Who is this?'

'My name is Serge Perrault. I'm a friend of—'

Perrault!

'I know who you are!' he interrupted.

There was a brief silence.

'I have to speak to you right away!' shouted Perrault.

His voice was hysterical.

'Where are you?' shouted Servaz. 'Where?'

'Meet me at the top of the cable cars in fifteen minutes. Hurry!'

Servaz felt another surge of panic.

'Which cable cars?'

'The ones up in Saint-Martin 2000, near the ski lifts! I'll be there. Get a move on, bloody hell! Don't you understand, it's my turn! Come alone!'

19

The sky was dark and the streets were white when Servaz turned the ignition. Outside the snow was coming down heavily. He started the windscreen wipers. Then he rang Ziegler.

'Where are you?' he asked as soon as she picked up.

'With the parents,' she said, lowering her voice, and he understood she was not alone.

'Whereabouts?'

'At the edge of town, why?'

In a few words, he summed up Perrault's call for help.

'You're closer than I am,' he concluded. 'Get there as quickly as you can! There's not a minute to lose. He's waiting for us up there.'

'Why not alert the gendarmerie?'

'There's no time. Hurry!'

Servaz hung up. He pulled down the sun visor stamped 'Police,' and stuck the magnetic revolving light on the roof. He turned on the siren. How long would it take him to get up there? Gaspard Ferrand did not live in Saint-Martin but in a village five kilometres away. The streets were covered in snow. Servaz figured a good quarter of an hour to get to the car park that was right in the centre of town by the cable car station. How long would it take him to get up there? Fifteen, twenty minutes?

He took off like a shot, siren howling, before the eyes of an astonished Ferrand standing in his doorway. There was a traffic light at the end of the street. It was red. He had started to go through it when he saw an enormous lorry coming from the right. He slammed on the brakes and immediately felt the car skid out of control. The Jeep swerved sideways right in the middle of the crossroads; the steel juggernaut narrowly missed him, horns blaring. The roar seemed to burst his eardrums just as the fear struck him like a fist in his gut. It took his breath away. His knuckles went white on the wheel. He put the car into first and set off again. No time to think! Maybe it was better that way. It was not just thirty-eight tons of steel that had narrowly missed him; it was death in a tin can.

At the following crossroads he took a right and left the village. The white fields stretched away in the distance; the sky was just as threatening, but it had stopped snowing. He accelerated.

He entered Saint-Martin from the east. At the first roundabout he took the wrong exit. He turned back, swearing and hitting the steering wheel; other drivers stared at him incredulously. Fortunately there was not much traffic. Two more roundabouts. He went by a church and found himself on the avenue d'Étigny, the commercial and cultural heart of the town with hotels, chic boutiques, plane trees, a cinema and cafés. There were cars parked all along the avenue. On the sides and down the middle of the road the snow had been transformed into a dark slush by dozens of passing vehicles. Just before the cinema he turned right. An arrow indicated, 'CABLE CARS.'

At the end of the street was a large car park, a vast esplanade in the looming shadow of the mountain. Opposite the car park its slopes rose to the sky, and a long white scar of the hanging gondolas sliced its way through the fir trees. He drove as fast as he dared past the rows of cars until he reached the lower station, where he braked abruptly, skidding again. A moment later he was outside, running up the steps to the building set on two huge concrete pillars. He hurried to the ticket window; a couple were buying tickets. Servaz flashed his card.

'Police! How long does it take to get up there?'

The man behind the window gave him a disparaging look.

'Nine minutes.'

'Any way you can speed it up a bit?'

The man stared at him as if his request were completely insane.

'To do what?' he asked.

Servaz tried to stay calm.

'I don't have time to argue. Well?'

'The maximum speed is five metres a second,' said the man with a scowl. 'Eighteen kilometres an hour.'

'Then move it, top speed!' said Servaz, jumping into one of the cabins, an egg-shaped shell with large Plexiglas windows and four tiny seats.

A pivoting arm closed the door behind him. Servaz swallowed his saliva. The car juddered on leaving the guiding rail, then dangled in space. Servaz decided it would be preferable to sit rather than stand in this unsteady shell; it rose quickly towards the first support tower, leaving the white roofs of Saint-Martin far below. He glanced briefly behind him and, as in the helicopter, he immediately regretted it. The cable was so steep that it struck him as one of those bold enterprises so common to men which are eloquent proof of their irresponsibility; and the cable was far too thin to reassure him. The roofs and streets were shrinking at an alarming rate. The gondolas ahead of him were separated from each other by thirty metres or so and swung to and fro in the wind.

He saw, down below, that the couple had decided not to go up and were headed back to their car. He was alone. No one was coming up; no one was going down. The gondolas were empty. Everything was silent, except for the wind moaning louder than ever.

Halfway up the slope they were suddenly surrounded by fog, and before he even knew what was happening, Servaz found himself in a surreal landscape of vague contours, his only company the fir trees standing in the mist like a ghostly army, and the blizzard that sent the snowflakes swirling round the gondola.

He had forgotten his weapon! In his haste, he had left it in the car. What would happen if he found himself face to face with the killer up there? Not to mention the fact that if someone was waiting for him at the top of the gondolas and was armed, Servaz would be a sitting duck. There was nowhere to hide. This plastic shell wasn't about to stop any bullets.

He found himself praying that Ziegler had got there before him. She should be ahead of him. *She's not the sort who forgets her weapon.* How would Perrault react on seeing her? He had told Servaz to come alone.

He should have asked the know-it-all at the ticket window if he had seen her. Too late now. He was headed into the unknown at an exasperating rate of five metres a second. He took out his mobile and dialled Perrault's number; he got his voicemail.

Shit! Why had he switched off his phone?

He could make out two dark figures in a gondola on its way down, roughly two hundred metres uphill. It was the first human presence he had seen since leaving the station below. He dialled Ziegler's number.

'Ziegler.'

'Are you up there?' he asked.

'No, I'm on my way.' She paused. 'I'm sorry, Martin, my motor-cycle skidded on the snow and I went flying. Nothing but scratches, but I had to borrow another car. Where are you?'

Shit!

'Roughly halfway up.'

The cabin with the two occupants seemed to be going faster and faster, the closer it came.

'You know there's a blizzard up there?'

'No,' he said. 'I didn't know. Perrault's not answering.'

'Are you armed?'

Even from this distance, he could see that one of the people in the opposite car was staring at him, just as he was staring at them.

'I forgot my weapon in the car.'

An oppressive silence followed.

'Be care—'

Her words were cut off. He looked at his mobile. Nothing! He dialled the number again. *No network.* That's all he needed! He tried twice more, to no avail. Servaz could not believe his eyes. When he looked up again, the occupied gondola was even closer. One of the men was wearing a black balaclava. All he could see were his eyes and mouth. The other man was bareheaded, wearing glasses. Both of them were staring at Servaz through the glass and fog. The first one was glaring.

And the other one was terrified.

In a split second Servaz understood, and the full horror of the situation became clear.

Perrault – the tall thin fellow from the photograph, with the thick glasses.

Servaz's heart leapt in his chest. As if in a dream, the gondola was coming towards him, terrifyingly quickly now. Less than twenty metres away. In two seconds it would pass him. Another detail caught his attention: on the far side the windowpane was missing.

Perrault was staring at Servaz, his mouth gaping, his eyes wide with fear. He was screaming. Servaz could hear his screams even through the windows, in spite of the wind and the noise of the pulleys and cables. He had never seen anyone look so terrified. It was if the man was going to shatter into pieces, to split apart from one second to the next.

Servaz swallowed. The moment the gondola went by his own and moved away behind him, all the details became clear: Perrault had a rope round his neck, and the rope went through the open window and into a sort of hook on the outside, just above. *Perhaps the hook was used to rappel any injured passengers down to the ground when the gondola was at a standstill,* thought Servaz in a flash. The man in the balaclava was holding the other end of the rope. Servaz had tried to see his eyes, but he'd thrown himself behind his victim just as the two gondolas passed each other.

I must know him! thought Servaz. *He's afraid I'll recognise him, even with a balaclava on!*

He fiddled desperately with his mobile. *No network.* In a panic, he looked around the cabin for an alarm button, an interphone, something, but there was nothing. Fuck it! You could die in one of these gondolas at the speed of five metres a second! Servaz turned round to look at the retreating car. One last time his eyes met Perrault's terrified gaze. If he'd had a gun, he could at least have . . . Have what? What would he have done? He was a lousy shot, anyway. During the yearly tests they took, he never failed to arouse the inspector's disbelief with his dismal results. The gondola and the two men melted into the fog.

He choked back a nervous laugh. Then felt like screaming.

In a rage, he slammed his fist into one of the windows. The minutes that followed were among the longest in his life. It took five minutes more for the upper station to appear, five interminable minutes punctuated only by the ghostly parade of fir trees, erect as foot soldiers in the mist. The station was a squat little building, set on thick concrete pillars like the one below. Beyond it Servaz could see the deserted ski slopes, the stationary tow lifts and buildings buried in fog. There was a man on the platform watching him approach. The moment the door opened, Servaz leapt out. He nearly went flying onto the concrete. His card in his hand, he rushed over to the uniformed man.

'Stop everything! Right away! Halt the cable cars!'

The cable operator shot him a stunned look from under his cap. 'What?'

'You can stop the gondolas, can't you?'

The wind was howling. Servaz had to shout even louder. His rage and impatience finally seemed to get through to the man.

'Yes, but—'

'Then stop everything! And call down below! Do you have a phone line?'

'Yes, of course!'

'Stop everything! Right away! And give me the telephone! Hurry!'

The operator rushed inside. He spoke feverishly into a microphone, gave Servaz a worried look, then pulled down the lever. The gondolas shuddered to a halt. Only afterwards did Servaz realise how terribly noisy it had been on the platform. He grabbed hold of the telephone and dialled the number for the gendarmerie. An orderly replied.

'Get me Maillard! Commandant Servaz calling! Hurry!'

A minute later, Maillard was on the line.

'I just passed the killer. He's on his way down, in one of the gondolas with his next victim. I've had them stop the cables. Take some men and get over to the gondola station! As soon as you've taken up position, we'll start them again.'

There was a moment of shock at the other end of the line.

'Are you sure?' stammered Maillard.

'Absolutely. The victim is Perrault. He called for help twenty-five minutes ago. He told me to meet him up there. I just passed him in a gondola that was on its way down – he had a rope round his neck, and next to him was a man wearing a balaclava!'

'Good God! I'll give the alarm. As soon as we're ready we'll call you!'

'Try to reach Captain Ziegler, too. My mobile isn't working.'

Maillard came back on the line after twelve minutes had passed, which Servaz had spent pacing back and forth on the platform, looking at his watch and smoking one cigarette after another.

'We're ready,' said the gendarme on the telephone.

'Good. I'll get the gondolas going again. Perrault and the assassin are in one of them! I'm coming!'

He motioned to the driver, then jumped into one of the gondolas. Just as it was pulling away, he could tell something was wrong. The killer had planned to push Perrault out into the void and watch him dangling from the end of a rope – and he certainly had no intention of reaching the bottom along with his victim. Servaz wondered if there was a place where the killer could jump from the moving gondola, and no sooner had he asked himself the question than he knew there must be.

Had Maillard and his men planned for such an eventuality? Were they checking all the paths leading up to the mountain?

He tried once again to dial Ziegler's number, but he got the same answer as before. As on the way up, he was moving through fog, unable to see anything but the shapes of the trees and the empty cars he met along the way. Suddenly he heard the *flap flap* of a helicopter's blades, but he could not see the aircraft. It did seem to him, however, that the noise was coming not from above but *from below*.

What was going on down there? With his nose on the windowpane he tried to see through the fog. But he could see no further than twenty metres. Suddenly the gondolas came to a halt, so abruptly that he almost lost his balance. For Christ's sake! He banged his nose against the window and the pain brought tears to his eyes. What were they doing down there? He looked around. The gondolas were swinging gently on their cables, like lanterns at a village fair; the wind had dropped and the snow was falling almost vertically now. He tried once again to use his mobile, with no more luck than before.

In the three-quarters of an hour that followed he was prisoner of his plastic bubble, observing the circle of fir trees and fog. After half an hour had gone by the gondola suddenly swerved, moved three metres further along, then stopped again. Servaz swore. What were they up to? He stood up, sat back down, stood up again. There was not even room enough to stretch his legs. When at last the gondolas jerked forward, he'd been sitting down for a long time, resigned to wait.

Just as he was approaching the lower station the fog lifted all of a sudden and the roofs of the town became visible. Servaz saw the flashing of revolving lights and many vehicles in the car park. Uniformed gendarmes were coming and going. He could also make out the white-clad figures of the CSIs, and the body laid out on a gurney beneath a silver tarp, next to an ambulance with an open tailgate.

He froze.

Perrault was dead.

They had stopped the gondolas in order to make the initial findings. Then they had taken him down and restarted the cars. Servaz knew at once that the killer had managed to get away. As soon as the pivoting arm opened the door, he burst out of the gondola and hurried across the concrete. He found Ziegler, Maillard, Confiant and d'Humières at the bottom of the steps. Ziegler was wearing a leather jumpsuit, but in several places the leather was torn: her knee and elbow were swollen, covered in bruises and scabs of dried blood. Clearly she hadn't even had time to dress her wounds. She was still holding her helmet in her hands, and the visor was cracked.

'What happened?' he asked.

'We should ask you that,' retorted Confiant.

Servaz glared at him. For a brief moment he wished that the young judge were a fragile figurine and that he were a hammer. Then he turned to Cathy d'Humières.

'Is it Perrault?' he asked, pointing to the body under the tarp. She nodded.

'He called me,' he explained. 'He wanted to speak to me in person. He sounded afraid; he must have felt threatened. He told me to meet him up there. I alerted Captain Ziegler and got up there as quickly as I could.'

'And you didn't see fit to ask for reinforcements?' asked Confiant.

'There wasn't time. He wanted me to come alone. He wanted to speak to me alone.'

Confiant stared at him, his eyes bright with fury. Cathy d'Humières was thoughtful. Servaz glanced again at the covered shape on the gurney: the investigators were folding the wheels and loading it onto the ambulance. He couldn't see the pathologist; he must have already left. Curious onlookers stood behind the police tape at the far end of the car park. There was a sudden flash. Then another one. The helicopter must have landed; he couldn't hear it anymore.

'And the killer?' he said.

'He got away.'

'How?'

'When we finally saw the gondola, there was a windowpane missing and Perrault was hanging underneath,' said Maillard. 'That's when we blocked everything. There's one spot where the gondolas go past a path that leads up to the resort. It's a fairly wide path, and in winter it doubles as a ski trail if you want to ski back down to Saint-Martin. There's a drop of about four metres between the gondolas and the path. But your guy probably got down using the other end of the rope he hanged Perrault with. After that, a good skier can be down here in three minutes.'

'Where does the path come out?'

'Behind the thermal baths.' Maillard pointed to the mountain. 'They're in the east part of town. The path winds round the mountain and comes out just behind the building – it's hidden from view.'

Servaz pictured the big building he'd gone by twice already. There was a vast rectangular esplanade, with the baths at one end, abutting the mountain. Around the other three sides of the esplanade there were hotels and cafés. In the middle was a car park. And, consequently, dozens of cars.

'That's where we lost his trail,' said Maillard.

'Did you include the path in the crime scene?'

'Yes, we closed off the entire area and a team of investigators is going over every metre from the gondolas to the car park at the baths.'

'He had it all worked out,' Ziegler commented.

'And yet he didn't have a lot of time.'

'How did he know that Perrault had called for help?' asked the gendarme.

They thought about it for a while, but no one came up with a satisfactory explanation.

'He used dynamic rope,' said Maillard. 'Good mountaineering equipment. He may have had it in his car all along, together with the skis. Then he could have put it in a backpack.'

'Someone sporty,' said Ziegler. 'A cool customer.'

Servaz nodded.

'He must have had a weapon. Perrault would never have gone up with him otherwise. But I didn't see any weapon, or skis, or backpack. It all happened so quickly. And I didn't really notice what else was there.'

Perrault's face, distorted by fear. He could not get it out of his mind.

'Where was he in relation to Perrault?' asked Ziegler.

'Perrault was closer to me, and the killer was behind him.'

'Perrault may have had a gun to his back. Or perhaps a blade.'

'It's possible. Brilliantly staged, once again. In spite of the lack of time. He's quick, and arrogant. Maybe too arrogant. When the gondolas came close to me, he hid behind Perrault,' Servaz added, frowning.

'Why would he do that, since he was wearing a balaclava?'

'So that I wouldn't see his eyes.'

Ziegler gave him a sharp look.

'You mean he was afraid you would recognise him?'

'Yes. Which means that I've already seen him. And that I've seen him close up. We have to question the man at the ticket window,' he said. 'Ask him if he saw anyone.'

'We already have. He recognised Perrault. After that, he's categorical: no one went up until you did.'

'How is that possible?'

'You can also reach Saint-Martin 2000 by road. It takes roughly ten minutes from the south end of town. The killer had plenty of time to get up that way.'

Servaz considered the lie of the land. From the square where the baths were located you left town on a road that ended twelve kilometres away, a stone's throw from the Spanish border. That was the way he had gone to Grimm's cabin. Another road branched off from that one and went up to the ski resort.

'In that case, he would have needed two cars,' he said. 'One to get up there, and one waiting below.'

'Yes. And probably someone waiting below,' Ziegler said. 'Outside the thermal baths. Unless a second vehicle had been parked there for a long time.'

'The first car may still be up there. Did you set up a roadblock on the way to the resort?' he asked Maillard.

'Yes, we're checking all the cars coming back down. And we'll check all the ones that stayed up there.'

'There are two killers,' said Ziegler.

Servaz looked at her.

'Yes. There were two of them at the power plant – and there were two of them this time, too.'

Something suddenly occurred to him.

'We have to call the Institute, right away.'

'We already have: Hirtmann is in his cell. He hasn't left it all morning. Two people from the Institute spoke to him, and Xavier himself went to check.'

Confiant was staring at Servaz, as if to say, 'I told you so.'

'This time, the press will go to town,' said d'Humières. 'We'll be all over the headlines, and not just the local press. I don't want anyone going off on their own, making statements that are out of line.'

Servaz and Ziegler didn't say anything.

'I suggest that Monsieur Confiant and I should take care of the press. The rest of you, absolute silence. The investigation is progressing; we have several leads. Nothing more. If they want details, let them come to me or to Martial.'

'On condition that His Honour doesn't use his statements to destroy our work,' said Servaz.

Cathy d'Humières shot him an icy look.

'What on earth do you mean by that?'

'Commandant Servaz gave Dr Propp and me a rough time on our way back from the Institute the day before yesterday,' said Confiant. 'He lost his cool; he seemed to have it in for everyone.'

The prosecutor turned to Servaz.

'Martin?'

'"Lost my cool" . . . that's a bit much,' said Servaz sarcastically. 'What I do know is that His Honour warned Dr Xavier that we were coming, and he didn't consider it necessary to inform you, or us, of the fact, even though we had all agreed that it was supposed to be a surprise visit.'

'Is that true?' asked d'Humières icily, turning to Confiant.

The young judge's face fell.

'Xavier is a friend of mine. I couldn't decently show up there with the police without warning him.'

'In that case, why didn't you tell us?' Cathy flung at him, her voice trembling with rage.

Confiant looked down, sheepish.

'I don't know . . . it didn't seem that important.'

'Listen! We're going to be in the spotlight.' She jerked her chin furiously towards the reporters clustered behind the police tape. 'We certainly mustn't treat them to the sight of a divided team. Since that is how things are, we will speak with one voice: mine! I hope we'll get somewhere soon with this investigation,' she said, walking off. 'And I want a meeting in thirty minutes to go over what we've got.'

The look Martial Confiant gave Servaz as he walked away was worthy of a Taliban fighter happening upon a porn star.

'Well, you certainly know how to make friends,' said Ziegler as she watched them leave. 'Did you say they were one behind the other in the gondola?'

'Perrault and the killer? Yes.'

'Compared to Perrault, was the killer shorter or taller?'

Servaz thought.

'Shorter.'

'Man or woman?'

Servaz took a moment to consider this. How many witnesses had he interviewed in the course of his career? He knew how difficult it had been for some of them to answer this type of question. Now it was his turn, and he realised how disloyal memory can be.

'Man,' he said, after hesitating.

'Why?'

Ziegler had noticed his hesitation.

'I don't know.' He paused. 'Because of the way he moved, his attitude . . .'

'Couldn't it be, rather, because you find it difficult to imagine a woman doing such a thing?'

He looked at her with a faint smile.

'Perhaps. Why do you suppose Perrault felt he had to go up there?'

'By the looks of it, he was running away from someone.'

'In any case, we've got another hanging.'

'But no severed finger, this time.'

'Perhaps it was simply because the killer didn't have time.'

'A blonde singer with a beard and big, feverish eyes, first name Kurt, 1993. Any idea who that could be?'

'Kurt Cobain,' answered Ziegler instantly. 'You saw him in one of the kids' rooms?'

'Alice's.'

'The official version is that Kurt Cobain committed suicide,' said the gendarme, limping over to Servaz's car.

'When?' he asked, stopping short.

'In 1994, I think. He shot himself.'

'You think or you're sure?'

'I'm sure. About the date, anyway. I was a fan at the time, and there were rumours that he was murdered.'

'In 1994 . . . if that's the case, then they weren't copycat suicides,' he concluded, starting to walk forward again. 'Have you seen a doctor?'

'I'll deal with that later.'

His mobile rang just as he was about to turn the ignition.

'Servaz.'

'It's Vincent. What the fuck's the matter with your mobile? I've been trying to reach you all morning!'

'What's going on?' he asked, ignoring Espérandieu's question.

'The signet ring: we found out what's inscribed on it.'

'And?'

'Two letters: a C and an S.'

'C S?'

'Yes.'

'What do you think it means?'

'No idea.'

Servaz thought for a moment. Then something else occurred to him.

'You haven't forgotten the favour I asked you?' he said.

'What favour?'

'About Margot.'

'Oh, blast, damn, hell. Yes, I did forget.'

'And what's the latest on the homeless bloke?'

'Oh, right, we got the results back for the prints: all three kids were there. But that doesn't change much – according to Samira, the judge is going with the drowning hypothesis.'

A shadow passed over Servaz's face.

'Someone must be leaning on him. The autopsy will settle it. It looks as if Clément's father has connections.'

'While the others certainly don't: the judge wants to interview the oldest one again, the son of the unemployed bloke. He thinks he's the instigator.'

'Well, well, what a surprise. And anything about Lombard?'

'I'm still looking.'

A large windowless room, lit by neon lights and divided into several aisles by tall metal bookshelves full of dusty files. Near the entrance were two desks, one with a computer that was at least five years old, the other with an ancient microfilm reader, a heavy, cumbersome machine. Boxes of microfilm were also stacked on the shelves.

The Wargnier Institute's entire history.

Diane had asked whether the files had been computerised and the archivist had practically laughed in her face.

She knew that there were electronic files on the occupants of Unit A. Xavier had entrusted eight more patients to her the day before, to 'cut her teeth on'. Evidently they were not important enough for someone to have taken the trouble to put their records into the computer. She walked down the rows, examining the folders, trying to determine what system governed the way they were stored. She had learned from experience that you couldn't always tell. Archivists, librarians and other software designers could have twisted minds.

But she was pleased to discover that the archivist was the logical sort, and had classified everything alphabetically. She grabbed the relevant binders and sat down at the little worktable. In the vast silent room, far from the turmoil of other parts of the Institute, she thought again about what had happened last night in the basement, and a chill came over her. From the moment she'd woken up she'd been seeing those gloomy corridors and recalling the icy humidity and smells from the basement, reliving the moment when she found herself plunged into darkness.

Who was going to Unit A at night? Who was the man she had heard screaming and sobbing at the holiday camp? Who was involved in the crimes committed in Saint-Martin? There were too many questions . . . One after the other they pounded against the feverish shores of her mind, like a returning tide. And she was dying to know the answers.

She opened the first file. There were painstaking records for each patient, from the very first signs of the pathology and initial diagnosis, through to the various hospital treatments they had received before eventually ending up at the Institute; there was also information about all the drugs they'd been given, and any side effects the treatment might have caused. The patients' dangerousness and the precautions to be taken in their presence were emphasised, reminding Diane, in case she had forgotten, that there were no choirboys at the Institute.

She took a few notes and went on reading. Then came the descriptions of the treatments themselves. Diane was not surprised to find out that antipsychotics and tranquillisers were administered in massive doses – doses far higher than current norms. This confirmed what Alex had told her. A sort of pharmaceutical atom bomb. She would not have liked to have her brain bombarded by these substances. She knew that the chemicals could cause terrible adverse reactions. Just the thought of it gave her a chill. Each file contained a separate sheet detailing the medication: doses, times, changes in treatment, delivery of the drugs to the relevant services. Whenever a patient needed a new batch of drugs from the Institute's pharmacy, the delivery slip was signed by the nurse in charge of their care and countersigned by the pharmacy manager.

Diane was feeling a need for caffeine by the time she started on the fourth file, but she decided to get to the end of her reading. She came last to the treatment schedule. As with the previous files, the doses gave her a chill up and down her spine:

Clozapine: 1 x 200 mg/day (3 x 100 mg tab 4 times a day).
Zuclopenthixol acetate: 400 mg IM/day.
Tiapride: 200 mg every hour.
Diazepam: Amp. IM 20 mg/day.
Meprobamate: 400 mg.

Good God! What sort of vegetables would these patients be? Then she remembered something else Alex had told her: after decades of very intense medical treatment, most of the inmates at the Institute were chemo-resistant. These guys were walking around the corridors with enough drugs in their veins to make a T-Rex space out, but they barely showed any signs of drowsiness. Just as she was about to close the file, she happened to notice something written in the margin: '*Why this treatment? Queried Xavier about it. No reply.*'

The writing was sloping and hurried. Just on reading it, she could imagine how frustrated and annoyed – and astonished – the person who had written the note must have been. She frowned and looked again at the list of medication and doses. She remembered that clozapine was used when other antipsychotics proved ineffective. In that case, why prescribe zuclopenthixol? In the treatment of anxiety there is no call for mixing two tranquillisers or two hypnotics. Yet that was what had been done. There might be other abnormalities that she had missed – she was neither a doctor nor a psychiatrist – but the author of the note had seen at least one. Apparently, Xavier had not bothered to answer. Puzzled, Diane wondered if this was cause for concern. Then she reasoned that this file was about one of her patients. Before starting any psychotherapy she had to know why this insane cocktail had been prescribed. The file spoke of schizophrenic psychosis, acute states of delirium and mental confusion – but there was a singular lack of anything more specific.

Should she question Xavier? Someone already had, to no avail.

She took the previous files and went through the signatures one by one for the consultant physician and the pharmacy manager. She eventually found what she was looking for. Above one of the signatures someone had written, '*Delivery delayed, transport strike.*' She compared the words 'transport' and 'treatment'. The shape of the letters was identical: the marginal note had been written by the pharmacy manager.

She would have to question him to start with.

With the file under her arm, Diane took the stairs up to the second floor. The Institute pharmacy was run by a male nurse in his thirties, who wore faded jeans, a white lab coat and scruffy trainers. It looked as if he hadn't shaved for three days, and his hair stood up in rebellious spikes. He also had circles under his eyes and Diane suspected he had an intense night life outside the Institute.

The pharmacy consisted of two rooms: one a reception area with a bell and a counter piled high with paperwork and empty boxes, and the other a room where the supplies of drugs were stored in locked glass cupboards. The nurse, whose name, according to the label embroidered on his chest pocket, was Dimitri, watched Diane come in, his smile just a touch too broad.

'Hey,' he said.

'Hello,' she replied. 'I'd like some information about the management of the pharmaceutical products.'

'OK. You're the new psychologist, right?'

'That's right.'

'What do you want to know?'

'Well, how it works.'

'Righty-ho,' he said, playing with the pen in his chest pocket. 'Come this way.'

She went behind the counter. He grabbed a big notebook with a cardboard cover that looked like an account book.

'This is the record book. We keep track of all the supplies as they come in and are dispensed. It's the job of the pharmacy to keep an inventory of the Institute's needs and make up the orders, then take delivery of the drugs, store them and distribute them among the various services. The pharmacy has its own budget. The orders are sent in roughly every month, but we can make special ones too.'

'Who, besides yourself, knows what comes in and goes out?'

'Anyone can consult the record book. But all the delivery slips and orders must be countersigned either by Dr Xavier himself, or, more often, by Lisa or Dr Lepage, the consultant physician. In addition, each drug has its own stock card.'

He took down a big binder and opened it.

'All the medication used at the Institute is in here and, thanks to this system, we know exactly how much we have in stock. Then we distribute the drugs. Each distribution is countersigned by both the charge nurse for each ward and myself.'

Diane opened the file she had in her hand and showed him the handwritten note in the margin of the supplementary sheet.

'This is your handwriting, isn't it?'

She saw him frown.

'That's right,' he replied, after a moment of hesitation.

'You don't seem to agree with the treatment this patient is receiving.'

'Well, I – I didn't see the point of – of prescribing two tranquillisers or zuclopenthixol acetate and clozapine at the same time. I, um, it's a bit . . . technical.'

'So you asked Dr Xavier.'

'Yes.'

'And what did he say?'

'That I was in charge of supplies, not a psychiatrist.'

'I see. Do all the patients receive such strong doses?'

'Most of them do, yes. You know, after years of treatment, almost all of them have become—'

'Chemo-resistant – yes, I know. Do you mind if I take a look at this?' She pointed to the record book and the binder containing the individual drug stock cards.

'No, of course not. Go ahead. Here, have a seat.'

He disappeared into the next room and she heard him make a phone call in a hushed voice. Probably to his girlfriend. He wasn't wearing a wedding ring. She opened the record book and began to turn the pages. January . . . February . . . March . . . April . . .

The inventory for the month of December was spread over two pages. On the second page, Diane's attention was drawn to a line in the middle: 'Delivery, order Xavier', dated 7 December. On the line were the names of three drugs. They were not familiar to her. She was sure they weren't commonly used. Out of curiosity, she jotted them down on her pad and called out to Dimitri. She heard him murmur, 'Love you'; then he came back into the room.

'What are these?'

He shrugged.

'I've no idea. I didn't write that. I was on holiday at the time.'

He leafed through the binder of stock cards and frowned.

'That's odd. There are no individual stock cards for these three drugs. Only invoices. Whoever filled in the record book didn't know what they were supposed to do.'

It was Diane's turn to shrug.

'Forget it. It doesn't matter.'

20

They went into the same incident room as before – Ziegler, Servaz, Captain Maillard, Simon Propp, Martial Confiant and Cathy d'Humières. At Servaz's request, Ziegler gave a brief summary of the facts. He noticed she was presenting them in a light that exonerated him of any errors of judgement; if anything, she was blaming herself for taking her motorcycle that morning, despite the weather forecast. She then drew attention to the detail that connected this new murder to the previous one: hanging. She did not mention the suicides, but did point out that Grimm and Perrault, along with Chaperon and a fourth man who had died two years earlier, had been charged with sexual blackmail.

'Chaperon?' said Cathy d'Humières, incredulous. 'That's the first I've heard of such a thing.'

'According to Saint-Cyr, the affair dates back to over twenty years ago,' said Servaz. 'Long before the mayor stood for office. The complaint was withdrawn almost immediately.'

He repeated what Saint-Cyr had told him. The prosecutor gave him a sceptical look.

'Do you really believe there's a connection? A drunken girl, some young men who were drunk as well, a few compromising photos . . . I don't wish to look as if I am defending that sort of behaviour, but it's not really much to make a fuss about.'

'According to Saint-Cyr, there were other rumours going round about the four men,' said Servaz.

'What sort of rumours?'

'More or less the same sort of thing – sexual abuse, rumours implying that once they got drunk they tended to be vicious and violent with women. Having said that, there were no other official complaints apart from this one – which, I repeat, was withdrawn very quickly. And then there are the things we found in Grimm's cabin. That cape, and those boots. The same ones, or near as dammit, as the ones we found on his corpse.'

Servaz knew from experience that it was better not to say too much to prosecutors and examining magistrates when you didn't have any solid proof, because they tended to come up with objections on principle. However, he could not resist the temptation to take it further.

'According to Saint-Cyr, Grimm, Perrault, Chaperon and their friend Mourrenx had been inseparable since their lycée days. We also found out that all four men wore the same signet ring: the one that should have been on Grimm's severed finger.'

Confiant gave them a puzzled look, knitting his brows.

'I don't see what this business about rings has to do with it,' he said.

'Well, we might see it as some sort of secret sign,' suggested Ziegler.

'A secret sign? Symbolising what?'

'At this point it's hard to say,' conceded Ziegler, glaring at the judge.

'Perrault's finger wasn't severed,' objected d'Humières, not hiding her scepticism.

'Precisely. But the photograph that Commandant Servaz found proves that at some point he did wear that signet ring. If the murderer didn't chop off his finger, perhaps Perrault was no longer wearing it.'

Servaz looked at them. Deep inside he knew they were on the right track. Something was coming to the surface, like roots emerging from the ground. Something dark and chilling.

And in this geography of horror, the capes and rings and severed or unsevered fingers were like little pebbles the murderer had left in his path.

'Clearly, we haven't been digging deep enough into these men's lives,' said Confiant suddenly. 'If we had done that instead of focusing on the Institute, perhaps we would have found something that would have warned us in time – to save Perrault.'

They all understood that the 'we' was purely rhetorical. What he really meant to say was 'you', and that 'you' referred to Servaz and Ziegler. At the same time, Servaz wondered whether Confiant wasn't right for once.

'In any case, the two murder victims were both charged in the complaint, and they were both wearing the ring,' he insisted. 'We cannot ignore these coincidences. And the third person who was involved in the complaint and who is still alive is none other than Roland Chaperon.'

He saw the prosecutor go pale.

'In that case, this is a priority,' she said.

'Yes. We have to do everything we can to find the mayor and place him under police protection – we haven't a minute to lose.' He checked his watch. 'I suggest we adjourn the meeting.'

When the first deputy mayor of Saint-Martin looked at them, the sting of fear in his gaze was as sharp as a needle. He was sitting at his desk on the first floor of the town hall, pale, nervously fiddling with his pen.

'I haven't been able to reach him since yesterday morning,' he said at once. 'We're very worried. Particularly after everything that has happened.'

Ziegler agreed with a nod of her head.

'And you have no idea where he might be?'

The deputy looked desperate.

'Not the slightest.'

'Any people he knows, whom he might have gone to see?'

'His sister in Bordeaux. I called her. She hasn't had any news. Neither has his ex-wife.'

The deputy looked at them both, uncertain and frightened, as if he were next on the list. Ziegler handed him a business card.

'If you hear anything at all, call us right away. Even if it doesn't seem important.'

Sixteen minutes later they were parking the car outside the bottling plant that Servaz had already visited two days earlier, where Roland Chaperon was both owner and boss. Lorries waited in the car park for their loads of bottles. Inside the plant there was an infernal racket. As on the previous occasion, Servaz saw an assembly line where the bottles were rinsed with a jet of clean water before they were shunted along to be filled, then the automatic process that sealed and labelled them, all without the slightest human intervention. All the workers did was check each stage of the operation.

Servaz and Ziegler went up the metal stairs leading to the manager's glassed-in soundproof office. The same big, hairy, unshaven man whom Servaz had seen the previous time was shelling pistachios, and he watched warily as they came in.

303

'There's something going on,' he said, spitting a shell into the wastebasket. 'Roland hasn't come by the factory, either yesterday or today. It's not like him to be gone without letting us know. With everything that's been going on, I can't understand why there aren't more roadblocks. What are you waiting for? If I were a gendarme . . .'

Ziegler had pinched her nose because of the smell of sweat that lingered in the office. She could see the huge dark stains spreading across the armpits of the man's blue shirt.

'But you're not a gendarme, are you,' she said sharply. 'Other than that, you have no idea where he might be?'

The fat man gave her a nasty look. Servaz could not help but smile. There were a few others like him round here who thought that city folk were incapable of acting intelligently.

'No. Roland wasn't the type to go on about his private life. A few months ago we found out about his divorce, almost overnight. He had never mentioned that he was having relationship troubles.'

'"Relationship troubles,"' echoed Ziegler, her tone openly sarcastic. 'That's nicely put.'

'Let's go straight to his place,' said Servaz, climbing back into the car. 'If he isn't there, we'll have to search the house from top to bottom. Call Confiant and ask for a warrant.'

Ziegler picked up the car phone and dialled a number.

'No answer.'

Servaz took his eyes from the road for a second. Clouds swollen with rain or snow were drifting across the dark sky like fatal omens, and the light was fading.

'Never mind. We don't have time. We'll do without.'

Espérandieu was listening to the Gutter Twins singing 'The Stations' when Margot Servaz came out of the lycée. Sitting in the shadow of the unmarked car, he observed the crowd as it scattered on the way out of the school; it did not take even ten seconds to spot her. That day, in addition to her leather jacket and striped shorts, Martin's daughter was wearing purple extensions in her black hair, fishnet tights and enormous fur ankle warmers that made her look as if she were heading off to an après-ski party. She stood out like a native headhunter at an elegant soirée. Espérandieu thought of Samira. He made sure he had his digital camera on the passenger seat, then opened the voice memo app on his iPhone.

'Five p.m. On her way out the lycée. Talking with schoolmates.'

Ten metres away, Margot was laughing and chatting. Then she pulled a tobacco pouch from her jacket. *That's not good for you*, thought Espérandieu. She started rolling a cigarette as she listened to her friends. *You seem to know what you're doing. Must be a habit.* He suddenly felt like some fucking voyeur ogling the cute chicks on their way out of school. *Shit, Martin, this is bloody unfair!* Twenty seconds later, a boy on a scooter pulled up to the little group.

Espérandieu was immediately on the alert.

The driver took off his helmet and spoke directly to his boss's daughter. She tossed her cigarette on the pavement and crushed it under her heel. Then she straddled the seat of the scooter.

Well, well. *'Leaving on scooter with individual aged seventeen to eighteen. Black hair. Not from lycée.'*

Espérandieu hesitated to take a picture. Too close. Someone might see him. As far as he could tell, the boy was good-looking, his hair gelled in spikes. He put his helmet back on and handed one to Margot. Was he the little bastard who was hitting her and breaking her heart? The scooter took off. Espérandieu followed. The boy drove fast, and recklessly. He slalomed between the cars, causing his scooter to zigzag where he shouldn't, while turning his head and shouting to make himself heard to his passenger. *Sooner or later, you'll be in for a nasty reality-check, amigo . . .*

Twice Espérandieu thought he'd lost him, but caught up again further along. He refused to use his siren; he didn't want to be noticed for a start, and besides, there was absolutely nothing official about his mission.

Finally the scooter stopped outside a villa surrounded by a garden and a tall thick hedge. Espérandieu immediately recognised the place: he had come here once with Servaz. This was where Alexandra, Martin's ex-wife, lived, together with her bloody airline pilot.

And, consequently, Margot.

She climbed off the scooter and removed her helmet. The two young people talked calmly for a moment, her on the kerb, him on his scooter, and Espérandieu worried they might notice him: he was parked in the deserted street not five yards away from them. Fortunately they were far too absorbed in their conversation.

Espérandieu saw that they were relaxed with each other. No shouts, no threats. On the contrary, they were laughing and nodding. *What if Martin were wrong?* Perhaps being a cop had made him paranoid, after all. Then Margot leaned forward and kissed the young man on both cheeks. He revved the engine so fiercely that Espérandieu felt like getting out and walking over to tell him off; then he pulled out and rode away.

Shit! Not the right one! Vincent had just wasted an hour of his time. He cursed his boss in silence, turned round and went back the way he'd come.

Servaz observed the dark façade between the trees. White, imposing, unexpectedly tall, with chalet-style carved wooden balconies and shutters on every floor. A sloping, pointed roof with a triangular wooden pediment under the eaves. Typical mountain architecture. The house was set at the far end of a steep garden in the shadow of tall trees; the light from the streetlamps did not reach that far. There was something faintly threatening about the place – or was it his imagination? He remembered a passage from *The Fall of the House of Usher*: 'I know not how it was – but, with the first glimpse of the building, a sense of insufferable gloom pervaded my spirit.'

He turned to Ziegler.

'Is Confiant still not answering?'

Ziegler put her mobile back in her pocket and shook her head. Servaz opened the creaking rusty gate. They walked up the drive. There were footprints in the snow; no one had bothered to clear it. Servaz climbed up the porch. Beneath the glass awning, he turned the door handle. Locked. No light inside. He turned round; the town was spread out below them, Christmas decorations pulsing like the living heart of the valley. There was a faraway sound of cars and horns, but here everything was silent. In this old hillside residential neighbourhood, there reigned the unfathomable sadness and crushing calm of stifling bourgeois lives.

Ziegler joined him at the top of the steps.

'What shall we do?'

Servaz looked all around. The house rested on either side of the porch on a millstone base with small basement windows. There was no way to get in through the basement: the windows were protected by iron bars. But the shutters of the big windows on the ground floor were open. In a corner behind a bush he noticed a little garden shed shaped like a chalet. He went back down the steps and up to the shed. No lock. He opened the door. A smell of turned earth. In the dim light he could see rakes, shovels, flower boxes, a watering can, a wheelbarrow, a ladder . . . Servaz came back to the house with an aluminium ladder under his arm. He set it against the wall and climbed up to the height of the window.

'What are you doing?'

Without answering, he pulled down his sleeve and smashed the windowpane with his fist. It took two tries.

Then with his hand still buried in his sleeve he removed the pieces of glass, turned the handle of the window catch and pushed it open. He expected to hear the shrill blare of an alarm, but there was nothing.

'Do you know that a lawyer could invalidate the entire procedure because of what you've just done?' said Ziegler from the bottom of the ladder.

'For the time being, the urgent thing is to find Chaperon alive. Not to convict him. We'll just say we found the window like this and took advantage of—'

'Don't move!'

They both turned round. Further down the drive, between two fir trees, a shadow was aiming a rifle at them.

'Hands up! Don't move!'

Instead of complying, Servaz plunged his hand into his jacket and brandished his warrant card before climbing back down the ladder.

'Steady, old man: police.'

'Since when do the police go round breaking and entering?' asked the man, lowering his gun.

'Since we found out it's urgent,' said Servaz.

'Are you looking for Chaperon? He's not here. We haven't seen him in two days.'

Servaz knew the type: the 'self-proclaimed concierge'. There was one in every street, or just about. The man who went nosing into other people's lives, simply because they had moved in next door. He seemed to think he had the right to keep an eye on them, to spy on them from over the hedge, particularly if there was anything *suspicious* about them. Deemed worthy of suspicion in the eyes of the self-proclaimed concierge were all gay couples, single mothers, shy, reclusive old bachelors and, more generally, anyone who had ever given him a funny look or did not share his rigid ideas. Very useful for house-to-house enquiries. Even if Servaz felt nothing but the deepest contempt for the type.

'You don't know where he went?'

'No.'

'What sort of person is he?'

'Chaperon? He's a good mayor. A regular bloke. Polite, smiling, always a friendly word. Always ready to stop for a chat. No-nonsense sort of guy. Not like the commie down there.'

He pointed to a house down the street. Servaz supposed that the 'commie down there' had become the self-proclaimed concierge's preferred target. You couldn't have one without the other. He almost felt like saying that the 'commie down there' had surely never been charged with sexual blackmail. That was the problem with self-proclaimed concierges: they went by first impressions, and they often chose the wrong target. They were generally to be found in pairs, husband and wife – a formidable duo.

'What's going on?' said the man, not hiding his curiosity. 'With everything that's been happening lately, everyone's barricading themselves in. Except me. Bring him on, the nutter – I'm ready for him.'

'Thanks,' said Servaz. 'Go on home.'

The man grumbled something and turned round.

'If you need any other information, I live at number five!' he called over his shoulder. 'The name's Lançonneur!'

'I wouldn't like to have him for a neighbour,' said Ziegler, watching him walk away.

'You should take more interest in your neighbours,' said Servaz. 'I'll bet you've got one just like him. They're everywhere. Let's go.'

He climbed back up the ladder and went into the house.

The broken glass cracked beneath his feet. In the half-light he could make out a leather sofa, rugs on a parquet floor, panelled walls, a desk. Servaz found the switch and turned on the overhead light. Ziegler appeared in the window and climbed over the sill. Behind her, the lights of the valley were visible between the trees. She looked around. They seemed to be in a study, either Chaperon's or his ex-wife's. There were bookshelves, and old photos on the walls depicting mountain landscapes or small Pyrenean towns from the turn of the previous century. Servaz recalled that there had been a time when the spas in the Pyrenees were popular with a certain

Parisian elite who liked to come and take the waters, and the local mountain villages enjoyed a brief renown as elegant resorts, on a par with Chamonix, Saint-Moritz or Davos.

'First of all, let's try to find Chaperon,' he said. 'And hope he's not hanging somewhere. Then we'll search the place.'

'What exactly are we looking for?'

'We'll know when we find it.'

He left the study.

A corridor.

At the end, a stairway.

He opened the doors, one by one. Drawing room. Kitchen. Bathroom. Dining room.

An old carpet kept in place by metal rods muffled his steps as he went up the stairs. Like the study, the stairway was panelled with light wood. On the walls were old ice axes, crampons with metal spikes, leather boots and rudimentary skis: ancient mountaineering equipment from a pioneering era. Servaz stopped to take a closer look at one of the pictures: a climber standing at the top of a rocky spur, vertical and sheer. Servaz immediately felt his stomach twist. How could the man not feel dizzy? There he was, standing at the edge of the void, smiling at the photographer who must have been equally high up, as if it were nothing. Then he saw that the mountaineer defying the summits was none other than Chaperon himself. In another picture he was dangling beneath an overhang, sitting calmly in a harness like a bird on a branch, with hundreds of metres of space below him, protected from a fatal fall by the thinnest of ropes. Servaz could just make out a valley with a river and villages below him.

Servaz would have liked to ask the mayor what it felt like to be sitting there. And, while they were at it, what it felt like to be the target of a killer. Was it the same sort of dizzy thrill? The entire interior of the house was a temple devoted to the mountain and the conquest of the self. The mayor was clearly made of stronger stuff than the chemist. Hewn from another wood altogether. This picture confirmed Servaz's first impression, from that day at the power plant: Chaperon might be a small man, but he was solid as a rock, a lover of nature and physical activity, with his white lion's mane and perpetual suntan.

Then he pictured Chaperon as he had been on the bridge and in the car: someone who was scared to death, in desperate straits. Between those two meetings, the chemist had been murdered. Servaz took a moment to reflect: the death of the horse, however dreadful it may have been, had not had the same effect on the mayor. *Why not?* Was it because it was a horse? Or because he did not feel targeted at the time?

Servaz went on exploring, tormented by the feeling of urgency that had gripped him ever since Perrault's death. Upstairs he found a bathroom, WC and two bedrooms, one of them a master bedroom. He walked around it and was immediately overcome by a strange sensation. He studied the room, frowning. There was something he could not get out of his mind.

A cupboard, a dresser. A double bed. But judging by the shape of the mattress, only one person had been sleeping there for a long time, and there was also only one chair and one night table.

It was the bedroom of a divorced man who lived alone. Servaz opened the wardrobe.

Women's dresses, blouses, skirts, jumpers and coats. And just below, pairs of high heels.

Then he ran his finger over the night table: a thick layer of dust – just like in Alice's room.

Chaperon didn't sleep in this room.

This had been the former Madame Chaperon's bedroom, before their divorce.

Just like the Grimms, the Chaperons had had separate bedrooms.

Something wasn't right. He felt instinctively he was on to something. The tension was there again and wouldn't leave. This persistent impression of danger, of impending disaster. Once again he saw Perrault screaming like the damned in his cabin, and his head began to spin. He grabbed hold of a corner of the bed.

Suddenly he heard a shout, '*Martin!*'

He rushed out onto the landing. Ziegler's voice, coming from below. His feet hardly touched the stairs. The door to the cellar was open. Servaz rushed through it and on down to a huge basement with rough stone walls. The boiler and laundry room. Plunged in darkness. There was a light further along . . . He hurried towards it. A big room lit by a bare light bulb. Its misty halo did not reach into the corners. A workbench, climbing gear hanging from big cork panels. Ziegler was standing in front of an open metal locker. A padlock was hanging from the door.

'What the—'

He broke off and went closer. Inside the cupboard was a black hooded waterproof cape and a pair of boots.

'And that's not everything,' said Ziegler.

She handed him a shoebox. Servaz opened it and held it under the dim light. He recognised it immediately: the ring. Stamped 'C S'. And a single yellowing dog-eared photograph. An old one. In it you could see four men standing side by side wearing the same capes as the one hanging in the metal cupboard, the same black hooded cape found on Grimm's corpse, the same cape that hung in the cabin by the river. The four men had their faces half hidden by the shadows of the hoods, but Servaz thought nevertheless that he could recognise Grimm's flabby chin and Chaperon's square jaw. The sun was shining on the four dark shapes, which made them seem even more sinister and out of place. A summer landscape, a bucolic vision all around – you could almost hear the birds singing. But the evil was there, thought Servaz. It was almost palpable: in that landscape flooded with sunlight, the form it had taken in the four figures, its presence, was even more obvious. Evil exists, he thought, and these four men were one of its countless incarnations.

He was beginning to get an idea of their set-up, a possible pattern.

The four men, in his opinion, had a shared passion: mountains, nature, hiking and camping rough. But there was something else, too, more secret. Deep in these valleys they were isolated from the world, in total impunity; they were exalted by the summits they knew so well, and they had finally come to believe they were untouchable. Servaz felt he was getting near the source from which everything flowed. Over the years, they had created a sort of mini-sect, living as they did in this remote part of the Pyrenees, where the outside world only reached them through television and newspapers; they were cut off both geographically and psychologically from the rest of the population, and even from their spouses – as the divorces and deep-rooted hatred proved.

Until reality caught up with them.

Until the first blood was spilled.

When that happened, the group had scattered, terrified, like a flight of starlings. And they were being shown up for what they really were: pathetic, terrified cowards and losers. Knocked brutally from their pedestals.

The mountains would no longer be the grandiose witness of their undetected crimes, but the theatre of their punishment. Who, now, was dispensing justice? What did he look like? Where was he hiding?

Gilles Grimm.

Serge Perrault.

Gilbert Mourrenx – and Roland Chaperon.

The 'club' of Saint-Martin.

There was a question tormenting him. What was the exact nature of their crimes? Because Servaz no longer had any doubt that Ziegler was right: the blackmail they had threatened the girl with was only the tip of the iceberg, and now he dreaded finding out what lay below the surface. At the same time he sensed there was an obstacle somewhere, a detail that did not fit with the pattern. It was too simple, too obvious, he thought. Somewhere there was a screen they couldn't see, and the truth was hidden behind it.

Servaz went over to the basement window that looked out onto the darkened garden. It was pitch black outside.

They were out there, waiting to exact justice. In the night, ready to strike. No doubt searching for Chaperon, as he and Ziegler were. Where was the mayor hiding? Far away, or still nearby?

Suddenly another question struck him. *Did this club consist only of the four men in the photograph, or were there other members?*

Espérandieu found the babysitter in the sitting room when he got home. She got reluctantly to her feet, apparently absorbed in an episode of *House*. Unless she had been hoping to make more money. *A first-year law student with an exotic name like Barbara, Marina or perhaps Olga,* he remembered. *Lyudmila? Stella? Vanessa?* He gave up on calling her by her first name and paid her for her two hours. He also found a note from Charlène under a magnet on the fridge: *Private view. I'll be late. Kisses.* He got a cheeseburger out of the freezer, put it in the microwave, then plugged in his laptop. There were several messages in his inbox, including one from Kleim162. The subject of the message was 'Re: Various questions about L.' Espérandieu closed the kitchen door, put on some music (the Last Shadow Puppets album *The Age of the Understatement*), pulled over a chair and began reading.

Hey, Vince.

Here are the initial results of my investigation. No scoop, but a few little things that will paint a rather different portrait of Éric Lombard from the one the public is fed. Not so long ago, during a billionaire's forum in Davos, our man adopted the definition of globalisation as postulated by Percy Barnevik, the Swedish former president of the ABB Group: 'I would define globalisation as the freedom for my group of companies to invest where it wants when it wants, to produce what it wants, to buy and sell where it wants, and support the fewest restrictions possible from labour laws and social conventions.' Which is also the creed of most multinational CEOs.

To get an idea of the increasingly powerful pressure these groups are exerting on governments, just think that in the early 1980s there were roughly 7,000 multinational corporations around the world, that by 1990 there were 37,000, and now 15 years later there are over 70,000, controlling 800,000 subsidiaries and 70 per cent of trade flow. And the tendency is only getting stronger. Consequently, there has never been so much wealth, and the wealth has never been so inequitably distributed: the CEO of Disney earns 300,000 times what the Haitian worker manufacturing the company's T-shirts gets. The 13 board members of AIR, to which Éric Lombard belongs, earned salaries of €10 million each last year – in other words, twice the total combined salaries of all 6,000 workers in one of the group's Asian factories.

Espérandieu frowned. Was Kleim162 about to rehash the entire history of socialism for him? He knew that his contact had a visceral mistrust of the police, politicians and multinational corporations, that he was not only a journalist but also a member of Greenpeace and Human Rights Watch, and that he had been in Genoa and Seattle during the anti-globalisation demonstrations that were held on the fringe of the G8 summits. He had been in the Diaz school in Genoa, which the demonstrators were using as a dormitory, when the Italian carabinieri had burst in and beat them up with such incredible brutality that the walls and floor were covered in blood. Eventually they called the ambulances. The final toll: 1 dead, 600 injured and 281 arrests.

Éric Lombard was groomed in the family's sporting goods company: a brand name that everyone knows thanks to the

313

champions who use their products. He succeeded in doubling the branch's profit in five years. How did he do that? By developing a veritable 'art' of subcontracting. Shoes, T-shirts, shorts and other sporting equipment were already being manufactured in India, Indonesia and Bangladesh, by women and children. Éric Lombard went out there and modified the existing agreements. Now in order to obtain a licence, the supplier has to agree to draconian conditions: no strikes, flawless quality and production costs so low that the workers receive a pittance. To keep up the pressure the licence is subject to revision on a monthly basis. A tactic his competitors had already used. Since he inaugurated this policy, the branch has been more prosperous than ever.

Espérandieu looked down. He studied his T-shirt, emblazoned with the words '*I'm next to a moron*', with an arrow pointing left.

Another example? In 1996, the pharmaceutical branch of the group bought the American company that had developed eflornithine, the only medication known to be effective against African trypanosomiasis, commonly known as sleeping sickness. A disease that affects 450,000 people in Africa every year and which, if left untreated, can lead to encephalitis, coma and death. The Lombard Group immediately stopped producing the drug. Why? *Not profitable enough.* To be sure, the disease affects hundreds of thousands of people, but they are people without real purchasing power. Countries like Brazil, South Africa and Thailand decided to manufacture the drugs to combat AIDS or meningitis, given the humanitarian urgency, disregarding the patents that belonged to the major pharmaceutical companies; Lombard joined forces with the companies to bring a suit against those countries at the World Trade Organisation. At the time, old Lombard was already dying, and it was Éric who took over the reins of the group, at the age of twenty-four. So are you beginning to see our handsome adventurer and media darling from another point of view?

Consequently, thought Vincent, *Lombard must have no lack of enemies. Which wasn't really good news.* He skipped over the following pages, which were more or less the same sort of thing, and figured he'd go back to them later. He did pause, however, to read a passage a bit further along:

For you the most interesting aspect might be the bitter conflict between the Lombard Group and the workers of the Polytex factory, near the Belgian border, in July 2000. In the early 1950s Polytex was manufacturing one of the first synthetic fibres in France, and they employed 1,000 workers. By the end of the 1990s there were only 160 workers left. In 1991 the factory had been bought by a multinational who handed it over almost imme- diately to a private equity firm: it wasn't profitable anymore because of competition from other less costly fibres. Although it certainly could have been – the superior quality of the product meant that it was ideal for surgical use. There was a market for it. Finally, after a series of firms had taken over the factory, a subsid- iary of the Lombard Group came forward.

For the workers, a multinational the size of Lombard seemed like a dream come true. They wanted to believe. The previous raiders had all given them the usual shutdown blackmail: salaries frozen, compulsory overtime including weekends and holidays. Lombard was no different: at first, he asked them to put in an even greater effort. In fact, the group had bought the factory for one purpose alone: to acquire the patents. On 5 July 2000, the commercial court of Charleville-Mézières ruled that the factory should be liquidated. For the workers this was a terrible blow. It meant compulsory redundancy, an immediate end to work and destruction of all the equipment. The Polytex workers were so angry that they decided to take the factory hostage, and declared they were ready to blow it up and pour 50,000 litres of sulphuric acid into the Meuse if their demands were not taken into consid- eration. They were well aware of the weapon they had: the factory contained a whole host of very toxic chemicals, which in the case of a fire or explosion would have caused a catastrophe even worse than the AZF disaster in Toulouse in 2001.

The authorities immediately ordered the evacuation of the nearby town, hundreds of policemen were positioned around the site, and the Lombard Group was ordered to begin immediate negotiations with the help of the unions. The affair lasted five days. As they were not making any progress, on 17 July the

315

workers poured 5,000 litres of sulphuric acid, symbolically coloured red, into a stream that fed into the Meuse. They threatened to do it again every two hours.

Politicians, trade unionists and leaders then denounced what they called 'indefensible eco-terrorism'. A major evening paper ran the deadly serious headline 'Advent of Social Terrorism' and spoke of 'suicidal Taliban'. Which is all the more ironic when you think that for decades Polytex had been one of the biggest polluters of the Meuse and the whole region. Finally, three days later the factory was captured by the GIGN special forces and the CRS riot police. The workers went home with their tails between their legs: they hadn't gained a thing. I imagine quite a few of them have still not digested what happened.

That's all I have for the time being. I'll keep on digging. Goodnight, Vince.

Espérandieu frowned. If this was relevant to the case, why now? Eight years later? Had any of the workers ended up in prison? Or after several years of unemployment had they killed themselves, leaving behind families filled with hatred? He made a note to find the answer to these questions.

Espérandieu looked at the time in the corner of his screen: 7.03 p.m. He switched off the laptop and stretched on his chair. He got up and took a bottle of milk from the fridge. The house was silent. Mégan was playing in her room; Charlène wouldn't be back for several hours; the babysitter had left. He leaned against the sink and took an anxiety supressant. Prompted by a sudden thought, he looked for the name of the laboratory on the box – only to find that, in order to calm the worry brought on by the doings of the Lombard Group, he had just taken one of their drugs!

He wondered how he could go about finding out more about Lombard, and remembered a contact in Paris – a brilliant young woman whom he had known at the police academy and who would surely be well placed to obtain juicy revelations.

'Martin, come and have a look.'

They had gone back to searching every floor. Servaz had started on a little room which, judging by the layer of dust, had not been used for ages. He opened cupboards and drawers, lifted up a mattress and pillows, was even trying to remove the metal sheet blocking the fireplace when Irène's voice reached him.

He went out onto the top-floor landing. On the other side was an inclined ladder with a handrail, like on a ship. And an open trap door directly above. A ribbon of light fell from the gaping hole and pierced the darkness on the landing.

Servaz climbed up and put his head through the opening.

Ziegler was standing in the middle of the room, and motioned to him to join her.

The attic consisted of one long, attractive space under the beams, and served both as bedroom and study. Servaz emerged from the hole and got his footing. The furnishing and décor were like something you'd find in a mountain chalet: rough wood, a wardrobe, a bed with drawers beneath the window, a table that served as a desk. On one of the walls was an immense map of the Pyrenees – with valleys, villages, roads and peaks. Right from the start Servaz had been wondering where Chaperon slept, as none of the bedrooms had seemed lived in; now the answer was before his eyes.

Ziegler looked all around the room, as did Servaz. The cupboard was open.

Empty hangers in a tangle inside; a pile of clothing lying on the floor.

On the desk, loose papers, and, under the bed, a gaping drawer revealed a tangle of men's underwear.

'I found it like this,' murmured Ziegler. 'What is going on here?'

Servaz noticed a detail that he had initially missed: on the desk, among the papers, was a box of bullets, open . . .

In his haste, Chaperon had dropped one on the floor.

They looked at each other.

The mayor had fled, as if he had the devil at his heels.

And he was afraid for his life.

21

Seven p.m. Diane had become very hungry and she hurried to the little cafeteria where something would be provided for the staff who did not go home. On her way in she greeted two guards eating at a table near the door, and picked up a tray.

She made a face as she looked through the glass display where the warm meals were served: chicken and chips. She would have to get organised if she wanted to eat a balanced diet and and not leave with ten extra kilos at the end of her stay. For dessert she took a fruit salad. She sat by the picture window and gazed out at the nocturnal landscape. Little lamps set around the building lit the snow at ground level, beneath the fir trees. The effect was magical.

Once the two guards had left, she was all alone in the silent room – even the server behind the counter had disappeared – and a wave of sadness and doubt overcame her. And yet as a student she would often be alone in her room, studying and working while others were scattered among the pubs and clubs in Geneva. Never had she felt so far from home. So isolated. So lost. It was the same thing every evening, as soon as night fell.

She told herself angrily to get a grip. What had become of her lucidity, of her human and psychological knowledge? Couldn't she do a better job of observing herself, instead of succumbing to her emotions? Was she simply *maladjusted* here? She knew the basic equation: maladjustment = torn = anxious. She brushed the argument aside. It wasn't as though she didn't know why she felt so ill at ease. It had nothing to do with her. It was because of what was going on here. She would have no peace of mind until she got to the bottom of it. She stood up to leave. The corridors were just as deserted as the cafeteria.

She went round the corner of the corridor leading to her office and froze. A chill, right down into her gut. Xavier was there. He was slowly closing the door to *her* office. He glanced first to the right then left, and she quickly stepped back behind the wall. To her great relief, she heard him head off in the opposite direction.

Audio cassettes.

That was the next thing that caught his attention. Among the loose papers on the mayor's desk were tapes of the kind no one used anymore but which, it would seem, Chaperon had kept. Servaz picked them up and read the labels: *Birdsongs 1*, *Birdsongs 2*, *Birdsongs 3*. He put them back down. There was a small stereo with a tape deck in a corner of the room.

Mountaineering, birdsongs: the man was truly passionate about nature.

And old things, as well: old photos, old cassettes . . . All these old things in an old house – what could be more normal?

Yet somewhere at the back of his mind an alarm bell was sounding. It had something to do with the things in this room. More precisely, with the birdsong. What did it mean? He tended to trust his instinct as a rule; it rarely warned him in vain.

He racked his brain, but nothing came. Ziegler was calling the gendarmerie to have them come and seal off the house, and bring forensics with them.

'We're getting near the truth,' she said when she had hung up.

'Yes,' he agreed solemnly. 'But clearly we're not the only ones.'

He could feel the fear in his guts again. At this point he no longer doubted that the foursome made up of Grimm, Perrault, Chaperon and Mourrenx, and their former 'exploits', were at the crux of the investigation. But the killer, or killers were at least two steps ahead. Unlike Ziegler and himself, they knew everything there was to know, and they had known it for a long time. And what did Lombard's horse or Hirtmann have to do with any of it? Once again, Servaz told himself that there was something he had failed to see.

They went back downstairs and out onto the lit porch. The trees tossed shadows about and painted the garden with darkness. Somewhere a shutter creaked. Servaz wondered why the birdsong obsessed him so. He took the cassettes out of his pocket and handed them to Ziegler.

'Have someone listen to this. And not just the first few seconds. The whole thing.'

She gave him a surprised look.

'I want to know if it really is birdsong on the tape. Or something else.'

His mobile vibrated in his pocket. He took it out and looked at the caller ID: Antoine Canter, his boss.

'Excuse me,' he said, going down the steps. 'Servaz here,' he replied, trampling on the snow in the garden.

'Martin? It's Antoine. Vilmer wants to see you.'

Divisional Commissioner Vilmer, the head of the Toulouse crime unit. A man Servaz did not like, and who returned the feeling. In Vilmer's opinion, Servaz was the sort of cop who had had his day: resistant to innovation, individualistic, working by instinct and refusing to follow the latest directives from the ministry to the letter. Vilmer dreamt of pliable, trained, interchangeable civil servants.

'I'll stop by tomorrow,' he said, glancing over at Ziegler, who was waiting by the gate.

'No. Vilmer wants you in his office tonight. He's waiting for you. Don't go pulling a fast one, Martin. You've got two hours to get there.'

Servaz left Saint-Martin shortly after eight o'clock. Half an hour later, he left the *départementale* 825 for the A64. He was overcome by fatigue as he tore down the motorway, with his headlights dipped, dazzled by the oncoming traffic. He pulled off into a service area for a coffee. After that he bought a can of Red Bull, opened it and drank the entire thing before he went back to the car.

A fine drizzle was falling when he reached Toulouse. He greeted the security guard, parked his car and hurried to the lift. It was half past nine when he pressed the button for the top floor. Ordinarily Servaz avoided coming here. The corridors were too vivid a reminder of his early days in the force, in the General Directorate of the National Police, which was full of people to whom 'police' was little more than a word to be typed, and who greeted any request on the part of a policeman in uniform as if it were a new strain of the Ebola virus. At this time of day most of the staff had gone home and the offices were deserted. He compared the atmosphere in these muffled corridors with the chaotic one of permanent tension that reigned in his own unit. Of course Servaz had also encountered a good number of competent, efficient people in the directorate. They were rarely the pushy sort. Even rarer among them was any tendency to wear the latest fashion. With a smile he recalled Espérandieu's theory, which posited that once you had a certain number of suits and ties per square metre, you entered a zone he called 'the zone of rarefied competence', and which he further subdivided into zones of 'absurd decisions', 'hogging the stage' or 'taking cover'.

He checked his watch and decided to let Vilmer wait five more minutes. It wasn't every day he had the opportunity to keep a navel-gazer like Vilmer hanging about. He took the time to go to the coffee room, and dropped a coin into the machine. Two men and a woman sat chatting around a table. When he came in, the volume of conversation dropped a few decibels; one of them told a joke in a low voice. *A sense of humour*, thought Servaz. One day his ex-wife had told him it was something he didn't have. Maybe it was true. But did that mean he was any less intelligent? Not if you went by the number of idiots who excelled at it. But it was certainly the sign of a psychological weakness. He would ask Propp. Servaz was beginning to like the shrink, despite his tendency to pontificate.

When he'd finished his umpteenth coffee, he left the room and the conversation resumed. The woman behind him burst out laughing. An artificial, graceless laugh, which grated on his nerves.

Vilmer's office was a few metres further down the hall. His secretary greeted Servaz with a friendly smile.

'Go on in. He's expecting you.'

Servaz told himself that this did not bode well, and wondered at the same time whether Vilmer's secretary was able to claim overtime.

Vilmer was a thin man with a neatly groomed goatee, an impeccable haircut and a commanding smile glued to his lips like a stubborn cold sore. He always wore the latest thing in shirts, ties, suits and shoes, and had an obvious penchant for hues of chocolate, chestnut and violet. Servaz viewed him as living proof that a moron can go far provided he has other morons ranked above him.

'Have a seat,' he said.

Servaz collapsed in the black leather armchair. Vilmer seemed cross. He joined his fingers beneath his chin and studied him wordlessly for a moment, as if to convey both profundity and disapproval. He would never have won an Oscar for his performance, and Servaz stared right back at him with a little smile. Which merely served to exasperate the commissioner.

'You find this situation amusing?'

Like everyone else, Servaz knew that Vilmer had spent his entire career cosily ensconced behind a desk. Apart from a brief early spell in vice, he had no idea what it was like out there. There were rumours that he had been the whipping boy, the laughing stock of his colleagues.

'No, sir.'

'Three murders in eight days!'

'Two,' corrected Servaz. 'Two murders and one horse.'

'What's the latest on the investigation?'

'We've been at it for a week. And we nearly caught the killer this morning, but he managed to escape.'

'You let him escape,' specified the commissioner, before hastening to add, 'Confiant has been complaining about you.'

Servaz shuddered. 'What do you mean?'

'He complained to me personally and to the Ministry of Justice. Who immediately informed the private secretary of the Ministry of the Interior. Who then called me.'

He paused for effect, then said, 'You have put me in a very awkward situation, Commandant.'

Servaz was stunned. Confiant had gone behind d'Humières's back. The judge wasn't wasting any time.

'Are you taking me off the case?'

'Of course not,' replied Vilmer, as if the thought had not even occurred to him. 'Besides, Catherine d'Humières came to your defence rather eloquently, I must say. She reckons that you and Captain Ziegler are doing a good job.'

Vilmer sniffed, as if it cost him to repeat something so inane.

'But I'm warning you: there are people in high places who are following the matter. We are in the eye of the storm. For the time being everything is calm. But if you fail, there will be consequences.'

Servaz could not help but smile. Sitting there in his chic little suit, Vilmer acted as if it were nothing, but he was shitting himself. Because he knew very well that the 'consequences' would concern not only the investigators.

'This is a sensitive case, don't forget that.'

Because of a horse, thought Servaz. *It's the horse they're after.* He repressed his anger.

'Is that all?' he asked.

'No. That man, the victim, Perrault, he called you for help?'

'Yes.'

'Why you?'

'I don't know.'

'You didn't try to dissuade him from going up there?'

'I didn't have time.'

'And what's all this business about suicide victims? What does that have to do with anything?'

'For the time being, we don't know. But Hirtmann mentioned it when we went to see him.'

'What do you mean?'

'Well, he . . . *advised* me to take an interest in the suicides.'

The commissioner looked at him with a stupefaction that was anything but feigned this time.

'You mean that Hirtmann is telling you how to conduct your investigation?'

Servaz frowned.

'That might be a somewhat . . . simplistic way of looking at things.'

'*Simplistic?*' Vilmer raised his voice. 'I get the impression that this investigation is all over the place, Commandant. You have Hirtmann's DNA, don't you? What more do you need? Since he couldn't have left the Institute, it means he has an accomplice inside. Find him!'

Isn't it wonderful how simple things can seem when you view them from a distance, when you leave out the details, and you know nothing about the case, thought Servaz. But basically, Vilmer was right.

'What sort of leads do you have?'

'A few years ago a complaint was filed against Grimm and Perrault for blackmail. Sexual blackmail.'

'So?'

'It would seem they weren't novices. They may even have gone further with other women. Or with teenagers . . . This could be the motive we're looking for.'

Servaz was aware that he was on shaky ground now, that they had very few clues to go on – but it was too late to back down.

'Revenge?'

'It could be.'

His attention was distracted by a poster on the wall behind Vilmer. A urinal. Servaz recognised it: Marcel Duchamp. The Dada exhibition at the Centre Georges-Pompidou in 2006. Clearly displayed, as if to prove to his visitors that here was a man of culture who was passionate about art and also had a sense of humour.

The director thought for a moment.

'What about the connection with Lombard's horse?'

Servaz hesitated.

'Well, if we go with the revenge theory, it would mean that these people – the victims – must have done something really ugly,' he said, repeating almost word for word what Alexandra had said. 'Particularly if they did it together. In Lombard's case, since they couldn't get at him directly, the killer or killers went after his horse.'

Vilmer suddenly went pale.

'Don't tell me . . . don't tell me that you suspect Éric Lombard of being involved in – in this—'

'Sexual abuse,' said Servaz, helping him finish his sentence, aware that he might be taking things too far; still, the fear he saw for a split second in his boss's eyes was like an aphrodisiac. 'No, for the time being there's nothing like that. But there is bound to be a link between him and the others, something to place him among the victims.'

At least he had managed one thing: to shut Vilmer up.

On leaving the crime unit offices, Servaz headed for the old centre of town. He didn't feel like going home. Not right away. He needed to offload the tension and rage that Vilmer aroused in him. It was still drizzling and he didn't have an umbrella, but he welcomed the rain like a blessing. As if it were cleansing him of all the muck he'd been drenched in over the last few days.

He let his footsteps take him to the rue du Taur, and found himself outside the brilliantly lit glass entrance of his assistant's wife Charlène's art gallery. The gallery was long and narrow and occupied two levels, and the white, modern interior was visible through the windows, a sharp contrast to the neighbouring façades of old red brick. There were a lot of people inside. A private view. He was about to continue on his way when he saw Charlène waving to him from the first floor. He went half-heartedly into the long room. His clothes and hair were dripping, his sodden shoes squeaked and left a damp trail on the light wood floor, but he attracted fewer gazes than he would have expected. *All these faces sought to appear eccentric, modern and open-minded, or at least so they thought. On the surface they were open and modern, but what about deep down? One sort of conformism banishes another*, he mused. He headed for the steel spiral staircase at the back, his eyes dazzled by the whiteness of the premises and the powerful spotlights overhead. He was about to put his foot on the bottom step when a huge painting against the back wall caught his attention and left him speechless.

In fact it wasn't really a painting but a photograph, twelve feet high.

A huge crucifixion scene in sickly bluish tones. Behind the cross a stormy sky was roiling with clouds torn by lightning. On the cross Christ had been replaced by a pregnant woman. Her head bent to one side, she was weeping tears of blood. Bright red blood also flowed from the crown of thorns on her bluish brow. Not only was she crucified, her breasts had been torn off and replaced by two bloody, bright red wounds, and her irises were a translucent milky white.

Servaz recoiled. The realism and violence of the picture were unbearable. What sort of madman could have conceived such a painting?

Why were people so fascinated by violence? he wondered. The avalanche of shocking images on television, in the cinema and in books – was it a way to stave off fear? Most of these artists only knew violence indirectly, abstractly. They had no real experience of it. If the cops who were confronted by unbearable crime scenes, or the firefighters who had to pull the victims of car accidents from the wreckage every week, or the magistrates who dealt day after day with atrocious cases – if they all began to paint, sculpt or write, who knows what they would portray, what would come out of them? Would it be the same thing, or something radically different?

The steel steps vibrated beneath his feet as he climbed upstairs. Charlène was chatting with an elegant man with silky white hair. She paused to motion to Servaz to come closer; then she introduced them. Servaz gathered that the man, a banker, was one of the gallery's best clients.

'Well, I shall go back downstairs and admire this very beautiful exhibition,' he said. 'Congratulations again on your flawless taste, my dear. I don't know how you manage, every time, to find such extremely talented artists.'

The man walked away. Servaz wondered if he had looked at him even once – he did not seem to have noticed the state Servaz was in. For men like him, Servaz did not exist. Charlène kissed Servaz on the cheek and he could smell the raspberry and vodka on her breath. She was radiant in a red maternity gown beneath a short white vinyl jacket, and her eyes, like her necklace, shone just a touch too brightly.

'It looks like it's raining,' she said, looking at him with a tender smile.

She waved around the gallery. 'You come here so rarely. I'm very glad you're here, Martin. Do you like it?'

'It's somewhat . . . unsettling,' he replied.

She laughed.

'The artist goes by the name Mentopagus. The theme of the exhibition is *Cruelty.*'

'Well, in that case, it's a great success,' he joked.

'You're not looking very well, Martin.'

'I'm sorry, I shouldn't have come in here in this state.'

She brushed away his apology with a wave of her hand.

'Here, the best way not to stand out is to have a third eye in the middle of your forehead. All these people think they are so avant-garde, cutting-edge, modern, anti-conformist – that they are *beautiful* inside – that they're so much better than everyone else . . .'

He was surprised by the bitterness he could detect in her voice and he glanced at her glass. Perhaps it was the alcohol.

'The cliché of the egocentric artist,' he said.

'If clichés become clichés, it's precisely because they contain a greater truth,' she retorted. 'In actual fact I believe I know only two people who have a true inner beauty,' she continued, as if she were speaking to herself. 'Vincent and you. Two cops. And yet where you're concerned, you keep that beauty well hidden.'

He was surprised by her confession. He wasn't expecting it at all.

'I hate artists,' she said suddenly, her voice trembling.

Her next gesture surprised him even more. She leaned over and kissed him, again on his cheek but this time at the corner of his mouth. Then she touched his lips furtively with her fingertips – a gesture of surprising restraint and astonishing intimacy – before she walked away. Her heels clicked on the metal steps as she went downstairs.

Servaz's heart was beating the same rhythm. His head was spinning. Part of the floor was covered with gravel, plaster and cobblestones, and he wondered if it was a work of art or a construction site. Opposite him on the white wall was a square painting where a multitude of tiny characters swarmed in a dense, colourful crowd. There were hundreds of them, perhaps thousands. Apparently, the first floor had been spared the *Cruelty* exhibition.

'It's brilliant, isn't it?' said a woman standing next to him. 'This sort of pop art, the comic-book side to it. It's like a miniature Lichtenstein.'

He was startled. Lost in thought, he hadn't heard her come up to him. She spoke as if she were doing singing exercises, her voice rising and falling.

'*Quos vult perdere Jupiter dementat prius,*' he said.

The woman looked at him, uncomprehending.

'It's Latin: "Those whom Jupiter seeks to destroy he first makes mad."'

He turned and headed quickly for the staircase.

At home he put *The Song of the Earth* on his stereo – the modern version by Eiji Oue with Michelle DeYoung and Jon Villars – and went straight to the breathtaking 'Farewell'. He wasn't sleepy and he took a book down off the shelf. *Aethiopica* by Heliodorus of Emesa.

And now is she my daughter with me here, my daughter I say, named by my name, and on her all my hopes depend. And beside other things, wherein she is better than I could wish, she has quickly learned the Greek tongue and has come to perfect age with such speed as if she had been a peerless branch, and so far doth she surpass every other in excellent beauty that all men's eyes, as well strangers as Greeks, are set on her.

Sitting in his chair by the bookshelf, he stopped reading and thought about Gaspard Ferrand, the broken father. His thoughts then drifted to Alice and the suicide victims, like a flock of crows above a field. Like the young Chariclea in Heliodorus' tale, all men's eyes had been set on Alice. He had reread the neighbours' statements: Alice Ferrand was a perfect child – beautiful, precocious, with excellent results at school, including in sports – and always ready to oblige. *But she had changed recently,* according to her father. What had happened to her? Then his thoughts returned to the Grimm-Perrault-Chaperon-Mourrenx foursome. Had Alice and the other suicide victims ever had anything to do with them? If so, when? At the holiday camp? But two of the seven suicide victims had never stayed there.

Once again he felt himself shivering. It was as if the temperature in the apartment had dropped several degrees. He wanted to go to the kitchen to fetch a bottle of water, but suddenly the sitting room began to spin. The books on the shelves were swaying while the lights from the lamp seemed glaring and venomous. Servaz dropped back into his armchair.

He closed his eyes. When he opened them again, the dizzy spell had passed. What was the matter with him, for God's sake?

He got up and rushed into the bathroom. He took out one of Xavier's tablets. His throat was on fire, and the cold water felt good for a split second; then the burning sensation returned. He massaged his eyes and went out onto the balcony for some air. He looked over the lights of the city and thought about how modern towns, with their unreal lighting and permanent noise, managed to transform their inhabitants into insomniacs and drowsy ghosts.

Then Alice was there again. He saw the room under the roof, the orange and yellow furniture, the purple walls and white carpet. The photos and postcards, the CDs and school things, her clothes and books. *A diary . . . a diary was missing*. Servaz was increasingly convinced that a girl like Alice could not have *not* had one.

There had to be a diary somewhere.

And then there was Gaspard Ferrand, the literature professor, globetrotter, yogi. Servaz instinctively compared him to his own father, who had also been a teacher, of Latin and Greek. A brilliant man, secretive, eccentric and also irascible on occasion. *Genus irritabile vatum*: 'the irritable race of poets'.

Servaz knew very well where this thought would lead him. Too late; he could not stop the rush of memories; they overwhelmed him, bore him away with nightmarish precision.

The facts. Nothing but the facts.

Which were as follows: on a warm July evening, the young Martin Servaz, aged ten, was playing in the courtyard of the family house when the lights of a car approached down the long, straight road. The Servaz home was an old farmhouse three kilometres from the nearest village. Ten o'clock at night. A gentle semi-darkness reigned, and in the neighbouring fields the chirring of crickets would soon be replaced by the sound of frogs; a muffled rumble of thunder came from the mountains on the horizon, and the stars grew ever sharper in the still pale sky. Then there came the imperceptible whisper of that car in the distance, coming down the road. The whisper became the sound of an engine and the car slowed down. It turned its lights towards the house and went slowly up the drive, bouncing over the ruts. The tyres crunched on gravel when it came through the gate and braked in the courtyard. A gust of wind caused the poplar trees to rustle as two men climbed out of the car. He could not see their faces because of the darkness under the trees, but he heard one of them say clearly, 'Hello, lad, where are your parents?'

At the same time, the door to the house opened and his mother appeared on the threshold. The man who had spoken went up to her and apologised for the disturbance, speaking very quickly, while the other one put a hand on Martin's shoulder. There was something about his hand that immediately felt unpleasant to young Servaz. Like an infinitesimal shift in the peaceful evening. Like a dull threat that the young boy alone could perceive, even though the man was acting in a friendly manner, and he could see his mother smiling. He looked up and caught a glimpse of his father in the window of his study on the first floor where he was correcting his students' homework; he was frowning. Servaz wanted to call out to his mother to be careful, not to let them into the house, but he had been taught to be polite and to keep quiet when adults were talking.

He heard his mother say, 'Come in.'

Then the man behind him pushed him gently forward, his big fingers burning his shoulder, and he thought the gesture was more authoritarian than friendly. Even today he could still remember every step they took, resounding in his brain like a warning. He remembered the strong smell of cologne and sweat. He remembered how the chirring of the crickets seemed to grow louder, shrill like an alarm. Even his heart was beating like an ominous drum. It was when they got to the top of the front steps that the man plastered something over his mouth and nose. A piece of damp cloth. In a split second a blade of fire burned his throat and lungs, and he saw white dots dancing before his eyes before he fell into a black hole.

When he came to, he was in the storage space under the stairs, nauseous and dazed, and the sound of his mother's pleading voice behind the door filled him with fear. When he heard the two men's growling voices threaten, reassure and make fun of her in turn, he could no longer control himself and he began to tremble. He wondered where his father had gone. He had known instinctively who these men were. They weren't quite human; they were the bad guys from the cinema; they were evil beings, the super-villains in his comic books: the Tinkerer and the Green Goblin . . . He guessed his father must be tied up somewhere, powerless, the way comic-book heroes often were, because otherwise he would already have come to save them. Many years later, he told himself that neither Seneca nor Marcus Aurelius had been of much use to his father when it came time to reason with the two visitors. But can you really reason with two famished wolves? It wasn't meat the two wolves were after; it was another flesh. If little Martin had had a watch, he would have seen that when he regained consciousness, it was twenty minutes past midnight, and five more hours would go by before the horror came to an end, five hours in which he heard his mother scream, sob, hiccup, swear and plead, almost without stopping. And as his mother's cries gradually changed into unintelligible murmurs, as the snot ran from his nose and urine flowed down his thighs, as the first sounds of dawn came through the door of the storage space – a cock crowing early, a dog barking in the distance, a car going by not a hundred metres away – and a vague grey light began to filter along the ground, silence fell over the house – a total, definitive and strangely reassuring silence.

Servaz had been in the police force for three years when he managed to get his hands on the autopsy report, fifteen years after it happened. With hindsight he could see this was a grave error. He had thought that the years would give him the necessary strength. He was wrong. It was with unspeakable horror that he had discovered in detail what his mother had been through that night. Once he had closed the report, he ran to the toilets and threw up.

The facts, nothing but the facts.

Which were as follows: his father had survived, but he had spent two months in hospital, while young Martin had been sent to stay with his aunt. Once he was out of hospital, his father had gone back to his teaching job. But it quickly became apparent that he could no longer fulfil his role: on numerous occasions he showed up drunk and dishevelled in front of his students, whom he then went on to insult fiercely. Finally the administration had placed him on indefinite leave and he had only sunk deeper. Little Martin was sent to stay with his aunt again. The facts, nothing but the facts. Two weeks after he met the woman who would become his wife, Servaz went to see his father, as summer was drawing near. When he got out of the car, he glanced briefly at the house. To one side the old barn was falling to ruin; the main part of the house seemed uninhabited; at least half of the shutters were closed. Servaz knocked on the front door. No answer. He went in. 'Dad?' Nothing but silence. The old man must be dead drunk again somewhere. Servaz threw his jacket and briefcase on a chair and went to drink a glass of water; once his thirst was quenched, he climbed the stairs. His father must be in his study. Young Martin was right: he was in his study. A faint music came through the closed door and he recognised it at once: Gustav Mahler, his father's favourite composer.

But he was wrong too: the old man wasn't drunk. Nor was he reading one of his beloved Latin authors. He was slumped motionless in his chair, his eyes wide open and glassy, a white foam on his lips. Poison. Like Seneca, like Socrates. Two months later, Servaz passed his exams to become a police officer.

At ten o'clock that night, Diane switched off the light in her office. She took some work with her to finish before bed, and went back up to her room on the fourth floor. It was still just as cold up there and she put her dressing gown on before sitting down to read. As she went through her notes she visualised the first patient she had seen that day: a man of sixty-four who looked harmless enough, with a shrill, rasping voice as if his vocal cords had been filed. A former philosophy teacher. He had greeted her very politely when she came in. The interview had been held in a small lounge with tables and chairs that were riveted to the floor. There was a wide-screen television sealed in a Plexiglas bubble, and all the corners and sharp edges of the furniture were padded with plastic. There was no one else in the lounge, but a nursing auxiliary was on guard at the entrance.

'How do you feel today, Victor?' Diane asked.

'*Like a fucking bag of shit.*'

'What do you mean?'

'*Like a huge turd, excrement, dog poo, a lump of dung, a—*'

'Victor, why are you being so vulgar?'

'*I feel like the stuff that comes out of your arse, Doctor, when you go to the—*'

'Don't you want to answer me?'

'*I feel like . . .*'

She reminded herself never again to ask him how he felt. Victor had killed his wife, his brother-in-law and his sister-in-law with an axe. According to the file, his wife and in-laws had treated him as if he were worthless, constantly making fun of him. In his 'normal' life, Victor had been a very well-educated and cultured individual. During his previous hospitalisation, he had assaulted a nurse who made the mistake of laughing in front of him. Fortunately he weighed only fifty kilos.

No matter how she tried, Diane couldn't manage to focus solely on the case. Something else was lurking at the edge of her awareness. She was eager to have done with this work in order to get back to the events at the Institute. She didn't know what she was going to find, but she was determined to take her investigation further. And now she knew where to begin. The idea had occurred to her after she had surprised Xavier coming out of her office.

When she opened the next folder, she immediately pictured the patient. A man in his forties with a feverish gaze, dirty hair and hollow cheeks beneath a scruffy beard. A former researcher specialising in marine biology, of Hungarian origin, and who spoke excellent French with a strong accent. György.

'We are connected to the great depths,' he had said at once. 'You may not know it yet, Doctor, but we don't really exist, we exist only as thoughts, we are emanations of the minds of the creatures of the deep, those that live at the bottom of the ocean, over two thousand metres below the surface. It is the realm of eternal darkness: daylight never reaches that far. It is *dark* there all the time.'

On hearing the word, she felt an icy wind of fear pass over her.

'And it's cold, very, very cold. And the pressure there is colossal. It increases by one atmosphere every ten metres. No one can bear it, except those creatures. They look like monsters, you know. Like us. They have enormous eyes, and jaws full of sharp teeth, and luminous organs all down their bodies. They are carrion eaters; they feed on the corpses that drop down from the upper layers of the ocean; they are terrible predators who can swallow down their prey in one gulp. There is nothing but darkness and cruelty down there. Like here. There is the viperfish, *Chauliodus sloani*, with a head like a skull, teeth as long as knives and transparent as glass, with a serpent's body that has hackles of luminous points. There are the *Linophryne lucifer* and the *Photostomias guernei,* uglier and more terrifying than piranhas. There are the *pycnogonids,* which look like spiders, and the hatchetfishes, which may look dead, but are alive. These creatures never see the light of day, never go up to the surface. Like us, Doctor. Can't you see the analogy? It is because we do not truly exist here, unlike you. We are secreted by the mind of those creatures. Every time one of them dies down there at the bottom, one of us dies here too.'

His eyes had glazed over while he was speaking, as if he had gone to the depths of the ocean darkness. His absurd speech had chilled Diane with its nightmarish beauty. She found it difficult to get rid of the images he had created.

Everything in the Institute went by opposites, she thought. Beauty/ cruelty. Silence/screaming. Solitude/promiscuity. Fear/curiosity. Ever since she had arrived, she had been in a constant turmoil of contra- dictory feelings.

She closed the folder for the patient called György and concen- trated on something else. All evening she had been thinking about the treatment Xavier was forcing some of his patients to undergo. The chemical straitjacket. And the clandestine visit he had paid to her office. Had Dimitri, the manager of the pharmacy, told Xavier that she seemed awfully interested in his treatment methods? It was unlikely. She had sensed that Dimitri felt a silent hostility towards the psychiatrist. She mustn't forget that Xavier had only been there a few months, that he had come to replace the man who had founded the place. Was he finding it difficult to relate to the staff?

She leafed through her notepad until she located the names of the three mysterious products Xavier had ordered. They were no more familiar to her than the first time.

She opened her laptop and went on to Google.

Keyed in the first two words of her search.

With a start she discovered that Hypnosal was a brand name for sodium thiopental, an anaesthetic that was one of the three products administered in the lethal injections used in the United States, as well as for euthanasia in the Netherlands. It was also marketed under a well-known name: Penthotal. For a time it had been used in narco- analysis, which consisted of injecting an anaesthetic to help the patient retrieve supposedly repressed memories – a technique that had been criticised and abandoned long ago, as the existence of repressed trauma had never been scientifically proven.

What was Xavier playing at?

The second entry puzzled her even further. Xylazine was also an anaesthetic – but for veterinary use. Diane wondered if she had missed something, and she read further down the various hits provided by the search engine, but found no other known applications. She was more and more bewildered. What was a veterinary drug doing in the Institute's pharmacy?

She moved on quickly to the third product. Now her eyebrows lifted. Like the two previous drugs, halothane was an anaesthetic agent. But given its toxic effect on the heart and liver, it had gradually disappeared from the operating theatre, except in developing countries. All marketing for human use had been stopped in 2005; like xylazine, halothane was used only for veterinary purposes.

Diane lay back against the pillows and thought. To the best of her knowledge, there were no animals at the Institute, not even a dog or a cat. (She had been led to understand that some of the residents had a pathological fear of pets.) She reached for her laptop and went back over the information she had, one element after another. Suddenly something caught her eye. She had almost missed the most important thing: the three products were not mentioned together except in one case. *To anaesthetise a horse* . . . The information was on a website for veterinarians. The author of the article, a specialist in equine medicine, recommended pre-medication with xylazine in a dose of 0.8 mg/kg, followed by an IV injection of sodium thiopental, and finally halothane at a dose of 2.5 per cent, for a horse weighing roughly 490 kilos.

A horse . . .

Something not unlike one of György's deep-sea creatures began to stir in her gut. Xavier . . . She thought again of the conversation she had overheard through the air vent. He had seemed so distraught that day, so lost, when that cop informed him that someone in the Institute was involved in the death of the horse. She could not imagine a single reason why the psychiatrist might have gone up there and killed the animal. Besides, the cop had said something about two people. There was one other thing, though. If it was Xavier who had provided the drugs to anaesthetise the horse before killing it, no doubt he was behind Hirtmann's DNA getting out.

The thought of it made the living thing wriggle in the hollow of her stomach.

To what end? What was Xavier's role in all this?

Had the psychiatrist known then that after the horse, a man would be killed? Why should he be an accomplice to the crimes if he had only been here for a few months?

She could not get to sleep. She tossed and turned in her bed, first on her back, then on her stomach, gazing at the faint grey light beyond the window, where the wind was howling. Too many unpleasant questions were keeping her mind busily awake. At around three o'clock she took half a sleeping tablet.

Servaz sat in his armchair and listened to the flute in the first recitative of the 'Farewell'. Someone had once compared it to a 'dream nightingale'. Then the harp and clarinet joined in, like a beating of wings. Birdsong, he suddenly remembered. Why did the memory of these songs trouble him persistently? Chaperon loved nature and mountaineering. And so what? Why should those recordings have any importance whatsoever?

No matter which way he turned it, he could not find the answer. But he was sure that there was something waiting to come to light. And it had to do with the recordings they had found at the mayor's house. He was eager to know if it really was birdsong on the cassettes. But this was not the only thing bugging him. There was something else.

He got up and walked out onto the balcony. It had stopped raining, but a faint mist clung to the wet pavement and left the streetlamps with vaporous halos. He thought again of Charlène Espérandieu, the surprising intimacy of her kiss on his cheek, and once again his stomach was in a knot.

On coming back in through the French doors he realised his mistake: it wasn't the birdsong, it was the tapes themselves that were significant. The knot in his stomach hardened as if someone had poured cement down his oesophagus. His pulse accelerated. He hunted through his notebook until he found the number, then rang it.

'Hello?' said a man's voice.

'May I come by your place in an hour and a half or so?'

A silence.

'But it will be after midnight!'

'I'd like to have another look at Alice's room.'

'At this time of night? Can't it wait until tomorrow?'

The voice on the other end of the line sounded truly dismayed. Servaz could put himself in Gaspard Ferrand's position: his daughter had been dead for fifteen years. How could anything suddenly be so urgent?

'Still, I really would like to have a look tonight,' he insisted.

'Fine. I never go to bed before midnight, anyway. I'll wait for you until half past. After that, I'm going to bed.'

At roughly twenty-five minutes past twelve he reached Saint-Martin, but instead of going into the town he took the road to the sleeping village five kilometres further along.

Gaspard Ferrand opened the door the moment Servaz rang the bell. He seemed extremely curious.

'Is there anything new?'

'I'd like to see Alice's bedroom again, if you don't mind.'

Ferrand shot him a questioning look. He was wearing a bathrobe over a jumper and an old pair of jeans and was barefoot in his slippers. He pointed to the stairs. Servaz thanked him and climbed them quickly. In the room he headed straight for the wooden shelf above the little orange desk.

The cassette deck.

It was neither a radio nor a CD player, unlike the stereo on the floor; it was an old cassette player that Alice must have found second-hand somewhere.

Except that Servaz hadn't seen any tapes the first time he visited. He picked up the cassette deck; it seemed a normal weight, but that didn't mean anything. He went through all the drawers of the desk and night tables again, one by one. No tapes, anywhere. Perhaps there had been some at one point and Alice had thrown them all out when she switched to CDs?

Then why would she have kept the bulky player? Alice's room was like a museum of the 1990s, with one single anachronism: the cassette deck.

Servaz grabbed it by the handle on the top and examined it from every angle. Then he pressed the button to open the compartment. Empty. He went back down to the ground floor. He could hear the sound of the television from the sitting room. A late-night cultural programme.

'I need a Phillips screwdriver,' said Servaz from the threshold. 'Is that something you might have?'

Ferrand was sitting on the sofa. This time, the look the literature professor gave him was frankly inquisitive.

'What have you found?'

His voice was imperious, impatient. He wanted to know.

'Nothing, absolutely nothing,' answered Servaz. 'But if I do find something, I'll be sure to let you know.'

Ferrand got up and left the room, returning a minute later with a screwdriver. Servaz went back up under the eaves. The three screws were very easy to twist. *As if they had been tightened by a child's hand.*

Holding his breath, he removed the front panel.

Found it.

You had to hand it to her. Part of the device had been painstakingly emptied of its electronic components. Held in place against the plastic shell with thick brown tape were three little notebooks with blue covers.

Servaz gazed at them for a long time without reacting. Could he be dreaming? *Alice's diary.* It had stayed here for years, unknown to everyone. And of course it was lucky that Gaspard Ferrand had kept his daughter's room intact. Very gingerly Servaz peeled off the dried-up adhesive tape and took out the notebooks.

'What is it?' came a voice from behind.

Servaz turned round. Ferrand was staring at the notebooks. His eyes were gleaming like a hawk's, burning with an almost unhealthy curiosity. The policeman opened the first notebook and glanced at it. He read the first words. His heart began to pound: '*Saturday, 12 August*' . . . *This is it.*

'It looks like a diary.'

'It was in there?' said Ferrand, stunned. 'All these years, it was in there?!'

Servaz nodded. He saw the professor's eyes fill with tears and his face contort with grief and pain. Servaz suddenly felt very ill at ease.

'I have to go over them,' he said. 'There might be some

explanation for her act in these pages, who knows? Then I'll give them back to you.'

'You did it,' murmured Ferrand in a flat voice. 'You did it where we all failed . . . It's incredible . . . How – how did you guess?'

'Not yet,' said Servaz to calm him. 'It's too soon.'

22

It was eight o'clock in the morning and the sky was growing pale above the mountains when he finished reading. He closed the last notebook and went out onto the balcony to breathe in the cold, sharp dawn air. Exhausted. Physically sick. Near breaking point. First the boy called Clément, and now this.

It had stopped snowing. The temperature had even risen slightly, but heaped layers of clouds drifted above the town. The roofs and streets shone with a silvery brilliance, and Servaz could feel the first raindrops on his face. They pitted the snow that had settled in a corner of the balcony, and he went back inside. He wasn't hungry, but he had to have at least a hot coffee. He went down to the large veranda that overlooked a town blurred with rain. The waitress brought him fresh bread, coffee, a glass of orange juice, butter and jam. To his surprise, he devoured everything. Eating felt like an exorcism; eating meant that he was alive, that the hell he had found in the pages of those notebooks did not concern him. Or that he could keep it at a distance at least a moment longer.

My name is Alice. I'm fifteen years old. I don't know what I'm going to do with these pages, or whether someone will read them someday. Maybe I'll tear them up or burn them as soon as I've written them. Or maybe I won't. But if I don't write them now, fuck, I'll go crazy. I've been raped. It wasn't just one bastard, either, but several disgusting pigs. On a summer night. Raped.

Alice's diary was one of the most difficult things he had ever had to read. It was chilling. The intimate diary of a teenage girl, consisting of drawings, poems, cryptic phrases. During the night, as dawn approached like a fearful animal, he had been tempted to throw it into the waste paper basket. And yet there was not much in the way of concrete information in the notebooks – it consisted, rather, of allusions and insinuations. A few facts, however, did appear clearly. In the summer of 1992, Alice Ferrand had gone to stay at Les Isards. The very same one Servaz had seen on his way to the Wargnier Institute, the one that Saint-Cyr had mentioned, the one visible in a photograph pinned in her room. At the time, Les Isards took in children from Saint-Martin and the surrounding valleys for the summer, from families too poor to send their children on holiday. It was a local tradition. Several of Alice's best friends would be there that summer, and she had asked her parents for permission to go with them. At first, they had hesitated, then finally agreed. Alice pointed out that their decision had not been made solely to please her but also because, in the end, it was in keeping with their ideals of social equality. She added that on that day they had taken 'the most tragic decision of their lives'. Alice did not blame her parents. Or herself. She blamed the *swines*, the *bastards*, the *Nazis* (written in capital letters with red ink) who had destroyed her life. She would have liked to *castrate them, emasculate them, slice off their cocks with a rusty knife and force them to eat them – and then kill them.*

It occurred to Servaz that Alice had several things in common with the boy named Clément: both of them were intelligent and precocious for their age. Both of them had also shown they were capable of incredible verbal violence. And physical, too, thought Servaz. Except that the boy had turned against a homeless man, and the girl against herself.

Fortunately for Servaz, Alice's diary did not describe what she had suffered in detail. It was not a diary in the strictest sense of the word: she did not record her life on a day-by-day basis. It was, rather, an indictment. A cry of pain. Still, because Alice was an intelligent child with a penetrating mind, her words were terribly distressing. The drawings were even worse. Some of them would have been extraordinary if their subject had not been so gruesome. Servaz immediately noticed the one of four men in capes and boots. Alice was talented. She had drawn in detail the folds of their black capes and the men's faces, obscured by the sinister shadow of their hoods. Other drawings showed the four men on their backs, naked, their eyes and mouths wide open, dead. *A fantasy,* thought Servaz.

On looking closer, he was disappointed to see that while the capes were faithfully reproduced and the naked bodies realistic, the faces, on the other hand, did not resemble any of the men he knew. Not

Grimm, nor Perrault, nor Chaperon. They were swollen, monstrous faces, caricatures of vice and cruelty that evoked the grimacing gargoyles from cathedrals. Had Alice intentionally disfigured them? Or did he have to accept that she and her friends had never seen their torturers' faces, that the men had never removed their hoods? He could, however, infer several things. First of all, there were always four men in the drawings: it was clear that the rapists belonged to the same foursome. And then the diary did answer another question that had arisen from Grimm's death: the boots. Until now, their presence on the chemist's feet had been an enigma, but now Servaz had found an explanation:

They always come on a stormy night, the scum, when it's raining. No doubt to be sure that no one will come to the camp while they're here. Because who would ever think of coming to this valley after midnight when it's pouring down?

They splash about on the path in their loathsome boots and leave their muddy tracks along the corridors and soil everything they touch, the foul pigs.

They have loud voices and coarse laughs: I've recognised at least one of those voices.

Servaz shuddered on reading this last sentence. He had gone through the notebooks in every direction, feverishly turning the pages, but nowhere had he found any other reference to the torturers' identity. At one point he also read, '*They each took their turn.*' Words that left him paralysed, incapable of reading any further. He had slept for a few hours, then resumed. After going over certain passages, he concluded that Alice had been raped only once – or rather, on one single night – but that she was not the only one affected, and that the men had come to the camp half a dozen times or so over that summer. Why hadn't she said anything? Why had none of the children sounded the alarm? There was a vague reference to a child who had died, who had fallen down a ravine. Was he an example, a warning to the others? Is that why they remained silent? Because they had been threatened with death? Or was it because they were ashamed and thought no one would believe them? In those days, denunciations were very rare. Alice's diary did not provide any answers to these questions.

There were also poems that displayed the same precocious talent as her drawings, even if her aim was not so much to imbue her text with literary qualities as to express the horror of what she had been through:

> Was I that little BODY full of TEARS?
> This Filthy Thing, this spot on the ground, this bruise:
>   that was Me? – and I
> Looked at the ground so close to my face, the shadow
> Of the torturer lying there;
> It doesn't matter what they did, what they said
> They cannot reach the hard seed, the kernel of me.
> 'Papa, what does it mean, WHORE?'
> Those words when I was six. This is their answer:
> PIGS PIGS PIGS PIGS.

One detail – the most sinister of all – had caught Servaz's attention: in her description of the events, Alice spoke several times of *the sound of the capes*, the rustling of the black waterproof fabric when her aggressors moved. '*That noise*,' she wrote, '*I'll never forget it. For ever, it will always mean the same thing: evil exists, and it has a sound.*'

These words left Servaz lost deep in thought. As he went on reading, he understood why he had not found any diaries in Alice's room, or any sort of writing at all:

> *I used to keep a diary. I wrote about my little life the way it used to be, day after day. I tore it up and threw it away. What would be the point of keeping a diary after THIS? Not only have those vermin ruined my future, they've also soiled my past for ever.*

He understood that Alice could not bring herself to throw out these notebooks: this was perhaps the only place where the truth could be found. But at the same time she wanted to be sure that her parents would not see them. So she found a hiding place. She probably knew that after her death her parents would not touch her room. Or at least so she must have hoped. As she must have hoped, secretly, that someday someone would find the notebooks. But she could not have imagined it would take all these years and that the man who would unearth them would be a perfect stranger. In any case, she had not chosen to 'castrate the bastards'; she had not chosen revenge. *Someone else had done it for her . . . Who?* Was it her father, also mourning the death of her mother? Or another parent? Or a child who had been abused but did not commit suicide, who had gone on to become an adult full of rage, filled for ever with a thirst for vengeance?

Once he had finished his breakfast, he went back up to his room and took two of Xavier's tablets. He felt feverish and nauseous. Fine drops of sweat were pearling on his forehead. The coffee he had just drunk was sitting on his stomach. He took a long, scalding shower, got dressed, took his mobile and went out.

The Cherokee was parked a short distance away, outside a shop that sold spirits and souvenirs. A cold, heavy rain was falling, and the streets were invaded by the sound of water rushing down the gutters. He sat behind the wheel of the Jeep and called Ziegler.

That morning Espérandieu picked up his phone as soon as he got to work. He called a ten-storey semicircular building located at 122, rue du Château-des-Rentiers in the 13th arrondissement in Paris. A voice with a slight accent picked up.

'How are you, Marissa?' he asked.

Commandant Marissa Pearl belong to the BRDE, the financial crime unit, a sub-directorate of the Ministry of Finance and the Economy. Her speciality was white-collar fraud. Marissa was unbeatable when it came to tax havens, money laundering, active or passive corruption, bogus invitations to tender, embezzlement, influence peddling, mafia-like networks and multinationals. She was also an excellent teacher, and Espérandieu had been enthralled by her course at the police academy. He had asked a lot of questions. After class they had a drink together and found they had other shared interests: Japan, graphic novels, indie rock. Espérandieu had added Marissa to his list of contacts and she had done likewise: in their job, a good network could help kickstart a flagging investigation. From time to time they would get in touch via a quick email or phone call, perhaps waiting for the day when one of them would need to ask the other for a favour.

'I've been sharpening my teeth on a big boss from the CAC 40 stock market index,' she said. 'First job I've had this big. No need to tell you they've been trying to put a spoke in my wheel. But keep it quiet!'

'You'll be the terror of the CAC 40, Marissa,' he reassured her.

'What can I do for you, Vincent?'

'Do you have anything on Éric Lombard?'

Silence on the other end. Then, 'Well, I never! Who tipped you off?'

'About what?'

'Don't tell me it's a coincidence: that's the very man I'm working on, Éric Lombard. How did you find out?'

He could hear the suspicion in her voice. The cops in the financial crime unit moved in a slightly paranoid world – in the shadow of giant transnational corporations. They were only too used to dealing with corrupt politicians and high-ranking civil servants who had been bought, not to mention crooked lawyers and cops.

'Lombard's favourite horse was killed a week or so ago. Here, in the Pyrenees. While Lombard was on a business trip to the US. The crime was followed by two murders, locally. We're thinking there's a connection between the events. That it might be revenge. So we're trying to find out as much as we can about Éric Lombard. Above all whether he has any enemies.'

She sounded somewhat more relaxed when she started speaking again.

'Well then, you know what? You're bloody lucky!' He could tell that she was smiling. 'We've been stirring up all sorts of muck. Someone blew the whistle on him. You can't imagine all the stuff that's coming to the surface.'

'I suppose it's strictly confidential?'

'Indeed. But if I come across anything that might be connected with your case, I'll let you know, all right? Two murders and a horse? What a strange story! I'm afraid I've got to go now, though.'

'Can I count on you?'

'You can. As soon as I have something for you, I'll pass it on. If I can ask the same of you, of course. But let's get one thing straight: I didn't say anything to you, and you don't know what I'm working on. In the meantime, here's the best one yet: in 2008 Lombard paid less in taxes than the baker downstairs from me.'

'How is that possible?'

'It's very simple: he has brilliant lawyers. And they know every single one of the four hundred and eighty-six tax loopholes that exist in this wonderful country of ours, mostly in the form of tax credits. The main one, obviously, being overseas loopholes. Which means more or less that overseas investments allow a tax reduction of up to sixty per cent in the industrial sector and up to seventy per cent for the renovation of hotels and yachts. Moreover, there's no limit on the amount of the investment so there's no ceiling for the reductions. We're talking investments that favour short-term gain, and couldn't care less about the project's economic viability. So of course Lombard doesn't invest at a loss, he can pull out if he has to. Add to that the tax credits he gets as a result of the international agreements on double taxation, and the purchase of artwork, and a whole bag full of accounting tricks like taking out loans to buy shares in his own group, and he doesn't need to go and set up shop in Switzerland or the Cayman Islands. So in the end Lombard pays less in taxes than the bloke who earns one-thousandth what he does. Not bad, is it, for one of the ten richest men in France?'

Espérandieu recalled what Kleim162 had told him one day: the watchword of governments and international financial institutions like the IMF was to 'create a favourable environment for investment' – in other words, to shift the tax burden from the wealthy onto the middle classes. Or, as an American billionaire imprisoned for tax fraud had cynically put it, 'Only little people pay taxes.' Perhaps he should introduce Marissa to his contact: they were made to get along.

'Thank you, Marissa, you've just made my day.'

He sat for a moment gazing at his screen. A scandal was about to break involving Lombard and his group. Could it have anything to do with their investigation?

Ziegler, Propp, Maillard, Confiant and d'Humières listened to Servaz without moving. Before them they all had croissants and bread rolls which one of the gendarmes had brought from the nearest boulangerie. They had tea, coffee, soft drinks and glasses of water. And there was something else they were all sharing: fatigue, visible on every face.

'Alice Ferrand's diary has opened up a new lead,' concluded Servaz. 'Or, rather, it confirms one of our theories. That of revenge. According to Gabriel Saint-Cyr, one of the leads he had after the suicides was sexual abuse. He'd had to abandon it for lack of evidence. But if we are to believe this diary, there were teens at the Les Isards holiday camp who were raped and tortured on several occasions. Which led some of them to suicide.'

'Although you are the only one who has read the diary up to now,' remarked Confiant.

Servaz turned to Maillard, who got up and walked round the table handing out piles of photocopies. A few had already eaten their croissants, leaving crumbs everywhere; others had not touched them.

'Obviously. For the simple reason that the diary was never meant to be read. It was very well hidden. And I only discovered it last night, as I told you. Thanks to a combination of circumstances.'

'And what if the girl made it all up?'

Servaz spread his hands.

'I don't think so. You'll be able to judge for yourself. It's too real, too . . . specific. And if that were the case, why would she have gone to such trouble to hide it?'

'Where is all this heading?' asked the judge. 'To a child who has grown up and is taking revenge? One of the parents? In that case, what is Hirtmann's DNA doing at the crime scenes? And where does Lombard's horse fit in? I've never seen such a muddle of an investigation!'

'It's not the investigation that is muddled,' said Ziegler in a sharp voice, 'it's the facts.'

Cathy d'Humières stared at Servaz for a long time, her empty cup in her hands.

'Gaspard Ferrand would have a very good motive for these murders,' she pointed out.

'As would all the parents of the suicide victims,' answered Servaz. 'And as would, obviously, the young people who were raped by the foursome and who are now adults.'

'This is a very important discovery,' said the prosecutor at last. 'What do you suggest, Martin?'

'Nothing has changed; the most urgent thing is to find Chaperon. That's our priority. Before the killer or killers find him. But now we know that the men did their dirty work at Les Isards. So we have to concentrate our search there, and on the suicide victims. Since we now know that there is a connection between them and our two victims, and that the connection is the camp.'

'Even if two of the young people never stayed there?' objected Confiant.

'It seems to me that these notebooks leave no doubt as to what happened there. Perhaps the other two adolescents were raped elsewhere, not at the camp. And should we consider them to be paedophiles? I don't really know . . . There doesn't seem to be any indication that they went after young children; it was more like adolescents and young adults. Does that make a difference? It's not for me to say.'

'Boys and girls equally, judging by the list of the suicides,' said Propp. 'But you're right, these men don't really have the profile of paedophiles; more like sexual predators with an extreme penchant for sadism and the most perverse sort of games. And beyond a shadow of a doubt, they were drawn to the youth of their prey.'

'Fucking depraved,' said Cathy d'Humières icily. 'How do you plan to go about finding Chaperon?'

'I don't know,' confessed Servaz.

'We've never been up against a situation like this,' she said. 'I wonder if we shouldn't ask for reinforcements.'

Servaz's response surprised everybody.

'I'm not against it. We have to find all the children who stayed at the holiday camp who are now adults, and interview them. And all the parents who are still alive. Once we manage to put a list together. It will be a painstaking job, and it will take time and means. But we haven't got time. We'll have to move quickly. So that leaves the means. We can get extra staff on this.'

'Fine,' said d'Humières. 'My understanding is that the crime unit in Toulouse are already swamped with investigations, so I'll call in the gendarmerie,' she said, looking at Ziegler and Maillard. 'Anything else?'

'The straps that were used to hang Grimm from the bridge,' said Ziegler. 'The factory that manufactures them contacted me. They were sold through a shop in Tarbes . . . several months ago.'

'In other words, we can't hope for any videotapes,' said d'Humières. 'Do they sell a lot of them?'

'They're a hypermarket specialising in sporting goods. The check-out assistants see dozens of customers every day, especially on the weekends. So we can't expect anything at that end.'

'Right. Anything else?'

'The company that handles the security at the Institute,' continued the gendarme, 'has provided us with a list of their staff there. I've started going through it: for the time being, nothing to report.'

'Perrault's autopsy is this afternoon,' said d'Humières. 'Who can be there?'

Servaz raised his hand.

'And then I'll go and see Xavier at the Institute,' he added. 'We need an exact list of everyone in contact with Hirtmann. And we have to ring the town hall in Saint-Martin. See if they can provide us with a list of all the children who went to the holiday camp. Apparently it was run and financed by the town. So these are our two main priorities, the Institute and the holiday camp. We've got to keep digging, find out if there's a connection between the two.'

'What kind of connection?' asked Confiant.

'Suppose we find out that one of the young people from the holiday camp – one of the victims – is now a staff member at the Institute?'

Cathy d'Humières gave him a sharp look.

'It's an interesting idea,' she said.

'I'll deal with the town hall,' said Ziegler.

Servaz gave her a surprised look. She had raised her voice. That wasn't like her. He nodded.

'Good. But our priority is to find Chaperon, wherever he's hiding. We have to question his ex-wife: she may know something. Go through his papers. There might be something in his bills, rent receipts, to lead us to his hiding place. You already have an appointment with the former Madame Chaperon this morning, so go ahead. You can go to the town hall after that.'

'Fine. Anything else?' said d'Humières.

'The psychological profile,' said Propp. 'I've begun to put together a fairly precise portrait, taking into account the elements we found at the crime scenes: the hanging, the boots, Grimm's nudity and so on. But the diaries change everything. I'll have to go back to the drawing board.'

'How long will you need?'

'We have enough material now for me to work fairly quickly. I'll bring you my conclusions on Monday.'

'On *Monday*? Let's hope the killers don't work on the weekend either,' said d'Humières curtly.

Her sarcasm made the psychologist blush.

'One last thing: good work, Martin. I always knew I made the right choice putting you on this case.'

As she said this, her gaze went from Servaz to Confiant, who preferred to stare at his fingernails.

Espérandieu was listening to the Raconteurs singing 'Many Shades of Black' when the telephone rang. He pricked up his ears when he found it was Marissa, calling back from the financial crime unit.

'You did say you wanted to know if anything strange had happened lately to do with Éric Lombard?'

'Basically, yes,' he agreed.

'I might have something for you. I don't know if this can help – at first glance it doesn't seem connected with your case – but it happened recently and did cause a certain stir, apparently.'

'Tell me anyway.'

So she told him. Her explanation took a while. Espérandieu had some difficulty understanding exactly what it was about: something to do with the sum of $135,000 earmarked in Lombard Media's account books for a television documentary commissioned from a certain production company. When they checked with the company in question, there was no record of any such documentary. Clearly, the accounting entry was hiding a misappropriation of funds. Once Marissa had finished, Espérandieu was disappointed: he wasn't sure he'd understood it all, and he didn't see how it might help them. But he did take down a few notes on his pad.

'Well, does that help you or not?'

'Not really,' he replied. 'But thanks all the same.'

There was something electric in the atmosphere at the Institute: Diane had been watching Xavier all morning, scrutinising his every little act and gesture. He seemed worried and tense – on the verge of exhaustion in fact. Several times over, their gazes met. *He knew . . .* Or more precisely, *he knew that she knew.* But perhaps she was imagining things. Projection, transfer: she knew all about that.

Should she inform the police? All morning the question preyed on her mind.

She wasn't convinced they would see as direct a link as she did between the drug shipment and the death of the horse. She had asked Alex whether anyone at the Institute had a pet: he seemed surprised, then said no. She also recalled that she had spent the morning with Xavier on the day she arrived – *the morning the horse had been discovered* – and that he certainly didn't look like someone who had stayed up all night beheading an animal, transporting it and hanging it up at an altitude of two thousand metres in temperatures of ten degrees below zero. He had seemed fresh and rested that day – and above all unbearably arrogant and condescending.

In any case, far from exhausted or stressed out.

She wondered whether she wasn't jumping to conclusions, whether the isolation and the strange mood that reigned in this place weren't making her paranoid. In other words, whether she was imagining it all. And wouldn't she look completely ridiculous if she contacted the police only for them to discover the true reason why the medication had been ordered, destroying completely any credit she might have with Xavier and the rest of the staff. Not to mention her reputation when she went back to Switzerland.

This prospect had a definite dampening effect.

'Aren't you interested in what I have to tell you?'

Diane came back to the present. The patient sitting across from her was looking at her sternly. Even now, he still had a working man's large, callused hands. A former worker who had attacked his boss with a screwdriver after an unwarranted dismissal. After reading his file, Diane felt that a few weeks in a psychiatric hospital would have been enough for the poor man. But he had fallen into the hands of a zealous psychiatrist; he'd been put away for ten years. In addition, they had given him massive and prolonged doses of psychotropic drugs. A man who on arrival was probably just suffering from depression had ended up completely crazy.

'Of course I am, Aaron. I am interested.'

'You aren't, I can tell.'

'I assure you.'

'I'm going to tell Dr Xavier that you're not interested in what I'm telling you.'

'Why would you do that, Aaron? If you don't mind, we could get back to—'

'Blah blah blah, you're just trying to gain time.'

'Gain time?'

'You don't have to repeat everything I say.'

'What's got into you, Aaron?'

'"What's got into you, Aaron?" For one hour I've been talking to a wall.'

'Not at all! I just—'

'"Not at all! I just . . . " Knock-knock-knock, what's going on in your head, Doctor?'

'Pardon?'

'What's the matter with you?'

'Why do you say that, Aaron?'

'"Why do you say that, Aaron?" Questions, all I ever get is questions!'

'I think we should postpone this interview until later—'

'No, I don't think so. I'm going to tell Dr Xavier that you are wasting my time. I don't want any more sessions with you.'

She could not help but blush, in spite of herself.

'Oh, come on, Aaron! This is only our third one. I—'

'You're somewhere else, Doctor. You don't feel concerned. Your mind is elsewhere.'

'Aaron, I—'

'You know what? You don't belong here. Go back to where you came from. Go back to Switzerland.'

She was startled.

'Who told you I was Swiss? We've never talked about it.'

He threw his head back and burst out laughing, an ugly laugh. Then he looked straight at her with a gaze as smooth and dull as a slate.

'What do you think? We know everything, here. Everyone knows that you are Swiss, *like Julian.*'

'No doubt about it,' said Delmas. 'He was dropped into space with the strap round his neck. We've got significant bulbar and medullary lesions, unlike the chemist, and there are also lesions round the cervical vertebrae due to the shock.'

Servaz avoided looking at Perrault's body, which was lying face down with the back of the neck and skull cut open. The spinal cord glistened like jelly in the light of the autopsy room.

'There are no signs of haematoma or injections,' continued the pathologist, 'but since you had seen him alive in the cabin just before . . . Basically, he followed his murderer of his own free will.'

'Or was threatened with a weapon, more like,' said Servaz.

'Well, that's not my jurisdiction. I'll run a blood test anyway. Grimm's blood has just shown minute traces of flunitrazepam. It's an antidepressant ten times more powerful than Valium, prescribed in cases of severe sleep disorders and marketed under the name of Rohypnol. It is also used as an anaesthetic. Grimm was a chemist; perhaps he took it for his own insomnia. It's possible . . . It has also been classified among the so-called date-rape drugs, because it provokes amnesia and it is a powerful anti-inhibitor, particularly when taken with alcohol, and because it is odourless, colourless and taste-less, is quickly absorbed, and leaves very little trace in the blood, making it virtually undetectable: any chemical trace disappears within twenty-four hours.'

Servaz let out a low whistle.

'The fact we found only tiny traces is certainly due to the lapse of time between absorption and the taking of the blood sample. Rohypnol can be administered orally or intravenously, swallowed, chewed or dissolved in a drink. The aggressor probably used it to make his victim more malleable. The man you're looking for is a control freak, Martin. And he is very, very clever.'

Delmas turned the body over onto its back. Perrault no longer had the terrified expression Servaz had seen in the gondola. Instead, his tongue was sticking out. The coroner picked up an electric saw.

'Right, I think I've seen enough,' said the cop. 'In any case, we already know what happened. I'll read your report.'

'Martin,' called Delmas just as he was about to leave the room.

He turned round.

'You don't look well,' said the pathologist, with the saw in his hand like a Sunday handyman. 'Don't start taking all this business too personally.'

Servaz nodded and left. In the corridor, he looked at the padded casket that was waiting for Perrault once he left the mortuary. Servaz went out of the hospital basement and up the concrete ramp, and took huge lungfuls of fresh air. But the memory of the odour of formaldehyde, disinfectant and corpse would stick to his nostrils for a long time. His mobile rang just as he was unlocking the Jeep. It was Xavier.

'I have the list,' announced the psychiatrist, 'of the people who were in touch with Hirtmann. Do you want it?'

Servaz looked at the mountains.

'I'll come over and get it,' he answered. 'See you later.'

The sky was dark, but it was no longer raining when he headed for the Institute. At every turn, the last vestiges of autumn, yellow and red leaves along the side of the road, lifted up from the snow and blew away as the Jeep went by. A bitter wind shook the naked branches, which reached out to scratch the car like fleshless fingers. At the wheel of the Cherokee he thought again of Margot. Had Vincent done his job of following her? Then he thought about Charlène Espérandieu, and the boy named Clément, and Alice Ferrand . . . Everything was whirling; everything was mixed up in his head.

His mobile buzzed again. He picked up. It was Propp.

'I forgot to tell you something: white is important, Martin. The white mountaintops for the horse, the whiteness of a naked body for Grimm, and again the snow for Perrault. White is for the killer. He sees it as a symbol of purity and purification. *Look for white*. I think you will find white around the killer.'

'White like the Institute?' said Servaz.

'I don't know. I thought we had ruled out that lead, right? I'm sorry, there's nothing more I can tell you at the moment. *Look for white*.'

Servaz thanked him and hung up. A knot in his throat. There was something threatening in the air, he could feel it.

It wasn't over.

PART 3
White

23

'Eleven,' said Xavier. He handed the sheet across the desk. 'Eleven people have been in contact with Hirtmann over the last two months. Here's the list.'

The psychiatrist seemed preoccupied, and his features were drawn.

'I had a long talk with each of them,' he said.

'And?'

'Nothing.'

'What do you mean, nothing?'

'Nothing came of it. No one seems to have anything to hide. Or else they all do. I don't know.'

He saw Servaz's questioning gaze and waved his hand in apology.

'What I mean is, we live in isolation here, far away from everything. In these circumstances, there is a kind of scheming that seems incomprehensible to outsiders. Little secrets, manoeuvring behind the scenes, plots hatched against one person or another; cliques are formed; it's a game governed by rules that would seem surreal to anyone else. You must wonder what I'm going on about.'

Servaz smiled.

'Not at all,' he said, thinking about the force. 'I know only too well what you mean, Doctor.'

Xavier relaxed slightly.

'Would you like a coffee?'

'Please.'

Xavier got up to go to the little coffee machine in the corner. The coffee was good, and Servaz made it last. To say that this place made him uncomfortable would be an understatement. He wondered how anyone could work here without going stark raving mad. It wasn't only the residents, it was also the place itself: the thick walls, the mountains.

'In short, it is difficult to see things clearly,' continued Xavier. 'Everyone here has their little secrets. Under these conditions, no one plays fair.'

Dr Xavier gave him an apologetic smile behind his red glasses. *And you're not playing fair, either, my friend,* thought Servaz.

'I see.'

'So I put together the list of everyone who has been in contact with Julian Hirtmann, but it doesn't mean I suspect them all.'

'No?'

'Our head nurse, for example. She is one of the longest-serving members of staff. She started when Dr Wargnier was here. So much of the everyday functioning of this establishment relies on her competence and her knowledge of the residents. I trust her implicitly. You needn't waste your time on her.'

Servaz looked at the list.

'Hmm. Élisabeth Ferney, that's her?'

Xavier nodded.

'Altogether trustworthy,' he insisted.

Servaz raised his eyes and looked closely at the psychiatrist, who blushed.

'Thank you,' he said, folding the sheet and putting it in his pocket. Then he hesitated. 'I have a question for you that has nothing to do with the investigation. A question for the psychiatrist, not the man or the witness.'

Xavier raised an eyebrow, intrigued.

'Do you believe in the existence of evil, Doctor?'

The psychiatrist remained silent longer than Servaz would have expected. All that time, behind his peculiar red glasses, he was staring at Servaz, as if he were trying to determine what the cop was driving at.

'As a psychiatrist,' he said finally, 'my answer is that the question is not a matter for psychiatry. It is a matter for philosophy. And more specifically, morality. From that vantage point, evil cannot be conceived without good; you cannot have one without the other. Have you heard of Kohlberg's stages of moral development?' he asked.

Servaz shook his head.

'Lawrence Kohlberg was an American psychologist. He was inspired by Piaget's theory of the stages of acquisition, and he postulated the existence of six stages of moral development in man.'

Xavier paused, leaned back in his chair and crossed his hands over his belly while he gathered his thoughts.

'According to Kohlberg, an individual's sense of morality is

acquired in successive stages during the development of his personality. None of these stages can be skipped. Once an individual
reaches a certain moral stage, he cannot go back: he will be at that
level for life. However, not all individuals attain the final level, far
from it. Many of them stop at a lower level. Finally, these stages are
shared by all of humanity, and are the same regardless of culture.'

Servaz sensed that he had aroused the psychiatrist's interest.

'At level 1,' began Xavier enthusiastically, 'good is rewarded and
evil is punished. As when you hit a child's fingers with a ruler to
make him understand he's done something wrong. Obedience is
perceived as a value in itself, and the child obeys because the adult
has the power to punish him. At level 2, the child no longer obeys
for obedience's sake, but to obtain gratification: this marks the beginning of an exchange.'

Xavier gave a little smile.

'At level 3, the individual reaches the first stage of conventional
morality, and seeks to satisfy the expectations of those around him.
It is the judgement of family or the group which matters. The child
learns respect, loyalty, trust, gratitude. At level 4, the notion of the
group is expanded to society as a whole. This is where respect for
law and order comes in. We are still in the domain of conventional
morality, and this is the stage of conformism: good consists in doing
one's duty, and evil is what society condemns.'

Xavier leaned forward.

'From level 5 on, the individual is freed from convention and
surpasses it. This is post-conventional morality. The individual moves
beyond selfishness to become altruistic. He also knows that values
are relative, that laws must be respected but that they are not neces-
sarily good. Above all he has the interests of the collective in mind.
Finally, at level 6, the individual adopts freely chosen ethical principles
which may come into conflict with the laws of his country, if he
considers those laws to be immoral. It is his conscience and reasoning
that will prevail. The moral individual at level 6 has a clear, coherent
and integral value system. A person like this is active in associations
and charities, and a sworn enemy of selfishness and greed.'

'This is very interesting,' said Servaz.

'Isn't it? I don't need to tell you that a great many individuals
remain stuck at levels 3 and 4. Kohlberg also envisaged a level 7.
There are very few individuals who ever attain it. The individual at

level 7 is bathed in universal love, compassion and holiness, far above common mortals. Kohlberg mentions only a few examples: Jesus, Buddha, Gandhi. In a way, we might say that psychopaths are those who remain stuck at level 0. Even if that is not a very academic notion for a psychiatrist.'

'And you think it would be possible to come up with a similar scale for evil?'

The psychiatrist's eyes sparkled behind his glasses when he heard Servaz's question. He licked his lips.

'That's a very interesting question,' he said. 'I confess I've often wondered the same thing myself. On such a scale, someone like Hirtmann would be at the far end of the spectrum, the mirrored opposite of a level 7 individual, basically.'

The psychiatrist was staring him straight in the eyes. He looked as if he were wondering what level Servaz had attained. Servaz felt himself sweating again, his pulse accelerating. Something was growing in his chest. Panic. Again he saw the headlights in his rear-view mirror, Perrault screaming in the cabin, Grimm's naked corpse hanging beneath the bridge, the headless horse, Hirtmann staring at him, Lisa Ferney's gaze along the corridors of the Institute. The fear had been there from the start, deep inside, like a seed, asking only to sprout and blossom. He wanted to flee from this place, this valley, these mountains.

'Thank you, Doctor,' he said, getting abruptly to his feet.

Xavier stood up and reached out his hand.

'Don't mention it.' He held Servaz's hand for a moment. 'You look very tired, Commandant, not at all well. You should get some rest.'

'That's the second time today someone has told me that,' said Servaz with a smile.

But his legs were shaky as he walked to the door.

Half past three. The winter afternoon was coming to a close. The silhouette of the mountain cut across a grey, threatening sky closing over the valley like a lid. He sat in the Jeep and looked at the list. Eleven names. He knew at least two of them: Lisa Ferney and Dr Xavier himself. He turned the ignition and backed round to drive away. On the pavement the snow had almost all melted, replaced by a black, oily film, soft and shining. There were no other cars on the narrow road, but a few kilometres further along, as he drew level with the holiday camp, he saw a car parked near the entrance to the drive. An old red Volvo 940. Servaz slowed down and tried to read the number plate in the glow of his headlights. The car was so dirty that half the numbers had disappeared under mud and leaves. Chance or disguise? He felt a gnawing anxiety come over him.

He glanced inside as he went by. No one. Servaz parked five metres further along and got out. There was no one about. The wind was making a mournful sound in the branches, like old papers rustling in an empty street. And the rush of the torrent. The light was fading fast. He reached for a torch in the glove compartment and walked over to the Volvo, trampling the dirty snow on the side of the road. There was nothing special about the inside of the car, though it was just as dirty as the outside. He tried to open the door; it was locked.

Servaz had not forgotten the episode of the cable cars: this time, he went back to get his gun. As he walked over the rusty little bridge, he could feel an updraught of chill air from the river. The minute he started slipping in the mud on the path, he regretted not wearing boots, which reminded him of what Alice had written in her journal. In a few strides his city shoes were in the same pitiful state as the Volvo. It began to rain again as he entered the forest. He started walking under the cover of trees, but as soon as the path led into a clearing, the rain drummed on his skull like dozens of little fingers, a diabolical rhythm. Servaz turned up his collar over his dripping neck. Hammered by the downpour, the holiday camp looked completely deserted.

As he drew near the buildings the path started up a gentle slope and he slipped in the mud and almost fell flat on his face. His weapon slid into a puddle. He swore and picked it up. He told himself that if someone was hiding somewhere watching him, they would be laughing at his clumsiness.

The buildings seemed to be waiting for him.

Servaz called out, but no one answered. His pulse was racing now. Every alarm signal, one after the other, was flashing red. Who could be wandering about the deserted camp, and why? And above all, why was there no answer to his call? It must have been audible, carried by the echo.

The three buildings were in the chalet style, but made of concrete, with just a few wooden embellishments; there were big slate roofs, rows of windows on each floor and large picture windows on the

361

ground floor. The buildings were connected by covered walkways open to the wind. There was no light at any of the windows. Half of the panes were broken; a few had been replaced by plywood boards. Water gushed from broken gutters, splattering the ground. Servaz swept the beam of his torch over the central building and discovered a faded motto painted above the entrance: 'There are no holidays in the school of life.' *Nor in crime*, he thought.

Suddenly something moved at the edge of his vision, to the left. He swung round. A moment later, he was no longer quite sure what he had seen. Perhaps it was branches shaken by the wind. Yet he was almost certain he had glimpsed a shadow. A shadow among the shadows.

This time he made sure the safety was off and a bullet in the chamber. Then he stepped forward, on the alert. Once he passed the furthest chalet, he had to be careful where he trod, because the ground rose steeply, slippery and unstable with mud. On either side the tall, straight beech trunks rose to their black branches far above, and if he looked up, he could see patches of grey sky and the pouring rain. The muddy slope careened down through the trees to a stream a few metres below.

Suddenly he saw something.

A glow of light.

As tiny and flickering as a will-o'-the-wisp. He blinked to chase the rain from his lashes; the glow was still there.

Shit, what is that?

A flame. Dancing, fragile, minute, a metre from the ground, against one of the tree trunks.

His inner alarm continued to sound. Someone had lit that flame, and that someone could not be far away. Servaz looked all around. Then he went down the slope to the tree. A candle. A tea light, the kind used in chafing dishes, or to give atmosphere to a room. It sat on a little wooden tray fixed to the tree trunk. The beam of his torch swept over the rough bark and he saw something that left him rooted to the spot. A few inches above the flame a large heart had been carved into the bark. And inside were five names:

Ludo + Marion + Florian + Alice + Michaël

The suicide victims. Servaz stared at the heart, petrified, speechless.

The rain snuffed out the candle.

And then came the attack. Ferocious, brutal. Terrifying. He sensed he was no longer alone. A fraction of a second later something cold came down over his head. Panicked, he reared up and fought like the devil, but his aggressor did not yield. He felt the cold thing close over his nose and mouth. His brain screamed in silence: *Plastic bag!* Then the man dealt a terrible blow to his knees and in spite of himself Servaz's legs collapsed beneath him. He was on the ground, his face in the mud, the man's entire weight on top of him. The bag was suffocating him. Through the plastic he could feel the soft, sticky mud. His assailant was pressing his head into the ground, pulling the bag round his neck, kneeling on his arms. As he gasped for breath Servaz remembered the mud in Grimm's hair, and an icy, uncontrollable fear came over him. He flailed, trying to throw the man off his back. No use: he did not let go. With a terrible rustling, sucking noise, the plastic came away from his face whenever he breathed out, then clung again to his nostrils, mouth and teeth the moment he breathed in, filling him with a horrible sensation of suffocation and panic. Struggling for air, his head bound in a prison of plastic, Servaz felt as if his heart was going to stop at any moment. Then suddenly he was pulled violently backwards and a rope closed round his throat, sealing the plastic bag. A searing pain shot through his neck as he was dragged over the ground.

He lashed out in every direction, his feet slithering through the mud to try and reduce the terrible pressure on his neck. His buttocks rose, fell again and slid over the soft earth, while his hands tried in vain to grab the rope. He didn't know where his gun had fallen. He was dragged over several metres, displaced, heaving, an animal being carted to the abattoir.

In less than two minutes he would be dead.

He was already struggling for air.

His mouth opened convulsively, but the plastic was blocking every intake of breath.

Inside the bag, the oxygen was getting scarce.

He was going to suffer the same fate as Grimm.

The same fate as Perrault.

As Alice.

They would hang him.

He was about to lose consciousness when the air hit his lungs as if a floodgate had been opened. Pure, unspoiled air. He could feel the rain streaming over his face. He gulped in the air and the rain, hoarse lungfuls that made a noise like a bellows.

'Breathe! Breathe!'

Dr Xavier's voice. He turned his head, took a moment to focus and saw the psychiatrist bending over him, supporting him. Xavier looked as terrified as he did.

'Where – where is he?'

'He got away. I didn't even see him. Be quiet, breathe!'

Suddenly they heard the sound of an engine and Servaz understood.

The Volvo!

'Shit,' he found the strength to say.

Servaz was sitting against a tree. He let the rain cleanse his face and hair. Crouching next to him, Xavier seemed equally indifferent to the rain soaking his suit, and the mud on his polished shoes.

'I was on my way down to Saint-Martin when I saw your car. I wondered what you were doing here. So I decided to come and see.'

The psychiatrist shot him a penetrating look and a tentative smile.

'I'm like anyone else: this investigation, these murders . . . it's terrifying – but also very intriguing. In short, I was looking for you, and suddenly I saw you there, lying on the ground, with that bag on your head . . . and that rope! The man must've heard my car and bolted. He certainly didn't think he'd be disturbed.'

'A – a trap,' stammered Servaz, rubbing his neck. 'He set me a – a trap.'

He puffed on his damp cigarette; it crackled. His entire body was shaking. The psychiatrist gingerly pulled the collar of Servaz's jacket to one side.

'That doesn't look too good. I'm going to take you to hospital. You should get it seen to right away. And have an X-ray of your neck and larynx.'

'Thank you for coming this – this way.'

'Good morning,' said Mr Atlas.

'Good morning,' replied Diane. 'I'm here to see Julian.'

Mr Atlas studied her, frowning, his enormous hands on the belt of his boiler suit. Diane held his gaze without flinching. She struggled to keep her composure.

'Isn't Dr Xavier with you?'

'No.'

A shadow passed over the huge man's face. Once again she looked him in the eyes. Mr Atlas shrugged and turned away.

She followed him, her heart pounding.

'You've got a visitor,' said the guard after opening the cell door.

Diane walked in. She could see the surprise in Hirtmann's gaze when their eyes met.

'Good morning, Julian.'

The Swiss man didn't answer. He seemed to be in a bad mood. His good spirits from before had vanished. It was all she could do not to turn on her heels and go back out before it was too late.

'I didn't know I'd have visitors today,' he said finally.

'I didn't know either,' she replied. 'At least not until five minutes ago.'

This time he seemed genuinely disconcerted and she felt something almost like satisfaction. She sat down at the little table and spread her papers before her. She waited for him to come and sit opposite, but he didn't; he merely continued to pace in front of the window like a beast in its cage.

'As we will be meeting regularly,' she began, 'I would like to clarify a few things, to set up a framework for our sessions and get an idea of how things work here.'

He stopped pacing to give her a long, suspicious look, then started up again wordlessly.

'You don't mind?'

No answer.

'Well, for a start, do you get a lot of visits, Julian?'

Once again he stopped to stare at her before continuing to pace to and fro, his hands clasped behind his back.

'Any visits from outside the Institute?'

No answer.

'And here, who visits you, Dr Xavier? Élisabeth Ferney? Who else?'

No answer.

'Do you ever talk with them about what goes on outside?'

'Has Dr Xavier authorised this visit?' he asked suddenly, stopping right in front of her.

Diane forced herself to raise her head. He looked down on her from his full height.

'Well, I—'

'I'll bet he didn't. What exactly are you doing here, Dr Berg?'

'Well, I just told you, I—'

He tutted. 'It's incredible how lacking in psychology you psychiatrists are. I may have good manners, Dr Berg, but I don't like to be taken for a fool.'

'Are you aware of what goes on outside?' she asked, abandoning her professional tone.

He seemed to be thinking. Then he sat down, leaning forward with his forearms on the table, his hands crossed.

'Do you mean those murders? Yes, I read the papers.'

'So, you get all your information from the papers?'

'What are you implying? What is going on outside that has got you in this state?'

'In what state?'

'You seem terrified. But not just terrified. You're like someone who's looking for something, or even like an animal, a little burrowing animal, that's what you look like just now, like some dirty rat. If you could see your face! Good God, Dr Berg, what is the matter with you? You can't stand it here, is that it? Aren't you afraid you'll disrupt the smooth running of this place with all your questions?'

'You sound just like Dr Xavier,' she said mockingly.

He smiled.

'Oh, no, please! Look, the first time you came in here, I could tell you weren't at home. This place . . . What did you expect to find? Evil genies? You'll find nothing but sorry psychotics, schizophrenics and pathetic paranoid patients here, Dr Berg. And I include myself in that. The only difference between us and the people outside is the violence. And believe me, it's not just among the patients.'

He spread his hands.

'Oh, I know that Dr Xavier has a – let's say *romantic* vision of things. That he sees us as maleficent beings, the emanations of Nemesis and other such rubbish. He thinks he has been entrusted with a mission. For him this place is some sort of Holy Grail of psychiatry. It's pure bullshit.'

While he was speaking, his expression grew ever darker and harder, and she could not help but recoil.

'It's no different here from anywhere else – there's nothing but filth, mediocrity, shoddy treatment and drugs in high doses. Psychiatry is the greatest swindle of the twentieth century. Look at the medication they use: they don't even know why it works! Most of it was discovered by chance.'

She stared at him intensely.

'Tell me where you get your information,' she said. 'Does it all come from the papers?'

'*You're not listening to what I'm saying.*'

He said this in a loud, authoritarian voice. She jumped. She sensed she was going to lose him; she had blundered, missed something. He was going to close himself off.

'I am, yes, I am listening—'

'You are not listening to me.'

'Why do you say that? I—'

Suddenly she understood.

'What did you mean by "It's not just among the patients"?'

A thin, fierce smile spread across his face.

'You can see, when you want to.'

'What is that supposed to mean, "It's not just among the patients"? What are you talking about? Madmen? Criminals? Murderers? Are there some among the *staff*?'

'I rather like talking to you, after all.'

'Who are you talking about, Julian? Who is it?'

'What do you know, Diane? What have you found out?'

'If I tell you, how do I know that you won't repeat it?'

He burst out laughing, a horrible, unpleasant laugh.

'Oh, come now, Diane! This sounds like a bloody film! What do you think? That I'm actually interested? Look at me: I will never get out of here. So there could be an earthquake out there and I wouldn't care one way or the other – or at least as long as it didn't break these walls in two.'

'They found your DNA at the place where the horse was killed,' she said. 'Did you know that?'

He observed her for a long time.

'And how did you know?'

'It doesn't matter. Well, did you know or not?'

He made a little grimace that might have been a smile.

'I know what you're looking for,' he said. 'But you won't find it here. And the answer to your question is: I know everything, Diane. Everything that goes on outside and inside. Rest assured, I won't tell

367

anyone about your visit. I can't be sure that Mr Atlas will be as discreet, though. Unlike me, he is not free to do as he pleases. That's the paradox. And you should go. The head nurse will be here in fifteen minutes. Get out of here! Leave this place, Diane. You're in danger . . .'

Espérandieu sat thinking at his desk. After Marissa's call an idea had come to him. He couldn't stop thinking about the money she had mentioned: $135,000. What could such an amount correspond to? At first glance, the $135,000 seemed to have nothing to do with their investigation. At first glance . . . and then he had his idea.

It seemed so ridiculous that he shoved it out of his mind.

But his stubborn idea would not go away. What would it cost to find out? By eleven o'clock he had made up his mind. He picked up the telephone. The first person he called was very reluctant to give him a straight answer at first. Such matters should not be discussed over the phone, even with a cop. When he quoted the figure of $135,000, however, he learned that that was roughly the rate charged for the distance involved.

Espérandieu felt his excitement growing.

Over the next thirty minutes he made half a dozen more calls. The first ones came up with nothing. Every time he got the same answer: no, nothing like that for that particular date. His idea was beginning to seem ridiculous again. The $135,000 could mean so many things. But then he had made one final call and this time, bingo! He listened to the answer with a mixture of incredulity and exhilaration. Had he hit the bullseye? Was it possible? A little voice tried to temper his enthusiasm: it might, of course, simply be a coincidence. But he didn't think so. Not with that exact date. When he hung up, he still couldn't believe it. Incredible! With just a few phone calls, he had progressed the investigation by leaps and bounds.

He looked at his watch: ten to five. He wanted to tell Martin about it, but then he changed his mind: he needed definitive proof. He grabbed the phone and feverishly dialled yet another number. Finally, he had a lead.

'How are you feeling?'

'Not great.'

Ziegler was staring at him. She seemed almost as upset as he was.

368

Nurses came in and out. A doctor had examined him and taken several X-rays before wheeling him back to the room on a gurney, even though he was perfectly capable of walking.

Xavier sat waiting in the hospital corridor for Ziegler to take his statement. There was also a gendarme posted outside Servaz's door, which was suddenly flung wide open.

'What happened, for the love of Christ?' cried Cathy d'Humières as she strode up to the bed.

Servaz tried to keep it short.

'And you didn't see his face?'

'No.'

'Are you sure?'

'All I can say is that he was bloody strong. And that he knew how to go about attacking someone.'

Cathy d'Humières gave him a long, dark look.

'This can't go on,' she said. She turned to Ziegler. 'Put a hold on any case that's not urgent and get all available staff on to this one. What have we got on Chaperon?'

'His ex-wife has no idea where he might be,' answered Ziegler.

Servaz remembered that Ziegler had gone to Bordeaux to meet her.

'What is she like?' he asked.

'Uppity. Snobbish, sunbed tan, too much make-up.'

He couldn't help but smile.

'Did you ask her about Chaperon's character?'

'Yes. It's interesting: the minute I mentioned him, she clammed up. All I got was the usual stuff: his mountain-climbing, politics, the friends who monopolised him, their divorce by mutual consent, lives that ended up heading in different directions and so on. But I got the feeling she was hiding something important.'

Servaz remembered Chaperon's house: their separate bedrooms. Like Grimm and his wife. Why? Had their wives discovered their terrible secret? Servaz thought that had to be the truth, one way or another. Perhaps – no, surely – they had merely suspected a fraction of the whole. But the widow Grimm's scorn for her husband, and her suicide attempt, and the former Madame Chaperon's reluctance to talk about her private life came from a common source: these women knew how deeply perverse their husbands were, even if they did not know the extent of their crimes.

'Did you ask her about what we found in the house?' he asked Ziegler.

'No.'

'Do it. There's not a minute to lose. Call her and tell her that if she is hiding something and her husband is found dead, she will be the prime suspect.'

'All right. I found something else of interest,' she added.

Servaz waited.

'Élisabeth Ferney, the head nurse at the Institute, had several brushes with the law when she was young. Petty crimes. Stolen scooters, insulting a police officer, drugs, assault and battery, extortion. She was up in court several times.'

'And she got a job at the Institute in spite of that?'

'It was a long time ago. She got back on track, did her training. She worked in several other psychiatric hospitals; then Wargnier, Xavier's predecessor, took her under his wing. Everyone is entitled to a second chance.'

'Interesting.'

'In addition, Lisa Ferney goes regularly to a bodybuilding club in Saint-Lary, twenty kilometres from here. And she belongs to a rifle club.'

Servaz and d'Humières were instantly on the alert. A thought occurred to Servaz: his intuition at the Institute might have been correct. Lisa Ferney had the profile . . . Whoever had hung the horse up there had to be very strong. And the head nurse was stronger than some men.

'Keep digging,' he said. 'You may be on to something.'

'Ah, yes, I almost forgot: the tapes.'

'Yes?'

'It was just birdsong.'

'Ah.'

'Right, I'm off to the town hall to see if they have that list of the children who went to the holiday camp,' she concluded.

'Ladies, I must ask you to let the commandant get some rest,' boomed a voice from the doorway.

They turned round. A doctor in his thirties wearing a white coat had just come in. He had a dark complexion and thick black eyebrows that almost met in the middle of his forehead. On his coat Servaz read 'Dr Saadeh.' He came up to them with a smile. But his eyes were not smiling, and his thick brows were knitted together in a stern expression that made clear that in this place, prosecutors and gendarmes must bow to a higher authority, the doctor's. As for Servaz, he had already started pushing back the sheets.

'There's no way I'm staying here,' he said.

'And there is no way I am letting you leave just like that,' retorted Dr Saadeh, placing a friendly but firm hand on his shoulder. 'We haven't finished examining you.'

'Well then, be quick,' said Servaz, resigned, flopping back against the pillows.

But as soon as they had all left, he closed his eyes and fell asleep.

At that very moment, a police officer picked up the phone in the massive stronghold of the Interpol General Secretariat at 200, quai Charles-de-Gaulle in Lyon. The man sat in the middle of a vast open-plan office full of computers and other machines, with a panoramic view over the Rhone. There was also a decorated Christmas tree, whose star rose above the cubicles.

He frowned when he recognised the voice of the person at the other end.

'Vincent? Is that you? How long has it been, my friend? What are you up to?'

Second only to the UN in terms of membership, Interpol covers 187 countries. Its central services do not, however, constitute an actual police force – it is, rather, an intelligence service consulted by the member states' police forces for its expertise and databases – which include files on 178,000 criminals and 4,500 fugitives. A service that issues several thousand international arrest warrants every year: the famous 'red notices'. The man who had just answered his phone was called Luc Damblin. Espérandieu had known Damblin, like Marissa, at police academy. The two men exchanged a few polite words; then Espérandieu got straight to the point.

'I need to ask you a favour.'

Damblin gazed absently at the posters in front of him: Russian mafiosi, Albanian pimps, Mexican and Colombian drug lords, Serbian and Croatian jewellery thieves, international paedophiles rife in poor countries. Someone had added red Santa Claus hats and white beards to the photos; it didn't make them look any more jovial. Damblin listened patiently to his colleague's explanation.

'You're in luck,' he replied in the end. 'There's a bloke at the FBI in Washington who owes me one. I gave him a nudge in the right direction on one of his cases. I'll call him and see what we can do. But why do you need to know?'

'An investigation I'm working on.'

'Something to do with the States?'

'I'll explain. Here, I've just sent you the photo,' said Espérandieu. Damblin checked his watch.

'It could take some time. My contact is fairly busy. How soon do you need an answer?'

'It's rather urgent, I'm afraid.'

'It's always urgent,' answered Damblin. 'Don't worry: I'll put your request at the top of my pile. For old times' sake. Besides, Christmas is coming: this can be your present.'

Servaz woke up two hours later. It took him a moment to recognise the hospital bed, the white room, the big window with blue blinds. When he figured out where he was, he looked for his belongings and found them in a plastic bag on a chair. He jumped out of bed and dressed as quickly as possible. Three minutes later, he was outside and calling a number from his mobile.

'Hello?'

'It's Martin. Is the inn open this evening?'

At the other end of the line, the old man laughed.

'I'm glad you called. I was about to make dinner.'

'I have a few questions for you.'

'And here I thought it was all about my cooking. What a disappointment! Have you found something?'

'I'll explain.'

'Good. I'll see you later.'

Night had fallen, but the street outside the lycée was well lit. Sitting in an unmarked car, Espérandieu saw Margot Servaz come out of the school. He almost didn't recognise her: her black hair had changed to Scandinavian blonde. She had two little bunches on either side of her head that made her look like a caricature of a German *Mädchen*. And a peculiar hat.

When she turned round, he also saw, even from this distance, that she had a new tattoo on her neck. An enormous, multicoloured tattoo.

Vincent thought about his daughter. How would he react if, later on in life, Mégan also went in for this sort of thing? Checking to see that his camera was where it should be on the passenger seat, he turned the ignition. Like the day before, Margot chatted on the pavement with her schoolmates for a moment and rolled a cigarette. Then her attentive escort with the scooter appeared.

Espérandieu sighed. At least this time if they got ahead of him, he would know where to find them. He wouldn't have to drive as recklessly as before. He pulled out and started after them. The driver of the scooter indulged in his usual acrobatics. On Espérandieu's iPhone, the Gutter Twins were singing, *O, Father, now I can't believe you're leaving*. At the next traffic light, he slowed and came to a halt. The car in front of him had stopped and the scooter was already four cars ahead of him. But Espérandieu knew that at the crossroads they would be going straight; he relaxed.

The hoarse voice in his headphones was declaring, *My mother, she don't know me | And my father, he can't own me* when the light turned green, and the scooter turned to the right, back-firing. Espérandieu spluttered with irritation. *What the fuck are they doing now?* This wasn't the way home. The queue in front of him was taking an exasperatingly long time to move. Espérandieu got nervous. The light changed to amber, then red. He went through on red, just in time to see the scooter turning left at the next traffic light two hundred metres further along. Fucking hell! Where were they off to in such a hurry? He made it through the next crossroads on amber and set about trying to catch up.

They were heading into the centre.

He was nearly behind them now. The traffic was much heavier, it was raining, and the beams from the headlights bounced off the wet pavement. In these conditions it was no easy thing to follow the zigzagging vehicle. Sixteen minutes later, the scooter dropped its passenger on the rue d'Alsace-Lorraine and took off again immediately. Espérandieu parked in a prohibited spot, pulled down the screen marked 'Police', and got out. His instinct told him that there was something going on. Then he discovered he had left his camera on the passenger seat; he swore, went back to get it, then ran to catch up with his target.

No panic: Margot Servaz was walking calmly ahead of him through the crowd. As he jogged to reach her he checked that the camera was working.

She turned into the Place Esquirol. The bright windows and Christmas lights gave a new life to the trees and the old façades. With only a few days left until Christmas, it was crowded. Which suited him fine: that way she wouldn't notice him. Suddenly, he saw her stop short, look all around, then turn abruptly and go into the Brasserie du Père Léon. Espérandieu's alarm bells started ringing: this was not the behaviour of someone with nothing to hide. He hurried to follow her as far as the café. Now he had a dilemma: he had already met Margot half a dozen times. How would she react if she saw him come in right behind her?

He looked through the window just in time to see her kiss someone on the lips, then sit down opposite him. She looked radiant. Espérandieu saw her laugh joyfully at what her companion was saying.

Then he turned to look at him. *Oh, fuck.*

On that cold December evening he gazed up at the stars scattered above the mountains, and the lights from the mill, reflected in the water, promised a welcoming warmth. A brisk wind stung his cheeks; the rain was once again turning to snow. Saint-Cyr opened the door and Servaz saw his face freeze with astonishment.

'Good Lord! What happened to you?'

Servaz had looked at his face in the hospital mirror, and knew it was frightening. He had dilated pupils and bloodshot eyes worthy of Christopher Lee's Dracula, his neck was bruised up to his ears, his lips and nostrils had been irritated by the plastic bag, and there was a horrible purplish scar where the rope had dug into his throat. His eyes were filling with tears from the cold, or the tension.

'I'm late,' he said in a scratchy voice. 'If you don't mind, I'll come straight in. It's cold out tonight.'

He was still trembling all over. Once he was inside, Saint-Cyr took a closer look at him.

'My God! Come along and get warm,' said the old judge, going down the steps to the spacious living room.

The table had been set, and a bright fire was crackling in the hearth. Saint-Cyr pulled out a chair for Servaz to sit down. He picked up a bottle and filled a glass.

'Drink. And take your time. Are you sure you'll be all right?'

Servaz nodded. He took a sip. The wine was a deep red colour, almost black, strong but excellent. At least as far as Servaz could tell; he wasn't really a connoisseur.

'Somontano,' said Saint-Cyr. 'I bring it back from the other side of the Pyrenees, from the High Aragon. So, tell me what happened.'

Servaz told him. He couldn't stop thinking about the holiday camp, and adrenaline shot through him every time, like a fishbone rammed down a cat's throat. Who had tried to strangle him? He played back his memories of the day. Gaspard Ferrand? Élisabeth Ferney? Xavier? But Xavier had come to his help. Unless at the last minute the psychiatrist had baulked at the idea of killing a policeman. One minute Servaz was being brutally assaulted, and the next Xavier was there by his side. Could it have been the same person? No, it couldn't, because they had heard the Volvo drive off! Then he summed up the last two days – Chaperon's sudden flight, his empty house, the discovery of the cape and the ring, the box of bullets on the desk.

'You are getting closer to the truth,' concluded Saint-Cyr with a worried look. 'You're almost there. But this,' he added, looking at Servaz's neck, 'what he did to you, it's unspeakably violent – it looks as if he'll stop at nothing. He's ready to kill a policeman if he has to.'

'He, or they,' said Servaz.

Saint-Cyr gave him a sharp look.

'This is very worrying for Chaperon.'

'You have no idea where he might be hiding?'

The magistrate was pensive.

'No. But Chaperon is very keen on mountaineering. He knows every trail and every refuge on either side of the border. You should enlist the help of the mountain gendarmerie.'

Of course. Why hadn't he thought of it earlier?

'I made something light,' said Saint-Cyr. 'Per your request. Trout in an almond sauce. It's a Spanish recipe. I'm sure you'll like it.'

He went to the kitchen and came back with two steaming plates. Servaz took another sip of wine, then started on the trout. An enticing aroma rose from his plate. The sauce was light but deliciously spiced, with a hint of almonds, garlic, lemon and parsley.

'Do you think someone might be taking revenge for the teenagers?'

Servaz nodded with a grimace. His throat hurt with every swallow. He soon lost his appetite and pushed back his plate.

'I'm sorry, I just can't,' he said.

'Of course. I'll get you a coffee.'

Servaz thought of the heart carved in the tree bark. With the five names. Five of the seven suicide victims.

'So the rumours were justified,' said Saint-Cyr as he came back with Servaz's coffee. 'It's incredible that we missed that diary. And that we didn't manage to find the least little clue to confirm the theory.'

Servaz understood that while the judge was relieved the truth was finally out, he was feeling what any person would when they've been chasing after something for years and suddenly, just when they have become resigned to the fact they will never reach it, someone else seizes it: the feeling that he had missed the very crux of the matter, that he had been wasting his time.

'In the end your hunch was correct,' Servaz pointed out. 'And apparently the men never took off their capes when they committed the appalling acts, never showed their faces to their victims.'

'But not one of their victims ever spoke out!'

'That is often the case, as you well know. The truth comes to light many years later, when the victims have grown up, when they've gained some confidence and are no longer afraid of their torturers.'

'I suppose you've already had a look at the list of the children who stayed at the holiday camp?' asked Saint-Cyr.

'What list?'

The judge looked surprised.

'The one I made of all the children who'd stayed at the holiday camp, the one in the box I gave you.'

'There was no list in the box,' Servaz said.

Saint-Cyr seemed offended.

'Of course there was! You think I've gone mad? All the documents are there, I'm sure of it. Including that one. At the time, I tried to find a link between the suicide victims and the children who had been at the holiday camp, as I told you. I figured that there might have been other, earlier suicides that had not been noticed because they were isolated incidents, other children who had taken their own lives. That would have confirmed my hunch that the suicides were connected with Les Isards. So I went to the town hall and I got a list of all the children who had been at the camp since it began. That list is in the box.'

Saint-Cyr did not like it when anyone cast doubt on what he said, thought Servaz. Or on his intellectual capacities. The man seemed absolutely sure of himself.

'I'm sorry, but I didn't find any list like that.'

The judge shook his head.

'You have everything. I was meticulous back then. Not like nowadays. I made photocopies of every document in the file. I am certain that list was there.'

He stood up.

'Follow me.'

They went along a corridor with fine floor tiles of aged grey stone. The judge went through a low door and switched on the light. Servaz found himself surrounded by utter chaos, a dusty little office in an indescribable mess. Bookshelves, chairs and coffee tables, covered with law books piled every which way, stacks of files and folders spilling reams of paper precariously held together. There were even some on the floor and in the corners. Saint-Cyr grumbled as he rummaged through a pile that was stacked thirty centimetres high on a chair. Then another. Finally, after five minutes had gone by, he stood up straight with some stapled sheets and handed them triumphantly to Servaz.

'Here we are.'

Servaz looked at the list. Dozens of names over two columns on three pages. He let his gaze wander down the columns, and at first none of the names gave him pause. Then there was the first familiar name: Alice Ferrand. He went on reading. Ludovic Asselin. Another suicide victim. He found the third one a bit further along: Florian Vanloot. He was looking for the names of the two other teens who had stayed at the camp before their suicide when his gaze came upon another name, a completely unexpected name.

A name that should never have been on that list.

It made him dizzy. Servaz shuddered as if he had just been given an electric shock. His eyes must be playing tricks on him. He blinked, opened them again. The name was still there, along with the other children. Irène Ziegler.

Shit, it can't be!

24

He sat at the wheel of the Cherokee for a long time, staring blankly through the windscreen. He did not see the snowflakes, or the layer of snow rising on the road. A streetlamp cast a circle of light over the snow; the lights in the mill went out one after the other, except for one, surely the bedroom. Servaz thought the old judge must read in bed. He didn't close the shutters. There was no point: a burglar would have to swim against the current and climb along the wall to reach the windows. That was at least as effective as a dog or a burglar alarm.

Irène Ziegler. Her name was on the list. What could it mean? He remembered how he had come back to the gendarmerie after his first visit with Saint-Cyr with that box in his arms. He saw her again, going off with it to sort the documents one by one. Saint-Cyr had been categorical: the list of children who had stayed at the camp had been there then. But what if the old man was senile? Perhaps he was losing his memory and didn't want to admit it. Perhaps he had put the list somewhere else. But there was another possibility, a far more disturbing one. Which held that Servaz had never seen the list *because Irène Ziegler had removed it*. She had shown very little inclination to remember the events when he had first spoken to her about them. Suddenly another image came to him, when he was stuck on the cable car and trying to reach her. She should have got there long before him, she wasn't as far away, but when he got to the cable cars she wasn't there. She had said that she'd had a motorcycle accident, that she was on her way. Only afterwards did he see her: by then Perrault was already dead.

He rubbed his eyelids. He was exhausted, at the end of his tether; his body was nothing but a tangle of pain, and suspicious thoughts were spreading through his mind like a lethal poison. Others came to him: she knew about horses; she handled her car and her helicopter expertly; she knew the region like the back of her hand. He remembered how that very morning she had spoken up to say that she would take care of the visit to the town hall – she already knew what she would find. That list was the only trace that could lead to her. Had she also gone through Chaperon's papers so she would know where to find him? *Was she the one who had tried to kill him at the holiday camp? Who'd been holding the rope and the plastic bag?* He couldn't believe it.

Fatigue was muddling his thoughts. He couldn't think straight anymore. What should he do? He had no proof she was guilty in any way.

He looked at the clock on the dashboard and picked up his phone to call Espérandieu.

'Martin? What's going on?'

Servaz told him about the retired judge and his files, then explained what he had just discovered. There was a long silence on the other end of the line.

'Do you think it's her?' said Espérandieu finally, sceptical.

'She wasn't with me when I saw Perrault in the cabin with the murderer. The person wearing a balaclava, who hid behind Perrault when we passed each other so that I wouldn't see his eyes. She should have got there before me – but she didn't. She only got there long afterwards. She went to the holiday camp and she never mentioned it. She's familiar with horses, she knows the mountains, she's physically fit, and I'm sure she can use a climbing rope.'

'Sweet Jesus!' exclaimed Espérandieu, shaken.

He was speaking in a low voice and Servaz guessed he must be in bed, Charlène asleep beside him.

'What do we do?' asked Servaz.

Silence. Despite the distance he could tell that Espérandieu must be stunned. He wasn't used to his boss handing the reins over to him.

'You sound funny.'

'I'm exhausted. I think I may have a fever too.'

He didn't tell him about the attack at the holiday camp; he didn't feel like talking about it.

'Where are you?'

Servaz looked down the deserted street.

'Outside Saint-Cyr's house.'

He glanced in the rear-view mirror. Behind him, too, the road was lifeless and deserted. The last houses, a hundred metres away, were tightly shuttered. The only movement was the snow, falling thick and silent.

'Go back to the hotel,' said Espérandieu. 'Don't do anything just now. I'm coming.'

'When? This evening?'

'Yes. I'll get dressed and be on my way. Do you know where Ziegler is?'

'I suppose she's at home.'

'Or out looking for Chaperon. Maybe you could call her, just to find out.'

'And say what?'

'I don't know – that you don't feel well, that you're sick. You're exhausted, you said as much yourself. It's clear from your voice. Tell her you'll stay in bed tomorrow, that you can't take it anymore. And then you'll see how she reacts.'

Servaz smiled. After what had happened, she would have no trouble believing it.

'Martin? What's going on?'

He listened carefully. The muted sounds of a television in the background. Ziegler was at home. Or at someone else's place. A flat? A house? He couldn't picture the place where she lived. In any case, she wasn't out of doors, roaming about like a famished wolf in pursuit of the mayor. *Or of him.* He saw her again in her black jumpsuit, her high boots, with her powerful motorbike; he saw her sitting at the helicopter controls. All of a sudden he was certain she was the one.

'Nothing,' he said. 'I'm just calling to say I'm taking a break. I have to sleep.'

'You're not feeling any better?'

'I don't know. I can't think straight anymore. I can't think, full stop. I'm exhausted and my throat is killing me.' No lie was better than the one that contained a portion of truth. 'Do you think you can cope alone tomorrow? We've got to find Chaperon, no matter what.'

'Right,' she said, after a moment's hesitation. 'You're not up to it just now, anyway. Get some rest. I'll call you as soon as there's anything new. In the meantime I'm going to get to bed, too. You said it: got to be able to think straight.'

'Night, Irène.'

He hung up and called his assistant.

'Espérandieu,' said Espérandieu.

'She's at home. Or in any case there was a TV on in the background.'

'But she wasn't asleep.'

'Like plenty of other people who stay up late. Where are you now?'

'On the motorway. I'll stop for petrol and carry on. I've never seen the countryside so dark. I'll be there in fifty minutes. Do you suppose we should go and wait outside her place?'

He hesitated. Would he have the strength?

'I don't even know where she lives.'

'You're joking.'

'No.'

'So what do we do?'

'I'll call d'Humières.'

'At this time of night?'

Servaz put his mobile on the bed, went into the bathroom and splashed cold water on his face. He would have liked to drink a coffee, but he couldn't count on it to help. Then he went back into the bedroom and rang Cathy d'Humières.

'Martin! For Christ's sake! Have you seen the time? You should be asleep, the state you're in.'

'I'm sorry,' he said. 'But it's urgent.'

He guessed the prosecutor must be sitting up in bed now.

'Another victim?'

'No. A stroke of bad luck. We have a new suspect. But I can't tell anyone about it at the moment. Except you.'

'Who is it?' said d'Humières, suddenly wide awake.

'Captain Ziegler.'

A long silence on the line.

'Tell me everything.'

He did. He told her about Saint-Cyr's list, and about how Irène was absent at the time of Perrault's death, her reluctance to speak about her childhood or her stay at the holiday camp, her white lies regarding her personal life.

'That doesn't prove she's guilty,' said d'Humières.

Typical jurist's point of view, he thought. From his own point of view, Irène Ziegler was now his number one suspect.

'But you're right, this is disturbing. I don't like this business with the list one bit. What do you want from me? I don't think you'd be calling me at this time of night just to tell me something that could have waited until tomorrow.'

'We need her address. I don't have it.'

'We?'

'I asked Espérandieu to meet me.'

'You're going to trail her? Tonight?'

'Perhaps.'

'Good God! Martin! You should be asleep! Have you looked at yourself lately?'

'I'd rather not.'

'I don't like this. Be careful. If it is her, it could become dangerous. She's killed two men already. And no doubt she can handle a gun just as well as you.'

A flattering understatement, he thought. He was a lousy shot. And his assistant wasn't exactly Dirty Harry.

'Call me back in five minutes. I have to make one or two calls,' she said.

Espérandieu knocked on the door forty minutes later. Servaz opened it. His assistant had snowflakes on his anorak and in his hair.

'Have you got a glass of water and some coffee?' he said, a bottle of aspirin in his hand. Then he looked up and saw his boss. 'Fucking hell!'

At roughly the time Servaz was leaving Saint-Cyr's house, Diane was still at her desk.

She wondered what she ought to do now. She felt she was ready to take action – but did that mean she really wanted to? She was still tempted to behave as if everything were normal, and to forget what she had found out. Should she talk it over with Spitzner? At first she was keen, but on second thoughts she changed her mind. To be honest, she didn't know who to turn to.

She was alone, left to her own devices. She checked the time in the corner of her screen.

Eleven fifteen.

The Institute was silent except for the wind gusting against the window. She had just finished entering the data from the day's interviews into an Excel spreadsheet. Xavier had left his office long ago. *It was now or never.* She had butterflies in her stomach. What would happen if she got caught? Better not to even think about it.

'There she is.'

Espérandieu handed him the binoculars. Servaz trained them on the little three-storey building at the bottom of the hill. Irène Ziegler was standing in the middle of the living room, a mobile phone to her ear. She seemed to be speaking loudly, and was dressed like she was about to go out, not like someone planning to spend their evening in front of the telly before going to bed.

'She doesn't look like she's about to go to sleep,' said Espérandieu, taking the binoculars again.

They were on a little rise at the edge of a car park, twenty kilometres from Saint-Martin. The car park was surrounded by a hedge. They had slipped into the space between two bushes. An icy wind rattled the hedge. Servaz turned up the collar of his jacket, and Espérandieu was sheltering beneath the hood of his anorak, which was turning white. Servaz was shaking with cold, and his teeth were chattering. It was forty-two minutes after midnight.

'She's coming out!' said Espérandieu; he saw her grab a biker's jacket near her front door.

A moment later she had slammed the door to the flat. He lowered the binoculars to the entrance of the building, where Ziegler appeared twenty seconds later. She went down the steps and headed towards her motorcycle, despite the snow.

'Shit! I don't believe it!'

They ran towards the car. The rear wheels skidded slightly in the bend at the foot of the hill, just in time for them to see the motorcycle turn right at the top of the street. When they reached the crossroads, the traffic light had turned red. They went through it. It was unlikely they'd run into anyone at this time of night, in this weather. They were on a long avenue white with snow. In the distance Ziegler was driving very slowly. Which made things easier for them, but also made it more likely they'd be noticed, because they were completely alone, just Ziegler and them, on the long white road.

'She'll spot us if this goes on,' said Espérandieu, slowing down.

They left the little town behind and drove for ten minutes or more at a slow pace, going through deserted villages, past fields of white, with the mountains on either side. Espérandieu had let her get quite far ahead, until they could only just make out the tail light of her bike shining through the darkness as faintly as the lit end of a cigarette.

'Where on earth is she going?'

Servaz could hear in Espérandieu's voice the same bewilderment he felt. He didn't reply.

'Do you think she's found Chaperon?'

Servaz stiffened at the thought. He felt his tension rising; he was filled with apprehension at the prospect of what might happen. Everything seemed to indicate that he was on the right track: she had lied to him; she hadn't gone to bed but was going out in the middle of the night, unbeknown to everyone. He couldn't stop mulling over all the evidence that pointed to her.

'She's turned right.'

Servaz strained to see ahead. She had just left the road for a car park outside a low rectangular building that looked like one of the countless commercial warehouses found along main roads. Through the snow they saw a neon light shining in the dark. It formed a woman's luminous profile; she was smoking a cigarette and wearing a bowler hat. The smoke from the cigarette spelled out the words 'Pink Banana'. Espérandieu slowed down again. They saw Ziegler stop the motorcycle and dismount.

'What is it?' asked Servaz. 'A nightclub?'

'A gay bar.'

'A what?'

'A lesbian club.'

They drove into the car park in first gear, just as she was greeting the doorman. She went past two plastic palm trees and disappeared inside. Espérandieu drove very slowly past the entrance to the night-club. Further on there were other rectangular buildings. Like gigantic shoeboxes. A commercial zone. He turned and backed into a pool of darkness, well away from the streetlamps and neon lights, but facing the entrance to the club.

'You wanted to find out about her private life, well, here you go.'

'What's she doing in there?'

'What do you think?'

'I mean, she's hunting for Chaperon, she knows that time is of the essence, and yet she wastes it to come here? At one o'clock in the morning?'

384

'Unless she's got an appointment with a contact.'

'In a gay bar?'

Espérandieu shrugged. Servaz looked at the clock on the dashboard. Eight minutes past one.

'Take me back,' he said.

'Back where?'

'To her place.'

He felt in his pocket and pulled out a little collection of skeleton keys. Espérandieu frowned.

'Whoa, steady . . . That's not a good idea. She might leave at any moment.'

'You can drop me off there, and come back here to make sure she's still inside. I won't go in until you give me the green light. Is your mobile charged?'

Servaz took his out. For once it was working. Espérandieu did likewise, shaking his head.

'Hold it right there. You can hardly stand up straight. If Ziegler is a murderer, she'll be extremely dangerous.'

'If you keep an eye on her, I'll have plenty of time to get out of there. We don't have time for games.'

'And what if a neighbour sees you and sounds the alarm? Confiant will destroy your career. The man hates you.'

'No one will know. Let's go. We've wasted enough time.'

Diane looked all around her. Not a soul. The corridor was deserted. There were no surveillance cameras in this part of the Institute, which was off limits to the patients. She turned the handle; the door was unlocked. She checked her watch. Twelve minutes past midnight. She went in. The room was bathed in the moonlight coming in through the window. Xavier's office.

She closed the door behind her. All her senses on alert, unbelievably sharp – as if the tension were giving her an animal's heightened vision and hearing. Her gaze swept the desk, empty except for a lamp, the computer and the telephone; there was a little bookshelf on the right, a filing cabinet on the left, a fridge in the corner and pot plants on the windowsill. Outside, the storm was raging, and at times, when the moon was hidden momentarily by clouds, the light grew so dim that all she could see was the grey-blue rectangle of the window.

On the floor, in a corner, was a pair of bar-bells. They were small but heavy, she noticed as she went closer. She wanted to open the top drawer, but it was locked. *Drat.* The second, however, was not. She hesitated and switched on the desk lamp. She searched through the folders and papers in the drawer, but nothing caught her attention. The third drawer was almost empty except for a few pens and felt tips.

She went over to the filing cabinet. It was full of hanging files. Diane pulled out a few and opened them. Files on the staff. She noticed there were none under the name of Élisabeth Ferney, but there was one for Alexandre Barski. As there were no other Alexandres, she concluded it must be the nurse. She held it up to the lamp to be able to read it better.

Alex's CV informed her that he was born in the Ivory Coast in 1980. He was younger than she had thought. Unmarried. He lived in a town called Saint-Gaudens; Diane thought she recalled having seen the name on a map of the region. He had been working at the Institute for four years. Before that, he had worked at the psychiatric hospital in Armentières. As a student he had completed several internships, including one in a child psychiatry unit, and Diane thought that this was something they could talk about in future. She wanted to get closer to Alex – to befriend him, make him an ally. He'd got good appraisals. Over the years, first Wargnier then Xavier had written comments such as 'good listener', 'competent', 'shows initiative', 'team spirit', 'gets along well with patients'.

Right, you haven't got all night.

She closed the file and put it back. With some misgivings, she looked for her own file. 'Diane Berg.' She opened it and found her CV and printouts of the emails she had exchanged with Dr Wargnier. She felt her stomach knot when she read a comment in Xavier's handwriting at the bottom of the page: '*Could be problematic?*' The other hanging files in the drawer were no more revealing. She glanced into the other drawers. Files on the patients. Administrative paperwork. The fact that there was no file for Lisa Ferney confirmed Diane's suspicions: perhaps she really was the one in charge here. Neither Wargnier nor Xavier had dared to put together a file on the head nurse.

She inspected the bookshelf on the other side of the room. Then once again the desk and the computer. Diane hesitated, and finally sat down in Xavier's chair. A stubborn odour of soap and an overly spicy cologne permeated the leather back of the chair. She paused to listen carefully, then turned the computer on. Something stirred and whined deep inside the machine, like a newborn roused from sleep.

The desktop wallpaper appeared – an ordinary autumn landscape – and the icons popped up one after the other.

Diane went over the icons, but nothing grabbed her attention. She opened his mailbox. Nothing of interest. The latest email was from that very morning, addressed to all the staff and entitled 'Calendar of therapeutic team operational meetings'. There were 550 messages in his inbox, including 12 unread ones; Diane didn't have time to open them all, but she looked quickly at the last 40 and didn't find anything out of the ordinary.

Then she went through the sent mail. Nothing to report there either.

She closed the mailbox and looked for his bookmarks. Several websites drew her attention, including a singles dating site, another one entitled 'Learn charm from a psychologist-sexologist', a third with 'ultimate' pornographic images, and a fourth one that referred to 'thoracic pain and cardio-circulatory distress'. She wondered whether Xavier actually had heart problems or was simply a hypochondriac. After seventeen minutes she switched off the computer, disappointed.

She looked again at the top drawer, the one that was locked.

She wondered whether Xavier kept an external hard drive or a USB in the drawer. With the exception of the porn sites, his computer seemed just a little bit too clean for someone with something to hide.

She looked all around her, found a paperclip, straightened it and slipped it into the little lock, trying to imitate what she had seen in films.

It was clear that her efforts were getting her nowhere when the paperclip broke in two and half of it remained stuck in the lock. She swore in a low voice. She picked up a paper knife and with some difficulty managed to extract the metal. After that, she thought through all the possibilities and suddenly an idea came to her. She swung round in the chair towards the window and stood up, then lifted each of the flower pots one by one. Nothing. Then she dug her fingers into the soil.

In the third pot her fingers closed round something. A piece of cloth, with something hard inside . . . She tugged and a small pouch appeared. The key was there. Her pulse accelerated. But on opening the drawer she was disappointed: no hard drive, no USB stick. Just a pile of papers about the Institute. Reports, correspondence with colleagues – nothing confidential. Why would Xavier lock the drawer, in that case? Why not just leave it open like the others? As she rifled through the pages she found a thin manila folder. She pulled it out of the drawer and placed it on the desk blotter. There were only a few sheets inside, including a list of names spread over several columns. Diane noticed that it bore the seal of the town hall in Saint-Martin, and that it was a photocopy. She picked them up and started to look through them.

On the second sheet was a yellow Post-it note. She peeled it off and held it closer to the lamp. Xavier had written several names on it, followed each time by a question mark:

Gaspard Ferrand?
Lisa?
Irène Ziegler?
Holiday camp?
Revenge?
Why the horse???

She wondered what she was looking at, but she could guess the answer. The questions echoed her own. Two of the names were unfamiliar to her, but the words 'holiday camp' inevitably reminded her of her unpleasant experience at the abandoned buildings two days earlier. What she was holding was a list of suspects. She remembered the conversation she had overheard through the air vent: Xavier had promised the cop that he would conduct his own investigation among the staff. And these questions scribbled on a scrap of paper proved that he had begun to do so. Which meant, obviously, that if Xavier was conducting a secret investigation, he wasn't the accomplice the police were looking for. In that case, why had he ordered the drugs?

Puzzled, Diane put the list back in the folder, and the folder back in the drawer, then put the key in the lock, pausing. She had never heard of the other two people – but there was at least one name on

388

the list she could look into. By putting the words 'holiday camp' at the end of the list was Xavier implying that all these people were connected in some way with that place? Again she pictured the screaming, sobbing man. What had happened there? And what did it have to do with the crimes committed in Saint-Martin? The answer must have something to do with the word the psychiatrist had written just below: *revenge*. Diane knew that there were far too many elements missing for her to get at the truth. Apparently Xavier was getting somewhere, but he still had quite a few questions.

Suddenly she froze, her hand still on the key locking the drawer. Footsteps in the corridor. Instinctively she sank deeper into the chair, her hand moving slowly towards the desk lamp. She switched it off. She was plunged in the grey-blue half-light of the moon and her heart began to pound wildly. The footsteps had come to a halt outside the door. Was it one of the watchmen on his rounds? Had he seen the light? The seconds ticked by endlessly. Then the watchman continued on his way and the footsteps faded.

The blood still throbbing in her ears, she gradually began to breathe normally again. There was only one thing she wanted: to go back up to her room and hide. She would also like to question Xavier about his investigation. But she knew that the moment she admitted to searching his office she would be sacked, and there would go her career. She had to find another way to make him talk to her.

'Her motorbike's still there. She's not left yet.'

Servaz switched off his mobile and hit the light switch on the landing. He looked at his watch – twenty-seven minutes past one – then at the door of the other flat. Not a sound. Everyone was asleep. He wiped his feet several times on the doormat, then took out his skeleton keys and began to try them in the lock. Thirty seconds later he was inside. She had not installed any additional security.

There were two doors on the right: the first gave on to a corridor; the second led into the living room. Servaz walked across the dark, silent living room, looking for a light switch. The light came on to reveal a spartan interior. He stopped, his heart pounding.

Look for white, Propp had said.

He walked slowly around the room. The walls were white. The furniture was cold, disembodied. Modern. He tried to picture the person who lived here, independent of what he knew about her.

Nothing came. It was like a flat that belonged to a ghost. He went over to the dozen or so books on a shelf among the sporting trophies, and gave a violent shudder. They were all about the same thing: sexual crimes, violence to women, the oppression of women, pornography and rape. It was dizzying. *He was getting close to the truth.* He went on into the kitchen. Suddenly something moved, on his right. Before he could even react he felt something touching his leg. Panicked, he leapt back. A long meow and a cat ran for refuge elsewhere in the flat. *Christ, you gave me one hell of a fright!* Servaz waited for his heart to stop pounding, then opened the cupboards. Nothing in particular. He noticed that Irène Ziegler kept to a careful diet, unlike him. He went back across the living room towards the bedrooms. The door to one of them was open; it contained a desk, a bed and a metal filing cabinet. He went through the drawers one by one. Files: taxes, electricity, courses at the gendarmerie academy, rent, healthcare, various subscriptions. On the night table there were books in English. *The Woman-Identified Woman, Radical Feminism: A Documentary History.* He was startled by the telephone vibrating in his pocket.

'How are you getting on?' asked Espérandieu.

'Nothing so far. Anything your end?'

'No, she's still inside. Did it even occur to you she might not live alone? We don't know anything about her, for Christ's sake!'

His heart skipped a beat. Espérandieu was right. He hadn't thought of that! There were three closed doors in the flat. *What was behind them?* At least one of them must be a bedroom. The one he was in right now did not seem lived in. He had made no noise on entering, and it was almost two o'clock in the morning, a time when most people are sound asleep. With a cramp in his stomach, he left the room and stood outside the next door. He listened carefully. Not a sound. He put his ear against it. Silence, apart from the rush of his own blood. Finally he put his hand on the door handle and turned it very slowly.

A bedroom. An unmade bed.

The bed was empty. Once again his heart was pounding like mad; he told himself it was due to the pathetic physical condition he was in. He really had to think about doing some exercise if he didn't want to die of a heart attack one day.

He opened the last two doors; they led to the bathroom and toilet.

He went back into the room with the desk and checked the drawers: nothing but pens and credit-card statements. Then his gaze was drawn to a spot of colour beneath the desk. A road map. It must have fallen onto the floor. Once again his telephone throbbed in his pocket.

'She's left!'

'Right. Follow her. And call me when you're a kilometre from here.'

'What are you doing?' asked Espérandieu. 'Get the hell out of there, for Christ's sake.'

'I might have found something.'

'She's already left! She's on her way!'

'Catch up with her. Hurry! I need five minutes.'

He hung up.

He switched on the desk lamp and bent down to pick up the map.

It was two minutes past two when Espérandieu saw Irène Ziegler come out of the Pink Banana in the company of another woman. While Ziegler, in her leathers and boots, looked like some fascinating Amazon, her companion was wearing a white satin jacket with a fur collar over tight jeans and white-heeled boots laced from top to bottom. Straight from the pages of a magazine. She was as dark as Ziegler was fair, her long hair falling onto her collar. The two young women went over to Ziegler's bike, and the gendarme got on it. They exchanged a few more words. Then the dark-haired woman leaned over the blonde. Espérandieu swallowed when he saw them kissing deeply.

Blimey, he thought, his throat suddenly dry.

Ziegler revved the engine, a leather-clad Amazon welded to the steel of her bike. *That woman may be a killer*, he thought, to pour a cold shower on his incipient lust.

Suddenly another thought came to him. *It had taken two people to kill Éric Lombard's horse.* He took a photo of the dark-haired woman just before she disappeared back into the club. Who was she? *Could the assassins have been two women?* He took out his mobile and rang Servaz.

'Shit!' he swore after hanging up. Martin was staying in the flat! He must be out of his mind. He should have got out of there at once. Espérandieu took off at top speed, passing the bouncer. He took the turn at the exit a bit too abruptly and skidded once again

391

before accelerating down the long straight road. He only lifted his foot from the pedal once he saw the motorcycle's tail light again, and glanced automatically at the clock on the dashboard: seven minutes past two.

Martin, for heaven's sake, get out of there!

Servaz was turning the road map every which way.

A detailed map of the High Comminges region. On a scale of 1/50,000. No matter how much he stared at it, he couldn't see anything. Yet Ziegler had looked at this map recently. *It's here, somewhere, but you can't see it,* he thought. See what? What was he supposed to be looking for? And then it came to him: Chaperon's hiding place!

It had to be there, of course – somewhere on this map.

There was a spot in the road, after a long straight stretch, where you had to slow right down to take the bends. The road zigzagged through a landscape of fir trees and snow-laden birches, among low white hills and a winding stream. A picture-postcard landscape by day, and eerie at night in the glow of the headlights.

Espérandieu saw Ziegler slow down and brake, then lean very carefully into the first bend before disappearing behind the tall fir trees. He lifted his foot from the accelerator and entered the bend with the same caution. He was almost in slow motion by the time he reached the spot where the stream flowed. But it was not enough.

At the time, he would have been incapable of saying what it was. A black shadow.

It burst out from the other side of the road and leapt into the beam of the headlights. Instinctively, Espérandieu slammed on the brakes: the wrong reflex. The car swerved sideways, rushing to meet the animal with a violent shock. Clinging to the steering wheel, he managed to right the car but too late. It came to a halt; he put on his hazard lights, took off his seatbelt, grabbed a torch and hurried outside. A dog! He'd hit a dog. The animal was lying in the middle of the road, and looked imploringly at Espérandieu in the beam of light, breathing heavily, a cloud of vapour at his muzzle; one of his paws was trembling.

Don't move, mate! I'll be right back! thought Espérandieu, almost speaking out loud.

He put his hand inside his anorak. His mobile wasn't there!

Espérandieu looked desperately down the road. The motorcycle was long gone. *Shit, shit, shit!* He rushed to the car, leaned in and ran his hand under the seats. Nothing! Not a trace of the damned phone. Not on the seat, or on the floor. Where was the fucking thing?

No matter how Servaz turned the map, he could find no hint of a place where Chaperon might be hiding. But maybe Ziegler hadn't needed to mark it. Maybe all she'd had to do was glance at it to check something she already knew. Servaz stared at Saint-Martin, with its ski resort, the surrounding valleys and summits, the road he'd taken to get here and the one that led to the power station, the holiday camp, the Institute and all the surrounding villages.

He looked around him. A sheet of paper on the desk caught his attention. One paper among many.

He reached for it. The deed to some property. His pulse began to race. A deed in the name of Roland Chaperon, resident of Saint-Martin-de-Comminges. There was an address: Chemin 12, sector 4, valley of Aure, municipality of Hourcade. Servaz swore. He didn't have time to go and consult the property register. Then he noticed that Ziegler had written a letter and number in red felt tip at the bottom of the sheet. *D4.* That was it. With moist palms he held the sheet of paper closer while his finger ran feverishly over the map.

Espérandieu retraced his steps and saw the mobile phone in the road. He rushed to pick it up. It was in two pieces, the plastic shell split open. He tried to dial Servaz all the same, in vain. He was suddenly overwhelmed with fear. Martin! The dog let out a heartbreaking whimper. Espérandieu looked at him. *What the fuck! What is this nightmare!*

He yanked open the rear door, went back to the dog and lifted him up. He was heavy. The dog growled, threateningly, but let himself be carried. Espérandieu settled him on the back seat, slammed the door and got back behind the wheel. He glanced at the clock. Twenty past two! Ziegler would be back any minute. *Martin, get out of there, now! For the love of Christ!* He took off like a shot into a sideways skid, righted the car at the last minute and tore down the white road, clinging to the wheel like a rally driver. His heart was going 160 a minute.

★

A cross, a tiny cross in red ink that he had originally failed to see. Right in the middle of square D4. Servaz was jubilant. On the map there was a tiny black square in the middle of a deserted zone of forests and mountains. A chalet, a cabin? It hardly mattered. Now Servaz knew where Ziegler would be headed.

Suddenly he remembered the time: twenty past two. There was something wrong. Espérandieu should have called him ages ago. Ziegler had left the club sixteen minutes earlier! That was more than enough time to . . . He felt a cold sweat down his spine. He had to get out of there, right away. He cast a panicked look at the door, put the map back where he had found it, turned off all the lights and went into the living room. He heard a rumbling outside. Servaz hurried to the window, just in time to see Ziegler's motorbike. He went cold all over. *She's here already!*

He quickly switched off the living-room light.

Then he hurried to the front door, left the flat and closed the door gently behind him. His hand was trembling so much he almost dropped the skeleton key. He locked the door and started down the stairs, then stopped short after a few steps. Where was he going? This would lead nowhere. If he went out this way, he'd find himself face to face with her. He had a shock when he heard the front door creak open, two floors further down. He was trapped. He went back up the stairs two at a time, as silently as possible, and found himself back where he had started: the second-floor landing. He looked all around. There was no way out, no hiding place – Ziegler lived on the top floor.

His heart was thudding in his chest, fit to tunnel right through it. He tried to think. She would show up any second and find him there. How would she react? He was supposed to be sick in bed, and it was almost two thirty in the morning. *Think!* But he couldn't. He had no choice. He got out the skeleton key once again, opened the door, then locked it behind him. Then he rushed into the living room. The damned flat was too bare. There was nowhere to hide! For a split second he thought about turning the light on, sitting down and greeting her like that, as casual as could be. He would tell her that he had let himself in. That he had something important to tell her. No! That was stupid! He was sweating, out of breath; she would see the fear in his eyes straight away. He should have waited for her out on the landing. What an idiot! Now it was too late! Would she go so far as to kill him?

With an icy shiver he thought that she had already tried. At the holiday camp, that very morning. The thought of it revived him. *You have to hide!* In a few strides he was in the bedroom. He slipped under the bed just as he heard a key in the front door.

As he crawled deeper, he could see her boots in the hall. His chin against the floor, his face dripping with sweat – it was like a nightmare. Something not quite real, something that could not happen.

He heard her drop her keys noisily onto the chest in the entrance. For a moment of absolute terror he thought she was coming straight into the bedroom.

But then he saw the boots vanish into the living room, and heard the squeaking of her leather jumpsuit. He was about to wipe the sweat off his face with his sleeve when suddenly he froze: he'd forgotten to switch off his mobile.

The dog was whimpering on the back seat. But at least he wasn't moving. Espérandieu started into the last bend the way he had in all of them: virtually out of control. The rear of the car seemed to want to pull away, but he declutched, swung the wheel the opposite way, stepped briefly on the accelerator and managed to straighten up.

Ziegler's building.

He parked outside, reached for his gun and leapt out. He looked up and saw that there was light in the living room. Ziegler's motorcycle was there, too. But no sign of Martin. He listened carefully, heard nothing but the moaning of the wind.

Shit, Martin, show yourself!

Espérandieu was desperately scanning the surroundings when an idea came to him. He got back behind the wheel and started the car. The dog protested faintly.

'I know, old boy. Don't worry, I won't let you down.'

He drove back up the short, steep hill that led to the car park, reached for his binoculars and crept into the space in the hedge just in time to see Ziegler walking out of her kitchen with a bottle of milk. She had tossed her jacket onto the sofa. He saw her take a drink, then remove the belt from her leather trousers and pull off her boots. Then she left the living room. A light came on in the small frosted-glass window on the left. The bathroom. She was taking a shower. Where had Martin got to? Had he had time to make his escape? If so, then where was he hiding, for Christ's sake? Espérandieu swallowed. There was another window between the bathroom and the big one in the living room. Since the blinds were up and the door was open, he could just make out what must be a bedroom. Suddenly a figure emerged from under the bed. The shadow stood up, hesitated for a moment, then left the bedroom and headed stealthily towards the front door. Martin! Espérandieu felt like shouting for joy, but merely trained his binoculars on the entrance to the building until Servaz appeared at last. A smile lit up Espérandieu's face. Servaz looked from left to right, hunting for him, until Espérandieu put two fingers in his mouth and whistled.

Servaz looked up and saw him. He pointed upwards and Espérandieu understood. He trained his binoculars on the windows; Irène Ziegler was still in the shower. He motioned to Servaz to go to the side of the building and he climbed back into the car. One minute later his boss was opening the passenger door.

'Shit, where were you?' asked Servaz, a puff of white coming from his mouth. 'Why didn't you—'

He broke off when he saw the dog lying on the back seat.

'What is that?'

'A dog.'

'I can see that. What's it doing there?'

Espérandieu described the accident briefly. Servaz got into the passenger seat and slammed the door.

'You let me down for a . . . *dog*?'

Espérandieu made an apologetic face.

'It's my Brigitte Bardot side. And besides, my mobile is in pieces. You scared the shit out of me! We really fucked up on this one.'

In the dark car Servaz was shaking his head.

'It's entirely my fault. You were right, it wasn't a very good idea.'

It was one of the things Espérandieu liked about Martin. Unlike so many bosses, he knew how to admit when he was wrong, and how to take responsibility for his mistakes.

'But I found something all the same,' he added.

He told him about the map. And the property deed. He took out a piece of paper where he'd written down the coordinates. They were quiet for a moment.

'We have to call Samira and the others. We'll need reinforcements.'

'Are you sure you didn't leave any trace?'

396

'I don't think so. Other than a litre of sweat under the bed.'

'OK, that's good,' said Espérandieu. 'We've got something more urgent to deal with.'

'What's that?'

'The dog. We have to find a vet. Right away.'

Servaz looked at his assistant and wondered if he were joking. Vincent looked as serious as could be. Servaz turned round and stared at the animal. The dog looked very weak; he was in a bad way. He lifted his nose from the seat and looked at Servaz with gentle eyes, sad and resigned.

'Ziegler is taking a shower,' said his assistant. 'She won't be going out again tonight. She knows she's got all day tomorrow to get Chaperon, because you're supposed to be staying at home. She'll do it in broad daylight.'

Servaz hesitated.

'OK,' he said. 'I'll call the gendarmerie and find out where there's a vet. In the meantime, you get Samira out of bed and tell her to get down here with two more officers.'

Espérandieu looked at his watch – a quarter to three – and took Servaz's phone. He was on the line with Samira for a good ten minutes. Then he hung up and turned to his boss. Next to him, his head against the door, Servaz was sound asleep.

25

The camp bed creaked when he sat up, swung his legs out from under the blankets and put his bare feet on the cold tiles. A tiny, unfurnished room. As he gave a yawn and switched on the bedside lamp, Servaz remembered that he had been dreaming about Charlène Espérandieu: they had been making love in a hospital corridor while the doctors and nurses walked past them, oblivious. *On the hospital floor?* He looked down at his morning erection, and burst out laughing from the strangeness of the situation. He found his watch, which had slid under the bed; it was six o'clock in the morning. He reached for the clean clothes that had been laid out on a chair. The shirt was too big, but the trousers were the right length. Servaz headed for the showers at the end of the corridor. Ziegler had been placed under constant surveillance, and he preferred to sleep at the gendarmerie rather than the hotel, to keep an eye on the operation.

The showers were deserted. There was a nasty draught, spoiling the feeble efforts of a radiator. Servaz knew that the gendarmes slept in the other wing, where they had their own accommodation; these premises did not get used very often. Which didn't stop him from swearing when he turned on the hot water tap and a trickle, scarcely lukewarm, condescended to emerge from the shower head.

Every movement he made caused him to wince in pain. He started thinking. He felt certain that Irène Ziegler was guilty, but there were still some grey areas, some doors to open in the long corridor that led to the truth. Ziegler had surely been raped by the four men, along with other women in the region. The books he had seen in her flat were proof that the trauma was still raw. Grimm and Perrault had been killed for what they had done – but why had they been hanged? Because of the suicide victims? Or was there another reason? There was one detail that obsessed him: Chaperon had fled as if he had the devil on his heels. Did he know who the assassin was?

Servaz tried to reassure himself: Ziegler was being watched, and they knew where Chaperon was hiding – they held all the cards.

It might have been the icy air, or the water that was getting colder by the second, or the memory of his head imprisoned in a plastic bag – for whatever reason, he could not stop trembling. In the deserted shower room, he felt pure fear.

He was waiting in the incident room with his coffee when the others started to arrive. Maillard, Confiant, Cathy d'Humières, Espérandieu and two other members of the squad – Pujol and Simeoni, the narrow-minded heavies who had it in for Vincent. Everyone sat down and checked their notes before they began and the room was filled with the sound of shuffling paper. Servaz observed their pale, tired faces; they were all on edge. The tension was palpable. He wrote a few words on his pad while waiting for everyone to get ready; then he began.

He summed up the situation. When he told them what had happened to him at the holiday camp, a heavy silence fell. Pujol and Simeoni were watching him closely. Both of them seemed to be thinking that it would never have happened to them. Perhaps it was true. They might well represent the worst side of the profession, but they were good in tough situations.

Then he began to detail Ziegler's guilt, and this time it was Maillard who went pale. The atmosphere was heavy. For the cops to suspect a gendarme of murder – this was a recipe for all sorts of conflict.

'I don't like the sound of this at all,' said d'Humières soberly.

He had rarely seen her looking so wan. Her careworn features gave her a sickly complexion. He glanced at his watch. Eight o'clock. Ziegler would be getting up soon. As if to confirm his thoughts, his mobile rang.

'We're on – she's getting up,' said Samira Cheung on the line.

'Pujol,' he said at once, 'get over there with Samira. Ziegler has just woken up. And I want a third car for backup. She's one of us, so I don't want her to spot you. Simeoni, you take the third car. Don't follow too closely. Besides, we know where she's headed. It would be better to lose her than have her find out you're following her.'

Pujol and Simeoni left the room without a word. Servaz got up and went over to the large map of the region on the wall. For a moment his gaze went back and forth between his pad and the map; then he stabbed his finger on the exact spot. He turned and looked at his colleagues.

'There.'

A twist of smoke rose from a chimney on the moss-covered roof of the hut. Servaz looked around him. Grey clouds were draped over the wooded slopes. The air smelled of damp, fog, mulch and wood smoke. Below the spot where they stood, they could see the cabin down in the hollow of a small snow-filled valley, accessible by a single path. Out of sight, three gendarmes and a park ranger were keeping watch on the approach. Servaz turned to Espérandieu and Maillard, who replied with a nod; accompanied by a dozen men or more, they began to head slowly downhill.

Suddenly they stopped. A man had just come out of the hut. He stretched in the morning light, sniffed the air, spat on the ground, and they could hear him let out a fart as loud as a shepherd's horn. Oddly, a bird with a mocking cackle called out in reply. The man looked round one last time, then went back inside.

Servaz recognised him instantly, in spite of the beard.

Chaperon.

They reached the clearing behind the cabin. The humidity was like a Turkish bath, although not nearly as warm. Servaz looked at the others; they split into two groups. They moved slowly forward, sinking into the snow up to their knees, then crouched down below eye level to go round to the front door. Servaz was leading the first group. Just as he went round the corner to the front of the hut, the door opened. Servaz stepped backwards, his gun in his hand. He saw Chaperon take three steps, undo his flies and piss copiously into the snow, humming a little tune.

'Finish pissing and get your hands in the air, Pavarotti,' said Servaz behind him.

The mayor swore: he had just splattered his shoes.

Diane had spent a hell of a night. She had woken up bathed in sweat four times, with such a feeling of oppression that it was as if she was wearing a corset. The sheets, too, were soaked. She wondered if she had caught something.

She remembered having a nightmare: she was bound up in a strait-jacket, tied to the bed in one of the cells in the Institute and surrounded by a horde of patients touching her face with damp hands. She was shaking her head and screaming, until her cell door opened and Julian Hirtmann came in, a nasty smile on his lips. A moment later Diane was no longer in her cell but in a much vaster space, out of doors; it was night time, there was a lake and fires, and thousands of huge insects with birds' heads were crawling on the dark ground, and she could see the naked bodies of men and women fucking, hundreds of them in the reddish glow of the flames. Hirtmann was one of them and Diane understood that he had organised this gigantic orgy. She panicked when she discovered that she was naked, too, on her bed, still tied up but without the straitjacket – and she struggled until she woke up.

She stood under the shower for a long while, trying to get rid of the sticky sensation left by her dream.

Now she was wondering how she should behave. Every time she thought of speaking to Xavier she remembered the shipment of veterinary anaesthetics and felt ill at ease. Was she throwing herself into the lion's jaws? It was like one of those 3-D photographs, where the picture changes depending on how you hold it: she could not keep the image stable. What was the psychiatrist's role in all of this?

Judging by the clues she had at her disposal, Xavier seemed to be in the same situation: he knew from the cops that someone at the Institute was involved in the murders, and he was trying to find out who. Except that he was ahead of her, and had a host of information she did not. But then only a few days before the animal's death he had received a shipment of drugs used to put a horse to sleep. Which always led her back to the same point: two completely contradictory facts, and yet both were true. Could it be that Xavier had merely passed the anaesthetics on to someone else, without knowing what was going to happen? In that case, the person's name should have shown up in her search. Diane just didn't get it.

Who were Irène Ziegler and Gaspard Ferrand? By the looks of it, two people connected to the Les Isards holiday camp. Like Lisa Ferney . . . That was where she should start. The only concrete lead she had: the head nurse.

Servaz went into the cabin. A low sloping roof: the top of his head touched the ceiling. At the back was an unmade bunk with white sheets and a brown blanket, and a soiled pillow. There was a big woodstove, whose black pipe vanished into the roof; next to it was a pile of logs. Under the window, a sink and a little countertop; a burner, connected no doubt to a gas bottle. A book of crossword puzzles lay open on the table next to a beer bottle and an overflowing ashtray; a storm lamp was hanging directly above. There was a smell of wood smoke, tobacco, beer and, above all, stale sweat. There was no shower. He wondered how Chaperon managed to get washed.

This is what's left of those bastards: two corpses and a pathetic bloke who's gone to earth like a stinking rat.

He opened the cupboards, slid his hand under the mattress, searched the pockets of the jacket hanging behind the door. Inside it he found keys, a change purse and a wallet. He opened the wallet and found an ID card, a chequebook, a national insurance card, a Visa and an American Express. In the purse he found €800 in €20 and €50 notes. Then he opened the drawer, where he found the gun and the bullets.

He went back outside.

In less than five minutes, the men had taken their positions. Ten of them around the cabin and in the woods; six others at strategic points above the valley and overlooking the path, so they would see her arrive; all of them as stocky as Playmobil figurines in their Kevlar jackets. Servaz and Espérandieu waited inside the hut with Chaperon.

'What the fuck,' said the mayor. 'If you've got nothing on me, I'm out of here. You can't hold me against my will.'

'As you like,' said Servaz. 'If you want to end up like your friends, you're free to go. But we're confiscating the gun. And the moment you take a step out of here, you'll have no protection – spies who lose their cover call it being "in the cold".'

Chaperon shot him a look full of hatred, weighed the pros and cons, shrugged and slumped back onto the bunk.

At nine fifty-four, Samira called to let him know that Ziegler was leaving her house. *She's taking her time*, he thought. She knows she's got the whole day ahead of her. She must have it all figured out. He reached for the walkie-talkie and warned all the units that the target was on the move. Then he poured himself a coffee.

By ten thirty-two, Servaz was on to the third coffee of the morning and his fifth cigarette, despite Espérandieu's protests. Chaperon sat at the table playing patience, in silence.

*

At ten forty-three, Samira called to say that Ziegler had stopped at a coffee bar, and she'd bought some cigarettes, stamps and flowers.

'Flowers? From a florist's?'

'Yes, hardly from a butcher's.'

She must have spotted them . . .

At ten fifty-two, Servaz learned that Ziegler was heading for Saint-Martin at last. To reach the small valley where the cabin was, you took a road leading to Saint-Martin from the town where she lived, then a second one that headed due south and finally a forest track.

'What the fuck is she doing?' asked Espérandieu, when it was well past eleven. They had not said three words in over an hour, except for the exchanges between Samira and Servaz.

Good question, thought Servaz.

At nine minutes past eleven, Samira rang to say that Ziegler had gone past the road leading to the valley without slowing down, and was now headed into Saint-Martin. *She's not coming here.* Servaz swore and went outside to get a breath of fresh air. Maillard emerged from the woods and went up to him.

'What do we do now?'

'We wait.'

'She's at the cemetery,' said Samira at eleven forty-five.

'What? What's she doing at the cemetery? She's taking you for a ride: she's spotted you!'

'Maybe not. She did something weird.'

'What do you mean?'

'She went into a tomb and stayed in there for five minutes. That's what the flowers were for. She came back out without them.'

'A family tomb?'

'Yes, but it wasn't hers. I went to check. It was the Lombard family tomb.'

Servaz jumped. He didn't know the Lombards were buried in Saint-Martin. The situation was getting away from him. *There was a blind spot.* It had all begun with Éric Lombard's horse; then the investigation had sidelined Lombard in order to concentrate on the Grimm-Perrault-Chaperon trio and the suicide victims. And now

Lombard had suddenly turned up in the game again. What did it mean? What was Irène Ziegler doing in that tomb? He didn't get it.

'Where are you now?' he asked.

'I'm still at the cemetery. She saw me, so Pujol and Simeoni have taken over.'

'I'm coming.'

He went out of the cabin, down the path to the forest track, then headed into the thicket on his right. He pulled aside the snow-laden branches that were hiding the Jeep, and slipped behind the wheel.

It was just after noon when Servaz parked by the cemetery. Samira Cheung was waiting for him. Despite the cold, she was wearing a simple leather jacket, hotpants over thick tights, and worn brown leather hiking boots. The music from her headphones was so loud that Servaz could hear it as soon as he got out of the Jeep. Beneath her hat her ruddy face made him think of a strange creature from a film, one that Margot had dragged him to see, full of magicians and magic rings. He frowned when he saw the skull on Samira's sweatshirt. *Rather appropriate*, he thought. She looked less like a cop than a grave robber.

They climbed up a small hill, through the trees and gravestones towards a copse of evergreen trees that marked the end of the cemetery. An old woman gave them a stern look. The Lombard tomb stood out. Its mere size made it practically a mausoleum, or a chapel. On either side stood a carefully pruned yew tree. Three stone steps led up to the entrance, which was guarded by a fine wrought-iron gate. Samira tossed her cigarette to one side, went round the monument and hunted for a moment before she came back with a key.

'That's what I saw Ziegler do,' she said. 'It's hidden underneath a loose stone.'

'She didn't see you?' asked Servaz sceptically, eyeing his subordinate's outfit.

Samira frowned.

'I know my job. When she spotted me, I was in the middle of setting out a bouquet of flowers on a tomb for a guy called Graves. Funny, don't you think?'

Servaz looked up, but there was nothing written on the triangular pediment above the entrance. Samira turned the key and pulled open the creaking door. Servaz followed her in. A dim light filtered through an opening on their right, not enough for them to make out anything other than the vague shapes of three tombs. Once again Servaz wondered why everything had to be so heavy and sad and filled with darkness – as if death were not enough already. Yet there were countries where death was almost light, almost joyful, where there were celebrations, where people feasted and laughed, instead of these dreary, cheerless churches and all these requiems and *lacrimae rerum*, these kaddishes and prayers full of vales of tears. *As if cancer and road accidents and hearts that gave way and suicides and murders were not enough*, he thought. He noticed a single bouquet placed on one of the tombs: a spot of light in the gloom. Samira took out her iPhone and loaded the 'flashlight' app. The screen went white, and she held it above each of the three tombs in turn: *Édouard Lombard . . . Henri Lombard . . .* the grandfather and father. Servaz told himself that the third tomb must be that of Éric's mother, Henri's wife – the former failed actress, the ex-call girl, the *whore*, according to Henri Lombard . . . Why on earth would Irène leave flowers on that tomb?

He bent down to read the inscription. And frowned.

He had thought they were one step closer to the truth. But now everything had become more complicated, once again.

He looked at Samira, then again at the inscription, in the glow of her mobile:

MAUD LOMBARD, 1976–1998

'Who is it?'

'Éric Lombard's sister, born four years after him. I didn't know she was dead.'

'Does it matter?'

'It might.'

'So why do you think Ziegler is leaving flowers on her tomb? Any idea?'

'Not a clue.'

'Did she ever talk about it with you? Or say that she knew her?'

'No.'

'What does it have to do with the murders?'

'I don't know.'

'Well, at least you have a link this time,' said Samira.

'What do you mean?'

'A link between Lombard and the rest of the case.'

'What link?' he asked, puzzled.

'Ziegler didn't come and put flowers on this tomb by chance. There's a link. And even if you don't know what it is, she does. All you've got to do is ask her.'

Yes, he thought. Irène Ziegler knew a lot more than he did about the entire case. Maud Lombard must have been about the same age as Ziegler. Had they been friends? Obviously, Irène Ziegler had more than one secret.

In any case, there was no sign of Henri Lombard's wife, Éric's mother. Repudiated even in death, she had not been allowed to share in the family's appalling eternity. As they made their way back to the entrance, Servaz thought about the fact that Maud Lombard had died at the age of twenty-one. It felt like a crucial point. How did she die? An accident, illness? Or something else?

Samira was right: Ziegler held the key. Once she was in custody, she might come clean, but he doubted it. He had had plenty of chances to learn that Irène Ziegler had a strong character.

In the meantime, where had she got to?

He was overwhelmed by anxiety. They hadn't had any news in a while. He was about to call Pujol when his mobile rang.

'We've lost her!' shouted Simeoni.

'What?'

'Dyke bitch – I think she spotted us! With her fucking motorbike, she had no trouble at all leaving us behind!'

Shit! Servaz felt the adrenaline rush through his veins, and a sinking sensation in his guts. He looked up Maillard's number on his mobile.

'Pujol and Simeoni have lost the target,' he yelled. 'She could be anywhere! Let Lieutenant Espérandieu know, and stand ready!'

'OK. No problem. We're waiting for her.'

Servaz hung up. He wished he could be as calm as the gendarme was.

Suddenly something else occurred to him. He took out his mobile and dialled Saint-Cyr's number.

'Hello?'

'Maud Lombard, does that mean anything to you?'

There was a hesitation at the other end of the line.

'Of course. Éric Lombard's sister.'

'She died at the age of twenty-one. That's a bit young, no? Do you know how she died?'

'She committed suicide,' replied the judge, without the slightest hesitation this time.

Servaz held his breath. Just what he had hoped to hear. The pattern was coming to the surface. More and more clearly . . .

His pulse accelerated.

'What happened?'

A second hesitation.

'It was a tragic business,' said the voice at the other end of the line. 'Maud was a fragile, idealistic person. While she was studying in the United States, she fell passionately in love, I think. And the day her young man left her for someone else, she couldn't take it. That, along with her father's death the previous year . . . She came back here and killed herself.'

'And that's it?'

'What were you expecting?'

'The topiary in the Lombards' garden – is that in her memory?'

There was another hesitation.

'Yes. As you know, Henri Lombard was a cruel, tyrannical man, but occasionally he could show he cared. Moments when his paternal love took over. He had the animals sculpted when Maud was six years old, if memory serves me. And Éric Lombard kept them. In honour of his sister, as you said.'

'She never stayed at Les Isards holiday camp, did she?'

'A Lombard at Les Isards, you must be joking! Les Isards was reserved for the children of poor families who couldn't afford holidays.'

'I know.'

'Then how could you think a Lombard child might set foot there?'

'One more suicide. You weren't tempted to include her on the list?'

'Five years later? The chain of suicides had stopped long before. And besides, Maud was a woman, not a teenager.'

'One last question: how did she do it?'

Saint-Cyr paused for a moment.

'She slit her wrists.'

Servaz was let down: no hanging.

At half past twelve, Espérandieu got a message on his walkie-talkie. *Lunch.* He looked at Chaperon sprawled on the bunk, gave a shrug and went out. The others were waiting at the edge of the forest. As a 'guest' of the forces of law and order, he had the choice between a Parisian sandwich consisting of baguette, ham and Emmental, a *pan-bagnat* or a Moroccan sandwich with kebab, tomatoes, peppers and salad.

Moroccan, he decided.

As Servaz climbed back into the Cherokee, a thought emerged slowly from the muddle of unanswered questions. *Maud Lombard committed suicide . . . Lombard's horse was the first on the list.* What if that was the key to the investigation, and not the holiday camp? He had a feeling this would open new perspectives. There was a door that had not yet been tried, and the name 'Lombard' was written on it. Why had Éric Lombard been one of the avenger's targets? He hadn't been paying enough attention to that. He remembered how Commissioner Vilmer had gone pale when he had suggested there might be a connection between Lombard and the sex offenders. At the time it was just a joke, meant to destabilise him. But beneath the joke lay a real question. Now Ziegler's visit to the Lombard tomb showed just how crucial the question might be: what exactly was the link between Lombard and the other victims?

'She's on her way.'

'Copy.'

Espérandieu sat up abruptly. He released the button of his walkie-talkie and looked at his watch. Fourteen minutes to two. He reached for his gun.

'Base 1 to command. I've got a sighting. She just left her motorcycle at the top of the path. She's headed towards you. Over to you, base 2.'

'Base 2 here. OK, she just went by.'

Some minutes later, then:

'Base 3 here. She has not gone by. I repeat, target has not gone by.'

'Shit, where is she?' barked Espérandieu into the walkie-talkie. 'Can anyone see her? Answer!'

'Base 3 here. No, no sign . . .'

'Base 4. I can't see anything either.'

'Base 5. No one in sight.'

'We've lost her, command. I repeat, we've lost her!'

★

Where the fuck was Martin! Espérandieu still had his finger on the walkie-talkie when the door to the cabin was flung open and bounced against the inside wall. He swung round, his weapon pointed . . . and found himself looking into the barrel of a standard-issue gun, the black eye staring right at him. Espérandieu swallowed.

'What the hell are you doing here?' asked Ziegler.

'You're under arrest,' he answered, his voice singularly lacking in conviction.

'Irène! Put down your weapon!' shouted Maillard from outside.

There was a terrible second of hesitation. Then she lowered her gun.

'Was this Martin's idea?'

Espérandieu saw a deep sadness in her eyes, just as an immense relief came over him.

At twenty-five to five, as an icy twilight was settling over the mountains, Diane left her room and went down the deserted corridor of the fourth floor. Not a sound. At this time, all the staff were assembled on the lower floors. Diane herself should have been with one of her patients or in her office, but she had slipped quietly back upstairs a quarter of an hour earlier. After leaving her door half open to listen out for any noise, she had concluded that the sleeping quarters were empty.

She looked quickly in both directions and hesitated only a fraction of a second before turning the handle. Lisa Ferney had not locked her door. Diane took this as a bad sign: if the head nurse had anything to hide, she would certainly have locked her door. The small room, bathed in a shadowy light, was exactly like her own. Diane felt for the light switch and a dim yellow glow lit the room. Like an old detective well versed in the art of searching, she felt underneath the mattress, opened the cupboards and the night table, looked under the bed, checked the medicine cabinet in the bathroom. There were not very many possible hiding places and hardly ten minutes had gone by before she left again empty-handed.

26

'You can't see her,' said d'Humières.

'Why not?' asked Servaz.

'We're waiting for two officers from the gendarmerie disciplinary body. There'll be no interview until they get here. We have to avoid any kind of faux pas. Captain Ziegler's interrogation will take place in the presence of her superiors.'

'I don't want to interview her, I just want to talk to her!'

'Please, Martin . . . the answer is no. We have to wait.'

'And how soon will they be here?'

Cathy d'Humières looked at her watch.

'In two hours. Give or take.'

'It looks like our Lisa is going out tonight.'

Diane turned to look towards the door of the cafeteria. She saw Lisa Ferney go up to the counter and order a coffee. Diane saw that the head nurse had changed her uniform for a long pale pink jumper, jeans, a white coat with a fur collar and thigh-high boots. Her hair fell loosely onto the silky fur, and she had not skimped on the eye shadow, mascara, lipstick and gloss.

'Do you have any idea where she's going?' asked Diane.

Alex nodded with a knowing smile. The head nurse did not even glance their way. She drank down her coffee and vanished. They heard her hurry down the corridor.

'She's on her way to meet her "mystery man",' he said.

Diane stared at him. Just then, he looked like a mischievous little boy about to share his greatest secret with his best friend.

'What's that all about?'

'Everyone knows Lisa has a lover in Saint-Martin. But no one knows who it is. When she goes out like that, she usually doesn't come back until the next morning. Some staff members have tried to tease her about it, to get her to talk, but every time she sends them packing. The strangest thing is that no one has ever seen them together, in Saint-Martin or anywhere else.'

'He's probably a married man.'

'In that case, his wife must work nights.'

'Or she has a job that means she's often away from home.'

'Unless it's something too shameful to mention,' suggested Alex, leaning across the table with a devilish expression.

Diane tried to seem indifferent. But she could not ignore what she knew, and the tension would not leave her.

'Such as?'

'Perhaps she goes to swingers' nights. Or maybe she's the murderer everyone is looking for.'

She felt a knot in her stomach. She was finding it increasingly difficult to hide her anxiety. Her heart began to beat faster: *Lisa Ferney out all night* . . . This was her chance.

'Not very practical, is it, a white coat with a pale pink jumper, for bumping people off,' she said, trying to joke. 'Might get a bit dirty, right? And then all that make-up just to—'

'Maybe she seduces them before she kills them. You know: the praying-mantis type.'

Alex seemed to think it was all very funny. Diane would have preferred to change the subject. Her stomach was like a block of cement.

'And then she goes and hangs her victim under a bridge? That's no praying mantis, that's the Terminator.'

'The problem with you Swiss is that you always look at things practically,' he said teasingly.

'I thought you liked our typical Swiss humour.'

He laughed. Diane stood up.

'I have to go,' she said.

He nodded. His smile was just a touch too warm.

'Right. I've got work, too. See you later, I hope.'

By half past six Servaz had drunk so much bad coffee and smoked so many cigarettes that he was beginning to feel downright ill. He hurried to the toilets to splash cold water on his face, and almost threw up. The nausea dissipated slowly, although it didn't vanish completely.

'Fuck, what are they doing?' he asked, going back into the little waiting room with its plastic chairs, where the squad members sat patiently.

★

411

Diane closed the door behind her and leaned against it, heart pounding.

The room was bathed in the same grey-blue light as Xavier's office the day before.

A stubborn perfume. Diane recognised it, Lolita Lempicka. On the smooth surface of the desk a bottle caught the dim light from the window.

Where to begin?

There were filing cabinets, as in Xavier's office, but she decided to start with the desk itself.

None of the drawers were locked. She switched on the light to examine them and found a very curious object on top of the blotting pad: a golden salamander, set with precious stones – rubies, sapphires and emeralds. Just sitting there, in plain sight, being used as a paper-weight. Diane concluded that, given its size, the stones must be fake and the gold merely plate. Then she turned her attention to the drawers. Binders of various colours. She opened them. All to do with her position as head nurse. Notes, invoices, interview summaries, follow-up reports. Nothing that seemed out of place. Or at least not until the third drawer.

A stiff folder, at the back.

Diane took it out and opened it. Press clippings. All about the murders in the valley. Lisa Ferney had carefully assembled everything there was to know about the deaths.

Simple curiosity – or something more?

The wind howled under the door and for a moment Diane paused in her search. The storm was intensifying.

The filing cabinets. The same hanging files as in Xavier's office. As she brought them to the light to go through them one by one, Diane sensed she was wasting her time. She wouldn't find anything here because there was nothing to find. Who would be stupid or mad enough to leave traces of their crimes in their office?

As she leafed through the papers, her gaze fell once again on the salamander, its jewels shining brightly in the halo of the lamp. Diane was no expert, but she had to admit it was a very fine imitation.

She stared at the object. *What if it were real?*

Even supposing it was, what did that tell her about the head nurse? On the one hand that she was sure enough of her power and authority to assume that no one would dare enter her office without her knowing.

Secondly, that her lover was a rich man, because if the jewels were authentic, the salamander was worth a small fortune.

All things considered, Diane felt that she was on to something.

The two representatives of the gendarmerie's disciplinary body were in plain clothes, and their faces were so expressionless they could have been made of wax. They greeted Cathy d'Humières and Confiant with a short, formal handshake, and asked to interview Captain Ziegler right away and on their own. Servaz was about to protest, but the prosecutor cut him off by agreeing. Half an hour went by before the door to the room where Ziegler was being held opened again.

'It's my turn to question Captain Ziegler in private,' said Servaz when they came out. 'I don't need long. Then we can compare our thoughts.'

Cathy d'Humières turned to him and was about to say something when their gazes met. She remained silent. But one of the two wax figures came to life.

'A representative of the gendarmerie cannot be interrogated by a—'

The prosecutor raised her hand to interrupt.

'You've had your time, haven't you? Ten minutes, Martin. Not a moment more. After that, the interview will continue with everyone present.'

He went through the door. The gendarme was alone in the little office, a light shining onto her face. Beyond the blinds snow was falling in the glow of a streetlamp, like the last time the two of them had been together in this room. He sat down and looked at her. With her blonde hair, her dark leather jumpsuit covered in zippers, buckles and protective patches at the shoulders and knees, she looked like a heroine from a science-fiction story.

'Are you all right?'

She nodded, her lips tight.

'I don't think you are guilty,' he said straight away.

She gave him an intense look but said nothing. He waited for a few seconds before speaking. He didn't know where to begin.

'You didn't kill Grimm and Perrault. Yet appearances are against you, you know that?'

Once again she nodded.

He listed the facts one by one: she had lied – or hidden the truth – about the holiday camp and the suicide victims; she had hidden the fact that she knew where Chaperon had gone.

'And you weren't there when Perrault died. You were close: you should have been there first.'

'I had a motorcycle accident.'

'You have to admit that's a fairly flimsy excuse. An accident with no witnesses.'

'It's the truth.'

'I don't believe you,' he replied.

Ziegler's eyes opened slightly wider.

'Make up your mind,' she said. 'Do you think I'm innocent, or do you think I'm guilty?'

'Innocent. But you're lying about the accident.'

She seemed astonished. But this time she surprised him: she had just smiled.

'I knew from the start that you were good,' she said.

'Last night,' he continued, 'when you went to that club, after midnight, I was hiding under your bed when you got back. I got out while you were taking a shower. You should lock your door with something more sturdy. What were you doing at the bar?'

She digested what he had told her and stared at him for a long time.

'I went to see a friend,' she answered finally.

'In the middle of the night, with an investigation on? A case we're on the verge of cracking and that requires all our energy?'

'It was urgent.'

'What was so urgent about it?'

'It's hard to explain.'

'Why?' he asked. 'Because I'm a man, a macho cop, and you're in love with a woman?'

She looked at him defiantly.

'What do you know about these things?'

'Nothing, you're right. But I'm not the one who's in danger of being convicted of a double murder. And I'm not your enemy, Irène. Or your typical narrow-minded homophobic prick. So make an effort.'

She held his gaze, unflinching.

'I found a note when I got home last night. From Zuzka, my girlfriend. She's from Slovakia. She said she'd decided to get some space. She gave me a hard time, said I was too involved in my work, said I was neglecting her, that I was there but not really there. That sort of thing. You've been through that, I suppose, since you're divorced – you know what I'm talking about. There are a lot of separations among cops – even gay cops. I needed an explanation. Right away. I didn't want her to leave just like that, without having the opportunity to talk to her. It felt unbearable. So I rushed over to the Pink Banana without thinking. Zuzka's the manager there.'

'Have you been together long?'

'A year and a half.'

'And are you in love?'

'Yes.'

'Let's get back to the accident. Or the so-called accident. Because there was no accident, was there?'

'Of course there was! Didn't you see the state of my clothes? And the scratches? How do you think I got them?'

'For a while I believed it was from jumping out of the cabin,' he replied. 'After you'd pushed Perrault into the void.'

She squirmed on her chair.

'And you no longer believe that?'

'No, because you're innocent.'

'How do you know?'

'Because I think I know who it is. But I also think that you're not telling me the whole truth.'

Once again she seemed stunned by his insight.

'After the accident, I came late on purpose,' she said finally. 'I took my time.'

'Why?'

'Perrault: I wanted him to die – or rather, I wanted to give the murderer the chance to get him.'

Servaz looked at her for a moment. He nodded.

'Because of what they did to you,' he said. 'Grimm, Chaperon, Mourrenx and him.'

She didn't answer but nodded.

'At the holiday camp,' he continued.

She looked up, surprise in her eyes.

'No. It was much later. I was studying law in Pau, and one weekend I ran into Perrault at a village fete. He offered me a lift. Grimm and Mourrenx were waiting for us at the end of a track, a few kilometres away. Chaperon wasn't there that night. I don't know why. That's why I made no connection between him and the others until you found that photograph. That weekend when . . . when I saw that

Perrault had turned off the road and was heading down that track, I knew at once. I tried to get out, but he hit me, again and again, as we were driving; then when we stopped, he called me a prick-tease, a bitch. I was covered in blood. Then . . .'

She fell silent. He hesitated for a long time, then asked, 'Why didn't you—'

'Press charges? I was . . . I was sleeping around quite a lot at the time. Men, women . . . Even one of my profs at university, a married woman with kids. And my father was a gendarme. I knew what would happen – there'd be an investigation; I'd get dragged through the mud; there'd be a scandal. I thought about my parents, and how they would react, and my brother and sister-in-law, too, who didn't know anything about my private life.'

This was why they had been able to keep their secret for so long, he thought. His initial hunch at Chaperon's house had been spot on. They had banked on the fact that ninety per cent of rape victims do not report it and, with the exception of the teenagers at the holiday camp who never saw their faces, their chosen prey would have been easy targets, people with non-conformist lifestyles that would dissuade them from going to the police. Intelligent predators. But their wives had seen right through them, had ended up suspecting something, moving to separate bedrooms – or leaving them altogether.

He thought again about the director of the holiday camp who had died in a motorcycle accident. A very convenient death there as well.

'Do you realise that you put my life in danger?'

'I'm sorry, Martin. Really. But as it stands, the main thing is that I'm being accused of murder,' she pointed out, with a sad little smile.

She was right. He was going to have to play a tight game. Confiant would not let go easily, now that he had an ideal suspect. And it was Servaz himself who had delivered her to him.

'What makes things complicated,' he said, 'is the fact you took advantage of my absence to follow Chaperon's trail, and you didn't tell anyone.'

'I didn't want to kill him. I just wanted to – to frighten him. I wanted to see the terror in his eyes, the way he had seen the terror in his victims' eyes and got such a kick out of it. I wanted to find him alone in that forest and put the barrel of a gun into his mouth, so he would think that his time had come. Then I would have arrested him.'

Her voice had faded to a thin, icy trickle.

'Another question,' he said. 'When did you figure out what was going on?'

She looked him straight in the eye.

'From the first murder I had my doubts. Then when Perrault died and Chaperon vanished, I knew someone was making them pay. But I didn't know who.'

'Why did you steal the list of children?'

'It was idiotic, a knee-jerk reaction. I found it while I was sorting that damned box. And you seemed to be so interested in everything there. I didn't want to be questioned. I didn't want people digging into my past.'

'One last thing: why did you go and put flowers on Maud Lombard's tomb this morning?'

Irène Ziegler kept silent for a moment. This time she did not look the least bit surprised. She had already realised that she'd been tailed all day long.

'Maud Lombard also committed suicide.'

'I know.'

'I've always known that one way or another she'd also been a victim. At one point I was tempted by that way out, too. There was a time when Maud and I were going to the same parties – before I left for university, and before she crossed paths with those bastards. We were fairly close, not really friends, just acquaintances – but I liked her a great deal. She was a private, independent girl who didn't say much, but she was trying to break away from her family. So every year, on the anniversary of her death, I put flowers on her tomb. And I wanted to send her a sign before arresting the last one of the bastards still alive.'

'But Maud Lombard never stayed at the holiday camp.'

'So what? She'd run away several times. She often hung out with people who were a bit sketchy. And got home late. She must have encountered them somewhere, the way I did.'

Servaz was thinking on his feet. His theory was getting sharper. An incredible solution . . . He had no more questions. His head was spinning again. He massaged his temples and stood up painfully.

'There might be another idea we haven't envisaged,' he said.

★

417

D'Humières and Confiant were waiting for him in the corridor. Servaz walked up to them, struggling with the sensation that the walls and the floor were moving and he was going to lose his balance. He massaged the back of his neck and took a deep breath – but it wasn't enough to rid himself of the strange feeling that his shoes were filled with air.

'Well?' said the prosecutor.

'I don't think she did it.'

'What?' exclaimed Confiant. 'You're joking, I hope!'

'I don't have time to explain it to you now: we have to move fast. In the meantime, keep her in custody if you want. Where's Chaperon?'

'We're trying to get him to confess to the rape of the teenagers at the holiday camp,' replied d'Humières frostily. 'But he refuses to say a thing.'

'There's no statute of limitations, is there?'

'Not in so far as new evidence will let us reopen the investigation. Martin, I hope you know what you're doing.'

They exchanged a look.

'I hope so too,' he said.

His head was spinning; his skull was pounding. He headed towards the reception and asked for a bottle of water, and took one of the tablets Xavier had given him before going out to the Jeep.

How could he tell them his theory without infuriating Confiant and putting the prosecutor in an awkward position? There was one question still nagging him. He wanted to be absolutely sure before he laid his cards on the table. And he needed a second opinion – from someone who could tell him if he were on the right track, above all someone who would tell him how far he could go without overreaching. He looked at his watch. Twelve minutes past nine in the evening.

The computer.

She switched it on. Unlike Xavier's, it required a password. *Well, well.* She checked the time. She'd already been in the office for an hour.

Problem: she was no hacker. For ten minutes or more, she racked her brains in search of a password, tried keying in various versions of Julian Hirtmann and Lisa Ferney, but none of her pathetic attempts worked. She went back to the drawer where she had seen a folder containing personal documents and started with telephone and Social

Security numbers, trying forwards and backwards, then date of birth, a combination of the head nurse's first and middle names, a mix of her initials and her date of birth, all to no avail. *Shit!*

Her gaze fell on the salamander.

She typed 'salamander' and 'rednamalas'.

Nothing.

She looked one more time at the animal. With a sudden wild thought she picked it up and turned it over. On its belly was inscribed, 'Van Cleef & Arpels, New York.' She keyed the names into the computer. Nothing. *Shit! This is ridiculous! Like one of those stupid spy films!* She tried reversing the names. Nothing there either. *What did you expect, girl? We're not at the cinema!* At a total loss, she tried the initials on their own: VC&ANY. Nothing. So, backwards now: YNA&CV.

Suddenly the screen began blinking, then loaded the operating system. Bingo! Diane could not believe her eyes. She waited for the desktop to appear.

The game can begin. But time was passing. Nine thirty-two.

She prayed that Lisa Ferney really would be out all night long.

The emails.

There were over a hundred, from a mysterious Demetrius.

For each of them, in the subject column was written: 'Encrypted email.'

She opened one and found nothing but incomprehensible symbols. Diane knew what this meant, for it had happened to her at university: the certificate used to encrypt the message had expired and as a result it was no longer possible for the recipient to decrypt it.

Her mind was racing.

As a rule, to avoid this problem, the recipient was advised to save the messages right away. That is what she would have done in Lisa Ferney's shoes. She opened 'My Documents' and then 'My Inbox' and saw it at once: a folder entitled 'Demetrius'.

Lisa Ferney had not taken any further precautions: her computer was already locked and she knew that no one would have dared to go into it anyway.

Lisa

I'm in New York until Sunday. Central Park is all white and

there's an arctic cold. It's magnificent. I think about you.
Sometimes I wake up in the middle of the night in a sweat and I
know that I've been dreaming about your body, your lips. I hope
to be in Saint-Martin in ten days' time.
     Éric

     Lisa
     I'm leaving Friday for Kuala Lumpur. Can we meet before
that? I'll be at the chateau. Come.
     Éric

Where are you, Lisa?
     Why haven't I heard from you? Are you still angry with me? I
have a present for you. I bought it at Boucheron. Very pricey.
You'll love it.

Love letters. Well, emails. There were dozens of them. Perhaps
even hundreds. Spread over several years.

Lisa Ferney had carefully saved them. All of them. And they were
all signed by 'Éric'. Éric travelled a great deal, Éric was rich, and
Éric's wishes were more like commands. Éric favoured striking images
and was a pathologically jealous lover.

Waves of jealousy wash over me and every one leaves me gasping
for breath. I wonder who you're fucking. I know you, Lisa: how
long can you go without a piece of meat to stuff between your
thighs? Swear to me that there is no one else.

And sometimes, when neither threats nor grievances seemed to
work, Éric would indulge in self-mortification.

You must think I'm a filthy bastard, a complete idiot. I don't
deserve you, Lisa. I was wrong to think I could buy you. Can you
forgive me?

Diane scrolled down to the end, moving forward in time to the
present day. She saw that his tone had changed in the more recent
emails. It was no longer just a love story. Something else was
going on.

You're right. The time has come to take action. I've waited too
long: if we don't do it now, we'll never do it. I haven't forgotten
our pact, Lisa. And you know that my word is my bond.

Seeing you so strong and determined gives me courage. I think
you're right: no legal system on earth will give us peace of mind.
We have to do it ourselves.

We have waited so long. But I think the time is ripe.

Suddenly her finger froze on the mouse. Footsteps in the corridor.
She held her breath. Whoever was coming knew that Lisa had gone
out; they would be surprised to see a light under the door.

But the footsteps went by without stopping.

She exhaled and went on scrolling through the messages, swearing
softly to herself. She felt more and more frustrated. So far she had
absolutely nothing concrete, only allusions and innuendos.

Five more minutes and she'd get out of there. She went through
the last thirty messages systematically.

We have to talk. I have a plan. A terrible plan. You know what a
gambit is, Lisa? In chess, a gambit is the sacrifice of a pawn at the
beginning of the game in order to gain a strategic advantage. That
is what I'm getting ready to do. The gambit of a horse. But the
sacrifice breaks my heart.

The horse, she thought, holding her breath.

Her heart felt as if it were going to burst out of her chest, but
when she opened the next message, she went deeper into the
darkness.

Did you get the order? Are you sure he won't notice that you
made it using his name?

Her eyes wide open, her mouth dry, Diane looked at the date:
6 December . . . There was no answer in the folder, for this or any
other messages, but she didn't need one: the last piece of the puzzle
had slotted into place. Now her two theories were one. Xavier was
investigating for the simple reason that he was innocent and knew

nothing: he hadn't placed the order for the anaesthetics. It was Lisa Ferney, in his name.

Diane leaned back in the chair and thought hard. The answer was obvious. Lisa and this man Éric had killed the horse – and probably the chemist as well.

In the name of a pact they had made together long ago – a pact they had finally decided to honour.

Her thoughts were racing. Time was short.

With what she knew now, she had enough to go to the police. What was the name of that cop who had come to the Institute? Servaz. She sent the last message to the printer under the desk and reached for her phone.

In the headlights the trees emerged from the night like a hostile army. This valley loved darkness and secrecy; it hated outsiders nosing around. Servaz blinked, his eyeballs aching, and stared through the windscreen at the narrow road winding through the woods. His temples felt like they were about to explode. Snowflakes were hurling towards the car, where they were lit like brief comets as they passed. He had Mahler on full volume, the Sixth Symphony. With its air of pessimism and foreboding it was the perfect accompaniment to the blizzard's howls.

How much sleep had he got in the last forty-eight hours? He was exhausted. For no apparent reason he thought about Charlène again. This, and the tenderness she'd shown him in the art gallery, warmed him slightly. His phone began to buzz.

'I'd like to speak to Commandant Servaz.'

'Who's calling?'

'My name is Diane Berg. I'm a psychologist at the Wargnier Institute and I—'

'He can't be reached at the moment,' interrupted the gendarme at the other end of the line.

'But I have to speak to him!'

'Leave me your number; he'll call you back.'

'It's urgent!'

'Sorry, he's gone out.'

'Maybe you could give me his number.'

'Listen, I—'

'I work at the Institute,' she said, her voice as reasonable and firm

422

as possible, 'and I know who it was who got Julian Hirtmann's DNA out. Do you understand what that means?'

There was a long silence at the other end of the line.

'Could you say that again?'

She complied.

'Just a minute. I'll connect you with someone.'

The line rang three times, then: 'Captain Maillard, how can I help?'

'Look,' she declared, 'I don't know who you are, but I need to speak to Commandant Servaz. It's extremely important.'

'Who are you?'

She explained for the second time.

'What do you want from him, Dr Berg?'

'It's about the deaths in Saint-Martin. As I just told you, I work at the Institute – and I know who got Hirtmann's DNA out of there.'

This last piece of information left the captain speechless. Diane wondered if he had hung up.

'Good,' he said finally. 'Do you have something to write on? I'll give you his number.'

'Servaz.'

'Good evening,' said a woman's voice on the other end. 'My name is Diane Berg. I'm a psychologist at the Wargnier Institute. You don't know me, but I know you: I was in the room next door when you were in Dr Xavier's office and I overheard your entire conversation.'

Servaz almost told her that he had no time, but something about her tone kept him from interrupting.

'Can you hear me?'

'I'm listening. What do you want, Madame Berg?'

'Mademoiselle. I know who killed the horse. And it's almost certainly the same person who got Julian Hirtmann's DNA out of there. Would you like to know who it is?'

'Just a minute,' he said.

He slowed down and pulled over onto the verge, in the middle of the woods. All around him the wind was twisting the trees; branches clawed against the light of the headlights, like in an old German Expressionist film.

'Go ahead. Tell me everything.'

★

423

'You say that the author of the emails is called Éric?'

'Yes. Do you know who it is?'

'I think so, yes.'

Parked at the edge of the road, in the middle of the forest, he thought about what this woman had just told him. The idea he had begun to entertain after the cemetery, and which had become even more plausible when Irène Ziegler revealed that Maud had surely been raped, had just been reconfirmed. And what a confirmation. *Éric Lombard* . . . He thought again about the watchmen at the power plant, their silence, their lies. Right from the start he had been certain they were hiding something. Now he knew that it wasn't guilt that had made them lie; they had lied because they'd been forced to. Either they'd been blackmailed or their silence had been bought – probably both at the same time. They had seen something but had preferred to stay silent and to lie, even if it meant drawing suspicion upon themselves, because they knew they weren't equal to the situation.

'Have you been digging into this for long, Mademoiselle Berg?'

She took a moment to reply.

'I've only been at the Institute for a few days,' she said.

'It could be dangerous.'

A new silence. Servaz wondered how much danger she was in. She was no cop; she had probably made mistakes. And she found herself in an inherently violent environment, where anything could happen.

'Have you told anyone else?'

'No.'

'Listen carefully,' he said. 'This is what you're going to do: do you have a car?'

'Yes.'

'Fine. Leave the Institute at once, get into your car and drive down to Saint-Martin before the snowstorm stops you. Go directly to the gendarmerie and ask to speak to the chief prosecutor. Tell her I sent you. And tell her everything you just told me. Do you understand?'

'Yes.'

He had already hung up when she remembered that her car wouldn't start.

★

424

In the beam of his headlights he saw the buildings of the riding academy. It looked dark and deserted. There were no horses or grooms in sight. The boxes had been closed for the night – or for the winter. He pulled up in front of the big brick building and got out.

Whirling snowflakes engulfed him. Servaz turned up his collar and headed towards the entrance. The dogs started barking and pulling on their chains. A silhouette appeared in a window; someone looking outside. The door was ajar, and there was a light on in the passage behind it. Servaz went in. On his right he saw a horse and rider circling the large indoor arena under rows of lamps, despite the late hour. Marchand came out of the first door on the left.

'What's going on?' he said.

'I have a few questions for you.'

The manager led him to another door further along. Servaz went in. It was the same office he had seen on his first visit. On the laptop screen was a photograph of a horse. A magnificent animal with a bay coat. Perhaps it was Freedom. Marchand walked past him again and Servaz smelled the whisky on his breath. A bottle of Label 5 stood on a shelf, already over half empty.

'It's about Maud Lombard,' he said.

Marchand gave him a surprised, wary look. His eyes were a bit too shiny.

'I know she committed suicide,' said Servaz.

'Yes,' said the old horse trainer. 'A bad business.'

'What do you mean?'

He saw that Marchand was hesitating. For a moment, the man looked away before finally turning his gaze on Servaz. *He was about to tell a lie.*

'She slit her wrists—'

'That's bullshit!' shouted Servaz, grabbing the trainer by the collar. 'You're lying! Look: an innocent person has just been accused of the murders of Grimm and Perrault. If you don't tell me the truth right now, I will accuse you of being an accessory. Make your mind up. I haven't got all night!' he added, pale with fury, reaching for his handcuffs.

The trainer looked terrified by Servaz's anger, as unexpected as it was violent. Then he went pale when he heard the clink of the handcuffs. His eyes opened wide. But he tried to probe the cop nevertheless.

'You're bluffing.'

A good poker player, not easily taken in. Servaz grabbed him by the wrist and spun him round.

'What are you doing?' asked Marchand, stunned.

'I warned you.'

'You have no proof!'

'Do you know how many people have been taken in without proof and are still rotting in custody?'

'Wait! You can't do this!' protested Marchand, suddenly in a panic. 'You have no right!'

'I'm warning you: there are photographers outside the gendarmerie,' lied Servaz, dragging him towards the door. 'But we'll put a jacket over your head when we take you out of the car. All you'll have to do is look at the ground and let us lead you.'

'Wait, wait! Shit, wait!'

But Servaz had a firm grip on him now. They were already out in the corridor.

'All right! All right! I was lying! Take them off!'

Servaz paused. The horse and rider had stopped and were watching them from the arena.

'First, the truth,' murmured Servaz in his ear.

'She hanged herself. In the garden at the chateau, damn it!'

Servaz held his breath. Another hanging. This was it. He released the handcuffs. Marchand rubbed his wrists.

'I'll never forget it,' he said, his head down. 'It was twilight, summertime. She was wearing a white dress, almost transparent. She was floating like a ghost above the lawn with her neck broken, in the setting sun. I can still see it, before my eyes. Almost every night.'

Summertime. The season she had chosen to die, like the others. A white dress. *Look for white*, Propp had said.

'Why did you lie?'

'Because *someone* asked me to, of course,' said Marchand, lowering his eyes. 'Don't ask me what difference it makes – I have no idea. The boss didn't want people to know.'

'It makes a huge difference,' answered Servaz, heading to the door.

Espérandieu had just switched off his laptop when the phone rang. He sighed, looked at the time – ten forty – and picked up. He sat up a fraction straighter when he recognised the voice of Luc Damblin, his contact at Interpol. He had been waiting for this call ever since he got back to Toulouse, and had begun to lose hope.

'You were right,' said Damblin straight off. 'It was him all right. What is it you're working on? I have no idea what's going on, but, Jesus, I get the feeling you've landed a big fish. Can you tell me any more about it? What does someone like him have to do with a crime squad case?'

Espérandieu had nearly fallen off his chair. He swallowed and sat up again.

'Are you sure? Your man at the FBI confirmed it? Tell me how he got his information.'

Over the next five minutes, Luc Damblin explained in detail. *Jesus wept!* thought Espérandieu when he hung up. It was time to get hold of Martin. Right away.

Servaz felt as if the elements were in league against him. A real blizzard. Tonight of all nights. He hoped that the psychologist had managed to get down to Saint-Martin, that the road was still open. A few minutes earlier, on leaving the riding academy, he had made one last call.

'Hello?' said the voice on the line.

'I have to see you. Tonight. And I'm a little bit hungry. It's not too late?'

Laughter at the other end. But then it suddenly broke off.

'New developments?' asked Gabriel Saint-Cyr, not trying to hide his curiosity.

'I know who it is.'

'Really?'

'Yes, really.'

Silence at the other end.

'And do you have a warrant?'

'Not yet. I'd like your opinion first.'

'What do you plan to do?'

'First of all I have to clarify a few legal points with you. Then I'll make my move.'

'Don't you want to tell me who it is?'

'Let's have dinner first; then we'll talk.'

Once again, a little laugh on the other end of the line.

'I have to admit you've got me on tenterhooks. Come on over. I have some chicken left.'

'I'm on my way,' said Servaz, and he hung up.

As Servaz was parking the car at Saint-Cyr's he could see that the windows of the mill were streaming with warmth and light through the storm. Servaz had not passed a single car on his way, or a single pedestrian. He locked the Jeep and, bent double against the wind, hurried towards the little bridge. The door opened at once. A lovely smell of roast chicken, wood burning in the fireplace, wine and spices. Saint-Cyr took his jacket and hung it up, then showed him into the living room below.

'A glass of mulled wine to begin with? The chicken will be ready in twenty minutes. That way, we'll be able to talk.'

Servaz looked at his watch. Half past ten. The coming hours would be decisive. He had to think several moves ahead, but was his mind clear enough? The old judge would help him avoid any blunders. Their adversary was formidable. Servaz couldn't trip up on the smallest detail. He was also terribly hungry; the smell of the chicken was giving him stomach cramps.

The fire was burning briskly in the hearth. The room was filled with the sound of crackling logs, of the wind keening in the chimney and the rush of the stream outside. No Schubert this time. Clearly Saint-Cyr did not want to miss a word of what Servaz was about to tell him.

Two balloon glasses half filled with a ruby-coloured wine were waiting on a coffee table. The wine was steaming.

'Sit down,' said the judge, pointing to a chair.

Servaz took the glass nearest him. It was hot. He turned it in his fingers and breathed in the enticing fragrance. He could smell orange, cinnamon, nutmeg.

'Mulled wine,' said Saint-Cyr. 'Invigorating and full of calories for a night like this. Above all an excellent remedy for fatigue. It will give you a boost. This will be a long night, won't it?'

'Is it that obvious?' asked Servaz.

'Is what obvious?'

'How tired I am.'

The judge's gaze lingered on him.

'You look exhausted.'

Servaz drank. He made a face when he burned his tongue. A powerful taste of wine and spices filled his mouth and throat. Saint-Cyr had set out a few little slices of gingerbread on a saucer to go with the mulled wine. Servaz ate first one, then another. He was famished.

'Well?' said Saint-Cyr. 'Aren't you going to tell me? *Who is it?*'

'Are you sure?' asked Cathy d'Humières into the speakerphone.

Feet propped up on his desk, Espérandieu stared at his Converse trainers.

'My informant was categorical. He works at Interpol headquarters in Lyon. A gentleman by the name of Luc Damblin. He got hold of a contact at the FBI. He is certain, two hundred per cent.'

'Good heavens!' exclaimed the prosecutor. 'And you haven't been able to get in touch with Martin?'

'I tried twice. Both times, it was engaged. I got his voicemail. I'll try again in a few minutes.'

Cathy d'Humières checked her watch, a Chopard in yellow gold that her husband had given her for their twentieth wedding anniversary. Ten to eleven. She sighed.

'I'd like you to do something for me, Espérandieu. Keep calling him. Again and again. When you do reach him, tell him that I'd like to be in bed before dawn, and that we won't spend all night waiting for him!'

At the other end of the line, Espérandieu gave a military salute.

'Very well, madame.'

Irène Ziegler listened to the wind outside the barred windows. She had stepped away from where she'd been standing with her ear to the wall. It was d'Humières's voice; the walls were as thin as cardboard in this gendarmerie – as they were in hundreds of others throughout France.

Ziegler had heard everything. Apparently Espérandieu was on to something major. Something that would radically change the course of the investigation. Ziegler thought she knew what it was about. And Martin had vanished into thin air. She had an idea where he might be, where he'd gone in search of advice before making his next move. She knocked on the door, which opened almost at once.

'I need to go to the toilet,' she said.

The officer closed the door in her face. It opened again on a young woman in uniform, who gave her a suspicious look.

'Follow me, Captain. No messing about.'

Ziegler stood up, holding her handcuffed wrists in front of her.

'Thank you,' she said. 'I'd also like to speak to the prosecutor. Tell her that. Tell her it's important.'

The wind was howling down the flue, flattening the flames. Servaz was on the verge of collapse. He put his glass down and saw that his hand was shaking. He held it close to his body so Saint-Cyr wouldn't notice. The spiced wine tasted good, but there was a bitter aftertaste. He felt tipsy, and he couldn't afford that. He told himself he would drink nothing but water for the next half-hour, and then ask for a strong coffee.

'You don't seem to be doing too well,' said the judge, putting his glass down and watching him attentively.

'I've done better, but I'll be all right.'

In all honesty he could not recall ever having been so exhausted and on edge: dog-tired, his head full of cotton wool, prone to dizziness – and yet he was on the verge of cracking the strangest case of his entire career.

'So, you don't think that Irène Ziegler is guilty?' continued the judge. 'Everything seems to point to her.'

'I know. But there's something new.'

The judge's eyebrows went up.

'I got a phone call this evening from a psychologist who works at the Wargnier Institute.'

'And?'

'Her name is Diane Berg; she's from Switzerland. She hasn't been there long. Apparently she thought there was something strange going on, and she conducted her own little investigation behind everyone's back. That's how she found out that the head nurse at the Institute got hold of horse anaesthetics . . . and also that this woman is the mistress of a certain Éric, a very rich man who travels a great deal, judging from the emails he sends her.'

'How did she manage to find all that out?' asked the judge sceptically.

'It's a long story.'

'And so, this Éric, you think it's . . . ? But he was in the States the night the horse was killed.'

'The perfect alibi,' said Servaz. 'Besides, who would suspect the victim to be the culprit?'

'This psychologist – is she the one who contacted you? And you believe her? How do you know she can be trusted? That Institute must be tough on a person's nerves when they're not used to it.'

Servaz looked at Saint-Cyr. He had a moment of doubt. What if the judge were right?

'Do you remember when you told me that everything that happens in this valley has roots in the past?' said Servaz.

The judge nodded.

'You told me yourself that Éric Lombard's sister, Maud, committed suicide aged twenty-one.'

'That's right,' said Saint-Cyr at last. 'So do you think that her death has something to do with the holiday-camp suicides? She never went there.'

'There were two other victims who didn't stay there either,' answered Servaz. 'How did Grimm and Perrault die?' he asked. His heart was pounding.

'They were found hanging.'

'Exactly. When I asked you how Éric Lombard's sister committed suicide, you told me she slit her wrists. That's the official version. Well, this evening I discovered that actually she hanged herself as well. Why did Lombard lie about that? Unless it was to prevent someone from making a connection between Maud's suicide and the murders?'

'Has that psychologist spoken to anyone else?'

'No, I don't think so. I advised her to go down to Saint-Martin and contact Cathy d'Humières.'

'So you think that—'

'I think that Éric Lombard is behind the murders of Grimm and Perrault,' said Servaz. He felt as if his tongue were sticking to his palate and his jaw muscles were seizing up. 'I think he's taking revenge for what was done to his sister, a sister he adored, and he is accusing them, rightfully, of causing her suicide and that of seven other young people. I think he came up with a Machiavellian plot to dispense justice himself, while removing all suspicion from himself, with the help of an accomplice at the Wargnier Institute.'

He looked at his left hand. It was jumping on the armrest. He tried to keep it still, without success. When he raised his eyes, he saw that Saint-Cyr was staring at it.

'Lombard is a very clever man: he understood that sooner or later whoever was investigating the murders would make the connection with the wave of adolescent suicides fifteen years earlier, including his sister's. He must have figured that the best way to divert suspicion was to include himself among the victims. So he had to be the target of the first crime. But how to do it? He couldn't possibly kill an innocent person. At some point he must have had a flash of inspiration; he could commit a crime no one would ever suspect him of, by killing something he loved more than anything: his favourite horse. He must have been sick at heart when he finally decided to do it, but what better alibi than a slaughter that took place while he was – or so he said – in the US? That's why the dogs at the riding academy didn't bark. And the horse didn't neigh. He might even have another accomplice at the academy, as well as the head nurse at the Institute. Because it would have taken at least two people to get the horse up there. And the alarm at the academy didn't go off, either. However, he would never have let someone else kill the animal. That isn't the way the Lombards do things, and Éric Lombard is an adventurer, a warrior, used to the most extreme challenges, used to assuming responsibility. And not at all afraid of getting his hands dirty.'

Was it exhaustion, or the lack of sleep? His vision seemed to be blurring, as if he was suddenly wearing glasses with the wrong prescription.

'I also think that Lombard, or one of his henchmen, blackmailed the two watchmen at the power station – no doubt by threatening to have them sent back to jail, or by buying their silence. And Lombard must have known fairly quickly that the Hirtmann lead would not go far. But that didn't bother him: it was only a smokescreen. At a push, the fact we were looking into suicides from fifteen years earlier would not trouble him either; it would only multiply the leads. The guilty party could have been any of the parents, or even one of the teenagers who'd been raped and was now an adult. I wonder how much he knew about Ziegler, the fact that she'd stayed at the holiday camp. And that she'd make an ideal suspect. Or perhaps that was simply a coincidence.'

Saint-Cyr didn't respond; he seemed glum, as if concentrating on something. With his cuff Servaz wiped away the sweat pouring into his eyes.

'So in the long run he must have figured that even if everything wasn't turning out exactly as he'd planned, he'd shuffled the cards

432

so well that it would be almost impossible to get at the truth – or to trace it back to him.'

'Almost,' agreed Saint-Cyr with a sad smile. 'But he failed to reckon with someone like you.'

Servaz noticed that the judge's tone had changed. The old man was smiling at him in a way that was both admiring and ambivalent. Servaz tried to move his hand; it was no longer trembling, but it felt as heavy as lead.

'You are a remarkable detective,' said Saint-Cyr frostily. 'If I'd had someone like you working for me, who knows how many cases I would have solved?'

Servaz's mobile began to ring. He tried to reach for it, but his arm felt as if it were bound in quick-setting cement. It seemed to take for ever to move his hand just a few inches. The mobile rang for a long time, piercing the silence that had fallen between the two men; then the call went to voicemail. The judge was staring at him.

'I – I – feel – feel really *strange*,' stammered Servaz, letting his arm drop beside him.

Shit! What was wrong with him? His jaw was stiffening and he was finding it incredibly difficult to speak. He tried to get to his feet. The room immediately began to spin. Drained of strength, he collapsed into the armchair. He thought he heard Saint-Cyr say, '*It was a mistake to involve Hirtmann . . .*' He wondered if he'd heard correctly. He struggled against the mist in his mind, tried to concentrate on the words coming from the judge's mouth:

'. . . predictable: Hirtmann's *ego* got the upper hand, as was to be expected. He wormed the information out of Élisabeth in exchange for his DNA; then he got you heading down the trail of those suicides simply for the pleasure of showing you he was in charge. It flattered his pride. His immense vanity. It seems he took a fancy to you.'

Servaz tried to frown. Was that really Saint-Cyr who was speaking? For a split second he thought he saw Lombard across from him. Then he blinked, trying to rid his eyes of the stinging drops of sweat, and saw it was indeed the judge. Saint-Cyr took a mobile phone from his pocket.

'Lisa? It's Gabriel. Apparently your little snoop didn't speak to anyone else. She only had time to ring Martin. Yes, I'm sure . . . Yes, I've got the situation under control.'

He hung up and turned his attention back to Servaz.

433

'I'm going to tell you a story,' he said. Servaz felt as if his voice were coming to him from the end of a tunnel. 'The story of a little boy who was the son of a tyrannical, violent man. A very intelligent little boy, a wonderful little boy. When he came to see us, he always brought a bouquet of flowers that he'd picked along the path, or some pebbles he'd gathered from the banks of the river. We didn't have any children, my wife and I. So you can imagine that when Éric came into our life, it was a gift from heaven, a ray of sunshine.'

Saint-Cyr made a gesture as if to keep the memory at a distance, to refrain from yielding to emotion.

'But there was a cloud in that blue sky. Éric's father, the famous Henri Lombard, terrorised everyone around him, both in his factories and at home. And although there were times when he was affectionate with his children, at other times he terrified them with his fits of rage, the way he'd shout, the blows that rained down on their mother. Needless to say, both Éric and Maud were profoundly disturbed by the atmosphere that reigned at the chateau.'

Servaz tried to swallow and couldn't. He tried to move. Once again, his phone rang for a long time, then fell silent.

'In those days, my wife and I lived in a house in the woods not far from the chateau, on the banks of this same stream,' continued Saint-Cyr. 'Henri Lombard may have been tyrannical, suspicious, paranoid and downright insane, but he never surrounded his property with fences or barbed wire or cameras, the way people do nowadays. It just wasn't done back then. You didn't have all the crime, the threats. No matter what people say, the world we lived in was still human. In short, our house was a refuge for young Éric, and he often spent the entire afternoon there. Sometimes he brought Maud with him; she was a pretty child with a sad expression; she almost never smiled. Éric loved her very much. By the time he was ten he seemed to have decided he would protect her.'

He paused for a moment.

'My professional life was very demanding and I wasn't often at home, but from the moment Éric came into our lives I tried to set aside as much free time as I could. I was always happy to see him coming down the path to our house, on his own or with his sister trailing behind him. I became a second father to him. I raised that boy as if he were my own. There is nothing I am prouder of. My greatest success. I taught him everything I knew. He was an extraordinarily receptive child. Just look at what he has become today! And it's not only because of the empire he inherited. No. It was thanks to my lessons, and our love.'

Dumbfounded, Servaz saw that the old judge was weeping, tears streaming down his furrowed cheeks.

'Then there was that bad business. I remember the day we found Maud hanging from the swing. Éric was never the same after that. He withdrew into himself, became glum and obstinate. Seemed to harden himself. I suppose it was useful in business. But he was no longer the Éric I had known.'

'And what . . . what . . . happened to . . . to . . . ?'

'To Maud? Éric didn't tell me the details, but I think she crossed paths with those bastards.'

'No . . . after that . . .'

'The years went by. Éric had just inherited the company when Maud killed herself; their father had died the previous year. He was overwhelmed by work – one day in Paris, the next in New York or Singapore. He never had a minute to himself. Then all the doubts and questions about his sister's death came back. He got it into his head that he had to go after the truth. He hired some private detectives. Men who weren't very particular about their methods or their morals – and whose silence could be bought at a very steep price. They must have followed more or less the same leads as you, and they uncovered the truth about the four men. From that point on, it wasn't hard for Éric to imagine what had happened to his sister and other women before her. He decided to take the law into his own hands; he had the means. He was well positioned to know that his country's judicial system could be trusted only so far. He also found precious support in Élisabeth Ferney. His mistress. Who also grew up round here, and she's not just Éric Lombard's lover – she too was a victim.'

The light from the candles and lamps hurt Servaz's eyes. He was soaked in sweat.

'I'm an old man and my time is running out,' said Saint-Cyr. 'One year, five, ten: what difference does it make? My life is behind me. And what remains will, in any case, be nothing but a long wait for the end. Why not shorten that time if my death can help someone as brilliant and important as Éric Lombard?'

Servaz felt the panic spreading through him. His heart was

pounding so hard that he was certain he was on the verge of a heart attack. But he still couldn't move. And the room around him was now a total blur.

'I'm going to leave behind a letter, claiming responsibility for the crimes,' announced Saint-Cyr in an astonishingly calm, firm voice. 'So that justice will be served at last. Many people know how obsessed I was by the case of the suicide victims. So no one will be surprised. I will say that I killed the horse because I thought that Henri, Éric's father, had taken part in the rapes. And that I killed you because you had found me out. But afterwards I decided that there was no way out of the situation and, overcome by remorse, I decided it was preferable to confess before taking my own life. A beautiful letter, both moving and dignified: I've already composed it.'

For a moment the terror Servaz felt roused him slightly.

'Is . . . is no point. Diane . . . Diane Berg has proof . . . guilty . . . talk to Cathy . . . d'Humières . . .'

'I'm afraid,' continued Gabriel Saint-Cyr unperturbed, 'that tonight the psychologist will be found dead. After the inquest, among her papers there will be proof that she came from Switzerland for one purpose: to help her compatriot and former lover Julian Hirtmann to escape.'

'Why . . . are . . . doing . . . this?'

'I already told you: Éric is my pride and joy. I raised him. I made him what he is today. Not only a brilliant businessman but also an upstanding man. The son I never had.'

'He's . . . mixed up . . . mis . . . propriation . . . funds . . . corruption . . . exploiting chil . . . children . . .'

'Those are lies!' shouted Saint-Cyr, leaping up from his armchair. *With a gun in his hand. An automatic pistol.*

Servaz opened his eyes wide. Saint-Cyr's voice, and every other sound, every smell had become excruciatingly intense. All his senses had been flooded by extremes, leaving his nerves raw.

'Hallucinogenics,' said Saint-Cyr, smiling once again. 'You cannot imagine the possibilities they offer. Rest assured, the drugs you've taken with every meal I've fed you are not lethal. The aim was just to weaken you and make your reactions seem suspicious both to yourself and to those around you. The drug I put in your wine will paralyse you for a while. But you won't have a chance to come back round: you'll be dead long before. I'm terribly sorry to have to go to such extremes, Martin: you are the most interesting person I have met in quite a while.'

Servaz's mouth was gaping, like that of a fish out of water. He stared glassily at Saint-Cyr. He felt a sudden surge of anger: because of this fucking drug, he would die looking like an idiot!

'I've spent my entire life fighting crime, and now I'm going to end it as a murderer,' said the judge bitterly. 'But you leave me no choice: Éric Lombard must remain free. He has so many plans. Thanks to the associations that he funds, children won't go hungry, artists will be able to work, students will receive grants . . . I'm not going to let some little cop destroy one of the most brilliant men of his era. A man who has done nothing more than assure, in his way, that justice is done, in a country where the word lost its meaning a long time ago.'

Servaz wondered if they were talking about the same man: the one who had colluded with major pharmaceutical companies to stop countries in Africa manufacturing drugs against AIDS or meningitis; the one whose subcontractors had been encouraged to exploit women and children in India and Bangladesh; the one whose lawyers had bought Polytex for its patents, then sacked all its workers. Who was the real Éric Lombard? The cynical, unscrupulous businessman, or the philanthropist and patron of the arts? The young boy who looked after his little sister, or the shark who exploited human misery? Servaz couldn't think clearly anymore.

'Me . . . the psychologist,' he stammered. 'Mur-ders . . . You go back . . . principles . . . end your life . . . as a . . . as a murderer.'

He saw a shadow of doubt pass over the judge's face. Saint-Cyr shook his head vigorously, as if to shake it off.

'I am leaving without regret. To be sure, there are certain principles I have never compromised in my entire life. But nowadays even those principles are trampled on. Mediocrity, dishonesty and cynicism have become the rule. Today's men want to be like children. Irresponsible. Stupid. Criminal. An unprecedented wave of barbarity will sweep over us before long; the first signs are already here. And frankly, who will mourn our fate? Our selfishness and greed have made us squander the legacy of our ancestors. Only a few men like Éric are still struggling on in the midst of the mire.'

He waved his gun in Servaz's face. Servaz sat glued to his chair, but he could feel the anger rising in his body like an antidote to the poison in his veins. He thrust himself forward. No sooner had he managed to hoist himself from his chair than he could tell his effort would be in vain. His legs folded beneath him. Saint-Cyr stood to one side and watched him fall; he hit a side table, knocking over a vase and a lamp. The vase shattered; the blinding light seared his optic nerves, burned his retina where he lay flat on his stomach. He'd gashed his forehead on the side table and blood was trickling into his eyebrows.

'Come now, Martin, it's no use,' said Saint-Cyr indulgently.

Servaz managed to raise himself painfully onto his elbows. The rage inside was burning like an ember. The light was blinding; black spots danced before his eyes. All he could see were shadows and gleams of light.

He crawled towards the judge and reached for him, but Saint-Cyr stepped back. Between the judge's legs Servaz saw the flames in the fireplace. He was dazzled.

Then it all went very quickly.

'Put down your weapon!' said a voice on his left, a voice he recalled having heard somewhere, but he could not put a name to it; his mind was paralysed.

A first shot rang out, then a second. He saw Saint-Cyr fall back against the fireplace. His body bounced against the stone mantelpiece, then fell towards Servaz, who ducked his head. When he looked up again, someone was tugging the heavy body to one side, like the carcass of a horse.

'Martin! Martin! Are you all right?'

He blinked. A blurry face hovered before his weeping eyes. Irène. Someone was standing behind her. Maillard.

'Water,' he said.

Irène Ziegler hurried to the kitchen, filled a glass of water, then held it to his lips. Servaz swallowed slowly, his jaw muscles aching.

'Help . . . me . . . bath . . . room.'

The two gendarmes lifted him under the arms and supported him. Servaz felt as if he were going to collapse with every step.

'Lom . . . bard,' he stammered.

'What?'

'Road . . . blocks . . .'

'It's done,' Irène hastened to answer. 'All the roads have been blocked off since we got the call from your assistant. No one can get out of the valley.'

'Vin . . . cent?'

'Yes. He found proof that Éric Lombard wasn't in the States the night Freedom was killed.'

'The . . . heli—'

'No way. He couldn't possibly take off in this weather.'

He bent over the sink. Ziegler turned the tap and splattered him with cold water. Servaz leaned in closer and put his face directly under the icy stream, which had the effect on him of an electric shock. He coughed and spat. How long did he stand there leaning over the sink trying to clear his mind? He could not have said.

When he stood up again, he felt much better. The effects of the drug were beginning to wear off. Above all, he felt an urgency throbbing through his blood, fighting his torpor. *They had to act. Quickly.*

'Where are . . . Cath—'

'They're waiting for us. At the gendarmerie.'

Ziegler looked at him.

'OK. Let's get going,' she said. 'We mustn't lose any time.'

Lisa Ferney closed her phone. In her other hand she held a gun. Diane didn't know anything about weapons, but she'd seen enough films to know that the cylinder at the end of the barrel was a silencer.

'I'm afraid no one will help you, Diane,' said the head nurse. 'In less than half an hour, that policeman you spoke to will be dead. It's just your luck that my evening out got cancelled because of that cop.'

'Do you know how to use that?' asked Diane, pointing to the weapon.

Lisa Ferney gave a faint smile.

'I've learned. I belong to a rifle club. Éric introduced me to the sport. Éric Lombard.'

'Your lover,' commented Diane. 'And your accomplice.'

'It's not nice to go digging into other people's lives,' said the head nurse. 'I know you might find it difficult to believe, Diane, but Wargnier had a choice between several candidates when he got it into his head that he needed an assistant – I might say I was very offended when he implied I wasn't up to the job – and I'm the one who chose you. I put pressure on him to give you the position.'

'Why?'

'Because you're Swiss.'

'What?'

Lisa Ferney opened the door and glanced out into the silent corridor, her gun still aimed at Diane.

'Swiss, like Julian. When I saw your application in the pile, I knew at once that it was a good omen.'

Diane was beginning to see what the explanation might be. And it sent a chill down her spine.

'What plans?'

'To kill those bastards,' answered Lisa.

'Who?'

'Grimm, Perrault and Chaperon.'

'Because of what they did at the holiday camp,' said Diane, remembering the Post-it in Xavier's office.

'Exactly. At the holiday camp and elsewhere. This valley was their hunting ground.'

'I saw someone at the camp. A man, sobbing and shouting. Was he one of their victims?'

Lisa gave her a penetrating look, perhaps wondering how much Diane knew.

'Yes, Mathias. The poor boy never recovered. He went mad. But he's harmless.'

'I still don't see what this has to do with me.'

'It doesn't matter,' said Lisa Ferney. 'You have come from Switzerland to help Hirtmann escape, Diane. And you are about to set fire to the Institute and lead him to safety. Bad luck that once you get out, that ungrateful Julian won't be able to resist his impulses, and will succumb to the temptation to kill his accomplice: you. End of story.'

Diane couldn't move, overcome by a terror as pure as water.

'In the beginning, we came up with several ways to cloud the issue. But I immediately thought of Julian. In the end, it was a mistake. Someone like him always wants something in return. In exchange for his saliva and his blood, he wanted to know why we needed them. But his demands did not stop there. I had to promise him something else. And that's where you come in, Diane.'

'This is absurd. People know me back home. No one will believe a story like this.'

'But it's not the Swiss police who'll be leading the investigation. Besides, everyone knows that this place can have a very disturbing effect on a fragile psyche. Dr Wargnier did have his doubts about

440

you. In your conversations and emails he detected a certain "vulner-ability". I will be sure to point that out to the police, when the time comes – and they in turn will be sure to question Wargnier. And Xavier, who didn't want you here in the first place, is not about to contradict me. So you see: there will be a great many witnesses against you, in the end. You shouldn't have got in my way, Diane. I had decided to spare your life. You would have spent a few years in prison, that's all.'

'But you can't pin the DNA on me,' ventured Diane in desperation.

'True. That's why we found another candidate for that. For several months now we've been giving money to Mr Atlas. In exchange, he turns a blind eye to my visits to Unit A and my little schemes with Hirtmann. But that will turn against him when the police find out that the payments were made from Switzerland and they find a syringe at his house with traces of Julian's blood.'

'So you're going to kill him, too?' asked Diane, feeling dizzy, as if she were falling into a bottomless pit.

'What do you think? Do you suppose I want to spend the rest of my days in prison? Let's go,' added Lisa. 'We've wasted enough time.'

27

'Were you waiting for me?'

Cathy d'Humières jumped when she heard his voice. She turned to the door and stared at Servaz for a long time before turning to Ziegler and Maillard, then back to Servaz.

'Good heavens! What happened?'

There was a photo in a frame by the door. Servaz was surprised by his own reflection in the glass: the black shadows under his hollow, bloodshot eyes.

'Tell them,' he said to Ziegler as he collapsed into a chair; the ground was still moving.

Irène Ziegler filled them in. D'Humières, Confiant and the two wax dummies from the gendarmerie listened in silence. It was the prosecutor who had decided to release Ziegler right after Espérandieu's phone call. And it was Ziegler's idea that Servaz must be with his mentor that had saved him. That, and the fact that it took only five minutes to get from the gendarmerie to the mill by car.

'Saint-Cyr!' exclaimed d'Humières, shaking her head. 'I can't believe it!'

Servaz dissolved an aspirin in a glass of water. The mist in his brain lifted almost immediately and he could picture the entire scene at the mill again. He opened his red eyes wide and looked at the others.

'Damn!' he roared. 'When I was starting to get woozy, Saint-Cyr called that . . . Lisa, at the Institute . . . to tell her that the psychologist hadn't spoken to anyone but me, that he had the situation under control . . . just before he tried to—'

The prosecutor went pale.

'This means the girl is in danger. Maillard, do we still have a team up at the Institute? Tell your men to move in right away!'

Cathy d'Humières took out her phone, called a number, then put it down after a few seconds.

'Dr Xavier isn't answering.'

'We have to question Lombard,' said Servaz with difficulty. 'And take him into custody. But how should we go about it? He could be anywhere: Paris, New York, on some island that belongs to him somewhere, or here – but I doubt they'll volunteer the information.'

'He's here,' said Confiant.

Everyone turned to look at him.

'Before I came I went to the chateau, at his request, to bring him up to speed. Just before your assistant called,' he said to Servaz. 'I didn't get around, um, to telling anyone. There was too much going on after that . . .'

Servaz wondered how many times the young judge had gone to the chateau.

'We'll deal with that later,' said d'Humières in a stern voice. 'Have all the roads to the valley been blocked off? Good. We'll get in touch with the national HQ. I want a search of Lombard's residence in Paris at the same time as the chateau. The operation must be perfectly coordinated. And discreet. Only the people we absolutely need will be let in on it. He was wrong to go after one of my men,' she added, looking at Servaz. 'His name might be Lombard, but he has over-stepped the mark. And anyone who does that has to deal with me.' She stood up. 'I have to ring the Justice Ministry. We don't have much time to get the operation set up. Then we'll act. There's not a minute to lose.'

Everyone round the table started talking at once. Not everyone agreed with the prosecutor. Lombard was a big deal. There were careers at stake, issues of hierarchy, risks of collateral damage.

'How did Vincent find out that Lombard wasn't in the US?' asked Servaz.

Ziegler explained. They'd been lucky. There'd been an anonymous denunciation, and the financial crime unit in Paris were auditing the books of a certain number of the group's subsidiaries. Apparently they were on the verge of uncovering a major scandal. A few days earlier, when they'd been going through the books of Lombard Media, they'd found a new irregularity: a transfer of $135,000 to a produc-tion company that made television documentaries, along with some invoices from the same company. After the usual crosscheck with the production company, it turned out that the work had never been done and the invoices were bogus. The financial unit then began to ask what the money might have been for and above all, why someone was trying to hide it. Was it a bribe? Misappropriation of funds? They obtained a new warrant, this time for the bank that had arranged the transfer, and demanded the identity of the true beneficiary. Unfortunately, those behind the transaction had taken every precaution: in the space of a few hours the money had been wired to an account in London, from there to another account in the Bahamas, and then to a third one in the Caribbean. After that they lost all trace. But why? One hundred and thirty-five thousand dollars was both a nice round sum and a drop in the ocean as far as the Lombard empire was concerned. They summoned the CEO of Lombard Media and threatened to charge him. The man finally came out with it: he'd made the false entry at the request of Éric Lombard himself, as a matter of urgency. He also swore that he had no idea what the money was for. As Vincent had asked the financial unit to let him know of any irregularities, his contact there had passed on the information, although at first glance it had nothing to do with the death of a horse.

'What does it have to do with anything?' asked one of the bigwigs from the gendarmerie.

'Well,' said Ziegler, 'Lieutenant Espérandieu had another idea. He rang an airline company that charters jets for wealthy businessmen, and it turned out that this was exactly what a return transatlantic flight on a private jet would cost.'

'Éric Lombard has his own planes and pilots,' objected the officer. 'Why would he go and use another company?'

'So that there would be no trace of the flight,' replied Ziegler. 'All they had to do was hide the expense itself.'

'Which explains the bogus documentary,' interjected d'Humières.

'Exactly.'

'Interesting,' said the officer. 'But it's all supposition.'

'Not really. Lieutenant Espérandieu figured that if Éric Lombard returned in secret from the States on the night the horse died, he must have landed not far away. So he called all the local airports: Tarbes, Pau, Biarritz . . . By the third one, bingo: an American private jet did indeed land at Biarritz-Bayonne on the night of Tuesday, 9 December. Judging from the information we have, Éric Lombard came in under a false name and using false papers. No one saw him. The plane stayed for twelve hours or so and left again early in the morning. More than enough time to make it from Bayonne to Saint-Martin by car, go to the riding academy, kill Freedom, hang him up at the top of the cable car and leave again.'

Everyone was staring at the gendarme now.

'And that's not all,' she said. 'The airport at Biarritz kept a record of the American jet. Vincent Espérandieu then called his contact at Interpol, who contacted the FBI. They went to see the pilot today. He has formally identified Éric Lombard, and is prepared to testify.'

Ziegler turned to look at Servaz.

'Lombard may already know what we are up to,' she said. 'He probably has his own people at the FBI or the Ministry of the Interior.'

Servaz raised his hand.

'I've had two of my men posted outside the chateau since early evening,' he said. 'Ever since I began to suspect what was going on. If His Honour's information is correct, Lombard is still there. Where is Vincent, by the way?'

'He's coming. He'll be here in a few minutes,' replied Ziegler.

Servaz was trying to stand up, but his legs could barely support him.

'You should get to hospital,' said Ziegler. 'You're in no shape to take part in a raid. You need to have your stomach pumped. We don't even know what kind of drugs Saint-Cyr forced down you.'

'I'll do that when it's all over. This is my investigation, too. I'll stay in the background,' he added. 'Unless Lombard lets us come in without a fuss – which would surprise me.'

'Assuming he's still there,' said d'Humières.

'Something tells me he is.'

Hirtmann listened to the wind. *A real blizzard*, he thought with a smile. This evening, sitting on his bed, he wondered what he would do first if he regained his freedom – a fantasy he envisaged often, and each time it led to long, delightful daydreams.

In one of his favourite scenarios, he recovered the money and documents he had hidden in a cemetery in Savoie, near the Swiss border. One amusing detail: the money – 100,000 Swiss francs – and the fake ID were in a waterproof, insulated box, hidden in the coffin belonging to the mother of one of his victims – the very place his victim had told him about just before he killed her. With that money he would hire the cosmetic surgeon in the Var who used to join in the 'Geneva soirées'; in another hiding place Hirtmann had stored a few videos that would be disastrous for the man's reputation, whom he had had the presence of mind to spare during his trial. While he had his head wrapped in dressings, he would stay at the good doctor's clinic in a room with a view onto the Mediterranean, and he would arrange for both a top-of-the-range sound system to listen to his beloved Mahler, and visits from a high-class call girl.

His dreamy smile vanished abruptly. He placed his hand on his brow and made a face. This fucking treatment was giving him terrible headaches. That imbecile Xavier, and all those fucking moron psychologists . . . All the same, with their quack religion!

He could feel the anger welling up. The fury found its way into his brain, gradually disconnecting all rationality until there was nothing left but a cloud of black ink spreading across the ocean of his thoughts, an eel slithering out of its hole to devour all lucidity. He felt like hurting someone, or pounding the wall with his fist. He clenched his teeth and rolled his head, moaning and whining like a cat being boiled alive, until at last he grew calm. Sometimes he found it incredibly difficult to control himself, but self-discipline helped. In the course of his various internments in psychiatric hospitals, he had devoted months to reading books by moronic psychiatrists; he had learned those mental prestidigitators' little tricks, their illusionists' schemes; again and again and again in the depths of his cell he had rehearsed, the way only an obsessive can. He knew their primary weakness: there was not a single psychiatrist on earth who didn't think very highly of himself. Only one had guessed what he was up to and taken his books away. One in all the dozens he had met.

Suddenly a harsh sound pierced his ears. He sat up straight, on edge. The siren out in the corridor: a deafening, searing sound.

He scarcely had time to wonder what was going on before the lights went out. He found himself sitting in semi-darkness. *The fire alarm!*

His heart began to pound. A fire at the Institute! This might be his chance . . .

The door to his cell opened and Lisa Ferney strode in, her silhouette etched against the lurid orange light flickering through the door.

In one hand she was holding a fleece windbreaker, a white hospital coat and trousers, and boots. She tossed them over to him.

446

'Get dressed. Quickly!'

On the table she put a pair of goggles and an anti-smoke mask.

'Put those on, too. Hurry up!'

'What's going on out there?' he asked as he hurried to put the clothes on. 'Things not going so well? You need someone to create a diversion, is that it?'

'You never believed in it, did you?' she said, turning to him with a smile. 'You only did it because you found it amusing. You never believed I would keep my part of the bargain.' She stared at him without flinching; Lisa was one of the few people who could. 'What did you have planned for me, Julian? Were you going to punish me?'

She glanced out of the window.

'Get a move on!' she said. 'We haven't got all night.'

'Where are the guards?'

'I've overpowered Mr Atlas. The others are running about trying to prevent the inmates from escaping. The fire has deactivated the security alarms. Open house tonight. Hurry up! There is a team of gendarmes downstairs; the fire and the other inmates will keep them busy for a while.'

He put the mask over his face. Lisa was satisfied with the result. With his white coat and mask and the dim lighting, he was almost unrecognisable – except for his height.

'Go downstairs to the basement.' She handed him a key. 'Once you're down there, all you have to do is follow the arrows painted on the walls; they'll take you straight to a hidden exit. I've kept my part of the bargain. Now you have to keep yours.'

'*My* part of the bargain?' His voice sounded strange behind the mask.

She took a gun out of her pocket and handed it to him.

'You'll find Diane Berg in the basement. Take her with you. And kill her. Leave her somewhere out there, then vanish.'

He could smell the smoke the moment he was out in the corridor. The blinding flashes of the fire alarm jarred his eyes, and the nearby wailing of the siren hurt his eardrums. The corridor was deserted, and all the doors were open. As he went by, Hirtmann could see that the cells were empty.

Mr Atlas was lying on the floor of the security cabin with a nasty wound at the back of his head. There was blood on the floor. A great deal of blood. They went through the open security door and this time they saw the smoke coming up the stairs.

'Hurry!' said Lisa Ferney, the first note of panic in her voice.

The glow from the alarm set her long chestnut hair ablaze and painted her face a grotesque orange colour, deepening the shadows around her eyes and along her nose.

They hurtled down the stairs. The smoke was thicker than ever. Lisa coughed. Once they had reached the ground floor, she pointed to the last flight of stairs to the basement.

'Hit me,' she said.

'What?'

'Hit me! On the nose. Quickly!'

He hesitated for only a moment. She fell backwards when his fist struck her. She let out a cry and held her hands to her face. He gave a brief look of satisfaction at the spurt of blood, then disappeared.

She watched him dissolve into the smoke. The pain was strong but, more than anything, she was worried. Even before she started the fire she had seen that the gendarmes hidden on the mountain were heading for the Institute. What were they doing here if that cop was dead, and Diane was still tied up, lifeless, downstairs?

Something hadn't gone as planned.

She got back up. She had blood on her chin and her hospital coat. She walked unsteadily towards the exit.

Servaz was standing outside the chateau. With him were Maillard, Ziegler, Confiant, Cathy d'Humières, Espérandieu, Samira, Pujol and Simeoni. Behind them were three vans from the gendarmerie, with armed men inside. Servaz had rung twice at the gate.

'Well?' said Cathy d'Humières, banging her gloved hands together to keep warm.

'No answer.'

They had trampled the snow outside the gate, their footprints crossing and overlapping.

'There can't be no one there,' said Ziegler. 'Even if Lombard is away, there are always guards and staff. They're refusing to answer.'

Their breath turned to white vapour, borne away on the wind.

The prosecutor looked at her gold watch. Thirty-six minutes past midnight.

'Is everyone in position?' she asked.

In less than five minutes the search would begin in an apartment in Paris in the eighth arrondissement, not far from the Étoile. Two frozen civilians were pacing back and forth off to one side: Dr Castaing and Maître Gamelin, the solicitor, required as neutral witnesses in the event of the proprietor's absence.

'Maillard, ask Paris if they're ready. Martin, how do you feel? You look exhausted. Perhaps it would be better if you waited out here and let Captain Ziegler take charge? She'll manage very well.'

Maillard hurried over to one of the vans. Servaz gazed at Cathy d'Humières with a smile. She had let her scarf and her dyed blonde hair flutter loose in the storm; apparently anger and indignation had prevailed over looks.

'I'll be all right,' he said.

They could hear shouting from inside the van. Maillard was losing his temper: 'Since I told you we can't! What? Where? . . . Yes, I'll tell them right away!'

'What's going on?' asked d'Humières when he came rushing out.

'Panic stations – there's a fire over at the Institute! Our men are there, and it's all they can do to keep the inmates from escaping. The security isn't working. We have to get over there as quickly as possible.'

Servaz stopped to think. *This was no coincidence.*

'It's a diversion,' he said.

Cathy d'Humières gave him a solemn look.

'I know.' She turned to Maillard. 'What did they say, exactly?'

'That the Institute is on fire. All the patients are outside, with only a handful of guards and the members of our team who were up there to watch over them. The situation could disintegrate at any moment. Apparently several inmates have already managed to get away. They're trying to catch them.'

Servaz went pale.

'Residents of Unit A?'

'I don't know.'

'They won't get far in this snow and cold.'

'I'm sorry, Martin, but this is an emergency,' said d'Humières decisively. 'I can leave you your team, but I have to send as many agents as possible over there. I'll ask for reinforcements.'

Servaz looked at Ziegler.

'Leave me the captain, too,' he said.

'You want to go in there without support? They might be armed.'

'Or there might be no one.'

'I'll go with Commandant Servaz,' said Ziegler. 'I don't think there's any particular danger. Lombard is a murderer, not a gangster.'

D'Humières looked at them all.

'Fine. Confiant, you stay with them. But don't do anything rash. At the first hint of trouble, you wait for reinforcements, is that clear?'

'You stay back,' said Servaz to Confiant. 'I'll call you for the search as soon as the coast is clear. We won't go in unless we're sure there's no danger.'

Confiant nodded sombrely. Cathy d'Humières checked her watch again.

'Right, let's get over to the Institute,' she said, heading towards her car.

They looked at Maillard and the other gendarmes climbing back into their vans. A moment later they were gone.

The gendarme who was watching the basement emergency exit put his hand on his gun when the metal door swung open. He saw a tall man come climbing up the steps with a woman in his arms; he was wearing a white lab coat and a mask with an air filter.

'She's passed out,' said the man through his mask. 'The smoke . . . Do you have a car? An ambulance? She has to see a doctor. Quickly!'

The gendarme hesitated. Most of the residents and guards had assembled on the other side of the building. He didn't know whether there was a doctor among them. His orders were to keep an eye on this exit.

'We must hurry,' insisted the man. 'I've already tried to bring her round. Every minute is vital! Have you got a car, yes or no?'

The man's voice was deep, cavernous and full of authority.

'I'll fetch someone,' said the gendarme, leaving at a run.

A minute later a car pulled up outside the door. The gendarme got out of the passenger seat, and the driver – another gendarme – motioned to Hirtmann to get in the back. The moment he had settled Diane on the seat, the car took off. They went round the building and Hirtmann saw familiar faces – residents and staff – clustered well away from the fire. A good part of the Institute was already engulfed by flames. Firefighters were unrolling a hose from their engine. Another hose was already spraying the building, but far too late – it wouldn't be enough to save it. Outside the entrance, paramedics were unfolding a gurney they had taken from the back of an ambulance.

As the burning buildings receded in the distance behind them, Hirtmann gazed at the back of the driver's neck, and felt the cold metal of the gun in his pocket.

'How do we get through the gate?'

Servaz examined it. The wrought iron looked strong, and only a battering ram would get the better of it. He turned to look at Ziegler. She pointed to the ivy winding its way round one of the pillars.

'We'll have to climb it.'

In full view of the camera, he thought.

'Any idea how many people are inside?' asked Samira.

She was checking the chamber of her gun.

'Maybe there's no one; maybe they all got away,' said Ziegler.

'Or maybe there are ten, twenty or thirty of them,' Espérandieu remarked.

He pulled out his Sig Sauer and a brand-new magazine.

'In that case, we have to hope they respect the law,' joked Samira. 'This is a twist: murderers going over the wall at the same time in two different places.'

'We have no proof that Lombard had time to go over the wall,' answered Servaz. 'I'm sure he's in there. That's why he'd like to see us all rush over to the Institute.'

Confiant said nothing. He was glaring at Servaz. They saw Ziegler grab hold of the ivy and, with great ease, scramble up the pillar, grab the closed-circuit camera at the top, regain her balance and jump down on the other side. Servaz motioned to Pujol and Simeoni to keep watch with the young judge. Then he took a deep breath and followed Ziegler's example, although he found it a lot harder, particularly with the flak jacket under his jumper. Espérandieu brought up the rear.

Servaz felt a sharp pain on landing and cried out. When he took a step, he felt the pain again. He had twisted his ankle.

'Is something wrong?'

'I'll be all right,' he answered curtly.

To prove his point, he set off with a limp, pain shooting through his leg with every step. He clenched his teeth. He made sure that, for once, he hadn't forgotten his gun.

'Is it loaded?' asked Ziegler next to him. 'Have a bullet ready in the chamber. *Now*. And keep it in your hand.'

He swallowed. Her comment set his nerves on edge.

It was five minutes past one.

Servaz lit a cigarette and gazed at the chateau at the end of the long, paved avenue, lined with centuries-old oak trees. The façade and the white lawns were brightly lit, the topiary animals as well; small projectors were shining in the snow. A few windows glowed at the centre of the building. *As if they were expected.*

Other than that, nothing was moving. No sign of life in the windows. They had reached the end of the road, he thought. A chateau. Like in a fairy tale. A fairy tale for adults.

He's in there. He hasn't left. Everything will be decided here.

It's been written. From the very start.

There was something phantasmagorical about the chateau in that artificial light. Its white façade was truly resplendent. Once again, Servaz thought of what Propp had said: *Look for white.*

Why hadn't he thought of it earlier?

'Stop.'

The driver turned his head slightly towards the rear without taking his eyes off the road.

'Pardon?'

Hirtmann put the cold metal of the silencer on the gendarme's neck.

'Stop,' he said.

The car slowed. Hirtmann waited until the driver had pulled over to the side, then pulled the trigger. The man's skull exploded into a puree of blood, bones and brains, splattering the upper left-hand side of the windscreen. A bitter smell of powder filled the car. Long brown streaks trickled down the glass and Hirtmann told himself he would have to clean it before he could set off again.

He turned and looked at Diane; she was still sleeping. He pulled off his mask, got out, then opened the door on the driver's side and pulled him out. He left the body in the snow and searched for a rag. He wiped off the blood splatter as best he could, then went to the back of the car and grabbed Diane. She was still droopy, but he sensed it wouldn't be long before she emerged from the mist of chloroform. He settled her on the passenger seat, fastened her belt tightly, then went to sit behind the wheel with the gun between his thighs. In the snow and the cold night, the gendarme's still-warm body began steaming, as if it were being consumed.

Ziegler stopped at the end of the long, oak-lined approach, at the edge of the large esplanade outside the chateau. The wind was arctic. The large topiary animals, the garden borders dusted with snow, the white façade . . . *everything seemed so unreal.*

And calm. *Deceptively calm,* thought Servaz, all his senses on alert.

Sheltering from the wind behind the trunk of the last oak tree, Ziegler handed one walkie-talkie to Servaz and the other to Espérandieu. She gave her instructions with authority: 'We'll split up. Two teams. One to the right, one the left. As soon as you two are in position to cover us, you and I will go in,' she said, pointing to Samira. 'If they resist, we'll fall back and wait for reinforcements.'

Samira nodded and the two women walked quickly towards the second row of trees, where they disappeared, before Servaz could react. He looked at Espérandieu, who shrugged. Then they too slipped in among the trees, in the other direction round the esplanade. All the way, Servaz did not take his eyes from the building.

Suddenly he shuddered.

Something moved. He thought he saw a shadow flit behind a window.

The walkie-talkie crackled.

'Are you in position?'

Ziegler's voice. He hesitated. Had he seen something, yes or no? 'I may have seen someone on the first floor,' he said. 'I'm not sure.'

'OK, we'll go in anyway. Cover us.'

He almost told her to wait.

Too late. The women were already moving quickly through the snowy borders, then running across the gravel. Just as they were making their way between the two topiary lions, Servaz felt his blood freeze: a window had opened on the first floor. He saw a gun at the end of an outstretched arm! Without hesitation, he took aim and pulled the trigger. To his great surprise, a windowpane shattered, but not the right one! The shadow vanished.

'What's going on?' said Ziegler in the walkie-talkie.

He could see her hiding behind one of the giant animals. Not really much protection. A single burst of gunfire through the bushes and it would all be over.

'Be careful!' he shouted. 'There's at least one armed man in there! He was about to shoot!'

She gestured to Samira and they rushed towards the chateau. They disappeared inside. *Dear Lord!* Each one of them had more testosterone than he and Espérandieu put together!

'Your turn,' said Ziegler in the walkie-talkie.

Servaz grunted. They should have fallen back. Nevertheless, he ran towards the entrance to the chateau, with Espérandieu following. Several shots rang out inside. They hurried up the steps of the porch and rushed through the door. Ziegler was firing from behind a statue at the back of the room. Samira was on the floor.

'What happened?' shouted Servaz.

'They shot at us!'

Servaz looked at the series of dark rooms. Ziegler was bending over Samira. She was wounded in the leg, bleeding profusely. There was a long bloody streak across the marble floor. The bullet had torn open her thigh, but not the femoral artery. Lying on the floor, Samira was already putting her hand on the wound to stop the bleeding. There was nothing else to do until help came. Ziegler took out her walkie-talkie to call for an ambulance.

'From now on we stay right here!' insisted Servaz when she had finished. 'We'll wait for reinforcements.'

'They won't get here for another hour!'

'Never mind!'

She nodded.

'I'll make you a compression bandage,' she said to Samira. 'You never know: you might have to use your weapon.'

In a few seconds, she fashioned a bandage, wrapping it tightly enough to stop the bleeding. Servaz knew that once the bleeding stopped, an injured person could stay like that without any real danger. He reached for his walkie-talkie.

'Pujol, Simeoni, get over here!'

'What's going on?' asked Pujol.

'They fired at us. Samira is hurt. We need support. We're in the entrance hall. The coast is clear.'

'Copy.'

He turned his head, and started.

Several stuffed heads were looking down at him from the walls. A bear. A Pyrenean chamois. A stag. One of the heads looked familiar. *Freedom . . . The horse was staring at him with golden eyes.*

Suddenly he saw Irène start running towards the depths of the building. *Shit!*

'Stay with Samira!' he shouted to his assistant, and bolted off after her.

Diane felt as though she'd been sleeping for hours. When she opened her eyes, the first thing she saw was the road rushing past the wind-screen, and thousands of snowflakes coming to greet them. Then she became aware of a string of crackling messages from the dashboard, slightly to her left.

She turned her head and saw him.

She didn't wonder whether she were dreaming. She knew that, unfortunately, she was not.

He saw that she had woken up and grabbed his gun. He aimed it at her, still driving.

He didn't say a word – there was no need.

Diane could not help but wonder where and when he would kill her. And how. Would she end up like the dozens of others who had never been found – at the bottom of a hole somewhere in the woods? The thought of it paralysed her. In this car she was like an animal caught in a trap. So unbearable was this realisation that anger and determination gradually replaced her fear. And a cold resolution, as icy as the air outside: if she had to die, it would not be as a victim. She would fight; he would pay dearly. The bastard didn't know what was in store for him. She had to wait for the right moment. There was bound to be one; the important thing was to be ready.

Maud, my beloved little sister. Sleep, little sister. Sleep. You are so beautiful when you sleep. So peaceful, so radiant.

I failed you, Maud. I wanted to protect you, you trusted me, you believed in me. I failed you. I wasn't able to keep you from the world, little sister; I could not stop the world from hurting you, dirtying you.

'We must go now, sir! Come on!'

Éric Lombard turned round, with the can of petrol in his hand.

455

Otto still held his gun, but his other arm hung limply at his side, and the sleeve was soaked in blood.

'Wait,' he said. 'Give me just a bit more time, Otto. My little sister . . . what did they do to her? What did they do to her, Otto?'

He turned back to the coffin. Around him was a vast circular room, brilliantly illuminated. Everything in the room was white: the walls, floor, furnishings. In the middle was a platform. A large ivory-white coffin lay on top of it. There were also two low tables with flowers in vases. The flowers were white, too.

Éric Lombard shook the petrol can over the coffin. It was open. Inside, lying among the ivory padding, Maud Lombard seemed to be sleeping in her white dress. Her eyes closed. Smiling. Immaculate. Immortal.

Plastination. The body's liquids replaced by silicon – like those exhibitions where real, perfectly preserved corpses were displayed. Éric Lombard stared at the angelic young face, now streaming with petrol.

Violence is risen up into a rod of wickedness: none of them shall remain, nor of their multitude, nor of any of theirs: neither shall there be wailing for them. The time is come, the day draweth near . . . neither shall any strengthen himself in the iniquity of his life. (Ezekiel 7:11–14)

'Do you hear me, sir? It's time to go!'

'See how she is sleeping. Look at how peaceful she is. She has never been more beautiful than in this moment.'

'She's dead, for God's sake! Dead! Get a hold of yourself!'

'Father read the Bible to us every evening, Otto. Do you remember? The Old Testament. Isn't that right, Maud? He taught us his lessons; he told us to deliver justice ourselves – never to let an insult or a crime go unpunished.'

'Rouse yourself, sir! We must leave!'

'But he was an unjust, cruel man. And when Maud grew up and started to go out with her friends, her boyfriends, he treated her the way he had treated our mother. *But they that escape of them shall escape, and shall be on the mountains like doves of the valleys, all of them mourning, every one for his iniquity. All hands shall be feeble, and all knees shall be weak as water. Horror shall cover them.* Ezekiel, chapter seven.'

Shots rang out over their heads. Otto turned round and went towards the stairway, brandishing his weapon. He grimaced from the pain in his wounded arm.

★

The man came round the corner. It all happened very quickly. The bullet passed so near that Servaz heard it buzzing. He didn't have time to react. Ziegler was already firing and he saw the man collapse. His gun bounced on the floor with a metallic sound.

Ziegler went over to him, still holding her gun in the air. She leaned over him. A large red spot was spreading across his shoulder. He was alive but in shock. She sent a message through the walkie-talkie, then stood up and stepped back.

Servaz, Pujol and Simeoni walked over to her. Behind the statue a stairway led downstairs.

'This way,' said Pujol.

A white spiral staircase. Curving white marble walls. Steep steps winding down into the bowels of the huge building. Ziegler went down first, her gun held in front of her. Then a shot rang out and she rushed back up for shelter.

'Shit! There's someone shooting down there!'

They saw her unhook something from her belt. Servaz knew immediately what it was.

Otto saw a black object bounce like a tennis ball down the stairs and roll towards him along the floor. Tick-tick-tick . . . He understood too late. A stun grenade. When it exploded, a blinding flash literally paralysed his sight. This was followed by a deafening explosion which shook the room, and the wave went through his body, giving him the impression that the room was spinning. He lost his balance.

By the time he came round, two figures had appeared. He felt someone kick him in the jaw and he let go of his gun. Then he was turned over on the floor and felt the cold steel of handcuffs closing round his wrists. That was when he saw the flames. They had begun to devour the coffin. His boss had vanished. Otto did not struggle. As a young man in the 1960s he had served as a mercenary in Africa under Bob Denard and David Smiley. He was well acquainted with the atrocities of postcolonial warfare; he had tortured and been tortured. After that, he had followed the orders of Henri Lombard, a man who was as hard as he was; then he had served his son. It took a lot to impress Otto.

'Go fuck yourselves,' he said simply.

★

The heat from the fire was scorching their faces. The flames filled the centre of the room, blackening the high ceiling. Soon it would be impossible to breathe.

'Pujol, Simeoni,' shouted Ziegler, pointing to the stairway, 'take him out to the van!'

She turned to Servaz, who was gazing at the burning platform. The fire was devouring the body inside the coffin, but they had had time to see the long blonde hair and youthful face.

'Dear God!' sighed Ziegler.

'I saw her tomb at the cemetery,' said Servaz.

'I suppose it must be empty. How did they manage to preserve her for so long? Was she embalmed?'

'No, that wouldn't be enough. But Lombard has the means. And there are techniques.'

Servaz stared at the angelic young face as it was transformed into a mass of charred flesh, bones and molten plastic. It seemed totally unreal.

'Where is Lombard?' asked Ziegler.

Servaz emerged from his trance and nodded to an open door on the other side of the room. They went round the room, hugging the circular wall to keep clear of the flames, then through the door.

Another stairway leading upwards. Much narrower, not as well maintained as the other one. Grey, weeping stone, stained with black streaks.

They came out at the back of the chateau.

Wind. Snow. Storm. Darkness.

Ziegler stopped and listened. Silence. The full moon came and went behind the clouds. Servaz scanned the moving shadows of the forest.

'There,' she said.

The triple tracks of a snowmobile in the moonlight. They followed a path that carved a gap through the trees. The clouds closed over and the tracks disappeared.

'Too late. He got away,' said Servaz.

'I know where the trail leads to: it goes first to a cirque two kilometres from here, then up into the mountain, over a col and back down. From there, the road to Spain.'

'Pujol and Simeoni could follow.'

'They would have to make a detour of fifty kilometres. Lombard will get there before them. He probably already has a car waiting on the other side.'

458

Ziegler walked over to a small building at the edge of the forest: the tracks of the snowmobile started there. She opened the door and turned a switch. Inside the hut were two more snowmobiles and, against the wall, a board full of keys, skis, boots, helmets and black jumpsuits, whose yellow reflective strips caught the light.

'Good heavens!' exclaimed Ziegler. 'I'd love to know what sort of dispensation he got!'

'What do you mean?'

'The use of these things is strictly regulated,' she said, taking one of the jumpsuits off its hook.

Servaz swallowed as he watched Irène get into it.

'What are you doing?'

'Put that on!'

She pointed to a jumpsuit and a pair of boots. Servaz hesitated. There must be some other way . . . Roadblocks, for example. But all their officers had been mobilised at the Institute. And Lombard must already have an escape plan. Irène rummaged among the keys, then started the vehicle and glided it outside. She turned on the lights and went back inside to grab two helmets and two pairs of gloves. Servaz was struggling with his jumpsuit: it was too big, and his flak jacket got in the way.

'Come on,' she said above the sound of the four-stroke engine.

He put on the red and white helmet and immediately felt he was suffocating. He drew the hood of the jumpsuit over the helmet and went out. The boots made him walk like an astronaut – or a penguin.

Outside, the blizzard had abated somewhat. The wind had dropped and there were fewer snowflakes in the tunnel of light created by the snowmobile's headlight. He pressed the button on his walkie-talkie.

'Vincent? How is Samira?'

'She's OK. But the other guy is in a bad way. The ambulances will be here in five minutes. And you?'

'No time to explain! Stay with her.'

He cut the contact, lowered the visor of his helmet and clumsily straddled the raised seat behind Ziegler. Then he settled against the back support. She took off at once. The snowflakes came at them like shooting stars. The vehicle slid easily over the packed trail, hissing softly against the snow. The clouds parted again and through his visor he saw the mountains, just above the trees in the moonlight.

*

'I know what you're thinking, Diane.'

His deep, hoarse voice startled her. She had been lost in thought.

'You have been wondering how I'm going to kill you. And you are looking desperately for a way out. You're waiting for me to make a mistake. I'm sorry to say I will make no mistakes. And so, yes, you will die tonight.'

On hearing his words, an immense chill came over her, spreading from her head down to her stomach and legs. For a moment she thought she was going to faint. She swallowed, but felt a painful catch in her throat.

'Or maybe I won't. Maybe I'll let you live, after all. I don't like being manipulated. Élisabeth Ferney might regret having used me. She always likes to have the last word, so perhaps this time she'll be disappointed. Killing you would deprive me of that little victory: *that gives you a chance, Diane*. To be honest, I haven't really made up my mind.'

He was lying . . . He had made up his mind. All her experience as a psychologist told her so. This was just one of his twisted little games, one of his tricks: give the victim a gleam of hope, all the better to take it from her later on. All the better to destroy her. Yes, that was it: another one of his perverse pleasures. Terror, mad hope and then, at the last minute, disappointment and despair.

He fell silent, listening attentively to the messages coming from the radio. Diane tried to do the same, but her mind was a welter of confusion and she found it impossible to concentrate.

'It seems our friends from the gendarmerie have their hands full up there,' he said.

Diane looked at the landscape rushing past the windows: the narrow road was white, but they were driving fast. The car must have snow tyres. Nothing disturbed the immaculate whiteness except for dark tree trunks and a few grey boulders here and there. In the distance the high mountains stood out against the night sky and straight ahead was a gap between the summits. Perhaps that was where the road was leading.

She looked at him again, at this man who was going to kill her. A thought flashed into her mind, as sharp as an icicle in the moonlight. He was lying when he said he would not make any mistakes. He just wanted her to believe it. He wanted her to give up and entrust herself to him, in the hope he would let her live.

He was wrong. She wouldn't do that.

★

They came out of the forest, speeding through two snowdrifts. Servaz saw the entrance to the cirque: a gorge of monstrous proportions. He thought back to the gigantic architecture he had seen on first arriving in this valley. Everything here was out of proportion – the landscape, the passions, the crimes. The blizzard grew stronger, the snow swarming around them. Ziegler clung to the handlebars, arched against the wind behind the flimsy Plexiglas windscreen. Servaz huddled down to make the most of the feeble protection his colleague could offer. His gloves and jumpsuit were not enough to keep him warm. Now and again the snowmobile bounced like a bobsleigh to the right or the left, and more than once he thought they would tip over.

Soon, in spite of the gusts, he saw they were approaching a huge amphitheatre streaked with scree and ice flows. Several waterfalls had frozen; from this distance the ice had transformed them into tall white candles dripping wax against the rock face. When the full moon came out from behind the clouds and lit up the landscape, its beauty took his breath away. There reigned a sense of expectation, of time suspended.

'I see him!' he shouted.

The snowmobile was climbing the slope on the far side of the cirque. Servaz thought he could make out the vague line of a path heading towards a breach in the rocky wall. The vehicle was already halfway up. The moonlight flooded the cirque, carving out every detail in the rock and ice. Servaz looked up. The silhouette had just vanished into the shadow of the cliff; then it reappeared on the other side. He leaned forward and hung on as best he could, while their powerful vehicle gripped the slope with ease.

Once they had gone through the breach, they were among fir trees again. Lombard had disappeared. The track continued to climb, zigzagging through the forest; the wind was gusting, a blinding grey and white curtain. The beam from the headlight bounced back at them. Servaz felt as if a wrathful, roaring god were spitting his icy breath into their faces. He was trembling from the cold, but he also felt sweat trickling between his shoulder blades.

'Where is he?' shouted Ziegler. 'Shit! Where has he gone?'

He could sense her tension, every muscle straining to control the snowmobile. And her rage, too. Lombard had almost managed to have her sent to prison in his place. He had used them. Servaz

461

wondered fleetingly whether Irène was altogether sane, whether she was leading both of them into a lethal trap.

Then the forest thinned. They went through a small pass and down the other side. The storm subsided and the mountains appeared all around them, like an army of giants waiting as reserves in a nocturnal duel. Suddenly they saw him, one hundred metres below. He had left the trail and abandoned his snowmobile. Bent double, he was reaching towards the ground.

'He's got a snowboard!' shouted Ziegler. 'The bastard! He's going to slip through our fingers!'

Lombard was standing at the top of a very steep slope scattered with huge boulders. Servaz recalled the articles boasting of the man's sporting feats. He wondered whether their snowmobile would be able to follow him, then decided that Lombard wouldn't have abandoned his own if that were the case. Ziegler was hurtling down the slope at breakneck speed now. She turned off to follow Lombard's tracks, and for a moment Servaz thought they were going to go flying. He saw their quarry abruptly turn his head towards them and raise his arm in their direction.

'Watch out! He's got a gun!'

He would not have been able to say exactly what Ziegler did, but the snowmobile made an abrupt ninety-degree turn and Servaz somersaulted into the snow. There was a flash in front of them, followed by a loud bang. The sound reverberated against the mountain, was returned and amplified by the echo. A second detonation followed. Then a third. The gunshots and their echo made a deafening thunder. Then the shooting stopped. Servaz waited, buried in the powdery snow, his heart pounding. Ziegler was lying next to him; she had her gun, but for some reason she had decided not to use it. The last echo was still rippling in the air when a second sound seemed to emerge from the first, an enormous cracking sound.

Something unfamiliar. Servaz could not tell what it was.

Still lying in the snow, he felt the ground vibrating beneath him. For a moment he thought he was passing out. He had never felt anything like it.

The crack was followed by a hoarser noise, deeper, broader, more muted. And just as unfamiliar.

The deep, muffled grumbling grew louder, as if it were running on rails, a train coming nearer . . . No, not one train, but several together.

He sat up and saw Lombard looking towards the mountain, motionless.

Suddenly, he understood.

He followed Ziegler's terrified gaze towards the slope on their right. She grabbed his arm and pulled him to his feet.

'Quick! We've got to run! *Quick!*'

She led him towards the path, and he followed, heavy and awkward in his jumpsuit and boots. He stopped for a moment to look back at Lombard. He had stopped shooting and was struggling with the bindings on his snowboard. Servaz saw him give a worried glance towards the top of the slope. He did likewise and it was like a fist landing in his guts. Up there, in the moonlight, an entire chunk of glacier was moving, a sleeping giant suddenly awake. Servaz plunged ahead, hopping and waving his arms to go faster, never taking his eyes from the glacier.

A gigantic cloud was plummeting down the mountain through the fir trees. *It's all over,* he thought. *It's all over!* He stopped looking, tried to hurry. The enormous wave hit only seconds later. He was picked up from the ground, catapulted, tossed like a wisp of straw. He let out a faint cry, immediately stifled by the snow. He was tumbling inside the drum of a washing machine. He opened his mouth, coughed, hiccuped, waved his arms and legs. He was drowning. He met Irène's gaze; her head was down; she was staring behind him with an expression of absolute horror on her face. Then she disappeared. He was lifted, shaken, turned over.

He couldn't hear anything.

His ears were whistling.

He was gasping for air.

He was going to die suffocated, buried.

It's all over.

Diane saw the cloud hurtling down the mountain before he did.

'Look out!' she screamed, as much to frighten and unsettle him as to warn him.

Hirtmann cast a surprised look at her and Diane saw his eyes open wide. Just as the huge wave of snow, debris and stones was about to reach the road and bury them, he swerved abruptly and lost control. Diane's head struck the window, and she felt the rear of the car skid sideways. In the same instant the avalanche hit them head on.

Sky and earth turned upside down. Diane saw the road spin like a ride at an amusement park. Her body was thrown this way and that, and her head banged against the car door. A white fog enveloped them with a dull, terrifying roar. The car flipped over several times on its way down the slope, its passage scarcely slowed by the bushes. Two or three times Diane lost consciousness, so that the whole sequence seemed like a series of unreal flashes. When at last with a sickening groan of metal the car came to a halt, she was dazed but conscious. The windscreen had shattered; the bonnet of the car was entirely covered with snow; small streams of ice and pebbles were flowing down the dashboard onto her legs. She looked at Hirtmann. He was unconscious. His face was covered in blood. *His gun . . .* Diane tried desperately to unfasten her own belt and managed only with difficulty. Then she leaned over and searched for the gun. Eventually she found it at the killer's feet, almost stuck beneath the pedals. She had to lean even further, and with a shudder she put her arm between Hirtmann's legs to reach for it. She looked at it, wondering if the safety catch were on. *There was one good way to find out . . .* She aimed it at Hirtmann, her finger on the trigger. But she was not a killer. Whatever this monster might have done, she was incapable of pulling the trigger. She lowered the weapon.

Only then did she become aware of the silence.

Other than the wind in the leafless branches of the trees, nothing moved.

She looked for a reaction on Hirtmann's face, some sign that he was going to come round, but he remained perfectly still. *Maybe he was dead.* She didn't feel like touching him to find out. Her fear lingered – and would be there as long as she was shut inside this metal box with him. She searched her pockets for her phone and found it had been taken. Hirtmann might have it, but there again, she did not have the courage to go through his pockets.

Still holding the gun, she struggled to climb over the dashboard and crawled through the shattered windscreen. She did not even feel the cold. The rush of adrenaline kept her warm. She slipped off the car bonnet and immediately sank up to her thighs in the surrounding snow. It was hard to make headway. Overcoming an initial wave of panic, she started to climb towards the road. The gun in her hand was reassuring. She looked one last time at the car. Hirtmann hadn't moved. Perhaps he was dead.

It looooks like he's coooooming rooooound.
  Can you heeeeear us?
Voices. Far away. They were calling him. And then the pain. A lot of pain. Exhaustion, a desire to rest, drugs . . . A flash of lucidity where he saw faces and lights – then the avalanche, once again, the mountain, the cold and, finally, darkness.
  Maaartin, caaan youuu heeeear meee?
He opened his eyes, slowly, dazzled by the circle of light on the ceiling. Then a figure leaned over him. Servaz tried to focus on the face speaking quietly to him, but the halo of light behind her hurt his eyes. The face went in and out of focus. Yet it seemed to him that it was beautiful.
A woman's hand took his own.
  Martin, can you hear me?
He nodded. Charlène smiled at him. She leaned down and kissed his cheek. It felt good. A faint perfume. Then a door opened and Espérandieu came in.
'Is he awake?'
'It looks like it. He hasn't said anything yet.'
She turned and gave him a wink, and suddenly Servaz felt wide awake. Espérandieu crossed the room with two steaming mugs. He handed one to his wife. Servaz tried to turn his head, but there was something in the way: a neck brace.
'What a business, fuck!' said Espérandieu.
Servaz tried to sit up, but he flinched with pain and decided against it. Espérandieu noticed.
'The doctor said you shouldn't move. You have three broken ribs, some minor injuries to your head and neck, and frostbite. And, um, they had to amputate three toes.'
'*What?*'
'Just kidding.'
'And Irène?'
'She made it. She's in another room. She's a bit worse off than you are, but she'll be fine. A few fractures, that's all.'

465

Servaz felt a huge wave of relief. But there was another urgent question.

'Lombard?'

'His body hasn't been found: the weather up there won't allow a search. Tomorrow. He probably died in the avalanche. You two were lucky: it only grazed you.'

Servaz flinched again. He would like to see how Espérandieu would get on if he were *grazed* in a similar fashion.

'Thirsty,' he said.

Espérandieu nodded and went out. He came back with the nurse and the doctor. He and Charlène left the room while Servaz was questioned and examined from every angle. Then the nurse handed him a glass with a straw. Water. His throat was incredibly dry. He drank it all and asked for more. The door opened again and Margot appeared. He could tell by her expression that he must look awful.

'You could star in a horror film! You're really frightening!' she laughed.

'I took the liberty of bringing her along,' said Espérandieu, his hand on the doorknob. 'I'll leave you now.'

He closed the door.

'An avalanche,' said Margot, not daring to look at him for too long. 'Brrr, that's really scary.' She gave an awkward smile; then it vanished. 'Do you realise you could have died? Fuck, Dad, don't ever do anything like that again!'

What sort of language was that? he wondered. Then he saw she had tears in her eyes. She must have come by before he regained consciousness; she'd had a shock. He had butterflies in his stomach. He pointed to the edge of the bed.

'Have a seat,' he said.

He took her hand. There was a long moment of silence, and he was about to say something when there was a knock on the door. He turned to look and a young woman in her thirties entered the room. He was sure he had never seen her before, and she had a few injuries on her face – on her right cheek and eyebrow, a nasty gash on her forehead. Her eyes were bloodshot with dark rings underneath. Had she too been caught in the avalanche?

'Commandant Servaz?'

He nodded.

'My name is Diane Berg. I'm the psychologist from the Institute. We spoke on the phone.'

'What happened to you?'

'I had a car accident,' she replied with a smile, as if there were something funny about it. 'I could ask you the same thing, but I already know the answer.' She glanced over at Margot. 'May I speak to you for a moment?'

Servaz looked at Margot, who made a face, looked the young woman up and down, stood up and went out. Diane came over to the bed.

'You know that Hirtmann has disappeared?' she asked as she sat down.

Servaz stared at her for a moment. He shook his head, in spite of the neck brace. *Hirtmann at liberty* . . . A shadow passed over his face; his expression become hard and dark. In the final analysis, he thought, that entire night was a wasted opportunity. Lombard may have been a murderer, but he was a danger only to a handful of evil individuals. Hirtmann's motivation was very different. The uncontrollable fury that burned like a relentless flame in his heart would for ever set him apart from other human beings. Boundless cruelty, a thirst for blood, a total absence of remorse . . . Servaz felt a tingling down his spine. What would happen now that the Swiss killer was roaming free? Out there, without the drugs, his impulses and hunting instinct would be revived. The thought of it turned Servaz's blood to ice. Major psychopaths like Hirtmann did not feel the slightest trace of humanity; the euphoria they experienced while torturing, raping and murdering was far too great. The moment he had the opportunity, Hirtmann would strike again.

'What happened?' he asked.

She told him what she had been through from the moment Lisa Ferney surprised her in her office until she began walking along the frozen road, having left Hirtmann behind in the car. She had walked for nearly two hours before she found another living soul, and by then she was frozen, suffering from hypothermia. When the gendarmerie reached the scene of the accident, the car was empty; there were footprints and blood leading up to the road – then nothing more.

'Someone gave him a lift,' said Servaz.

'Yes.'

'A car that was just going by, or else . . . an accomplice.'

He turned to look out of the window. It was pitch dark.

'When did you realise that Lisa Ferney was in league with Lombard?' he asked.

'It's a long story. Do you really want to hear it now?'

He smiled at her. He sensed that although she was a psychologist, she was the one who needed to talk to someone. It had to come out. *Now* . . . This was as good a time as any, for both of them. He could tell that she was feeling the same sense of unreality as he was – a feeling born of a strange night of terror and violence, of all the days leading up to it. At that moment, although they were strangers, they were close.

'I have all night,' he said.

She smiled.

'Well,' she started, 'I got to the Institute the day they found that dead horse up on the mountain. I remember it very well. It was snowing, and . . .'

Epilogue

Crimen extinguitur mortalite
(Death extinguishes crime)

When Caesar realised, he gave the signal they had agreed on to the fourth line he had made up of six cohorts. The troops rushed forward at great speed, and in assault formation they made such a vigorous charge against the horsemen of Pompey that no one was able to resist.

'There they are,' said Espérandieu.

Servaz looked up from *The Gallic Wars*. He rolled down his window. At first sight he saw only a dense crowd rushing about under the Christmas lights; then, as if he were zooming in on a group photo, he saw two figures emerge from the crush. A sight that left his chest aching. Margot. She was not alone. *A man was walking at her side. Tall, elegant, dressed in black, in his forties.*

'That's him,' said Espérandieu.

'Are you sure?'

'Yes.'

Servaz opened the door.

'Wait for me here.'

'Don't do anything stupid, all right?' said his assistant.

Not answering, he lost himself in the crowd. One hundred and fifty metres ahead of him, Margot and the man turned right. Servaz hurried to reach the street corner in case they were headed down a side street but, once they had gone over the crossroads, they went straight towards le Capitole and its Christmas market. He slowed down, then hurried to the vast square with its small wooden chalets. Margot and her lover were wandering along the stalls. He noticed that his daughter looked perfectly happy. Although they did not make a display of it, their gestures betrayed an obvious physical closeness. Servaz felt a pinch of jealousy. When was the last time he had seen

Margot look this joyful? He was beginning to think that perhaps Espérandieu had been right, that the man was harmless.

Then they crossed the square in the direction of the cafés beneath the arcades and he saw them take a seat outside, despite the cold. The man only ordered for himself, and Servaz concluded that Margot would not be staying. He hid behind a chalet and waited. Five minutes later, his suspicions were confirmed: his daughter got up, gave the man a light kiss on the lips and walked away. Servaz waited a little longer. He used the time to study Margot's lover in detail. A good-looking man, sure of himself, with a high forehead and expensive clothes that testified to his social standing. Well preserved, but Servaz thought he must be a few years older than he was. *A wedding ring on his left hand.* He felt a surge of anger. *His seventeen-year-old daughter was going out with a married man who was older than her own father.*

He took a deep breath, covered the last few yards with a decisive stride and sat down in Margot's place.

'Hello,' he said.

'The seat is taken,' said the man.

'I don't think so; the young woman has left.'

The man gave him a surprised look and studied him. Servaz returned his gaze, without betraying the slightest emotion. An amused smile lit up the man's face.

'There are other free tables. I would prefer to sit by myself, if you don't mind.'

He had put it nicely, and his ironic tone confirmed his self-assurance. It would not be easy to unsettle this man.

'She's not yet of age, is she?' said Servaz.

Now the smile faded from the man's face. His gaze hardened.

'What business is it of yours?'

'You haven't answered my question.'

'I don't know who you are, but you're going to get the fuck out of here.'

'I'm her father.'

'What?'

'I'm Margot's father.'

'The cop?' asked his daughter's lover, incredulous.

Servaz felt as if he had just been kicked by a mule.

'Is that what she calls me?'

'No, that's what *I* call you,' answered the man. 'Margot calls you "Dad". She loves you very much.'

Servaz would not be swayed by emotion.

'And what does your wife think?'

The man immediately regained his coldness.

'That's none of your business,' he retorted.

'And have you talked to Margot about it?'

He saw with satisfaction that he had managed to rattle him.

'Listen, even if you are her father, it's none of your business. Yes, I told Margot everything. She doesn't care. Now I must ask you to leave.'

'And if I don't feel like leaving, what are you going to do: call the cops?'

'You shouldn't play that sort of game with me,' said the man in a low but threatening voice.

'No? What if I went to see your wife and discussed it with her?'

'Why are you doing this?' asked his daughter's lover – but to Servaz's great surprise, he seemed more puzzled than frightened.

Servaz hesitated.

'I don't like the idea that my seventeen-year-old daughter is being toyed with by a man your age who couldn't care less.'

'What do you know about it?'

'Would you get a divorce for a seventeen-year-old?'

'Don't be ridiculous.'

'Ridiculous? Don't you think it's ridiculous for a bloke your age to be having it off with a kid? Isn't there something *profoundly pathetic* about it all?'

'I've had enough of this,' said the man. 'Drop it right there. Stop acting the policeman.'

'What did you say?'

'You heard me.'

'She's a minor. I could arrest you.'

'That's bullshit! The age of consent in this country is fifteen. And you'll find yourself in deep water if you go on like this.'

'Oh, really?' said Servaz sarcastically.

'I'm a lawyer,' said the man.

Shit, thought Servaz. *That's all I need.*

'Yes,' confirmed his daughter's lover. 'A member of the bar of Toulouse. Margot was afraid you might find out about our . . . *affair.*

She has a great deal of respect for you, but, naturally, where certain things are concerned she finds you somewhat . . . *old-fashioned*.'

Servaz remained silent.

'Beneath her rebellious exterior, Margot is a wonderful girl, brilliant and independent. And a lot more mature than you give her credit for. Having said that, you're right: I have no intention of leaving my family for her. And she knows it very well. Besides, she sees boys her own age, too, occasionally.'

Servaz wanted to tell him to shut up.

'How long has this been going on?' he asked, in a voice that sounded strange to his own ears.

'Ten months. We met in the queue at the cinema. She's the one who started it, if you must know.'

So she was sixteen when it happened . . . His blood was throbbing. The man's voice were being drowned out by the buzzing of a thousand bees.

'I understand your concern,' said the lawyer, 'but it's misplaced: Margot is a self-confident, well-balanced girl – she can make her own decisions.'

He found the strength to react: 'Self-confident? Haven't you seen her lately, how *sad* she is? Is it because of you?'

The man looked genuinely embarrassed, but he held Servaz's gaze.

'No,' he said, 'it's because of you. She can see how lost and distraught you are. She can tell that loneliness is getting you down, that you would like to spend more time with her, that your job is eating away at you and you miss her mother. And it's breaking her heart. I'll say it again: Margot cares very deeply for you.'

There was a moment's silence. When Servaz spoke again, it was in a very cold voice.

'A brilliant defence, mate,' he said. 'But you should keep that sort of patter for the courtroom. You're wasting your time with me.'

Out of the corner of his eye, he was pleased to see that the man had taken offence at his familiarity.

'Now listen carefully. You're a lawyer, you have a reputation, and without your reputation you are dead, professionally. Whether my daughter is legally of age or not doesn't change a thing. If the rumour gets out that you're sleeping with a kid, it will be over for you. You will lose your clients one after the other. And your wife may turn a blind eye to your behaviour now, but she'll be less willing to do so when the money dries up, believe me. So you're going to tell Margot that it is over between you, as tactfully as possible. You can tell her what you like: palaver is your strong point, after all. But I don't want to hear of you ever again. And by the way, I've recorded this conversation, except the end. Just in case. Have a good day.'

He stood up and walked away, without even turning to check the effect his words had had. He already knew. Then he thought of Margot's pain, and felt a twinge of remorse.

On Christmas Day, Servaz got up early and went downstairs without making a sound. He felt full of energy. He and Margot had stayed up talking till the small hours, after everyone else had gone to bed: father and daughter in a living room that was not theirs, sitting at the end of the sofa next to the Christmas tree.

At the foot of the stairs, he glanced at the thermometer. One degree above zero outside. And fifteen degrees indoors: his hosts had turned down the heat for the night and the house was cold.

Servaz stood for a few seconds listening to the silence. He could imagine them under their duvets: Vincent and Charlène, Mégan, Margot. It was the first time in a long time that he'd been away from home on a Christmas morning. A strange feeling, but not an unpleasant one. The opposite in fact. Sleeping under the same roof were his best friend and assistant, a woman who filled him with desire and his own daughter. Bizarre? The most bizarre thing was that he accepted things as they were. When he had told Espérandieu he would be spending Christmas Eve with his daughter, Espérandieu had immediately invited them. Servaz was about to refuse, but to his great surprise he found himself accepting.

'But I don't even know them!' Margot had protested in the car. 'You told me there'd be just the two of us, not that we'd be spending the evening with a bunch of cops!'

But Margot had got along very well with Charlène, Mégan and above all Vincent. At one point she'd got quite drunk, and waving the bottle of champagne, she exclaimed, 'I never imagined a cop could be so nice!' It was the first time Servaz had ever seen his daughter tipsy. Vincent was almost as drunk as she was, and he wept with laughter. As for Servaz, at first he had felt awkward in Charlène's presence, and he couldn't help but remember her kiss at the gallery. But with the help of the alcohol and the atmosphere, he had eventually relaxed.

He was heading barefoot into the kitchen when his toes struck an object that began to flash, making a strident noise. A Japanese robot. Or Chinese. He wondered whether there were more Chinese products on the market in this country now than French ones. But then a black shape burst out of the living room and came rushing at his legs. Servaz bent down and gave the dog a brisk rub; it was the same mutt Espérandieu had run over on the road to the nightclub. He'd gone to get the vet out of bed at three o'clock in the morning and the dog had been saved. He had turned out to be very gentle and affectionate, so Espérandieu decided to adopt him. In memory of that freezing, terrifying night, he had named him Shadow.

'Hey, boy,' said Servaz. 'And Merry Christmas. Who knows where you'd be right now if you hadn't had the bright idea of crossing the road?'

Shadow replied with several approving yaps, his black tail banging against Servaz's legs. Apparently he was not the first one up: Charlène Espérandieu was already awake. She had started the kettle and the coffee machine, and was dropping bread into the toaster. She had her back to him and he gazed at her for a moment, at her long auburn hair falling onto her dressing gown. He was about to leave, a lump in his throat, when she turned towards him, her hand on her round belly.

'Good morning, Martin.'

Through the window he saw a car go down the street very slowly. All round the edge of the roof, Christmas lights were twinkling, as they must have done all night long. *A real Christmas night,* he thought. He started forward and stepped on a soft toy, which let out a squeak. Charlène laughed and bent down to pick it up. Then she stood up straight, put a hand on his neck, pulled him close and kissed him. Servaz immediately felt the blood rush to his cheeks. What if someone came in? At the same time, he felt an instant desire, in spite of the round belly between them. It wasn't the first time he'd been kissed by a pregnant woman, but this time the woman wasn't pregnant by him.

'Charlène, I—'

'Sshhh. Don't say anything. Did you sleep well?'

'Very well. May I – could I have a coffee?'

She caressed his cheek affectionately and went over to the coffee machine.

'Charlène—'

'Don't say anything, Martin. Not now. We'll talk about it later. It's Christmas.'

He took the cup of coffee and drank it down, his head empty. His mouth was furry. He was suddenly sorry he hadn't brushed his teeth before coming down. When he turned round, she had vanished. Servaz leaned against the countertop, feeling as if there were ants gnawing away in his stomach. He could feel in his bones the scars of his expedition on the mountain. This was the strangest Christmas he had ever known. And also the most terrifying. He could not forget that Hirtmann was out there. Had he left the area? Was he thousands of miles away? Or was he lurking somewhere nearby? Servaz couldn't stop thinking about him. And about Lombard, too: they had finally found his corpse. Frozen. Servaz shivered every time he thought about it. What a horrible way to die . . . *and he had almost died the same way.*

The icy, bloody interlude of the investigation seemed so unreal now. And already so far away. Servaz knew there were things that would probably never be explained. Like the initials 'C S' on the rings. What did they stand for? And when had the foursome's series of crimes begun? Who had been the ringleader? The answers would remain buried for ever. Chaperon had walled himself up in silence. He was waiting in prison to be tried, but he hadn't revealed a thing. Then Servaz remembered something else. He would be forty years old a few days from now. He'd been born on 31 December – and, according to his mother, on the stroke of midnight: she had heard the champagne corks popping in the next room at the very moment he let out his first cry.

The thought of it struck him like a slap in the face. *He was about to turn forty . . . What had he done with his life?*

'Basically, you're the one who made the most important discovery in the whole case,' declared Kleim162 the day after Christmas. 'Not your boss – what's his name again?'

Kleim162 had come down to spend the holidays in the Southwest. He'd arrived in Toulouse the night before on the TGV.

'Servaz.'

'Well, anyway, your Monsieur I-quote-proverbs-in-Latin-so-I'll-look-clever, he may be the king of cops, but that doesn't hide the fact that you were ahead of him.'

'Don't exaggerate. I was lucky. And Martin did a remarkable job.'

'Where does he stand sexually, your living god?'

'Straight, a hundred and fifty per cent.'

'Pity.'

Kleim162 swung his legs out of the sheets and sat on the edge of the bed. He was naked. Vincent Espérandieu took a moment to admire his broad, muscular back as he smoked, one hand behind his neck, his back propped against the pillows. A faint film of sweat shone on his chest. When Kleim162 stood up and walked over to the bathroom, the cop could not help but check him out again. Outside it was snowing, at last, on 26 December.

'I don't suppose you're in love with him,' said Kleim162 from the bathroom.

'My wife is.'

The blond head peered back round the door.

'What do you mean? Are they sleeping together?'

'Not yet,' said Vincent, blowing smoke towards the ceiling.

'But I thought she was pregnant? And that he's the future godfather?'

'True enough.'

Kleim162 studied him with genuine stupefaction.

'And you're not jealous?'

Espérandieu just smiled, raising his eyes to the ceiling. The young journalist shook his head as if he were deeply shocked, and vanished into the bathroom. Espérandieu put his headphones back on. The marvellously hoarse voice of Mark Lanegan in reply to Isobel Campbell's dreamy murmuring in 'The False Husband'.

One fine April morning, Servaz went to pick up his daughter at his ex-wife's place. He smiled as she came out of the house with her backpack and sunglasses.

They took the motorway towards the Pyrenees, then the Montréjeau/ Saint-Martin-de-Comminges exit, causing Servaz to frown and the base of his skull to itch. Then they drove due south, heading for the mountains. The weather was incredibly beautiful. The sky was blue; the summits were white. Through the open window the pure air was exhilarating, like ether. Margot had put her favourite music on full blast in her headphones, and was singing over it – but even this could not mar Servaz's good mood.

The idea for this outing had come to him a week earlier, when Irène Ziegler had called to ask how he was doing. He drove through picturesque villages, the mountains coming ever nearer until they were so close he could no longer distinguish them, and the road began to climb. With every bend in the road they came upon grandiose views: hamlets tucked away at the end of valleys, streams sparkling in the sun, layers of mist suffused with light surrounding the cattle. The landscape, he mused, didn't look at all the same anymore. Then they reached the little car park. The morning sun, hidden behind the mountains, had not yet reached it. They were not the first ones there. A motorbike was parked at the end. Two people were waiting for them, sitting on the rocks.

'Good morning, Martin,' said Ziegler.

'Good morning, Irène. Irène, let me introduce Margot, my daughter. Margot, Irène.'

Irène shook Margot's hand and turned to introduce the pretty woman by her side. Zuzka Smatanova had a firm handshake, long jet-black hair and a dazzling smile. They spoke few words before heading off, like no time had passed since they'd last seen each other. Ziegler and Martin went in front; Zuzka and Margot let them get ahead. Servaz could hear them laughing behind him. Somewhat further along, during the long climb, he and Irène began to talk. The pebbles on the path cracked beneath the thick soles of their shoes, and the murmur of water rose from the stream below. The sun was already warm on their legs and faces.

'I went on looking,' she said suddenly, when they had just gone over a little wooden bridge.

'Looking for what?'

'Information about the four men.'

He gave her a cautious look. He did not want to spoil this fine day by stirring up unpleasant memories.

'And?'

'I found out that at age fifteen Chaperon, Perrault, Grimm and Mourrenx were sent by their parents to a holiday camp. By the sea. You know what the colony was called?'

'Tell me.'

'The Colonie des Sternes.'

'So?'

'You remember the letters on the ring?'

'Yes.'

'Do you think that – that maybe that is where they began . . .?'

'It's possible.'

The morning light filtered through the leaves of an aspen grove rustling in the light breeze.

'Fifteen years old. The age where you find out who you really are. Where you make your lifelong friendships. The age of sexual awakening, too,' said Servaz.

'And the age of your first crimes,' added Ziegler, looking at him.

'Yes, that could be it.'

'Or it could be something else,' said Ziegler.

'Or it could be something else.'

'What's going on?' called Margot, coming up to them. 'Why did you stop?'

Zuzka gave them a penetrating look.

'Let it go,' she said. 'Shit, let it go!'

Servaz looked all around him. It really was a magnificent day. He spared a thought for his father. He smiled.

'Yes, *time to let it go*,' he said, and started walking again.

Author's Note

Some of the facts and information contained in this book may seem the product of an overactive imagination; this is not at all the case. The subterranean power plant two thousand metres up does exist; I simply moved it by a few dozen kilometres. Similarly, some of the psychiatric techniques described here, such as aversion treatment or penile plethysmography, are, unfortunately, practised in hospitals in Europe and other parts of the world. So is electroshock – and while it has certainly changed from the era of Lou Reed and 'Kill Your Sons', it is still very much in the news in twenty-first-century France.

As for the music that Espérandieu listens to, you can always download it.

Acknowledgements

As far as acknowledgements are concerned, the number one suspect must be Jean-Pierre Schamber. An ideal culprit, who combines impeccable taste, a passion for crime novels and other literary forms, and a knowledge of music that I sorely lack. He is the one who, from the very first pages, made it clear to me that I couldn't stop there. Thank you, friend.

The other suspects, whatever their degree of guilt, are also partly responsible for the crime: my wife, who knows what living with a writer means, and who has made life infinitely easier; my daughter, a globetrotter for whom the very planet is far too small – I would need three lives to catch up with her; my son, who knows a lot more than I do about the latest technology and who will hopefully put it to one side long enough to read this book.

Dominique Matos Ventura is surely another lead: without his encouraging words, his talent and our friendship, this book would not exist. His songs, moreover, were the soundtrack for this book while I was writing it.

Greg Robert might not be guilty, but he is definitely suspicious: a tireless tracker of abnormalities and a patient proofreader, whose only fault is that he loves fantasy. Greg is as much a friend as he is my nephew.

Then there are the accomplices: the entire team of Éditions XO, beginning with Bernard Fixot himself, an uncompromising kingmaker; Édith Leblond, for her skill and support; Jean-Paul Campos, for saying he's my number one fan; Valérie Taillefer, for her know-how and communication skills; Florence Pariente, Gwenaëlle Le Goff and of course, last but not least, Caroline Lépée, who could transform scrap metal into gold.

Finally, thanks to Gaëlle for her photographs, Patrick for his special sense of humour, Claudine and Philippe for oiling the wheels, my sister and Jo for always being there, and all the rest of the K clan: Loïc for his Brittany, Christian for his cellar (and his tools), Didier for being an ideal friend, Dominique, Ghislaine, Patricia and Nicole for their laughter.

When all is said and done, contrary to what I once thought, writing is not such a solitary activity after all.